Meghann Whistler grew up in Canada but spent her summers on the beaches of Cape Cod. Before settling down with her rocket scientist husband and raising three rambunctious boys, she worked variously as a magazine writer, a model and a marketing communications manager at a software company. She loves to hear from her readers, who can reach her at meghannwhistler.com.

Books by Meghann Whistler

Love Inspired

Falling for the Innkeeper
The Baby's Christmas Blessing
Their Unlikely Protector

Visit the Author Profile page at LoveInspired.com.

Their Unlikely Protector

MEGHANN WHISTLER

LOVE INSPIRED
INSPIRATIONAL ROMANCE

LOVE INSPIRED®
INSPIRATIONAL ROMANCE

Recycling programs for this product may not exist in your area.

ISBN-13: 978-1-335-93668-4

Their Unlikely Protector

Love Inspired
22 Adelaide St. West, 41st Floor
Toronto, Ontario M5H 4E3, Canada
www.LoveInspired.com

Printed in Lithuania

MIX
Paper | Supporting responsible forestry
FSC® C021394

For with God nothing shall be impossible.
—*Luke* 1:37

For my grandparents

Frank & Myrtle
Bill & Frances

Rest in peace

Acknowledgments

Many thanks to Melissa Endlich and the team
at Love Inspired for believing in this book
and bringing it to life.

Thank you, as well, to the ladies in
my FHLCW critique group—Kristi, Krystina and Janet—
for their support with the early chapters of this
manuscript, and to my critique partner, Beth Pugh,
who motivated and encouraged me from start to finish.

I'm grateful to my husband, family and friends
for always being there to cheer me on.
And thank YOU, dear reader, for joining me
on another trip to Cape Cod!

Enjoy!

Chapter One

When Brett Richardson first saw the plume of smoke as he drove through the streets of Wychmere Bay, his hometown on Cape Cod, he thought he was imagining things. It was like a bad flashback to that horrible night at Half Shell two months ago—except he actually hadn't been there that night to do anything about the fire that had burned his parents' restaurant to the ground.

He blinked and looked back toward the beach. Nope, his mind wasn't playing tricks on him. It was after two o'clock in the morning and he'd been driving for hours, but there was enough moonlight that he could see it clearly: the smoke was definitely there.

He reached for his phone before remembering that it had died in the middle of his catering gig up in Boston.

All right, everything's fine. Just drive by and make sure the fire department's there before you head home.

He shouldn't even have been on this street right now. No, he should have been on his way to the Sea Glass Inn, where he was staying until he found a cheap apartment to rent. But after getting off the highway, he'd gone on autopilot and headed for his childhood home—the one he and his sister had put on the market last spring so that he could buy out her share of Half Shell.

The sale had closed two months ago.

One week before the restaurant had gone up in flames.

But maybe the fact that he hadn't been paying enough attention to where he was going was a good thing, a God thing, because as he turned the corner onto the next street, he could see what was causing all the smoke.

A house. On fire.

And no lights or sirens anywhere.

He threw his car into Park in the middle of the road and leaped out, adrenaline shooting through his body. The garage of the small Cape Cod cottage in front of him was blazing, and there was no one else in sight.

There was a car parked in the driveway, though. Were the residents still inside asleep?

For a split second, Brett weighed his options. Go bang on the neighbors' doors, then wait for someone to answer and call 911. Or go break down the door of this house, and make sure everyone was safe.

He charged up the front walk. The fire was loud—the roar of it like a continuous roll of thunder—and hot, hotter than he'd expected.

He pounded on the door. "Fire!" He couldn't hear anything inside over the rumble of the flames. "Wake up! Wake up! Fire!"

He tried the handle. Locked.

He threw his shoulder against the door and winced at the pain. Then he did it again, and again. Nothing. The skin on the left side of his face felt like it was being seared by the heat from the flames.

He ran to the back of the house. It was quieter back here, with the fire emanating from the front of the garage. He banged on the sliding glass door. "Get up! Get out! Fire!"

Still, nothing. No signs of life.

Maybe nobody's home.

But maybe they were. There was no way he was leaving until he knew for sure.

Glancing around the back patio, he spotted a relatively large garden planter, picked it up and heaved it through the slider.

The tempered glass shattered—like a windshield, the shards weren't sharp—and Brett rushed inside. It wasn't hot in here, but it was smoky. "Fire!" he yelled, putting his arm over his mouth in an attempt to keep out the smoke. "Anybody home?"

"Help!"

It was a woman's voice, but now he thought he could hear a kid crying, too. He hurried toward the sound. "Where are you?"

"Upstairs!"

The cottage had a dormer roof, so there couldn't be more than one or two small rooms up there. He charged up the stairs, taking them two and three at a time.

He found the woman in the middle of a child's room, looking frantic, a toddler on her hip, and a sense of déjà vu hit him hard between the ribs.

Did he know her?

Even in pajama shorts and a ratty T-shirt, with her black hair haphazardly pulled back from her face, she was stunning.

Where had he seen her before?

If he hadn't been in such a hurry to get her and the boy out of there, he might have stopped to think about it more. "There's a fire. We have to go!"

"My brother! I can't find him!"

Brett gestured to the boy in her arms. "He's not…?"

"There's another one! They're twins!"

"Take him and get out," he ordered. "Call 911."

"I can't leave without—"

"Go!" he yelled. "I'll find him. Get out!"

In the span of two seconds flat, the expression on her face went from startled to mad. She was probably a foot shorter than him and half his weight, but she looked about ready to challenge him to a fistfight.

"Get him to safety," Brett said, nodding at the boy clutching her neck. "Please."

As quickly as the fight had entered her, it fled. Her shoulders sagged. Her lower lip quivered. "His name's Dylan. Find him, Brett. I'm begging you."

She knew his name, which meant he really did know her. But how? He coughed—the room was getting smokier. He'd have to figure it out later.

"I will," he said. "I promise."

Maybe it wasn't a promise he could keep, but he'd die before he'd let a little kid burn in a fire.

The woman turned and ran toward the stairs, the toddler in her arms crying in fright. Brett got down on his hands and knees to peer under one of two cribs. "Dylan? Buddy? Where are you? There's a fire. We have to go."

The boy wasn't there.

Brett crawled to the other crib, checked underneath it. No one.

"My name's Brett. I'm here to help you. Your sister took your twin outside. We need to go, too."

He scooted over and opened the closet. The kid wasn't there, either.

"Where'd you go, Dylan? Your sister's worried about you."

He looked in the corners of the room and behind the door. No Dylan.

The smoke was getting bad now, and Brett's eyes were stinging. He charged into the hallway. From the top of the stairs, he could see that the fire had moved into the house, flames licking the wall the living room shared with the garage. Adrenaline shot through him all over again. This was serious. He and the kid really could die up here. "Come on, come on. Where are you?"

He banged into the restroom and checked the bathtub and the shower stall. Nothing.

"Dylan!"

No answer.

The first flare of panic went off in Brett's chest. What if he couldn't find him?

Stay calm, stay calm. You'll find him. You have to.

There was one more small room up here, barely big enough for a bed and a dresser. "Are you in here, Dylan?" Brett called out, getting back onto his hands and knees to look under the bed. "Your sister's worried about you, buddy. The house is on fire, and we have to get you out."

The boy wasn't there.

Had he gone downstairs by himself? Maybe he'd already made it outside.

Brett started for the stairs, but before he could take the first step down, he heard something. A squeak. A sob.

He froze. "Dylan? Call out if you can hear me. It's Brett. I'm here to help you."

Downstairs, the fire had whooshed from one wall to three, the sound loud and hungry, like animals scrapping for food. The smoke was getting thicker, the heat traveling up. Brett was sweating profusely, perspiration dripping into his eyes. If he didn't get out of here soon, he'd have to jump out a window to avoid the flames.

Lord, if the kid is up here, show me where he is.

The panic receded, just a little. If he had to jump out a window, he'd do it, but he wasn't leaving without the little boy.

He heard another sound. A bang. A yelp.

He pulled his shirt up over his mouth and nose and turned his back on the stairs, determined to find the kid this time. In the boys' room, he once again checked the cribs and the closet. He even pulled out the bureau drawers.

Nothing. Still, nothing.

And now it hurt to breathe.

Where were the firefighters? Why weren't they here?

"Dylan!" he yelled, then listened hard. It was difficult to hear anything over the roar of the flames downstairs, but something—maybe a sound, maybe just a feeling—told him to go back in the bathroom.

He went in, and he saw that the door to the cupboard under the sink was slightly ajar.

"Dylan?" he called, getting down on his knees as he opened the cupboard.

The boy was squished in beside the pipes, chubby hands curled around his knees, eyes squinched shut, tears rolling down his face.

"Hey, buddy. I'm Brett. I'm going to pick you up so we can get out of here."

He lifted the boy, whose body was small but solid. The kid squirmed and kicked him, so Brett tightened his hold.

"It's okay, dude. Your sister asked me to get you. There's a fire so we have to leave."

Brett jogged to the top of the staircase, but the flames had already reached the bottom steps. If he wanted to go that way, he'd have to run through the fire, and although he'd have been willing to risk it if it were just him, he wasn't about to subject the boy to the flames.

"Scawy," the boy said, not fighting anymore, but clinging tightly to Brett's neck.

"Yeah, it is scary, isn't it?" Brett took the boy into the bedroom with the cribs, where there were lots of windows. The woman's bedroom only had one.

"Stinky."

"Yup, stinky, too."

He tried to open one of the windows, but it was stuck shut. Went to the second one. It, too, wouldn't budge.

"Come on," he muttered before yanking on the third and

final window, which was also sealed closed. He set the boy down at his feet and rubbed his temples. His eyes were watering, and he was starting to wheeze. He had to get them out of here, and fast.

He crouched down so he could look Dylan in the eye. "Hey, buddy, can you go crawl under that crib right there for a second? I've gotta punch out the window, and I don't want you getting hit by the glass."

After Valerie Williams woke her neighbors, screamed at them to call 911 and unceremoniously dumped Derrick on their living room couch, she ran back outside.

What she saw terrified her.

The house was burning. Her father's whole house was in flames.

Dylan's in there. Dylan's still in there.

Her heart was pounding, and she felt sick.

She shouldn't have left without him. Why had she left without him?

Because Brett Richardson, loudmouth Brett Richardson, told you to.

Shame curdled in her belly. Why had she listened to him? Why had she trusted him? She'd only known the guy for a few years in junior high and high school, but if there was one thing she remembered about him, it was that he was an annoying jerk.

An annoying jerk who was still in there, searching for her little brother. An annoying jerk who might have passed out from smoke inhalation, who might be dead.

She took a couple of steps toward the house, but some of her neighbors had collected on the lawn around her, and one of them caught her by the elbow. "You can't go in there."

She tried to shake him off. "My brother's in there. He's just a baby."

"I'm sorry. I can't let you do it."

"Let go of me, Martin!" She wrenched her arm, almost pulling it out of the socket when her neighbor tightened his grip.

"No."

"Please," she said, her voice cracking. *Please, please, please...*

There were only two things her father had asked of her before he died. One, that she take over his role at the town's fall fundraiser this year, spearheading the silent auction. And two, that she assume custody of her little brothers.

Although neither request was convenient given that she was in the running for a life-changing promotion at work, she'd instantly agreed.

How could she not? After her mother had left when she was seven, her father had been everything to her.

He'd been everything to those two boys, too. Her stepmother hadn't even bothered to stick around for the entire pregnancy. She'd simply filed the divorce papers, signed away her parental rights and dropped the twins off on Valerie's father's doorstep when they were two days old.

Now they were almost three, and for the past two weeks, they'd been Valerie's responsibility.

God willing, they'd be her responsibility for the next fifteen years.

Please don't let anything happen to Dylan, Lord. Please, please, please...

She heard one of the neighbors gasp, and she snapped her head up to see Brett clearing shattered glass out of one of the second-story windows.

"Dylan!" she screamed, and a few seconds later, Brett held up her little brother for her to see.

He found him. Thank God.

Her neighbor let go of her elbow, and she fell to her knees in the grass. Before she could even catch her breath, though, she turned to him, her voice shaking as the panic inside her spiraled back up. "We have to go get him. Martin, can you catch him?"

Martin's mouth opened and closed soundlessly, doubt and hesitation flashing across his face.

Which was precisely when she heard the sirens.

The fire department was coming.

She could only pray they'd reach her brother before the flames.

Chapter Two

"**I** think I liked you better when you couldn't talk back." Brett's sister, Chloe, smirked as she leaned her hip against the door to his hospital room.

Brett scrunched his brow and gave her a look that was half exasperated, half amused. "I haven't even said two words to you yet." He'd been here for a little over forty-eight hours now, and although his voice was still froggy, it wasn't nearly as bad as it had been when they'd first removed the breathing tube.

"Oops. Well, that right there was—how many?" She counted on her fingers. "Nine, and you just proved me right." She blew her blond bangs out of her face, then settled herself into the well-worn armchair in the corner of his balloon- and flower-filled room. "You were *much* easier to take when you were on the ventilator."

He rolled his eyes. He'd been intubated for less than twenty-four hours, but it was something he hoped he'd never experience again. "Thanks a lot, sis." Then, to annoy her, he squinted at her outfit. "That yellow dress of yours is giving me a headache." Chloe had always loved hunting for wacky thrift store clothes.

"This old thing?" His sister smiled. "How about these?" She pointed her toes to show off her pink loafers.

Brett chuckled. "You know how much I love a pink pair of shoes."

"Seriously, though, how're you feeling?"

He sat up straighter in the bed. After they'd removed the breathing tube yesterday, he'd asked the nurses to take all the balloons and give them to the kids in the pediatric ward, and to distribute the flowers amongst any adult patients who needed a lift. Apparently, there weren't that many patients at Cape Cod Memorial Hospital right now, though, because most of the balloons and flowers had made their way back to his room. "Can't wait to get out of here."

"How's your hand?"

He held it out for her to see. Punching out that window had done more damage than he'd expected, and he had lacerations up to his elbow, many of them deep enough that they'd required stitches. He'd also broken two of his fingers—a boxer's fracture, the doctor had called it. It would be a while before he could get back to work.

Which was a problem, given how badly he needed the money from those catering gigs. Before the restaurant had burned down, he'd been the owner, manager and head chef at Half Shell, but he'd stupidly let its property insurance lapse before the fire.

After putting all his money into renovating the restaurant a year and a half ago, then giving Chloe his half of the proceeds from the sale of their parents' home to buy out her share, he was dead broke.

With nothing to show for it and no way to recoup any of his loss.

If his friends Jonathan and Laura hadn't already agreed to let him stay at the Sea Glass Inn, he'd be homeless right now. Chloe and her husband, Steve, certainly didn't have room for him—their house only had three bedrooms, and they were all taken. One by the newlyweds, one by Brett's nephew, Aiden, and another by Steve's great-aunt.

Brett rubbed his face with his good hand. The meager savings he'd managed to scrape together from his catering gigs over the last eight weeks would almost certainly amount to dust by the time he paid the hospital bill for this little adventure.

At the rate he was going, he'd never raise enough money to rebuild the restaurant, and his dream of carrying on his parents' legacy would go unfulfilled.

Chloe made a face at the sight of his mangled hand. "Gross. You should've karate kicked the window. Your shoes would've protected your feet."

If he'd thought of it, he would have, but the only thing he'd been thinking about at the time was getting him and Dylan out of there as fast as he possibly could.

He wiggled the fingers that weren't broken, although, because of the stitches, even that hurt. "You don't think the ladies are going to like my Franken-fist?"

His sister pursed her lips. "If you'd ever actually go out and meet some ladies, they might. It's not every day you get to see a hero's war wounds up close and personal."

Brett waved that off. "I'm not a hero."

Chloe snorted and motioned toward the balloons and flowers. "Tell that to your adoring fans. And all the news outlets calling to interview you."

His eyebrows shot up. "What?"

"Your good buddy Rudy from the *Cape Cod Community Times* called me this morning begging for an exclusive with you."

Brett felt his blood pressure spike. "I hope you told him to get lost."

"Of course I did. But there's a slew of other reporters calling and asking to interview our very own local hero." She placed her hands under her chin and gave him a simpering smile. "What do you want me to say?"

Brett wrinkled his nose. He was no hero. He'd simply been

in the right place at the right time, and he'd done what anyone else would have done. "Tell them no. If I never talk to another reporter again, it'll be too soon."

"Okay, but I doubt anyone could spin this story to paint you in a negative light."

"Not taking that chance, sis." And as for his so-called adoring fans… He nodded his chin at all the balloons and flowers. "I thought I told the nurses to give all this stuff to other patients."

"They did," Chloe informed him, her eyes alight with laughter. "These are all new as of today."

"Really?" Brett shook his head. People were weird. Why would they think he wanted a bunch of flowers? But if it meant that not everyone in this town thought he was a moron, he'd take them and be grateful.

Settling back against his pillow, he asked, "How's the kid? Dylan?"

"He's good. They let him go home yesterday."

"He's not that much older than Aiden, is he?" Buying out Chloe's share of Half Shell had been Brett's belated wedding gift to his sister and Steve. Knowing that their small but growing family had some financial cushion gave him peace of mind.

"Year, year and a half older, I'd guess."

"I hope he wasn't too scared."

"Were *you* scared?"

He thought about telling her how frightened he'd been when the smoke was so thick he could barely see and the fire was so loud he could barely hear and the heat was making him sweat through his shirt and he still—*still*—couldn't find Dylan.

He didn't want to worry her more than he already had, though, so he didn't. "Yes."

Chloe looked away, shaking her head. "You scared me, too."

He wanted to get out of bed and comfort her, but he was still hooked up to a bunch of monitors. "I'm fine, sis."

She picked at her nail polish. "Steve and I, we want to give you back the money from the sale of the house."

"What?" Brett said. "I thought he bought all that new equipment for the clinic." Steve was a physical therapist who owned his own practice in town.

"He did, but he can get a line of credit."

"Chloe, no. That's your money. Don't go into debt for me."

"But you worked so hard on the renovation, and then to see it all come crashing down like that—"

"It's nobody's fault but my own," Brett said, a bite in his tone.

"How was it your fault? You didn't cause the gas leak."

"The fire wasn't my fault, but the insurance? That was definitely on me."

His sister leaned forward, all earnestness. "It was just an oversight, Brett. If I'd still been acting as the general manager, it would've been on me."

"But you weren't. And you hadn't been for over a year, Chlo. I should've hired someone. I shouldn't have tried to do everything myself."

"Be that as it may, we want to help you."

"You need that money. Pretty sure you'll need a bigger house when the new baby arrives."

Chloe's eyes bugged as her hand dropped to her stomach. "How do you know about the baby?"

Brett shook his head, feeling smug. "You've never been able to keep secrets from me."

"Seriously, Brett. How? I'm only eight weeks along. We haven't told anyone yet."

"You were on the phone with Steve yesterday when you thought I was sleeping. I couldn't talk 'cause I was still intubated, but I heard you. Congratulations!"

Chloe laughed and did a facepalm. "Of course that's how you found out. Well, there you go. You're going to be an uncle again!"

Brett grinned. He loved kids and couldn't wait to meet the newest member of the family. "I'm happy for you guys. Aiden's going to be a great big brother."

Chloe smiled. "He is, isn't he?"

"So, keep the money. I won't take it back."

She sighed. "You're too noble for your own good, you know that?"

Lying back, he fake yawned and stretched his good arm above his head, flexing his bicep as he did it. "And humble, too, right?"

She laughed. "How long before the stitches come out? You're going to lose all your muscle tone!"

Brett frowned. He hadn't thought about that. He probably wouldn't be able to do much at the gym until his fractured fingers healed.

Not that he was a gym rat. But he liked to keep in shape.

Still, though… "I'm just glad everyone got out of that house okay."

"I feel the same way," Chloe said, serious now. "And I know Valerie does, too."

He shot her a questioning look. "Valerie?"

"Valerie Williams? From high school?"

That was a blast from the past. He hadn't thought about Valerie Williams since she'd moved away from Wychmere Bay fifteen years ago. "What's she got to do with anything?"

"That was her father's house you were in, Brett. That was her brother you saved."

His mind zinged to a memory of the shy, studious girl he'd known in school—the one with the long, tangled hair and the long, skinny legs and an entire constellation of freckles on her face—and then to a snapshot of the beautiful woman from the other night. His jaw dropped. "*That* was Valerie Williams?"

Chloe gave him an odd look. "You didn't know?"

"How would I know that?"

"You didn't recognize her?"

"Kinda busy trying to get her out of a house that was *on fire*." Besides, the stunning woman from the fire looked *nothing* like the girl he'd known when he was a kid.

"She stopped by yesterday, but you were sleeping."

"Oh, great. She saw me when I was intubated?"

Chloe's lips tipped up into a smile. "Are you worried she didn't like what she saw?"

"No," Brett scoffed, crossing his arms over his chest.

"Liar! You're totally worried! You *like* her!"

"I do not. I saw her for all of, like, three seconds in the middle of a fire, and I spent most of that time yelling at her to get out."

"But you saved her brother, so trust me, it all evens out in the end."

He shook his head. Chloe didn't know what an idiot he'd been when it came to Valerie. After she thanked him for getting Dylan out of the fire, he doubted he'd ever see the woman again.

Chloe wasn't paying attention to his hesitation, though, and she clapped her hands in the weird way she did whenever she got excited. "This is perfect! You have to ask her out!"

"What? No."

"Pleeeeease? You guys could double-date with me and Steve. It would be fun!"

"You and Steve already double-date with Laura and Jonathan. You don't need me."

"But think of how great it would be for Aiden to have some friends his own age."

"Aiden has plenty of friends his own age at day care."

Chloe pouted. "Come on. Humor me."

Brett sighed and shifted in the bed. "Chloe, I lost everything when Half Shell burned down. I don't have a house. I don't have a steady job. And now that I've wrecked my hand, I probably won't be able to pick up any catering gigs for a while. Now is not the right time to start dating."

Her shoulders fell. "It's just been such a long time since you were interested in anyone."

"I'm not interested in Valerie Williams."

There was a small gasp from the doorway, and Brett's heart sank as he turned in that direction, because who was standing there, a hurt look on her lovely, freckled face?

Valerie.

Valerie's hands tightened around the tin of cookies she and the boys had baked as a thank-you gift for Brett. Some things never changed, did they?

Well, that's fine, Brett Richardson. I'm not interested in you, either.

"Is this a bad time?" she asked, pushing her hurt feelings to the floor. Her mentor was constantly telling her that she was too sensitive, that she'd never rise above the level of an associate if she didn't toughen up. "I can come back later."

Although she'd really prefer to get this over with now.

"No." Brett sat up straighter in his hospital bed, sunlight streaming in from the window overlooking the golf course next door. "Now's good. Come in. Chloe was just leaving," he added, shooting his sister a meaningful look.

"Sorry about that, Valerie." Chloe's face flushed with embarrassment. "We were just…"

"Goodbye, Chlo," Brett said firmly, and Valerie's opinion of him took another hit.

She worked with guys like him every day at her investment banking firm in New York. Guys who were big and broad-shouldered, arrogant, ambitious and willing to step on anyone who got in their way.

Not this time, Brett Richardson. This time I'm going to stand up for myself.

"Sorry," he said, looking her straight in the eye. "What I said before you came in wasn't personal—I meant I'm not interested in starting up anything romantic with *anyone* right now."

Valerie shrugged, trying to play it off. The only reason it had stung was because the man was undeniably handsome—even in his hospital gown he was all dark, scruffy jaw and unruly brown hair and muscles. Lots and lots of muscles.

Ew, she needed to stop that right now. You could slap lipstick on a pig, but it'd still be a swine. It was what was on the inside that mattered; she'd learned that lesson early and she'd learned it well.

"How's Dylan?" Brett asked, and Valerie was surprised that he remembered her brother's name.

"He's fine. Back to running around like a hurricane."

"And the other one? His twin?"

"Derrick's good, too."

"Dylan and Derrick?" Brett said, smiling. "That's cute."

She felt an answering smile pull at the corners of her mouth, and it confused her. After the way he and his friends had treated her in school, she definitely shouldn't be smiling at him. But two nights ago, he'd come out of nowhere and literally saved the day.

She'd driven to the hospital feeling magnanimous and wanting to repay him for risking his own life for Dylan's. But then she'd overheard him talking about her to Chloe, and all the old, icky feelings had rushed right back.

And now? She didn't know what to feel. Was he really interested in how the twins were doing?

The guys from her office couldn't care less about her personal life. Aside from her boss, Gary, and her mentor, Gloria, the only coworker who'd even bothered to ask why she was taking a leave of absence had seemed downright gleeful when she'd told him about the twins. Probably because he assumed she'd burn through her twelve weeks of family leave before she could formulate a long-term plan for caring for twin toddlers while working full-time, and the promotion they'd both been chasing would be his.

No way, dude. I've worked too long and too hard to get where I am today. Nobody's taking that job from me. Nobody.

"Well, I came by to say thank you for what you did for us. I don't know what would have happened if it hadn't been for you."

Brett waved that off. "You'd have figured it out. Little guy was hiding under the bathroom sink. He probably would've come out sooner if he'd heard your voice instead of mine."

She held out the tin of cookies. "We baked you some cookies."

"You did?" His eyes lit up as he took the tin and awkwardly pried off the lid with his uninjured hand. "Chocolate chip. My favorite."

His enthusiasm was gratifying, and she felt that smile trying to creep back onto her face. "The boys helped."

Brett held out the tin. "Want one?"

"No, thanks."

He ate one of the cookies in two bites. "Mmm. So much better than the food they serve here." He set the tin down on his bedside table.

"I'm sorry you got hurt," she said, nodding toward his splint and stitches. She'd been frantic when she'd seen how much blood was on Dylan's pajama shirt that night, and she'd only calmed down after the EMTs had assured her it wasn't Dylan's blood—it was Brett's. "Is it bad?"

"It'll heal. But it turns out broken glass is sharp. Who knew?"

She cocked her head to the side. "Um…everybody?"

Brett laughed, and she felt a little burst of pride in her chest. See? She could make the class clown laugh. She wasn't the same sad, shrinking violet she'd been as a teenager.

"You got me there, I guess," Brett said, splaying the hand that hadn't been cut up by the glass. "Where are the kids, by the way?"

"A friend's watching them."

"You could've brought them."

She scrunched her nose. "The twins and small spaces aren't always a great combination."

He chuckled again. "I believe it. Once I get out of here, maybe I can stop by and say hi to them. Where are you staying? How long have you been back in town?"

"A few weeks. My dad passed away recently. I came back to settle his affairs and pick up the twins."

Brett's dark eyes filled with compassion. "I'm sorry about your dad."

Valerie shrugged and looked away. These days, kindness made her weepy, and she didn't want to be vulnerable like that in front of Brett.

Probably picking up on the fact that she didn't want to talk about it, he changed the subject. "Where do you live?"

"New York."

"City? Or state?"

"City."

"Wow. I've heard it's crowded there."

She stifled a giggle. Understatement of the year. "You've never been?"

"I'm not really a city guy."

"Not even Boston?"

He made a face. "I go when I have to. That's where I was

driving back from when I saw the smoke from your house the other night. But honestly? Even Providence is too big for me. I hate the traffic. And how impersonal everything is. People look right through you, like you don't even exist."

He was right about that, although Valerie didn't mind the anonymity. After sticking out like a shoe in a sandal factory in school, she liked the fact that in New York she could blend right in.

"Why were you in Boston so late that night?"

"Working."

"What do you do?" Maybe he was a dockworker or a bouncer at a nightclub or some other job that required him to stay in excellent physical shape.

"I'm a chef."

Her mouth dropped open. "You're kidding."

"No. Why?"

"You don't look like a chef."

He laughed. "What do chefs look like?"

Not like you. "Um…" Flustered now, she could tell she was blushing.

He took mercy on her and changed the subject again. "What do *you* do for work?"

Based on past experience, she knew the tables were about to turn. "Investment banking."

His eyebrows shot up. "Really?"

"Really." She gave him an overly sweet smile. "Why? Do I not look like an investment banker?"

He smirked. "Touché, mademoiselle. Touché."

They smiled at each other for a second, and the strangest sense of calm cinched around her, like a warm blanket, or a big, fluffy robe.

What in the world…?

She broke his gaze. This was Brett "The Dog Ate My Homework" Richardson. Brett "No Time to Study Because of Football Practice" Richardson. Brett "In Love with a Queen Bee Cheerleader" Richardson.

Whatever this weird attraction was, it was clearly one-sided. Besides, she and the twins would leave Cape Cod soon after the Cranberry Harvest Festival, and she would never see him again.

"Uh… I should go," she said.

"Wait. New York City—is that where you moved in the middle of tenth grade?"

He remembered when she'd left? "No. My dad pulled me out and sent me to boarding school in Boston."

Well, first he'd sent her to a residential treatment center for three months, but Brett didn't need to know about that.

"Boarding school?" He cringed. "Yikes."

"It was a good thing, actually. I wasn't bullied there like I was here."

His face went pale. "Was it really that bad?"

She bit back a sigh of frustration. "Maybe you don't re-member this, but you and your pals on the football team used to call me Sticks and Dead Girl because I was so skinny. And your girlfriend started a rumor that I was a freak because of my eyes. Created a whole fake social media profile just to humiliate me."

Valerie had sectoral heterochromia: her right eye was gray, but her left eye was a mix of gray and blue.

Until her mom left when she was seven, Valerie had loved her mismatched eyes. Her twin sister, Vanessa, whose eyes had been the same, had liked them, too.

But after Vanessa died, her mom had said that looking at Valerie was like looking at a ghost, and she couldn't do it anymore.

Then she'd left. And Valerie hadn't spoken to her since.

Was it any wonder she'd struggled with her mental health—and an eating disorder—as a teen?

She was just grateful that, since then, God had shown her who she really was. Chosen. Loved. Forgiven. A daughter of the Most High King.

Even so, sometimes looking back on her childhood and adolescence still hurt.

Brett rubbed a hand across his jaw, his face drawn. "Tracy did that?"

Valerie gave him a tight smile. "She did."

"I'm sorry. I didn't know."

Valerie hiked her shoulder. "How is she, by the way?"

It was Brett's turn to shrug. "No idea."

"You two didn't…stay in touch?" Granted, they'd all been young back then, but Brett and Tracy—the jock and the cheerleader—had seemed like they'd go the distance.

And sure, Valerie had been jealous. Not of Tracy, per se, but of any girl who had a long-term boyfriend who clearly adored her.

Valerie certainly hadn't had that in high school. And although she'd dated a bit since, she'd never felt *adored*.

"We stayed in touch for a while." Brett looked away, and she saw a muscle in his jaw twitch. "Not anymore."

"Sorry," she said, because it was polite.

"Water under the bridge."

She didn't know what to say to that, and it seemed like he didn't, either, because they were both silent until it started to feel awkward. She shuffled her feet on the linoleum tiles.

"Well, um—" she started, just as he said, "I always liked your eyes. And your freckles."

"Oh." Her hand flitted to her face. Her heart fluttered in her chest.

Was he…*flirting* with her? Or just saying something nice in an attempt to make up for the fact that his ex-girlfriend had called her names?

"How much longer are you staying in town?" he asked.

"I don't know. Before he died, my dad made me promise to help out with the Cranberry Harvest Festival, so at least until that's over, but now we'll probably have to stay until I get this whole mess with the house sorted out…"

Brett was staring at her, and it made her squirmy. "What?" she said.

"I'm the one who nominated the charity the festival is backing this year, so I'm pretty involved, too."

"Oh. What's the charity?"

"Parents Against Drunk and Distracted Driving."

"Nice." That was a good cause. It made her feel a little less anxious to know that the proceeds from the silent auction she was supposed to organize would support a worthy charity.

Her dad had given her all his notes, including his goal for how much money he wanted the auction to bring in. It was a lot, but he'd been adamant that Valerie could do it. "Look at all the money you help those companies raise through your job," he'd said. "It'll be a piece of cake for you."

But it wasn't. At all.

At work, she spent 99 percent of her time on the computer analyzing financial information and putting together presentations for her boss. She rarely had face time with clients, and she was *never* the one asking them for anything.

Organizing a silent auction meant seeing people she hadn't laid eyes on in fifteen years. Talking to people she hadn't spoken with since tenth grade. And then putting her hand out and pleading for a favor.

Ugh.

She'd promised, though, and she never went back on her word. Especially not to her dad.

Brett nodded down at his injured arm. "I'm supposed to help with the setup and the teardown on the day of, but I'm not sure I'm going to be much use for that anymore."

"How long before the stitches come out?" she asked.

"A week or so for the stitches, but they said it could take as long as six weeks for the broken fingers to heal."

She winced. "I'm sorry." The cookies she'd brought seemed entirely inadequate in light of the injuries he'd sustained.

He studied his fist before catching her gaze and holding it. "A hundred percent worth it."

And there it was again, that feeling of warm serenity—like a smooth stone skipping across the still surface of a calm lake.

But the rational part of her mind screamed, *Brett "Can I Copy Your Homework" Richardson is not someone you can start crushing on. You have the boys to think about, and your job in New York—the job you've poured your whole self into for years!*

"We could, uh, trade volunteer jobs," she suggested. She might not be particularly big or strong, but surely an able-bodied woman would be better equipped to help set up and clean up the festival than broken-handed Brett.

"What are you supposed to do?"

"Organize the silent auction. My dad said it would be easy, but I don't know any of the shop owners here, so I'm having trouble psyching myself up to go ask for donations."

His chest puffed out. "Well, I know everyone in town, so I can definitely help with that. When should we go? I'm supposed to get out of here tomorrow, so how about the day after?"

"Oh." Like so many things about this conversation with him, that caught her off guard. "You want to go together?"

"Well, yeah," he said, as though it were completely obvious.

"I thought you could handle the auction, and I could do the setup and whatnot."

"Aw, come on. You know I'm not going to leave you on your own to set up the venue. And it never hurts to have a pretty girl with you when you're asking for free stuff."

"Oh, um…." Her face heated again. He thought she was pretty?

She willed her heart to stop beating so fast. It wasn't like he was asking her on a date. He just wanted her to tag along while he solicited donations for the auction.

But the fact that she was reacting like he'd asked her out? Huge red flag.

"Uh, no," she said, glancing at the door. "That's not... No. I have to go."

"Wait." He reached out a hand. "You never told me where you were staying."

Nope, I didn't. And I'm not going to.

She had to get out of here before she did something she knew she'd regret. Teaming up with him now would be just as bad, just as pointless and every bit as pathetic as helping him with his homework back in middle school.

Worse, actually.

She was a grown woman now. Not a sad little girl desperate to be accepted by her peers.

Ignoring his comment, she raised her hand in what she hoped was a friendly goodbye wave, although she suspected it looked more like a manic brush-off. "I've really got to go. Enjoy the cookies!"

Then she sped out of the hospital like a hyena was chasing her, proud that she'd stood her ground and refused to spend more time with Brett.

And if there was a small part of her that regretted leaving so awkwardly and abruptly?

She'd get over it. She always did.

Chapter Three

The next evening, Brett sat on the back porch of Chloe and Steve's house, a soda in hand as Steve manned the grill, cooking a rainbow trout they'd caught that afternoon. The scent of charcoal, crackling fish skin and fire-licked onions floated on the fresh autumn breeze.

Brett liked it out here, at Frog Pond. It was almost like Steve and Chloe lived in the forest, with large trees looming all around their cozy cottage and the small, still body of water.

Today had been just what he'd needed. From the moment they'd picked him up from the hospital, it had been pure relaxation.

Steve and Chloe's toddler, Aiden, was running around the deck in footie pajamas. Brett chuckled when he saw that the little guy was chewing on a pine cone. Aiden was an endless source of amusement, and it made Brett wonder, for the umpteenth time that day, how Dylan was doing.

Not that he had a way to find out. If Valerie had agreed to work with him on the Cranberry Harvest Festival, he'd have had an excuse to get her number, but the way things stood, she'd practically sprinted out of his hospital room yesterday in her haste to get away from him.

Chloe scooped Aiden up and plopped him onto her lap. "No, silly boy," she scolded, prying the pine cone out of his hands. "You're not a squirrel. You don't eat pine cones!"

Brett had worried about his sister when she'd first reconnected with Steve, but his fears had been unfounded. Steve was a quiet, serious guy, but Chloe seemed to bring out his lighter side, and he clearly adored her.

Chloe held Aiden out to Brett. "Want to play one last round of horsey with him? I'm going to put him down for the night in a minute."

"Hosey! Hosey!" Aiden cried, reaching for Brett.

Brett let his sister settle Aiden on his lap, then wrapped his uninjured arm around the boy's waist. When Brett started bouncing him up and down on his knee, Aiden laughed, the sound bubbling out of him like flashes of quicksilver.

"All right," Chloe called out, laughing. "Let's not get him completely riled up right before bed."

Brett stopped and let Chloe retrieve Aiden. She held him up and said in a singsong voice, "Night, night, Daddy. Night, night, Uncle Brett."

"Night, night, buddy." Steve abandoned his post at the barbeque to ruffle the boy's blond hair and kiss him on the forehead.

"Sleep tight, little dude," Brett added.

Chloe went inside and slid the screen door shut.

"How're you doing on your soda?" Steve asked. "Need a refill?"

Brett took a sip. "Nope, I'm good."

Steve picked up a set of tongs and poked at the food on the grill. "Glad you could make it tonight." Brett was rarely available for dinner during the Cape's busy summer season, when the restaurant was going full tilt. Not that he had to worry about that right now, although if he hadn't gotten injured, he'd have been at a catering gig tonight.

"Thanks for picking me up. This was fun today."

"You deserve to relax and kick back a little. I can't even imagine what it must have been like, running into that house."

Wind whispered through the trees, shaking the leaves, which were just starting to change colors. "Running into it wasn't the scary part. It was being upstairs with all the smoke and the heat, and not being able to find the kid."

"Thank God you did, though."

"Amen to that, brother," Brett said.

Steve took a sip of his soda, then used a spatula to take the fish off the grill and slide it onto a serving plate. "Chloe said you know the woman who owns the house."

Brett shifted in his chair. "Used to." Once again, he pictured the shy, skinny girl who used to hide behind her hair. It was hard to reconcile his memory of her with the beautiful woman who'd visited him in the hospital.

After they'd been paired up for an assignment in middle school, she'd helped him with his homework almost every afternoon. That had changed once they got to high school, though, and it had been 100 percent his fault.

He could remember in vivid detail the first time he'd heard one his football teammates call her Sticks—the way her eyes had shot to his, silently begging him for help, even as his buddies laughed and fist-bumped each other.

Even then, he'd known that averting his gaze was the wrong thing to do. But he'd been new to the team, and he hadn't wanted any of his teammates asking him how he knew her or why he needed so much help with his schoolwork.

And so he'd watched, feeling ashamed, as she'd turned, shoulders slumped, and walked away. Half of him had wanted to run after her and apologize, while the other half had had all the maturity of a fourteen-year-old boy.

For the next year and a half, she'd ignored him, and he'd ignored her back. He'd always been aware of her, though, like a sliver he couldn't quite pull out.

Until one day, she'd been gone, along with any chance he had of making amends.

Well, he might have been an idiot in high school, but he hoped he'd have a chance to make it up to her now.

For some reason, he'd thought the nickname Sticks was related to the chopsticks she'd occasionally worn in her hair. If he'd realized it was a comment about her weight, he might have tried to put a stop to it. Even as a clueless teenager, his interactions with his sister, as well as Tracy, had made him aware that weight was a touchy subject for teenage girls.

He'd also had no idea that they called her Dead Girl, or that Tracy had called Valerie a freak.

Would he have done something about that if he'd known about it? He wanted to think he would have, but he'd been full-on infatuated with Tracy in high school.

And afterward, too.

Right up until eight years ago when he was down on one knee with a ring in his hand and she'd said no.

He'd heard she'd be at the Cranberry Harvest Festival this year, which some of the members of his graduating class were using as an unofficial high school reunion.

His stomach churned at the thought of seeing her again.

He'd only seen her once since she'd turned down his proposal. After marrying some other guy less than a year after breaking his heart, she'd actually had the audacity to bring her new husband to dinner at Half Shell right before they left on their honeymoon.

Although it had hurt—badly—at the time, ultimately it had helped him let the last of his feelings for her go. But he really had no desire to see her at the festival and dredge up all that ugliness from the past.

Steve studied Brett as he lifted his soda can to his lips. "Chloe thought you might be thinking about asking Fire Girl out."

"Fire Girl?" Brett chuckled. "Nope." He tried to hide the wince that accompanied the memory of Valerie hightailing it out of his hospital room. "She's an investment banker in New York City. Way out of my league."

And not just because she was beautiful.

She was smart—that's one thing he definitely remembered about her. And it had been thoughtful of her to bring cookies to the hospital.

Plus, he really did like her eyes. He didn't understand why Tracy had thought they were freaky. To him, the swirl of gray and blue in her left eye was like a mosaic: so pretty, so kaleidoscopic, so rare.

When they were talking yesterday, it had seemed like they had some kind of connection. It had clearly spooked her, though. Thanks to his high school stupidity, she wanted nothing to do with him now.

All thoughts of romance aside, he'd at least like to know how she and the twins were doing. After everything that had happened the other night, he felt protective of them. He wanted to make sure they were all okay.

Chloe came back outside carrying the baby monitor. "Who's out of your league?" she asked, her gaze ping-ponging between the two men.

"No one," Brett said.

Chloe narrowed her eyes at him. "Don't leave me hanging. What were you two talking about?"

"How beautiful you are," Steve said smoothly, bending to give her a kiss on the cheek.

"Ha ha," she replied, swatting him on the chest.

"Seriously." He caught her hand and drew her into a loose embrace. "You're very beautiful. Even your crusty old brother agrees."

Brett snorted—at twenty-nine, he was just one year older than Chloe and a whole year younger than Steve. "Enough PDA, people. Food's ready, right? Let's eat."

Steve laughed and added the vegetables to the serving plate, while Chloe went inside to get the salad and rice.

"You were talking about Valerie Williams, weren't you?" she asked, after she came back out and they'd all filled their plates.

Brett shot Chloe a wary glance. "Maybe. But I already told you I'm not interested in dating right now."

"Did I say anything about dating?" She batted her eyelashes like a beauty queen.

Brett wagged a finger at her. "Not subtle, sis. Not subtle at all."

"Can I help it if I want the best for you? She's smart. And nice. Way nicer than Tracy."

"How would you know?" Brett asked. "You weren't in her class."

"I hung out with her a bit at church camp. And reading club."

"Reading club?" he repeated incredulously. "Was that an actual thing?"

"Yes, Brett," Chloe said with exaggerated patience. "Some of us actually *like* to read."

"It's not that I don't like it…"

"I know," she said quickly. "I'm sorry. I didn't mean it like that."

Brett had always disliked school and done poorly on tests. For a long time, he'd thought he was just stupid—a dumb jock—and then, in his senior year of high school, he'd had an English teacher who'd referred him to an outside reading specialist for dyslexia.

The coaching had helped, but aside from audiobooks, reading wasn't something he'd ever consider a pleasure. He hated paperwork, too, which was probably why he'd ignored it—and let the restaurant's insurance policy lapse—after Chloe quit as the general manager at Half Shell.

The conversation moved on, and when they finished their meal, dusk was deepening into night. The wood frogs around the pond croaked and an owl hooted from the trees. Chloe brought out some oatmeal raisin cookies from the kitchen. Brett ate a couple, then sat back and closed his eyes, enjoying the cool night breeze on his face.

Steve went inside to put the dishes in the dishwasher, and Chloe studied Brett across the table. "In all seriousness, if you like her, you should ask her out. You can even sweeten the deal by telling her I'll babysit the twins."

Brett shook his head. "You've got to stop trying to set me up with every single woman who crosses your path." Ever since Chloe had gotten serious with Steve, she'd been obsessed with finding someone special for Brett, too.

"I know I've been a little...overzealous in the past, but I like Valerie. I think she'd be good for you."

"You don't even know her anymore, Chlo."

She waved her hand dismissively. "People don't change that much."

Brett fingered his stitches. Valerie's appearance had changed a lot, but he got what his sister was saying. The *essence* of a person was what generally stayed the same.

But if that was true, and he'd been someone who hadn't stood up for her against a bunch of bullies, what did that say about him?

Nothing good, that was for sure.

"Her job's in New York."

"So? Steve and I made the whole long-distance thing work."

"That was different," Brett said. "You were always going to come back home." The very same day Chloe had finished her student teaching internship in Boston last year, she'd moved back to Wychmere Bay and Steve had proposed. They'd married six months later.

She shook her head. "Not necessarily. If I hadn't found a job here, Steve was willing to sell the clinic and come with me."

"Really? He'd have sold his business?"

His sister shrugged. "If he'd had to."

Brett ran a hand through his hair. To reopen the restaurant, he had to stay here. Relocating would never be an option for him. "You two are too much."

"You're never going to meet anyone if you don't put yourself out there again."

Chloe was right—he knew she was. And Brett *did* want to find someone he could build a life and a family with.

But not until he got the restaurant back up and running. And not with someone who lived in New York City and worked as an investment banker.

"I just saw the girl for the first time in fifteen years. I'm not asking her out."

His sister's eyes sparkled with mischief. "Sometimes when you know, you know."

"I don't *know* anything."

Chloe hooted. "He finally admits it!"

Brett rolled his eyes. "You're a brat."

She stuck out her tongue. "Takes one to know one."

"Enough of that now, kids," Steve said, smirking as he walked onto the deck with fresh soda cans in hand. "Let's all play nice."

He handed out the drinks and then sat next to Chloe, looping his arm around her shoulders. She leaned into his embrace and looked up at him, tenderness written all over her face.

Brett felt a pang of longing. Valerie might not be the right woman for him, but once he put together a plan for reopening the restaurant, he *should* start dating again.

He wanted a wife and a family. He just hoped that God wanted him to have those things, too.

* * *

Mornings with the twins were…loud. Fun, but loud.

The high volume hadn't been a problem when they were staying at their dad's house, but now that the house was gone and her friend Laura had let them move into the Sea Glass Inn, Valerie was constantly worried they were wearing out their welcome.

"Valwee! Dilly Dally!" Derrick called, using his nickname for his twin. "Come see da truck!" He waved a purple monster truck over his head, and Dylan ran right over.

"That's a nice one, honey, but let's keep our voices down."

"Vroom, vroom!" he shouted, shooting the truck into the wall.

Dylan yelled, "Bang!" and started laughing.

"Boom!" Derrick grabbed the truck in his chubby hands and shot it back into the wall.

"Shh," Valerie said, cringing, her finger to her lips. "It's too early to be yelling." Then she turned up the enthusiasm in an attempt to get them excited about something else. "Let's get dressed and go have breakfast!"

She'd been amazed at how her father's community had rallied around her and the boys in the wake of the fire, dropping off clothes, toys and toiletries for them at the inn. Laura, too—her old friend from boarding school—had been amazing, insisting that since the inn wasn't open for business during the offseason anyway, Valerie and the twins could stay as long as they needed…for free.

Valerie had tried to protest—she had a healthy emergency fund saved up from her six years working at the investment bank—but Laura wouldn't take no for an answer.

Good thing Laura and her husband, Jonathan, also had small children. Their daughter, Emma, was seven, and their baby, Hunter, was just four months old.

Valerie managed to get the twins dressed in different color

shirts. Although she could easily tell them apart—Derrick was the loud alpha twin, while Dylan was his slightly shyer, more cuddly counterpoint—it helped others when she could tell them that Dylan was the one in the red shirt and Derrick was wearing blue.

"Daddy have brekkie with us?" Dylan asked as the three of them descended the wooden staircase to the first floor.

Closing her eyes, Valerie said a quick prayer. She'd explained this to the boys countless times since her father's death, but it wasn't sinking in. "No, honey. Remember? Daddy's in Heaven now."

"We go visit Heaben?" Dylan asked, his big blue eyes blinking up at her, all innocence.

She ruffled his curly black hair, which was due for a haircut. "No, honey. It's not somewhere we can go visit."

"On da phone?" Derrick chimed in, no doubt remembering the many times their father had let them talk to her on the phone using video chat.

Valerie shook her head. "I'm sorry, guys, but we can't call him on the phone. You can still talk to Daddy, but you won't hear him answer. That's okay, though, because he'll always be there when you need him, in your heart."

She laid her hand on her chest to emphasize her point, but the boys just looked up at her in confusion, their little heads cocked to the side.

"Maybe Daddy at da beach!" Derrick suggested to Dylan.

"I lub da beach!" Dylan cried.

"We go swimming with Daddy and da fishies!"

"And crabs!"

"Sharks!"

"Nemo!"

"Mermans!"

"Beach, Valwee?" Dylan asked, turning to her. "We go to da beach today?"

Valerie sighed and forced a smile. She didn't want to have to keep explaining the concept of death to the twins, but she could see no way around it. Their three-year-old minds couldn't grasp the idea that their daddy was gone for good.

"Sure, guys, we can go to the beach today, but let's have breakfast first."

"Brekkie!" Derrick shouted, running for the swinging wooden door that separated the inn's quaint parlor from the dining room. Dylan charged right after him.

Valerie fingered her necklace. Had she and Vanessa been this much of a handful as little girls? Seeing the boys together made Valerie miss not just her father, but her twin sister, too.

Cancer was a beast. A vicious, awful beast.

She followed the boys into the dining room, which was big and sunny, filled with farmhouse tables that probably overflowed with guests during the inn's high season in the summer. It was mid-September now and quiet, although the weather today could have fooled anyone into believing it was still mid-July.

Jonathan was nursing a cup of coffee at one of the tables. Emma sat next to him, mopping up syrup with her last bite of pancake.

"Morning." Jonathan raised his mug to Valerie. He was a lawyer with the juvenile court system, and he was dressed for work.

"Good morning," she replied, noting that there was a platter of pancakes and a plateful of scrambled eggs on the sideboard. "Is that up for grabs?"

Jonathan nodded. "Help yourself."

Valerie started putting together plates for the boys. They, meanwhile, ran to sweet little Emma. "Come to da beach with us, Emma! We see crabs and mermans!"

"That sounds fun," she said brightly, "but I have school."

"We swim with da fishies and da sharks," Derrick announced.

"And Daddy. And Nemo. And crabs," Dylan added.

"That's so cool," Emma told them. "Maybe we can all go on the weekend."

"Da weekend!" Derrick cheered. "We go on da weekend!"

"Sit down, guys," Valerie instructed. "I have pancakes for you."

The twins clambered into chairs next to Emma. "I lub pancakes!" Dylan said.

"Did you and your dad make them, Emma?" Valerie asked, setting the plates down in front of the boys. "They smell delicious."

Emma shook her head, her mouth full of eggs.

"Oh, is your mom up already?" Valerie glanced over her shoulder at the swinging door from the dining room into the kitchen. She'd heard Hunter crying a couple of times in the night, so she was surprised that Laura was awake and alert so early in the morning.

But just as she finished asking, the door swung open, and a man called out, "All right! Who wants bacon?"

"Me!" Emma cried, and the boys started yelling, "Me!" too.

Valerie's eyes flew to Jonathan's face. *Was that...?*

"Wow, that's what I like to hear!" Brett said as he strode into the room like a rock star, wearing a chef's hat and carrying a sizzling plate of bacon. "A little enthusiasm!"

His dark eyes widened in surprise when he saw her, but he recovered immediately, winking at her before he started chanting, "Ba-con! Ba-con! Ba-con!"

The kids all joined in. "Ba-con! Ba-con! Ba-con!"

Valerie darted another confused glance at Jonathan, who smiled, shrugged and plucked a piece of bacon off the plate. It was dark and crispy, and the smell was enough to make Valerie's mouth water.

What was Brett doing here so early in the morning?

After the way she'd reacted to him in the hospital, she'd

needed a clean break, but here he was, cooking fantastic food and wearing that chef's hat like a boss and…and *winking* at her.

"Valwee!" Dylan said happily, his mouth full. "Da fire man maked us bacon!"

Valerie pressed her palms to her cheeks, which she was certain—after that wink—were bright red.

One thing was for sure: someone had a lot of explaining to do.

Chapter Four

Valerie gaped at Laura, who was sitting on the couch in the inn's pretty, blue-hued parlor, Hunter on her shoulder. She'd just learned that Brett was staying here, at the Sea Glass Inn, for the foreseeable future because he'd sold his house a couple of months ago and then his restaurant had *burned down*.

Attempting to compose herself, Valerie glanced at the twins, who were playing with their monster trucks by the window overlooking the ocean, and lowered her voice as she asked, "Did they…did they investigate him for arson?"

"What?" Laura burst out laughing, startling Hunter, who started to cry. "Shh, you're okay, little man." Once she'd calmed him down, she turned back to Valerie. "You're not serious, are you?"

Valerie caught herself chewing on her nails—an old nervous habit—and moved her hand away from her mouth. "It's a pretty weird coincidence, isn't it? His restaurant burns down and then he's there when *my* house goes up in flames a few weeks later?"

Laura scrunched her brow. She was still in her pajamas, with a fluffy robe thrown on top. There were dark circles under her eyes and her wavy brown hair obviously hadn't been brushed. "You do realize that Brett is Jonathan's best friend, right?"

Valerie nodded.

"And that I've known him and his sister for, like, ever?"

Valerie nodded again.

"So, you think—what? That he goes around burning down buildings for fun?"

Did she think that? No, Brett wasn't evil, but he'd proved back in school that he was definitely okay with cutting corners. "What if he burned down his restaurant for the insurance money, and then he set my house on fire and ran in to save us to throw the investigators off the scent?"

Laura chuckled and shook her head. "You watch a lot of crime shows, don't you?"

"I wouldn't say I watch a lot of them…" Although she did turn them on sometimes when she needed to unwind after a long day at work. There was something very satisfying about watching a show where everything was good or bad, right or wrong—and where the bad guys always came to justice in the end.

"It's an interesting theory," Laura said, "but Brett didn't have insurance at the time of the fire, so I can tell you for a fact he wouldn't have done it for the insurance money."

Valerie's mouth fell open again. What kind of small business owner didn't have business insurance? That was just asking for trouble.

Laura yawned and shifted Hunter from her shoulder to her lap. The sweet little boy had fallen fast asleep in her arms. "There was a gas leak at the restaurant. The fire department's already cleared him. And didn't you say they thought it was an electrical fire at your dad's place?"

Valerie nodded, feeling terrible now for letting her mind leap to the worst possible scenario.

"Brett's a good person, Val. If he can help someone, he'll do it, even if it's hard or inconvenient for him."

Valerie shook her head. Laura's description simply didn't jibe with her memories of him from high school. "I left town because of him and his friends, Laura. I had to go to that eating disorder treatment center because of them."

That last part wasn't the whole truth, but it had felt true enough back then.

Laura reached over and squeezed Valerie's forearm. "I'm sorry they picked on you so much. I know it was hard on you."

Valerie ducked her head, tears pricking her eyes. She hadn't felt this emotional about the bullying in a long time, but being back here where it had all happened was bringing it straight to the surface. "I never thought I'd see any of them again, but here he is, everywhere I go."

"Did Brett know about Tracy's social media antics?"

"He said he didn't." But Valerie found that hard to believe. Brett and Tracy had practically been glued to each other back then.

And no, she didn't remember Brett himself ever calling her a name, but he also never spoke up when his buddies did it, either.

The worst part was, up until he'd joined the football team, she'd thought they were friends. Or friendly, at least. She'd thought that because she'd helped him out with his homework, he'd tell his teammates to knock it off with the name-calling and tell his girlfriend to shut down her awful posts.

But he hadn't.

Not once in a whole year and a half.

Laura gave her a sympathetic look. "Guys can be kind of clueless sometimes. If he said he didn't know about the online stuff, I'm sure he didn't."

"Why didn't you tell me he was staying here, too?"

"I didn't know he was part of the group that used to pick on you. I honestly didn't think you'd mind."

Valerie blew out a breath. She *shouldn't* mind. She just felt so discombobulated around him. Was he the kid who'd copied her homework and let his friends call her horrible names? Or the man who'd rushed into a fire to save her and her brothers? The one who'd called her pretty, who'd said he'd always liked her mismatched eyes?

She liked things to be cut and dried, and Brett was confusing her.

"He said he and Tracy aren't together anymore. Does she still live here?"

Laura shook her head. "She got married and moved to Chicago six or seven years ago. Brett was pretty upset about it back in the day. He proposed to her after he got out of the navy, but she said she didn't want to stay on Cape Cod for the rest of her life. Turned him down cold in front of all their friends."

A twinge of sympathy tugged at Valerie. She couldn't imagine how awful it would be to propose to someone you'd loved for years only to be rejected in such a public way.

A monster truck hit her foot, and Valerie glanced at the twins, who were watching her from across the room and snickering. She gave them a stern look. "Please don't shoot monster trucks at me or Mrs. Laura. It's not nice, and someone could get hurt."

"We tired of trucks," Derrick announced. "Me and Dilly Dally want to go to da beach now!"

Valerie turned to Laura. "Should we wait until Hunter wakes up so you two can come with us?"

"You guys go. I'm just going to sit here for a while and close my eyes while he's napping."

Valerie glanced at the baby, whose little chest was rising and falling with each baby-sized breath he took. "He sleeps so well during the day…"

"I know! You'd think the light and the noise would be a deterrent, but no. Having things going on around him seems to lull him to sleep."

Valerie chuckled. "Well, any time you need the twins to make a ruckus, you just let me know!"

* * *

Brett had been happy to escape the inn after breakfast for a walk on the beach. School was back in session, so there weren't many people around. A couple of middle-aged women out walking their dogs, some teenagers who were probably skipping school, a grizzled older guy out running.

He hadn't realized Valerie and the twins were staying at the inn, too, but it didn't surprise him. During the offseason, Laura and Jonathan were always opening their home to people who needed a temporary place to stay.

Last winter, they'd taken in a family who'd lost their house after the father had been laid off from work. Fortunately, the man had found a new job within a few weeks, and the family had managed to save enough money to get a rental home before the holidays.

Brett hoped his trajectory would be similar. But with his bum hand, there wasn't much he could do in the way of work. Whipping up a few pancakes and strips of bacon was one thing, but he couldn't really cook. Nor could he safely drive a car while his hand was in a sling, so even delivering food was out.

During the summer, Wychmere Bay's small population tripled thanks to all the tourist traffic, but it was September now, and no one in town needed retail help. Maybe Steve could give him a ride up to the Cape Cod Mall in Hyannis, and he could see if anyone there was hiring.

It would be good to get out of the inn for a while, anyway. Having breakfast with Emma, Jonathan and the twins this morning had been fun, but Valerie had hardly even looked at him. Her discomfort had been palpable, and he felt lousy about it.

He didn't want her to feel awkward around him, especially if they were both going to be staying at the inn through the end of the Cranberry Harvest Festival. But if saving her and her brothers from a fire hadn't swayed her opinion of him, he wasn't sure what else he could do.

Sand fleas dancing across his feet, he stared out to sea. The ocean was a swell of muted gray churn this morning—no waves, just a rhythmic back and forth swaying. The air was briny, and the primordial brown shells of washed-up horseshoe crabs dotted the sand all the way down to the jetty.

A few years ago, Brett had read an article about how the medical industry harvested horseshoe crab blood for use in medical testing, and how the animals would be caught, cleaned, hung upside down and bled from the heart before being released back into the wild.

He felt an affinity with them. Since the night his parents had died in a car crash, he'd donated blood, like clockwork, every fifty-six days.

And that's when it hit him, how he could potentially change Valerie's opinion of him: the Cranberry Harvest Festival, which she was only involved in because she'd made a death-bed promise to her father.

She might not want to work with him on getting donations for the silent auction, but that didn't mean she wanted to do it herself—she'd told him as much at the hospital. He could take that burden off her shoulders by visiting some of the local businesses this afternoon, then presenting her with the donations as a peace offering.

In fact, he might as well go get started on that now. He turned to head back to the inn when—

"Look! It's da bacon man!" Derrick and Dylan raced over the dunes toward him, one in a red bathing suit and sun shirt, the other dressed in blue.

"Bacon man!" the other twin shouted, before they both barreled into Brett's legs.

Brett laughed and patted them on the head. "Hey, guys. How are ya?"

"We go swimming with da fishies and da sharks!" the red-suited twin announced.

"Derrick! Dylan! What did I tell you about staying where I can see you?" Valerie demanded as she came jogging over a dune and saw the boys clustered around Brett.

"We sawed da bacon man! He at da beach!" This time, it was the blue-suited twin who answered.

Valerie, who was wearing black athletic shorts, a black ball cap and a white T-shirt, shot him a quick glance, an apology in her eyes. "I see that, Derrick. Did you say hello to Mr. Brett before you jumped all over him?"

"Hullo, Mr. Bacon Man," Derrick said dutifully.

"Not Mr. Bacon Man," Valerie corrected. "Mr. Brett."

"You da fire man *and* da bacon man," the red-suited twin chirped.

Brett chuckled. "Yup. And you must be my man Dylan."

"Dat's me!" the boy said, beaming.

"You build a sandcastle with us, Mr. Bacon Man?" Derrick asked.

"Mr. Brett," Valerie interjected.

"Mr. Brett Man," the boy corrected himself, much to Brett's amusement. "We bringed buckets and shobbels."

Brett glanced at Valerie, who was holding the sand toys, and raised his eyebrows. He'd be happy to play with the kids, but only if she was comfortable with it.

"Is it safe for you to get sand on your arm?" she asked. "With the stitches and all?"

He pulled a plastic garbage bag out of his pocket. His injured hand was in a sling, but he wasn't taking any chances. "I came prepared. I'll just wrap it up in this baby, and then it should be good to go." He glanced at the twins. "I'll be like Captain Hook and only use one hand!"

The boys cheered. Valerie, meanwhile, chewed on one of her nails. "You don't have to stay if you don't want to."

"I like building sandcastles." And the boys were a hoot.

"Are you sure?" she asked.

"Are *you* sure?" he countered.

She handed the sand toys to the twins. "Boys, go pick a good spot for your sandcastle."

The two of them ran off to inspect the sand next to the life-guard tower. Valerie sighed.

Brett gave her a sympathetic smile. "They seem like a handful."

"You have no idea." She took off her ball cap to redo her ponytail. The wind blew a strand of hair into her face. It stuck to her lip gloss, and she had to peel it off her lips before pulling it back into her elastic band.

No, *she* had no idea how much trouble Brett was having looking away from her. All he could think about was smoothing a hand through Valerie's shiny black hair.

He absolutely did *not* need to be thinking about her beautiful long hair or her kaleidoscope eyes or the dainty freckles dotting the porcelain skin on her pretty face. He needed to prove that he'd grown up since high school—that he was trustworthy and that she didn't need to be on guard around him.

He shoved his good hand into his pocket and turned his attention to the twins, who had already started digging. "Should I go over there and help them?"

"The beauty of twins—they play great together." She slipped her ponytail through the opening at the back of her ball cap, then tugged the hat down lower on her head. "They'll let us know when our services are needed."

He nodded and watched the boys collect sand in their buckets for a minute or two, aware of her small and delicate frame next to him but determined to focus on something else.

Lord, he prayed. *Take my thoughts captive. Make them obedient to Christ.*

"Sorry about the Mr. Bacon Man thing," she said, playing with the thin gold chain around her neck.

"Aw, don't worry about that. They can call me Mr. Bacon Man. It's funny. Makes me sound like a superhero."

"Well," she said, glancing up at him while obviously trying to hold back a smile, "that bacon *was* pretty good."

Like a match sparking against kindling, that hint of a smile lit something up inside him. He wanted to make her smile at him again, and again.

"And sorry about this morning," she went on. "I hope I didn't come off as rude. I just didn't expect to see you at the inn, so it took me by surprise, that's all."

"I didn't expect to see you guys there, either."

"It was nice of you to make breakfast."

"Least I can do for Jonathan and Laura. They're the best."

She glanced at his sling. "I'm surprised you're still able to cook with your injured hand."

He shrugged. "I can't do much. No chopping. No peeling. No lifting. But apparently I can handle bacon and pancakes with one hand tied behind my back."

"There you go." She grinned. "It's your superpower."

Oh, man. When she turned on her smile full blast, it was enough to make the world fall away. He grinned back, then lifted his good arm in the classic superhero pose. "Mr. Bacon Man to the rescue!"

She giggled, and he felt like he was flying. But then she said, "Laura told me what happened to your restaurant. I'm so sorry."

That took him crashing back down to earth. "Thanks." He raked his hand through his hair. "My parents started that restaurant before I was born. Losing it like that—it's been a nightmare."

"And you didn't have insurance?"

He shook his head.

"Why not?"

He gave her a pained smile. "'Cause I'm an idiot." She waited for him to go on, but he didn't. The more he talked about it, the angrier with himself he got.

"Well," she said, "if it's any consolation, my dad's home-owner's insurance will cover your medical expenses from the other night. I'll give you the phone number for the rep when we get back to the inn. She said all the medical bills will be covered, one hundred percent."

Relief poured through him. His small savings wouldn't be enough to rebuild Half Shell, but at least the hospital bills wouldn't wipe out what little funds he already had. "Phew, that's a big weight off my shoulders."

"Sorry I didn't tell you sooner. I should've mentioned it at the hospital."

"Valwee! Mr. Bacon Man! We founded a shell in da sand!" Dylan called out, waving a tiny shell over his head.

"Mr. Brett!" Valerie countered.

Brett chuckled. "I think that's a lost cause."

"Come on, then," she said. "Let's build them a sandcastle."

Chapter Five

When it was time to go back to the inn for lunch, the twins were loath to leave their sandcastle. Despite his one-handedness, Brett had somehow managed to help them build a tower that was almost as tall as they were, complete with a moat and a retaining wall that the boys had decorated with shells, feathers and seaweed.

Brett was the one who finally convinced them to leave by promising to make them spaghetti and meatballs, one of their all-time favorite meals.

Valerie and Brett were in the kitchen now, the boys settled on the couch in the parlor, watching one of their favorite cartoons.

"Thanks for your help back there," she said. "You're a good sport." And patient, too. He'd never come across that way in school—he was always goofing off—so that had surprised her.

He shrugged. "I enjoy kids. They're a lot of fun."

"Please don't worry about lunch. I can open a can of pasta for the boys."

"*Canned* pasta?" Brett tsked. "Absolutely not. You'll offend my culinary sensibilities." He poked around in the cupboards and all three of the inn's big fridges, pulling a few things out and setting them on the counter: basil, garlic, milk, eggs, hamburger meat, bread and tomatoes.

Valerie watched, wide-eyed. "How are you going to cook all that with one hand?"

He smirked. "I'm not. You are."

"Me?" Her voice went so high it squeaked.

He laughed. "Don't worry. I'll tell you what to do."

She didn't move. He didn't understand. She lived in New York City in a one-bedroom apartment with a kitchen the size of a postage stamp. Takeout was her middle name.

She toed the linoleum floor with her flip-flop. "I can't cook, Brett. The most I can do is heat something up in the microwave."

"You baked cookies the other day."

Her face heated with embarrassment. "I bought a roll of refrigerated dough from the store."

He cocked his head to the side and gave her a quizzical look. "Your mom never taught you how to cook?"

She hiked her chin. "My mom left when I was seven."

"Sorry." He held up his non-injured hand in a placating gesture. "I didn't realize."

"My dad never taught me, either. He was the king of grilled cheese sandwiches."

"Hey, nothing wrong with grilled cheese. You think the boys would be up for that instead of spaghetti?"

She nodded, feeling relieved that she wouldn't have to show him how inept she was in the kitchen. Although why she cared so much, she wasn't sure.

He put away most of the food he'd taken out, then grabbed the ingredients for grilled cheese sandwiches, including—weirdly—mayonnaise.

"Mayo?" she asked.

"Put it on the bread instead of butter, and it comes out of the pan perfect," he said, doing a chef's kiss. "What do you think? Will the boys go wild if we make them grilled cheese and *bacon* sandwiches?"

She smiled. "You're really enjoying this Mr. Bacon Man thing, aren't you?"

His cheeks colored and he shrugged, ducking his head. "After my big screwup with the restaurant insurance, what can I say? It's nice to feel appreciated, even if it's for something stupid like crispy bacon."

Something about the way he said it gave her pause. When she'd visited him in the hospital, she'd assumed he was arrogant, but there was a thread of insecurity woven into the way he talked about what had happened with his restaurant. "Being a good cook's not stupid. I'd kill to have more confidence in the kitchen."

"Ever taken a cooking class?" He handed her a loaf of bread, then turned on one of the burners on the stove.

She shook her head as she removed a few slices and started slathering them with mayo. "I work a hundred hours a week. No time."

His eyes bugged. "A hundred hours a week? That's insanity."

She hitched her shoulder. "I'm exaggerating. It's usually more like eighty or eighty-five. And it's not so bad when you're single. It's harder for my married coworkers. But you're banking on the future, you know? That the hard work and the long hours will eventually pay off."

Not that money was the be-all and end-all for her. Back when she'd dreamed of becoming a doctor, it hadn't been for the money; she'd simply wanted to do something good in the world.

But now that she had absurdly large student loans from college and business school to repay and twins to raise—not to mention the astronomical cost of living in Manhattan—it sure would be nice to get to a point in her career where she didn't have to worry about money so much anymore.

Besides, math was easy for her. Numbers were unambiguous. Unlike people, they followed clearly defined rules. Why not work hard at something she was good at and earn a comfortable living?

That was the argument her mentor, Gloria Parker, had used when she'd recruited Valerie, and Valerie had wanted to live up to Gloria's expectations ever since.

Brett held out a pan, and she laid the bread inside. "How are you going to handle those hours when you take the twins back to the city with you?"

She plucked at her necklace while he positioned the pan on the stovetop. She'd been thinking of almost nothing else since she'd first gotten the call about her dad's diagnosis, and she still didn't have a great answer. "I've really got to start calling nanny agencies."

And looking for a bigger apartment.

Or a house in Connecticut.

She wanted the boys to have a backyard. But if they moved to Connecticut, it would mean a long commute, and then she'd have even *less* time with them.

"Too bad you're not staying here. Chloe works at a day care. They've got a great program."

Valerie gave a slow nod. "My dad mentioned that. I guess he'd been considering it for the boys before he got sick. After he got the news…he just wanted to spend as much time with them as he could."

"I'm glad he had the chance to say goodbye."

She twisted her hands. "Not much of one. He only had three weeks after his diagnosis. Colon cancer. Stage four."

Brett grimaced. "I'm sorry."

She started tearing up, so she turned away. "Sorry. It's just so unfair. I hate cancer. It took my sister, too. It's the *worst*."

"You had a sister?"

She nodded, wiping away a couple of tears, her back still turned to him. "My twin. She was seven. A brain tumor."

"Valerie," he said, helplessness woven into his tone.

She put her hands over her eyes, trying to get ahold of herself. "It's okay. It was a long time ago. It doesn't usually hit me this hard, but with my dad's passing…"

"I get it," he said. "It's rough."

She sniffled and wiped her face again, then turned so he wouldn't have to keep talking to her back. "The doctors said that the kind of cancer she had wasn't hereditary, but with those kinds of things, you never really know…"

He frowned. "Have the boys given you any reason to be worried about their health?"

"Aside from the smoke inhalation after the fire? No. But it's one of my biggest fears. That one of them will have to grow up alone, and that it'll be because *I* missed something. Or didn't catch it soon enough."

Brett was quiet for a moment. She ran her fingers under her eyes, clearing away the moisture. Good thing she wasn't wearing mascara.

"That's a lot of pressure to put on yourself."

"I know. But I can't help it. It's a lot of responsibility, and my dad gave them to me because he trusted me to do everything right."

He was quiet again, thoughtful, and she realized that although he'd been loud and annoying in high school, that wasn't how she'd describe him now.

"Are you religious?" he asked. "Can I pray for you?"

"What, like right now?" She had faith, but it was more of a quiet, slip-into-the-back-row-of-the-church kind of faith than a pray-out-loud type of devotion.

"Well, let me flip the grilled cheese first," he said, then did it one-handed like the pro he was. "Okay, now I'm ready."

"Um, okay."

"Is that a yes?"

She took a deep breath. "Yes."

"Can I put my hand on your shoulder?"

She nodded.

He laid his hand on her shoulder, and she startled, even though she'd been expecting his touch.

Up close, he smelled like pine and wind and sea salt, and she had a hard time resisting the urge to step closer and bury her nose in his shirt.

He was so much taller than her, so much bigger. Would he wrap his arms around her to comfort her? Run his hands through her hair, over her shoulders, across her tear-streaked cheeks?

The thoughts were so out of character for her that she almost laughed. But telling people about her sister was out of character for her, too, yet here she was, spilling out all her secrets to him. Spilling out her tears, too.

What is going on with you? Brett Richardson is the last person you should be looking to for comfort. He's the last person you should trust.

He bowed his head. "Father God, we come before you today to ask you to sit with Valerie in her time of grief. Lord, you said, 'Blessed are they that mourn: for they shall be comforted,' and we're asking you to send that comfort now. Valerie's been through a lot, and she has two young boys to take care of. Give her strength, give her comfort and let her rest in the knowledge that she can cast her cares on you because you love her. In Jesus's name we pray. Amen."

He took his hand off her shoulder. She looked up, feeling both touched and embarrassed. No one had ever prayed for her like that before.

"Was that okay?" he asked. "You look freaked out."

She didn't feel freaked out, though. She actually felt calmer. Lighter. Refreshed. "That was really nice. Thank you."

"You're welcome."

Had it only been a couple of hours ago that she'd been wondering if he was capable of arson? She'd been wrong about him. So, so wrong.

"So," he said, "if your mom left when you were seven, I'm guessing your dad got remarried and the boys are your half brothers, right?"

She nodded.

"How come you're taking care of them? Where's their mom?"

Valerie scowled. "That woman is *not* their mother."

"Okay," Brett said, "but where is she? Does she know your dad passed?"

"She knows."

"And she doesn't want to…?"

"Nope. My dad was a rebound relationship for her. When the guy who broke her heart came crawling back, she couldn't sign the divorce papers fast enough. Thing is, the other guy didn't want to raise another man's children, so she signed away her parental rights, too. Dad begged her to reconsider after he got sick, but she flat-out refused."

"Ouch. That stinks."

She smelled something smoky and glanced at the stove. "Is the grilled cheese burning?"

"Ack!" He lunged for the spatula, then the pan.

Sliding the two sandwiches that had been cooking onto a plate, he said, "They're not too bad, but I can have those ones. I'll make fresh ones for you and the boys."

"I don't mind mine a little crispy."

"You think I can't eat two sandwiches in one sitting?"

She laughed. "I *know* you can eat two sandwiches in one sitting. I remember one day in the lunchroom when someone dared you to eat *five*."

"Oh, man, I forgot about that. Five was nothing for a teenage boy who had football practice every afternoon. I think I even had dessert after that."

"You did. Cookies. Big ones."

He smirked. "You were watching me, huh?"

And just like that, all of her good feelings toward him evaporated. He'd been an irritating jock with a big ego in high school, and he was just as irritating now. Why would he assume she'd been watching him? Did he actually think she'd been attracted to him back in high school?

Or was he trying to flirt with her now?

Either way, nope. Nuh-uh. No way.

"Everyone was watching you. You made sure of it."

He sighed. "Yeah, I was a bit of a showboat, wasn't I?"

"You were a *huge* showboat. Always clowning around and making it hard for the rest of us to concentrate."

He scrubbed his hand across his jaw. "I owe you a big apology."

Her heart leaped, and suddenly she was nervous. Like, super nervous. Blood-running-cold nervous. He'd clearly triggered her anxiety, but she didn't know why. "It's okay."

"It's not. You were nothing but nice to me, and I should have stood up for you. I'm sorry."

"It's fine." She tried to wave it off. If she accepted the apology—truly accepted the apology—it meant she'd have to forgive him and let it go, and she wasn't sure she was ready to do that just yet.

No matter how sincere he seemed to be.

"Really?" he asked. "Just like that?"

"Just like what?"

"Most of the women I know want to talk things through before they'll put them to rest."

If she'd been a hedgehog, her quills would have stuck straight out at that, because how many women did he have these kinds of deep conversations with?

A lot, surely.

Just look at him. It had to be a lot.

She folded her arms over her chest. "What do you want me

to say? That being the shy little nerdy girl with the dead sister and the deadbeat mom that the football team and cheerleaders badgered every day was no big deal?"

He gave her a steady look. "No, I can tell it *was* a big deal."

Her arms were still folded. Her jaw was still tight. "You know that now."

"I wish I'd seen it then. If I could go back and change it, I would."

"Uh-huh, sure." *Easy to say that now.*

He turned his attention back to the grilled cheese, using a spatula to take the two new sandwiches off the stove. "Look, I'm sorry I brought it up. It's obviously a sore subject, but if you ever do want to talk about it, you can tell me." He put the spatula down and wiped his hand on his shorts. "And I get it, why you're upset. Words are cheap. It's just—we're kind of stuck here together at the moment, but if you want me to buzz off and get out of your way, I will."

At that, she softened. Because yes, words *were* cheap, but what he was doing right now? Cooking her lunch and praying with her and helping her with the boys after saving them all from a house fire—those things meant just as much as the hard time he and his buddies had given her in high school.

More, maybe.

Probably.

Or at least they should.

Shouldn't they?

She wasn't the same person she'd been in high school. She was smart and successful with an amazing career path laid out in front of her. If she got the promotion she was hoping for, she could be a millionaire by the time she was thirty-five.

So why was she holding on so tightly to things that had happened fifteen years ago?

"You don't have to do that," she said. "Buzz off, I mean."

"Truce, then?" he asked, holding out his good hand for her to shake.

She nodded, taking his big, warm hand in hers. "Truce."

Brett polished off the last of his grilled cheese sandwich as Derrick chirped, "Ice cream, Valwee? We get ice cream now?"

Valerie rubbed her temples. "Are you guys sure you don't want to take a quick nap first?"

Derrick shook his head, his black curls bouncing. "Naps are for babies!"

"Me and D-Wex aren't babies!" Dylan added in an equally loud voice, adorably mangling the pronunciation of his brother's "D-Rex" nickname. "We're big boys!"

"Let's use our inside voices," Valerie said, wincing as she glanced at the door to the parlor and put a finger to her lips.

It looked like *she* could use a nap, but Brett knew better than to say any such thing out loud. "I can take them," he offered, "if you want to stay here and rest."

Valerie shot him a weird look. "You'd have to cross Main Street, and you can't hold both their hands."

Brett held up his good hand and waggled it around. "What do you think, guys, can I hold both your hands at the same time?"

Dylan reached his little hand out to grab Brett's, and Derrick followed suit. Brett easily wrapped his fingers around both of their wrists, lifting them off their feet for a quick second, then grinned at Valerie.

Derrick jumped up and down. "Mr. Bacon Man's hands is big!"

"Huge!" Dylan added.

"Ginorminous!"

Valerie stifled a laugh as she said, "Mr. Bacon Man is very tall, so it makes sense he has ginorminous hands." Then she turned to him. "How tall *are* you, Mr. Bacon Man?"

"Six-three, Madam Grilled Cheese. Why? How short are you?"

"Not short at all. I'm five-five, which is above the average height for women in the US."

"Is it now?" He raised an eyebrow. "You look pretty short to me."

She gave him a pert look before telling the boys to go put on their shoes. "You don't have to come with us. I'm good now. Sometimes being in the sun tires me out, but their antics always perk me up."

Brett shrugged. "I was going to head over to Main Street anyway, see if I can rustle up a few donations for the silent auction."

Her mouth fell open in surprise, and a zing of satisfaction zipped through him. He'd meant it when he'd said he wished he could go back and change how he'd treated her in high school, and he'd take every opportunity to show her it was true.

She scrunched her brows. "But I told you—"

"That you didn't want to team up? I remember."

She scratched her cheek and cocked her head to the side. "So why…?"

He shrugged. "Like I said back in the hospital, I know everyone in town, so it's no big deal."

"Oh. Well—"

Their conversation was interrupted by a knock on the inn's front door. Valerie got there first, and when she opened it, Rudy Valentini stood there in all his slick-haired glory.

"Hi, there. My name is—"

Brett's shoulders tensed, and he practically had to hold back a snarl. "What are you doing here, Rudy?"

Rudy sniffed, rocked back on his heels and gave the pencil he was holding an insouciant little twirl. "Chasing the scoop, naturally."

Brett snorted. "You really think I'm going to talk to you ever again?"

"Come on, now," Rudy tutted. "You know I was just doing my job."

"Yeah, right." If Valerie hadn't been standing in the way, Brett would have slammed the door in Rudy's smug face.

Rudy waved his hand as if Brett's reaction were neither here nor there, then gave Valerie an unctuous smile. "You're the woman from the fire last week, aren't you?" He stuck his pencil behind his ear. "Valerie Williams?"

"Yes…" Valerie replied tentatively, throwing a quick glance at Brett. Protectiveness surged inside him, and he wanted to bundle her back inside and get her far, far away from the irritating reporter.

"I'm Rudy Valentini with the *Cape Cod Community Ti*—"

"Leave her alone, Rudy," Brett huffed.

"Now, now, Bartholomew. Let the lady speak for herself."

"Bartholomew?" Valerie repeated, giving Brett a questioning look.

He groaned. "Don't ask." He hated his given name. *Hated it.*

Rudy made a clicking noise to get her attention, then gave her another ingratiating smile. "I'd love to get your take on what happened during the fire."

"Oh, um…"

"All I need is a few moments of your time," Rudy said, steepling his hands and leaning toward her.

Valerie shot Brett another look, and seeing the uncertainty in her eyes, he gave his protectiveness free rein. "Sorry, Rudy. We're on our way out. Now's not a good time."

"Oh, of course." Rudy took his business card out of his pocket and held it out to Valerie. "Forgive the intrusion. Here's my card. Call me when you have a free moment. I'm entirely at your service."

Valerie took the card. "Thanks. I'll give you a call."

"Please do." Rudy bowed as Brett reached past Valerie and tipped the door shut—not quite in Rudy's face, but close.

Valerie tapped Rudy's card against her thigh. "Not a fan?"

"Ugh, no," Brett said, shaking out his non-injured hand. "I can't stand that guy."

"He's a reporter?" Valerie asked.

"He's a creep."

She tilted her head to the side. "Is your real name Bartholomew?"

"I don't know that I'd call it my real name, but it's the name on my birth certificate."

"Wow. I've never met a Bartholomew before. Why don't you go by Bart?"

He wrinkled his nose. "Do I look like a Bart to you?"

Her eyes sparkled with laughter. "Well, you do now."

"Whatever you say, Valwee," he replied, imitating the twins. She snorted, and he grinned at her. Man, he loved making her laugh. "Just please don't start calling me Bart."

"Why name you Bartholomew and then call you Brett?" Her eyes widened as an idea struck her. "Or did you change your name to Brett?"

He shook his head. "It's a family name. But my father only let my mom give it to me under the condition that they never ever use it. They always called me Brett."

Compassion replaced the light of laughter in her eyes, and she paused before she asked, "Called?"

"They passed away right before I got out of the navy. Car accident with a drunk driver. That's why I nominated the drunk driving charity to the festival committee."

"Oh, I'm so sorry." She laid her hand on his arm. "I won't call you Bartholomew. Or Bart."

He liked the feel of her hand on his arm way too much. "Thanks."

"It's nice that you have a family name, though."

"Would you be saying the same thing if your name was Bartholomaya?"

She arched an eyebrow. "Bartholomaya? That's not even a real name."

"Sure it is," he replied. "And it's awful."

She laughed. "Agreed. Awful."

The boys thundered down the stairs in their Velcro sneakers. "Ice cream time?" Dylan asked.

"Ice cream time," Valerie confirmed, and the twins cheered.

It didn't take them long to walk up Sand Street past all the charming, cedar-shingled cottages and their sand-strewn front lawns. Before they hit Main Street, Brett nodded toward a path through the woods. "Here. I'll show you guys the secret passageway."

"Ooh!" Valerie said, while the boys shouted, "Yeah! Secret!"

"Well, more of a shortcut, really," Brett amended. "It lets us cut onto Main Street behind the movie theater." He pointed at the white clock tower peeking over the large oak trees whose leaves were just starting to change from green to gold and rust.

"Didn't this used to be a church?" Valerie asked.

"Yeah. You haven't been to the theater before?"

She shook her head.

"It's neat. It's not stadium seating like in a regular theater—they have couches and coffee tables. You can order dinner, too, and they'll bring it out to you. And it's not hot dogs and nachos, but real food, like chicken piccata or a Greek salad or pasta. It's pretty nice."

"I lub hot dogs," Dylan chirped.

Brett held his hand out for a fist bump. "Me, too, dude." Then he turned his attention back to Valerie. "I know the owner pretty well. I'll stop by after ice cream and see if she'll give us a donation."

"That'd be great," Valerie said. "Provided the boys aren't too whiny, we'll come with you."

At the ice cream shop, which had a real soda fountain at the counter and ice cream memorabilia hanging on the walls, Dylan ordered shark tooth ice cream—black raspberry with white chocolate chips—while Derrick opted for tiger tail: orange ice cream with a black licorice swirl. Brett ordered himself a root beer float, then looked to Valerie.

"What's good here?" she asked, playing with her necklace.

"Everything. It's all homemade."

She smiled and asked for a small cup of cranberry ice cream.

Brett approved. He'd always enjoyed using local cranberries in his dishes at Half Shell. Aside from Thanksgiving and Christmas, most people didn't think to use cranberry sauce, but he'd invented some killer cranberry sauces and chutneys that paired well with salmon, halibut, shrimp and scallops. He'd even created a tangy cranberry steak sauce that a number of his customers had requested he bottle and sell.

His dessert menu had also featured the tart, tasty berries. His cranberry crème brûlée and pumpkin cranberry cheesecake were perennial favorites, although he liked his cranberry-pineapple upside-down cake the best.

He really needed to figure out how he was going to raise the money to reopen the restaurant, because he couldn't imagine never having the freedom to set his own menu again.

The four of them got their ice cream and took it down the block to the park so the boys could run off their sugar high. As soon as the twins finished their cones, they zipped onto the play structure.

"So." Valerie took a small spoonful of her ice cream, then set it beside her on the bench. "What's the story with you and Rudy Valentini?"

Brett grimaced.

"You clearly didn't want him talking to me. How come?"

He sighed and pulled his phone out of his pocket. Then, one-handed, he navigated to an article about the fire at Half Shell and handed it to her. "Read that."

Valerie picked up the phone. Immediately, her eyebrows shot up to the sky, and Brett knew exactly what she was reading. The headline of Rudy's front-page article about him: "Beloved Local Business Owner Bankrupts Self Through Sheer Stupidity."

She read on, flicking concerned glances at him every few seconds.

When she reached the end of the article, Brett said, "And that's why I don't want you talking to Rudy Valentini."

"What did you do to him?"

Brett gaped at her. "What did *I* do to *him*?"

"He's clearly got it out for you. You must have done something."

Brett's lips flattened. "I didn't do anything. His dad bought a bunch of the local papers a couple of years ago and put Rudy in charge of revitalizing them. He farms out most of the writing to freelancers, but he loves shock value and clickbait headlines. And he's always there in person when there's big local news, nosing around for the scoop."

She gave him a weak smile. "At least he called you a 'beloved' local business owner."

Brett dropped his head and raked his good hand through his hair. Everybody had loved Half Shell. It had been a Cape Cod institution that his parents had opened before he was born.

When Brett had made the decision to remodel the restaurant a couple of years ago, he'd been determined to carry on their legacy and make them proud.

He could still picture the newly renovated space: floor-to-ceiling windows that overlooked the harbor, soaring cathedral ceilings and clean, contemporary lines to complement the crisp white linens that had adorned each table.

Man, he missed it.

It was going to take years to save up enough money to rebuild it from scratch.

But no matter how long it took, he'd do it. He wouldn't let his parents down.

Valerie took another small spoonful of her ice cream. "Can I ask you something?"

"Sure."

"If you own a restaurant, aren't you required to have insurance?"

He hated talking about this, but if he wanted her to trust him, he needed to suck it up and admit the extent of his idiocy. "Yes, but only a few select kinds. I had separate policies for workers comp and unemployment—which are the ones required by law—and then I also had general liability and property insurance. My property insurance expired, but because the renewal notice was buried under a pile of paperwork on my desk, I didn't realize it until it was too late."

She winced. "That's awful."

"The worst part is that I'd just invested a ton of money in a big renovation the year before the fire. I didn't have to officially declare bankruptcy, but I'm definitely broke."

"The article said you own the land. That's prime real estate. Can you sell it?"

He lifted his chin. "I'd never sell that property. I don't care if I have to work for a hundred years before I can reopen the restaurant. It's going to happen."

"Have you thought about finding an investor?"

"Like a business partner?"

She nodded.

He shook his head. "I like being my own boss, being able to do my own thing."

"There's plenty of investors who'll let you do your own thing."

Brett gave her a skeptical look. "I don't want to give some random stranger equity in my parents' restaurant, either."

She shrugged, watching the boys zoom down a curved red slide. "If you change your mind, I can put out some feelers. I mostly work on deals in the health care sector, but I have friends who work in the restaurant space."

It was weird to hear her talk about her work when she was dressed in shorts and a T-shirt. His mental image of investment bankers was slick dudes in fancy suits and glamorous women with tight skirts, high heels and purses that cost more than his car. Valerie was way more down-to-earth than that.

"What do investment bankers do, anyway? I've never understood that. Are you like a stockbroker or a financial advisor?"

She ate some more ice cream and shook her head. "We don't work with individual investors like financial advisors do. We help companies buy other companies or go public on the stock market—stuff like that." She set her ice cream down. "But most of what I personally do is spreadsheet math, and when that's done, I create PowerPoint slides so the senior bankers can present my math to our clients."

Okay, maybe he'd gotten it wrong when he'd thought investment banking was a glamorous profession. Who wanted to do math all day, every day?

"How'd you get into investment banking, anyway? I thought you wanted to be a doctor."

She gave him a startled look. "You remember that?"

"Sure. You talked about it a couple times in class."

"Oh. Well." Her hand fluttered, and she looked away. "I was premed for a little while in college, but I found out pretty quickly that I didn't have the stomach for it. I get woozy at the sight of blood, and I hate seeing people in pain. Not ideal for becoming a doctor."

She had a soft heart, and although he was sorry it had prevented her from achieving her dream of going into medicine, he had to admit that it made him like her even more. "You did okay with Dylan the other night."

She hitched her shoulder. "That was different—I'm his legal guardian now. You do what you have to do in those situations. But anyway," she continued, "I was still good at math and science, and I met a female alum who encouraged me to go into finance. Said if I did as well in business school as I did in college, she could pretty much guarantee me a job at her firm."

"Sweet deal."

"Yeah, it's been good. Her name's Gloria, and she's been my mentor ever since I joined the bank. My dad used to joke that she was more of a mother to me than my own mom ever was."

"I'm glad you've got someone there who's looking out for you." Although he wished her own mother was still part of her life.

"She pushes me, for sure. She's very focused. Talks all the time about how women *can* have a career and a family, even in banking. She's checked in on me a few times since my dad passed. Said she'll do whatever she can to help me find the right childcare for the twins so that I can clinch a promotion to VP."

All right, he'd known she was smart, but he was talking to a future Wall Street vice president who'd gone to business school. She must think he was a total loser. "You must be great at what you do."

"It's long hours, but the number crunching isn't too hard."

"Do you like it?"

"I—" She paused. "I don't mind the work."

"But…?"

"It's kind of a frat boy culture, which isn't my favorite."

"Lots of partying?" Brett asked.

"Yeah, a lot of them subscribe to the 'work hard, play hard' idea. They laugh at me for staying home Saturday nights so I can get up for church the next morning."

"The restaurant industry can be like that, too."

"Really?"

"Part of why I like being the boss. You can foster the culture you want to create."

"That's smart," she said, and the rush of exhilaration that accompanied her words caught him by surprise.

He wanted her to think he was smart and capable. Even if he never saw her again after the Cranberry Harvest Festival, he didn't want her to leave Cape Cod thinking he was the laughingstock Rudy had made him out to be in that stupid article.

He'd do whatever he could do to show her that, despite his idiocy with the restaurant's property insurance, he could be sharp and savvy.

Getting her a bunch of donations for the silent auction would be an excellent start.

Chapter Six

Although Valerie had moved away from Wychmere Bay before the Cranberry Harvest Festival had gotten off the ground, this year would mark its tenth anniversary, and she could tell that it was going to be a big deal.

Cape Cod prided itself on being one of the largest producers of cranberries in the country. Wychmere Bay, especially, loved its cranberries—its two bogs produced roughly two million pounds of them a year.

Harvest season ran from September until early November, and although people always tended to think of cranberry bogs as wet, swampy places, the truth was that the berries didn't grow in water. They grew dry on vines, and the best berries were dry harvested and sold fresh in stores.

The wet harvest that held such pride of place in the public's imagination was actually just to get the berries that had fallen off the vines or were too hard to reach. It happened quickly, too, with growers aiming to get the berries out of the water within a few hours so they didn't get moldy before they were frozen, dried or made into jelly.

The festival took place in the very park they'd just left, on the first Saturday in October, and she'd been told there was live music, a craft fair, food trucks, a mock cranberry bog where kids got a chance to tromp around in rain boots and harvest berries, a couple of big inflatable bounce houses, a variety of carnival games and, to top it all off, a professional fireworks display.

The goal of the Cranberry Harvest Festival was to bring the town together after the busy summer season, support local artists and musicians and raise money for charity. Her dad had been involved since the very beginning, when the town had elected to support Autry-Carter's Pediatric Cancer Institute in memory of her sister.

It touched her heart that, this year, the town was supporting a cause that was important to Brett. Knowing that he'd lost his parents in a car accident made her feel…softer toward him. Like maybe he could actually relate to her losing her sister and her dad.

She admired him for wanting to reopen his restaurant in his parents' honor, although she disagreed that he needed to do it all by himself.

The right investor would enhance his vision, not hamper it.

She'd make a few calls on his behalf and see if she could find someone awesome. An angel investor, rather than a corporation, would probably be the best fit.

Mind spinning about where to start her search for Brett's perfect business partner, she followed him and the twins into the movie theater that used to be a church.

Inside, there was an intricate stained glass window over the doorway, along with ornate woodwork on the door. The lobby had a red carpet, and several small tables where people could congregate before or after a show. The boys, mouths open, were looking around in awe.

Brett led them to an office behind the concession stand. "Hey, Cynthia," he said, and a middle-aged woman in jeans and a white blouse looked up from her desk.

"Brett," the woman replied, pushing her glasses up her nose, her face breaking into a smile. "To what do I owe the pleasure?"

"Here on official business for the Cranberry Harvest Festival." He gestured to Valerie. "This is Valerie Williams and her little brothers."

"A pleasure, sweetheart," Cynthia said, getting up and taking Valerie's hand in a warm, two-handed shake. Then she turned her attention to the twins. "And you two! What handsome, well-mannered boys. Would you like some popcorn?"

"Popcorn!" Derrick shouted, while Dylan bobbed his head up and down and said, "Yes, please."

Cynthia led them out of the office to the concession stand, where she scooped two small bags of popcorn for the boys and then directed them to a table in the lobby where they could sit and eat it.

"Cutie pies," she said, giving them a wistful look. "I'm so glad they weren't hurt in the fire. We're all so proud of Brett."

"Aw, Cyn," he replied with a teasing lilt to his voice. "You're making me blush."

"I'm serious, hon. You're a hero." She turned to Valerie, her expression earnest. "He deserves a medal, don't you think?"

Valerie blinked. A medal. Why hadn't she thought of that?

He deserved way more than a tin of chocolate chip cookies, that was for sure.

She'd have to call the fire department when they got back to the inn and see if there was some way to nominate Brett for an award.

"Stop it," he protested. "I was just in the right place at the right time, that's all."

"Such modesty." The older woman shot Valerie a playful smile. "Who are you and what have you done with our Brett?"

"Excuse me?" he said, his voice full of mock affront. "What exactly are you trying to say?"

Cynthia laughed and patted his arm. "Nothing, hon. We like you just the way you are."

He snorted. "Thanks… I think."

"So," Cynthia said. "The Cranberry Harvest Festival?"

"We're trolling for donations to the silent auction."

Cynthia smiled. "Count me in."

Valerie blinked again. Her dad had been right. This *was* easy. At least for Brett.

"For...?" he prompted.

Cynthia put her hands on her hips and looked up at the ceiling, thinking. "How about a date night certificate? Dinner and a movie for two?"

"Perfect," Brett pronounced. "Thanks a million."

"Will you need a tax receipt?" Valerie asked, her mind, as usual, on the numbers. "Could you give us an estimated value of the donation?"

"About fifty dollars," the theater owner replied. "Ten each for the tickets, and fifteenish for each of the dinners."

"Aw, Cyn, you're selling yourself short," Brett said.

The older woman laughed. "Not all of us are gourmet chefs, hon." She glanced at Valerie. "Last year, this one donated a two-hundred-and-fifty-dollar gift certificate to his restaurant, and it sold for more than a thousand dollars. Can you believe that? A thousand dollars!"

Honestly? It was impressive.

He was impressive.

As a person, of course. Not as a man.

"Well," Brett said, shifting uncomfortably, "sad to say I can't do the same thing this year."

"You're a smart boy," Cynthia said. "You'll think of something."

He chuckled. "You know I'm turning thirty this year, right, Cyn? Hardly a boy anymore."

She laughed and patted his cheek. "You'll always be a boy to me."

"Okay, well, thanks for the donation. We'll come back and pick it up a few days before the festival."

Cynthia gave him a jaunty little salute. "Righto. Thanks for stopping by. And great to meet you, Valerie. I hope to see you and the boys again soon."

Brett led her and the twins out of the theater and nodded at a sandwich shop across the street with a striped awning and a big glass window front. "Want to hit up Lettuce Feed You next?"

Valerie chuckled as she read the sign above the door. "Is it a salad bar?"

Brett shook his head. "Sandwiches."

The shop was adorable with its lacquered red-brick floor and wooden countertops. Her favorite part, though, was the carefully constructed dessert display next to the cash register.

"You want something?" Brett asked, following her gaze.

She gave her head a quick shake. "Just looking."

"You sure?" He raised his voice as a worker came out from the back room, drying his hands on a hand towel. "Mikey here's a good baker."

Valerie froze as Michael Carpenter—one of the football players who'd picked on her the most—shook Brett's hand and said, "Good to see you, buddy." Then he turned his gaze on her, giving her a smile that she was sure was supposed to be charming. "And who's this?"

"Valerie, Mikey. Mikey, Valerie. You might remember her from school."

Michael pursed his lips, trying to place her. Then his eyes went wide. "Sticks! Is that you?"

"It's me," she replied dully, grabbing a twin in each hand and shooting Brett a quick look. "We're going to wait outside."

As the door closed behind her, she heard Michael snort and say, "Was it something I said?"

Instead of waiting for Brett, she gripped the boys' hands tighter and started dragging them back to the inn.

Brett shot Mike a disappointed look.

"What?" Mikey said, holding up his hands. "I barely said hello."

"She never liked that nickname."

"Well, it sure doesn't suit her now." Mike grinned at him. "Two words. Gor. Geous."

Brett's shoulders tightened. This was one of the main reasons he didn't hang around with his old football friends anymore. He didn't like the way they talked about or treated women.

And he especially didn't like Mike talking about Valerie that way. "Knock it off, man. I'm serious."

"Oh, you already staked a claim." Mike was still grinning. "Sorry. My bad."

The tension in Brett's shoulders ratcheted up a notch. "It's not like that. She's a friend."

"Riiight."

And another notch. "We're working on the Cranberry Harvest Festival together."

"Sure, you are."

And another. "We are, Mikey, and you need to go apologize to her for being a jerk in high school. Now."

Mike glanced out the window. "Can't, dude."

If Brett's shoulders got any tighter, they were going to explode. "Why not?"

"She's already gone."

Brett spun around. Valerie and the twins were across the street, speed walking away from him.

No, no, no.

Every time high school came up, things between them just got worse and worse.

Brett pushed open the door and jogged after them. "Valerie! Wait up!"

The boys turned to look at him, but Valerie did not.

He picked up the pace and caught up with them a minute later, winded. The doctors had warned him that the smoke he'd inhaled during the fire could cause coughing, chest pain and shortness of breath for a few weeks, but this was the first time since the hospital that he'd noticed any ill effects.

It was also the first time he'd tried to run anywhere.

Go figure.

"Valerie," he panted, "I'm sorry about that. Mikey's got a big mouth."

"It's fine," she said, but her voice was hard. "We needed to get back, anyway."

Derrick wiggled out of Valerie's grasp and latched on to Brett's leg. "Mr. Bacon Man's legs is big!"

A second later, Dylan managed to attach himself to Brett's other leg. "Da biggest!"

Brett took a couple of big, exaggerated steps, like he was a dinosaur or a giant robot. The boys laughed. Still winded, Brett coughed, then kept coughing.

And coughing and coughing.

Valerie sighed. "You okay there, Mr. Bacon Man? Did they give you an inhaler before you left the hospital?"

He made a *yikes* face. They'd given him one, but he'd left it at the inn.

"Boys, let go."

The boys detached themselves from his legs. Valerie took Brett's arm and led him to a bench. "Sit. Catch your breath."

The boys clambered up next to him. "Breave," Dylan said, resting his head on Brett's arm. Derrick was on his other side, his little hand on Brett's shoulder. A verse from the Gospel of Mark ran through his mind: *Suffer the little children to come unto me, and forbid them not: for of such is the kingdom of God.*

He slowed his breathing, trying to cough through his nose. After a minute of that, it was under control.

He couldn't help wondering, though, if maybe it was a sign. He'd spent all day chasing after Valerie, and no matter how hard he tried to make things right between them, they kept falling straight back to square one.

He closed his eyes for a second. *Are you trying to tell me something, Lord?*

"You all right?" Valerie asked, watching him, a storm in those mismatched, gray-blue eyes.

He nodded, trying to figure out what she was thinking, but before he could get a good read on her, she looked away.

"You probably shouldn't be running right now."

"Wouldn't have," Brett said, "if I hadn't been trying to catch up with you."

"Are you okay to walk? We should get back to the inn."

He stood, and the boys stood with him. "I told Mike to apologize, but you were already across the street."

She reached for her necklace and started fiddling with it. "I don't want him to apologize."

"He'll give us a good donation. I'll make sure of it."

She shook her head. "I don't want to see him again. I don't want to see *anyone* from high school again."

Her words landed like a punch to his gut. A couple of times that day, he'd wondered if she was nervous around him because she was attracted to him, but now he knew: she was nervous because he reminded her of high school, and she'd hated high school.

Forget about Mikey—if she had her way, she'd never want to see *him* again, either.

"I'll handle it." He would, too. He'd go back to his original plan of soliciting the donations *for* her instead of *with* her. He'd stay out of her way.

"Thanks." She tugged at her necklace. The pendant was weird-looking: a teardrop with a jagged edge.

"What is that?" he couldn't help asking, nodding toward it with his chin.

"What?" She looked down.

"Your necklace."

"Oh." She glanced at the twins, who'd run a few paces ahead to look at a bug on the sidewalk, and lowered her voice. "The other half was Vanessa's."

"And Vanessa was…your twin?" he guessed.

She nodded, her knuckles going white as she squeezed the pendant harder.

"What shape is it supposed to be?"

"It's half a heart. The other half was hers. We buried her with it."

He gave a slow nod. "It's nice you have something to remember her by." But he also thought it was kind of sad, walking around with only half a heart—no way to make it whole.

They caught up to the boys and prodded them to keep walking. As they approached the inn's sprawling, rose-rimmed lawn, Valerie looked up at Brett, her multicolored eye flashing in the sunlight. "You should probably carry your inhaler with you."

"I know. Stupid mistake."

"Maybe you should go back to the doctor."

"Worried about me?" he teased, although secretly he *wanted* her to be worried about him. If she lived here, and if they didn't have such a crummy history, he would have asked her out sometime between the sandcastle and the grilled cheese and the ice cream.

She looked away. "No. I just…wouldn't want you to suffer for helping us that night."

"I'm not suffering."

"Okay, well…" She trailed off.

"Don't worry about that donation from Mike. I'll get it from him later this week. You won't have to see him again."

She nodded. "I appreciate that."

"Sure."

"And thanks for the ice cream. The boys had fun."

What about you? he wanted to ask. *Did you have fun, too?*

But he knew she hadn't. Certainly not after running into Mike.

"Anytime."

If things were different between them, if they were on good terms, he might have leaned down and given her a quick hug, seen if her hair smelled like flowers or strawberries or vanilla. But since an uneasy truce seemed to be the best the two of them could manage, he simply raised his good hand in a quick wave, then turned and strode into the inn.

When he came back out a few minutes later with his inhaler, she and the twins were gone.

Chapter Seven

Valerie didn't see much of Brett for the next few days, and by Saturday morning, it had started to feel personal. Like he was avoiding her.

He smiled and said a quick hello on the rare occasion they ran into each other in the parlor or the dining room of the inn, but he hadn't joined them at the beach or tried to cajole her into learning how to cook or invited himself along on another trip to go get ice cream, and she…missed him. His big, loud presence. His easy way with the boys.

You're losing it, she chided herself. *You should be relieved that he's not around more.*

But she wasn't.

It didn't help that she'd spent a lot of time the past few days researching awards she could nominate him for. There was a local one from the Wychmere Bay Fire Department that he'd almost certainly receive, as well as awards from organizations like the American Red Cross, the Carnegie Hero Fund Commission and a couple of New England car dealerships.

Some of them came with gifts and grants—like a new car or a cash stipend—and some were simply meant to recognize life-saving efforts.

Either way, Valerie thought he deserved every single one of them. The more she thought about what could have happened the night of the fire, the more she wrote it all down on the award applications, the more grateful she was that he'd barged in.

Would she have found Dylan if he hadn't been there? Would she and Derrick have made it out of the house?

In addition to nominating Brett for awards, she'd also spent time combing the internet for places in and around Boston that might donate an item to the Cranberry Harvest Festival. She'd come up with quite a list: the Boston Children's Museum, the Red Sox, the John F. Kennedy Presidential Library and Museum, the Celtics, Six Flags New England, the Boston Symphony Orchestra and the Boston Bruins, to name just a few.

The best part was that Valerie could submit all those requests via online forms and email—saving her from any more awkward face-to-face encounters like the one at Lettuce Feed You with Michael Carpenter.

Had Brett gone back there yet? If not, she could do it—she just had to mentally prepare.

She was still trying to nail down a grand prize to bring in the top bids. This item wouldn't be part of the silent auction— they'd auction it off live at the end of the event. For the past few years, she and Gloria had attended a gala hosted by the Women's League of NYC, which featured a bachelor auction that brought in thousands of dollars in donations. Valerie couldn't see herself asking any of the men around here to get up on stage to do something like that, though.

And she definitely couldn't see someone like Michael Carpenter bringing in the big bucks.

No, the grand prize would have to be something like a VIP pass to a concert or a helicopter tour. Something that would bring in a ton of money, so that she could do her father proud.

She heard the twins stirring in the room next to hers and went to get them dressed.

Downstairs, they were greeted by happy chaos. Chloe and Laura were sitting together in the dining room, Hunter in

Chloe's arms, as they watched Emma chase Chloe's son around one of the tables. The twins immediately joined the chase, whooping as they ran around the room.

Valerie plopped down in the chair next to Chloe, who was wearing jeans and a pink T-shirt that read Best Mom Ever. Laura was still in her pajamas. "Morning."

"Hey, girlfriend," Chloe said, smiling brightly. "Aiden's going to get tackled, isn't he?"

"By the twins? For sure."

"Aiden!" Chloe called. "Come here." The boy ran to her, his blond hair flopping and his face red. "Say hi to Dylan and Derrick."

He waved at the twins. "Hi."

The boys waved back and said, "Hi!" in unison.

"Why don't you guys go show Aiden and Emma your monster trucks?" Valerie suggested. Chirping excitedly, the twins ran off to find their toys.

"Phew! Not sure how much more my ears could take," Chloe joked. "Those kids are *loud.*"

Laura smirked at her. "Ha! Get used to it, my friend. Once Aiden has a playmate, you're done for. It's all over."

Valerie looked back and forth between Chloe and Laura. "Are you speaking hypothetically, or…"

Chloe grinned. "I'm pregnant!"

"Oh, wow!" Valerie said, genuinely pleased for her old friend. "Congratulations!"

"Thank you! Steve and I are thrilled."

"That's why the guys went out to get doughnuts," Laura added. "We're celebrating."

Hunter started bobbing up and down on Chloe's shoulder, looking for food. "And I'm practicing my baby-handling skills, but I can't help him with that." She handed him to Laura. "Go feed your cute baby."

"Come on, mister," Laura said to the little guy, then got to her feet. "Time for your morning snack."

She walked out of the dining room. Valerie and Chloe moved to the parlor so they could keep an eye on the older kids, all four of whom were busy bashing monster trucks into each other.

Valerie turned to Chloe. "How far along are you?"

"Just nine weeks. So keep it on the down-low, please. We're only telling our very closest friends."

Honored to be included, Valerie mimed zipping her lips. "Are you feeling good? No morning sickness?"

"Not yet." Chloe rapped her knuckles on the coffee table. "Knock on wood."

"Did you get morning sickness with Aiden?"

"This is actually my first pregnancy. Aiden is Steve's biological nephew."

"Oh! I'm sorry. I didn't realize."

"It's fine. Please. How would you have known?"

Valerie gestured to Chloe's hot pink T-shirt. "I saw your shirt and I just assumed—"

"Legally, Steve and I are his guardians. But in reality? I'm his mom."

"Is his biological mother in the picture at all?"

Chloe shook her head. "She died giving birth."

Valerie gasped. "I'm so sorry! I'm just going to stop talking now."

"It's okay," Chloe assured her. "Really."

They watched the kids play a little more.

"Are you going to adopt him, do you think?"

"I don't know. We're going to wait until he's older and ask him. If we adopt him, it'll change his birth certificate, and he might want to keep that connection to Steve's sister."

Valerie hadn't even thought about that. "Good point."

"What about you and the twins? Are you going to adopt them?"

"That would be a little weird, don't you think? I'm their sister, not their mom."

Chloe smiled. "Believe me, they're never going to think of you as their sister. You're definitely going to be their mom."

Valerie's stomach swooped. It was a lot of responsibility, but her dad had thought she was up for the job. She had to trust him, and trust God, that she'd be a better mom than her own mother had been.

"I hope I don't mess it up too badly. I almost lost Dylan already. If it hadn't been for Brett..."

Chloe grabbed her hand, cutting her off. "You're not going to mess it up, Valerie. I mean, yes, you will sometimes. That's part of being a parent. We're not perfect. But you didn't set that fire. You'd never let them down on purpose. And the fact that Brett was there? Well, sometimes God has a plan."

At that moment, the guys burst in the front door, carrying several boxes of pastries, a carrier full of coffees and a carton of juice. "Special delivery!" Brett called out.

Emma dropped the monster truck she'd been playing with and cried, "Doughnuts!"

Dylan, Derrick and Aiden all cheered.

Then, as the men moved into the dining room, Dylan ran over to Valerie and exclaimed, "Mr. Bacon Man bringed doughnuts!"

"I know, honey. It's very exciting!"

"I lub doughnuts!"

"Well, go get one."

He charged into the dining room, and Valerie chuckled. Chloe, meanwhile, lifted an eyebrow. "Mr. Bacon Man?"

"First morning Brett was here, he cooked them bacon. Apparently, it made an impression."

Chloe laughed. "That's priceless. I bet Brett loves it, doesn't he?"

Valerie laughed, too. "Yeah, kinda."

Chloe shook her head. "Figures." Then she paused. "But after all the bad press he got this summer, it probably feels really nice to have some affirmation of his talent. Even if it's just from a couple of kids."

Valerie's heart squeezed. The thought that tall, confident Brett might need affirmation was…unexpected.

And yet, it made sense. Who wouldn't feel a little insecure after losing everything the way Brett had?

Despite her initial reaction to seeing him again, he was anything but a loudmouth jerk. Big? Yes. Loud? Check. A bit of a joker? Sometimes, sure.

But he'd apologized to her, listened to her and even prayed for her.

After she submitted the award nominations on his behalf, she'd get cracking on finding him an investor. Because what could be more affirming than having someone believe in you enough to bankroll your vision?

As soon as she and Chloe entered the dining room, Steve pulled out a chair for Chloe. "Here, lovely." Then he set a plate in front of her. "It's your favorite. Boston cream."

Chloe smiled up at him. "You know me so well."

He kissed the top of her head, then went to help Aiden. Chloe turned to Valerie, her eyes twinkling. "So solicitous. I should get pregnant more often."

Valerie laughed. "He seems great."

"Yep, I'm blessed." She took a bite of her doughnut, her eyes closing in pleasure. "Hey, what are you and the twins up to today?"

"We're going to go into town and try to get some donations for the silent auction."

Chloe's face scrunched in confusion. "But I thought…" She glanced at her brother. "Oh. He didn't tell you."

Valerie followed Chloe's gaze over to Brett. "Tell me what?"

"Brett already got donations from basically every store and restaurant in town."

Valerie's eyes whipped to him, then back to Chloe. "What? Why would he do that?"

Chloe shrugged, but her eyes were sparkling so much they were practically lighting up the whole room. "Better go ask him," she said, trying—and failing—to hold back a laugh as she made a shooing gesture with her hands.

Valerie's cheeks heated. Could Chloe tell that she had a weird, confusing crush on Brett?

Oh, well. Hadn't she just been thinking that she'd like to see more of him? She threw her shoulders back in an attempt to marshal her courage, then headed his way.

He was sitting next to the twins, cutting their doughnuts in half. When she reached them, all three of them grinned at her.

"Valwee!" Dylan beamed. "Da bacon man bringed us *bacon* doughnuts!"

"Wowee. Those must be good."

"They're incredible," Brett said, handing her a disposable plate with a maple-glazed doughnut complete with bacon sprinkles on top.

"Thanks." She took a cautious bite. Whoa. Delicious.

Brett sipped his coffee. "Nobody makes doughnuts like the Barnacle Bakery."

She had another bite, then got up to pour the twins some milk. She poured herself a glass for good measure and grabbed an apple, too. Doughnuts were a nice treat, but she tried to keep her meals at least somewhat balanced. If she didn't, she got lightheaded a lot more often thanks to her orthostatic hypotension—a condition she'd developed when she was anorexic, and one that had never fully gone away.

When she wasn't staying hydrated, or when she got stressed, her blood pressure could go especially low, and she had to wear compression stockings to work and sip electrolyte drinks all day. Although she'd struggled with the lightheadedness a lot when she'd first started her job, she'd managed to control it pretty well over the last couple of years.

Ever since she'd gotten word of her dad's diagnosis, though, it had gotten worse. The day after the fire had been especially bad, and she'd spent a fair amount of time lying on the floor with her legs propped up against a wall in an attempt to boost her circulation. The last few days, however, had been okay, and she was determined to do her absolute best to keep it that way.

"So," she said, taking a seat. "Chloe said you got a bunch of donations for the silent auction?"

Brett rubbed the back of his neck. "Oh. Yeah. I went back to get the donation from Lettuce Feed You, then figured I might as well get them from other places, too. Like I told you, I know everyone, so it wasn't a big deal."

Jonathan leaned over from where he was sitting with Emma. "He spent all week going to just about every business in Wychmere Bay, Valerie. Don't let him play the 'it was nothing' card."

Brett shot his friend an irritated look and mimed throwing a doughnut at him. Jonathan laughed and turned his attention back to Emma, but Valerie's cheeks were on fire. Was Jonathan implying that Brett had gotten those donations because he liked her? Or was he teasing his friend because that's just what the two of them did?

"Seriously," Brett grumbled, motioning to his injured hand. "It's not like I have anything better to do."

Okay, then. Clearly, he and Jonathan just liked to tease each other. "Well, um, thanks. I was going to go today with the boys."

"Were you? I was thinking it would be good to head over to Chatsworth and see if any of the businesses there want to contribute."

Chatsworth, the town next to Wychmere Bay, was also a popular tourist destination during the summer, with a population that quadrupled from about six thousand in the offseason to twenty-four thousand in July and August. Known for its amazing seal tours and beautiful beaches, its shops and restaurants had always been a little more high-end than those in Wychmere Bay.

"That's a great idea," she said. "The boys and I can do that."

"But Valerie," Chloe cut in, obviously eavesdropping, "Steve and I want to take the twins to the beach with Aiden. They were having so much fun together before breakfast."

"It's okay," Brett said. "I'm happy to go to Chatsworth."

"How are you going to get there, brother-dear? Steve and Jonathan will both be at the beach." Then she gave them both a beatific smile. "Hey, I know! Why don't we watch the twins for you, Valerie, and you and Brett can—"

"Chloe," Brett warned, but she ignored him.

"—go to Chatsworth together. You don't mind driving, do you?"

"Uh…no." She looked between Chloe and Brett, who seemed to be having an intense, unspoken conversation with their eyes. Did he not want her to go with him? Chloe was probably pushing them together because she could tell Valerie had a thing for him, but this felt awkward. "But are you sure you want to babysit the twins? Watching three is a lot different than watching one."

"Trust me," Chloe said, emphasizing her words with dramatic hand gestures. "I'm a kindergarten teacher. I know all about keeping an eye on a whole variety of little hooligans."

Valerie glanced at the twins. "Do you guys want to go to the beach with Emma and Aiden?"

"Emma!" Derrick yelled. "We show you da fishies and da crabs!"

"And da sharks," Dylan added. "And our ginorminous sandcastle!"

Chloe beamed. "I think that's a yes."

* * *

Brett folded himself into the passenger seat of Valerie's little car. This whole broken hand thing was really getting old.

Another thing that was getting old? His sister. More specifically, her ridiculously transparent ploy to push Valerie into spending the day with him.

He'd told Chloe about what had happened when he and Valerie had seen Mikey at Lettuce Feed You. His sister knew that Valerie didn't want to keep getting high school shoved in her face.

Somehow, though, Chloe had chosen to forget the fact that he'd been part of Valerie's bad high school experience, too. And when she'd offered to babysit so that he and Valerie could go to Chatsworth on their own, he hadn't been able to figure out a graceful way to remove himself from this whole scenario.

"You okay over there?" Valerie asked, watching him as he tried to find the button that would slide the seat back. "You don't have to come with me if you have something else to do."

"No, it's fine. How do I push the seat back?"

"There's a bar underneath."

He fished around with his uninjured hand and found the lever, and the seat jolted back. "Whoa. That's got a kick."

Valerie smiled. "At least your knees aren't up at your chin anymore."

"How do you fit the twins in here? It's tiny."

"They're small. I figure I can hold off on buying a bigger car for a couple of years, at least." She turned her key in the ignition. "I don't drive much in the city, anyway."

"No?"

"I can walk to work, and if it's late, I just take an Uber home."

"Fancy."

She shrugged as she backed out of her parking space. "I've never had a problem, but it's good to be cautious."

Brett didn't like the images that flashed through his mind of all the things that could go wrong in the city. But things could go wrong here, too. For instance, both of the recent fires.

"You see yourself staying there long-term?" he asked.

"Lately I've been thinking about buying a house in Connecticut. I want the boys to have a backyard. And a community."

"Is it hard to find that in New York?"

"With the hours I work? Basically impossible."

He shifted around in his seat. He felt like he was in a clown car. It was not at all comfortable. "But won't you still be working the same hours if you move to Connecticut?"

She sighed. "It'll probably be even worse, since I'll have to commute into the city on top of my actual job."

He wasn't sure what to say about that, so after a few moments of silence, he fell back on a bad joke. "I once turned down a job where I'd be paid in vegetables." She gave him a funny look, so he finished with a flourish, "I couldn't live with the *celery.*"

She groaned. "Did you really just whip out the world's worst dad joke?"

"Why was the chef arrested?"

She gave him a big serving of side-eye before giving in and saying, "I don't know. Why?"

"He was caught beating an egg!"

She shook her head. "Stop. These are terrible." She was laughing, though, so he kept going.

"When does a normal joke turn into a dad joke?" He paused, then pulled out the punch line. "When it becomes *apparent.*"

Before he could launch into another one, she rapped on the dashboard. "Knock, knock."

He grinned. "Who's there?"

"Boo."

"Boo who?"

"Don't be sad," she said. "It's just a joke!"

He chuckled. "And you thought the celery joke was bad."

"You can thank the twins for that one."

"They're funny little guys."

Valerie smiled as she turned onto Main Street, then fiddled with the radio. "If you want, I can let you out somewhere along here."

His forehead furrowed. "Why would I want to get out here?"

She slowed the car and pulled into a metered parking spot. Then she started playing with her necklace. "I know Chloe goaded you into coming to Chatsworth with me. Honestly, though, you're off the hook. I know I made things uncomfortable after the whole Lettuce Feed You thing. I get why you've been avoiding me all week."

"Wait, wait." He turned in his seat so that he could see her better, even though the movement shoved his shoulder up against the window. "You think I've been avoiding you because you made *me* uncomfortable?"

She tugged harder on her necklace. "I overreacted. We shouldn't have walked away without waiting for you."

He was so surprised by the turn this conversation had taken, it took him a solid ten seconds to find the words to reply. "Valerie. I'm not mad at you. I thought *you* were mad at *me*."

She slid her broken heart pendant back and forth on her chain. "You—what? Why?"

"You said you didn't want apologies—you just didn't want to see anyone from high school ever again."

"Oh." She blinked, then reached out and touched his forearm. "I didn't mean *you*."

Their eyes locked, the moment stretching like a piece of saltwater taffy. The feel of her soft hand on his arm made his whole body warm. The car was small, and he was suddenly aware of the light, floral scent of her perfume buzzing around him.

Did she feel it, too—this pull between them?

Itching to draw her into his arms, he shifted again so that he wasn't staring straight at her—her pale skin, her cute freckles, her exotic, mismatched eyes.

She's leaving, she's leaving, she's leaving. If he forgot that fact, he might do something stupid, something that would make it hard on him when she took the twins and went back to New York.

Clearing his throat, he placed his gaze squarely on the road. "Okay, good. Then what are we hanging around here for? Let's go."

She took her hand off his forearm, and he felt the loss of it in the center of his chest. *Help me out here, Lord*, he prayed. He'd never felt an attraction even half this intense.

Valerie pulled out of the parking space and back onto Main Street. As they passed all the familiar sights, Brett's equilibrium started to come back.

When they passed Wychmere Community Church, he glanced over at her. "Have you been to a service at WCC yet?"

She nodded. "The boys were up early last Sunday. We went at eight."

"Cool. I usually go at ten thirty. Jonathan and I do sports with the kids afterward if you want to bring the twins."

"What kind of sports?"

"Depends on the weather, but we've done pretty much everything. Ball hockey, basketball, soccer, badminton. If the majority of the kids are little, we'll do Red Light, Green Light or even Simon Says."

"Sounds like something they'd enjoy." She took her eyes off the road to study him for a second. "It's nice that you're involved at church. Are you very religious?"

He tapped his fingers on his thigh. This question always felt loaded to him, and he was never sure he knew how to answer it well. "I mean, I grew up with religion. My parents always took us to church. But as you probably know, I didn't really live out my faith that much when I was younger."

"What changed?"

"The car accident. Losing my folks so young."

"Ah."

"Yeah, that's what it took for me to see that, without God, I had nothing. I came crawling to Him on my knees. Like, 'Here I am, Lord, I have nothing without you. I am nothing without you.' And He met me down there when I was at my lowest and lifted me onto my feet."

Brett was forever grateful. God was mighty. God was merciful. And He wanted His children to turn to Him and harness His strength.

"So, yes," he went on, "I go to church. I spend some time each day reading the Bible, even if it's just a verse or two. But sometimes when people say they're religious, it seems like it's more about following a set of rules than developing their relationship with God, and to me, that's missing the whole point."

"Hmm." She cocked her head to the side, considering his words. "That's deep."

He chuckled. Guess he'd handled that with some finesse after all. "What about you?"

"My dad walked away from church for a while after my sister died, so I didn't really grow up with a strong faith."

"And now...?"

She took a quick breath. "Before I went to boarding school, I went to a Christian treatment center for a few months. It opened my eyes to a bunch of stuff."

His mind swirled. Treatment centers were for alcohol and drug addiction, weren't they? He couldn't imagine that teenage Valerie had ever struggled with that. "What were you there for?"

"Behavioral health."

He wasn't sure exactly what that meant, but she didn't seem inclined to elaborate, so he let it go. "Well, I'm glad it helped you get back in touch with your faith."

She blushed. "Thanks."

"What about your dad? Did he have the chance to get right with God before he passed?"

"He did."

Relief rinsed through him. He was always glad to hear that someone had come to the Lord, but he was especially glad that Valerie could rest easy knowing that she'd see her father again someday.

"If you want," he said, "we can go to church together tomorrow and I can introduce you around."

She glanced at him, appreciation—and maybe even a little admiration—in her eyes. "That's nice of you."

It was hard not to feel a rush of affection for her. He hadn't done much, but suddenly he felt ten feet tall.

If only she weren't leaving in a few short weeks.

They kept driving, passing by an amusement center that housed a mini golf course, a trampoline park, batting cages and go-karts. "That looks fun," Valerie said.

Brett nodded. "Spent many an evening there in high school goofing off."

"With Tracy, right?" she asked, and it felt like she'd dumped a bucket of cold water over his head. He didn't want to talk about his ex-girlfriend right now. Not with her.

He shrugged. "Sometimes."

Valerie gave him a sideways look. "I know I left in tenth grade, but rumor had it you two were going to get married."

Brett sighed. It didn't seem like Valerie was going to let this go. "We talked about it."

"What happened?"

He rubbed his face. More stupidity on his part was what

had happened. An inability to read the writing on the wall. "She wasn't too excited when I left the navy. She'd moved to Boston by that time, and she wanted to travel. See the world."

"How long were you in the navy?"

"Just for my initial service commitment. I enlisted right after high school. I would've re-upped and stayed in longer if my parents hadn't died."

She fidgeted in her seat. "Thank you for your service."

He waved that away. The war vets were the ones who deserved recognition. "I was stationed in Japan. Tracy liked that. Said she wanted to get married and live on base over there, learn Japanese. So, I saved up for the ring she wanted, but by the time I had enough money to buy it, I'd left the navy and moved back home."

It still hurt, even eight years later. Brett worried it would always hurt—not because he was still in love with Tracy, but because he'd been so wrong about her and her feelings for him.

All he wanted was to find a woman who was kind and loyal—someone who'd stick by his side when life got tough, someone who'd be happy with a simple, quiet life in Wychmere Bay—but here he was yet again, developing feelings for a woman who had no intention of settling down in a small town.

"Wait," Valerie said. "She told you which ring to buy and then turned you down *after* you bought it?"

That was about the size of it. "Yup."

"Because she didn't want to move back to Cape Cod?"

"She did not," he confirmed.

"Were you able to return the ring at least?"

He shook his head. "The store wouldn't take it back. But I took it to the diamond district in Boston and got a pretty good price. I only ended up losing a couple hundred bucks."

She got that fierce, fighting look he'd seen on her face the night of the fire. "Unbelievable. If I weren't already mad at her because of that stupid social media profile, I'd be mad at her for you."

What was with her fixation on him and Tracy? "Don't be mad. We were both young back then. Probably too young to get married, anyway."

Valerie sighed. "You guys just always seemed…kind of perfect together. I mean, the way you looked at her…"

Perfect? Ha. But why would she think that? Tracy had been downright mean to her back then, and he'd been oblivious.

But he wasn't oblivious now, and hearing her gush about how he used to look at Tracy? Not ideal. "Gettin' a little weird here, Grilled Cheese."

She bit her lip. "Sorry."

"Let's leave the past in the past, shall we?"

"Of course," she said, eyes on the road. After a minute or two, she nodded to the large oak trees lining the street. "The leaves are starting to change."

Although Cape Cod was best known for its seashore, it was also highly forested. In many of the less built-up residential areas, the homes seemed to emerge from the trees—a mix of oak, pitch pine and the occasional maple tree.

"Wait 'til October. It's wicked colorful."

She smiled and ducked her head.

"What?"

"Your accent."

"Bad?" He didn't sound strange to himself, but he knew he talked like a local, all dropped *r*'s and unrounded consonants. Before he'd joined the navy, his accent had been even stronger.

She shook her head. "I couldn't even hear the New England accent until I'd been away at college for a couple of years. Then I realized I could hear it because I was losing it."

"Where'd you go to school?"

"New York University."

"City girl," he teased.

She slanted a glance at him. "Do you regret not staying in the navy for her?"

They were back to Tracy again? He bit back a groan of frustration. "If coming home to take care of my sister after our parents died was the straw that broke the camel's back, I'm glad I found out when I did."

"That's true. I guess it was a good thing she showed you what her priorities were before you got married and had a couple of kids."

"Right," he said.

Although it would have been nice if Tracy had been the person he'd thought she was. And it would definitely be nice to have a couple of kids.

Brett wondered what Valerie's kids would look like. Would they have black hair, like her and the boys? Would they have the same amazing, mismatched eyes?

He doubted having kids was on her radar right now, though. Aside from the twins, Valerie's priorities were getting back to her job and securing her promotion.

And that, unfortunately, wasn't going to change just because he was starting to wish it would.

Chapter Eight

Like Wychmere Bay, Chatsworth was highly walkable. A little bigger than Wychmere Bay, a little more fashionable, its main street featured home goods boutiques, antique stores, art galleries, a shop where you could buy artisanal oils and vinegars, and the biggest independent bookstore on Cape Cod.

Over the last two hours, Valerie and Brett had visited almost every shop on the block, and the vast majority had agreed to donate an item or a gift card to the Cranberry Harvest Festival. Valerie was by no means surprised, because they'd been greeted by a female staff member at almost every store they'd walked into, and as soon as those ladies had seen Brett, they'd stood taller, smiled brighter and—more often than not—started playing with their hair.

It had immediately, and irrationally, driven Valerie up the wall, even though Brett hadn't flirted back with any of them. But he had an easy charm that women couldn't help responding to. Case in point, herself.

She'd been more open with him than she'd ever been with any man, and considering their history, that was saying something. But just because he made her feel safe, seen and appreciated, it didn't mean they were going to take things in a romantic direction. They couldn't. She was only here for a few more weeks. And once she went back to work, she wouldn't have time for romance, anyway.

So this whole jealousy thing she had going on right now? Pointless.

What might *not* be pointless, however, was harnessing his good looks and easy charm to benefit the Cranberry Harvest Festival. And if her idea also happened to help her get over these inconvenient feelings for Brett? All the better.

"Hey, so remember how Cynthia at the movie theater said the gift certificate to your restaurant sold for four times its value at last year's auction?" she asked as they walked out of a shop that sold goat's milk products like high-end soaps, lotions, face scrubs and body butter.

"Yeah. Sweet, huh?"

They'd come to the end of the row of shops on Main Street. The cottage in front of them had a bird bath and fairy statuettes woven in among the roses growing in the front yard. It also sported cedar shingles and a gabled roof, just like her dad's old house.

A pang of nostalgia hit Valerie square in the chest. She'd miss it here on Cape Cod. She really would.

"Would you be willing to donate something again this year?"

He flashed her a skeptical look. "Um, you do remember that Half Shell burned down, correct?"

"Yes, but your stitches are coming out on Monday, aren't they? And then how much longer until you're out of the splint?"

"Doc said to give it two to three weeks."

"So, it could be off pretty soon after the Cranberry Harvest Festival, right?"

"Hopefully, yeah."

"What if you donated a home-cooked meal…"

"I can do that," he said slowly, probably sensing that she wasn't quite done.

"…and then stayed to eat it with the winner?"

He cocked his head to the side in confusion. "Why would they want me to stay and eat with them?"

"Not them," she said. "Her."

He stared at her for a beat. He hadn't shaved this morning, and he looked especially rugged. "How do you know the winning bidder would be a 'her'?"

"Because we wouldn't just be auctioning a home-cooked meal," she said. "We'd be auctioning off a date. With you."

"A date?" His eyebrows shot up. "Like one of those cheesy bachelor auctions?"

"I've been doing a ton of online research this week, and I'm waiting to hear back from a bunch of places up in Boston, but lots of people won't want to travel to redeem an auction item. They want something local. Something fun." And if there was one word Valerie would use to describe Brett, it would be fun.

"But that's what I've been doing all week. Collecting local donations."

"And gift baskets and gift cards are great," she conceded, "but what gets the really high bids are experiences. Things people can't get anywhere else."

"So, we auction off some tickets to a whale watch. Boom. Done." They'd walked down to the beach, and he flung out his arms to indicate the ocean in front of them. It was windy today, and the roar of the sea was loud.

"Everyone here's already been on a whale watch. That's not special."

"And a dinner date with me is special?" He threw her a skeptical look.

It would be to me.

Whoa. She needed to stop that. *Focus on making the auction a success, not your feelings for Brett.*

It might sting to see him go out on a date with someone else, but it also might be exactly what she needed to kick this crush to the curb before she headed back to New York.

"You're a bona fide hero," she said. "We should lean into that."

Unease flickered across his face, and he stroked his jaw with his uninjured hand. "You've got to stop saying stuff like that. I'm not a hero."

"You *are* a hero," she insisted. "If it weren't for you, the twins and I might have died that night."

"You would have gotten out."

She stared at the white-capped waves. "Maybe. Maybe not. I was pretty frazzled. Even if I'd gotten Derrick out, I don't know that I would have been able to find Dylan."

"People keep acting like it was this big act of bravery, but it wasn't. I saw the flames, and I reacted. There wasn't a lot of thought behind it."

"That's exactly what made it courageous, though. You weren't thinking about protecting yourself. You put us first, above your own safety."

"Any man in my position would have done the same thing."

"Nope." Valerie shook her head. "Not buying it. You're a Good Samaritan, Brett Richardson. Accept it."

"Doesn't mean anyone's gonna pay good money to go on a date with me," he grumped.

She laughed. "Any one of the women in all those stores we just visited would jump at the chance to go out with you if they were single."

Brett snorted. "Now you're just being ridiculous."

"I'm not! Know how much the Women's League in New York raised at its most recent bachelor auction? Eight thousand dollars! And besides, I know what it looks like when a woman wants to catch a man's attention. Oh, Brett," she said, twirling her hair and making her voice high-pitched in an over-the-top imitation of one of the ladies from the home goods store. "So glad you came by. Of *course* we'll donate to the auction for you."

Brett wagged his head, but there were twin spots of color on his cheeks. "They were just being nice."

"Prove it. Put yourself up for auction so we can see which one of us is right."

"Not happening."

She put her hands together in supplication. "Come on, I know you want the charity to get a big donation."

"Not. Happening."

"Why not? This is one of the last things I can do for my dad. I want it to be a huge success."

Brett scrubbed a hand over his face. "Look, Valerie. I get it that I'm like a hero to you. But you read Rudy's article about me. To most of the people around here, I'm just the idiot who lost his business because he was too stupid to renew his insurance."

She took a small step back, upset on his behalf. "That's not true. No one thinks you're an idiot."

"Why do you think I was always asking for your help with my homework back in the day? It wasn't because I have a high IQ."

She frowned. "You were busy with other things."

He took off his sunglasses and pinched the bridge of his nose. "You went to college and business school. I barely made it into the navy. I had to get tutoring to pass the vocational aptitude test. And even then, it was by the skin of my teeth."

"So what? You passed. And lots of people get tutoring."

"Did you ever get tutoring?"

"Well, no—"

"See?"

She put her hands on her lips. "Nobody cares if you needed help with your homework fifteen years ago, Brett."

"But they *do* care that I can't read well enough to submit paperwork on time now."

That stopped her frustration dead in its tracks. "You can't… what?"

"I can't read very well." He tapped his temple. "Dyslexia."

It wouldn't compute. Big, loud Brett had a learning disability? "I'm sorry."

He sat down in the sand. "It's fine. Obviously, I didn't do so great in school, but most of the time I manage. I should've hired an office manager, though. I shouldn't have tried to do all that stupid paperwork myself."

She dropped down beside him, sifting her fingers through the sand. "When did you find out?"

"Senior year of high school."

"Wow, that late?"

"Yup." He gave her a rueful smile. "I guess I had everybody fooled."

"Is that why you were always so obnoxious in class? You were trying to deflect from the fact that you had trouble reading?"

He tilted his chin down. "Probably. To some extent, at least."

"And here I thought you were just a loudmouth jerk."

He squinted at her. "Do I need to apologize again?"

"No, I've forgiven you." When she searched her heart, she knew that she really, truly had. She smiled. "And I didn't always think you were a jerk. Just after you joined the football team."

"Yeah, well, there was probably a part of me that was scared that if I stood up for someone else, they'd turn it around on me."

For some reason, that admission made her feel like a mama bear, fierce and protective. "You know that having a learning disability doesn't make you stupid, don't you?"

"Intellectually? Sure. I still feel stupid sometimes, though. Especially lately, since I lost the restaurant."

"God gives us all different gifts and talents. You're brave, you're charming, you can cook a mean slice of bacon…"

He laughed.

"So focus on your strengths."

He waggled his eyebrows. "You think I'm charming, do you?"

She pointed at the shops on Main Street. "Those ladies back there sure did. So use those talents and do your civic duty, Mr. Bacon Man. Get us a big donation for the festival."

"My civic duty, huh?" he asked, lips twitching.

She worked hard to keep a straight face. "I know you want to be a good citizen."

"Fine. I'll do it. But if the bidding's slow, you have to bail me out. I don't want to be embarrassed up there."

"I promise, you won't be embarrassed."

He shook his head at her. "Famous last words."

Despite agreeing to put himself up for auction, Brett didn't have much time to worry about it over the next few days. Valerie and the boys went to church with him on Sunday, then stayed for the kids' sports program afterward. Later, they all went to the beach with Jonathan, Emma, Chloe, Steve and Aiden while Laura stayed home with a sleeping Hunter.

On Monday morning, Brett, Valerie and the twins drove to another of the neighboring towns to ask for donations to the auction, scoring a gold-plated sand dollar necklace, a tote bag made from a recycled sail and a family pack of tickets to the local pirate museum, which of course they had to check out themselves while they were there.

The boys were super into it, touching the pirate coins and searching the museum for treasure. There was also a water play area where they could build and race paper boats, and Brett played with them there for over an hour.

On Tuesday, the four of them took the ferry to Martha's

Vineyard, where they once again pled their case for the silent auction, collecting a unique oyster mug, a photography book, a set of island-inspired candles, a gift certificate for a night at a B and B and a lavender-scented eye mask.

"You're going to have so many donations, you won't know what to do with them," Brett said on the boat ride home. They were on the top deck, the boys pressed up against the railing to watch the birds soaring through the sky, the sparkle of the sun on the water and the whitecaps on the waves.

"I think we can group some of them together in themed baskets."

"Ah." He tapped his forehead. "Smart."

As they approached the harbor, Brett held each of the twins up in turn to see all the seals that were sunning themselves on the buoys, and everything seemed so right and easy. Like this was exactly where he was supposed to be.

That night, they took the kids to dinner at Franco's, the pizzeria in town that Brett had been frequenting since he was a teen.

The food here was fast and fresh, the atmosphere laid-back. They fed a ten-dollar bill into the change machine in the corner, stuffed the boys' pockets full of quarters, then let them loose on the arcade games.

Franco himself, who was merrier than a caroler on Christmas but lean as a racehorse, came out from behind the counter to make sure the twins had a step stool so they could reach the games.

Brett and Valerie found a booth where they could keep an eye on the twins while they waited for their food: fig and prosciutto pizza for the two of them, spaghetti and meatballs for the boys.

Before the food came, though, Irene Perkins and Bill Anderson walked into the store. Irene was a spitfire in her seventies, the no-nonsense proprietor of Wychmere Bay's beloved

Candy Shack, which sold a wide variety of saltwater taffy, homemade fudge, penny candy and dozens of other sugary treats. A few years younger than Irene, Bill was a retired teacher Brett often ran into at the gym.

When they caught sight of Brett and Valerie, they made a beeline to their table. Brett stood to greet them, kissing Irene on the cheek and fist-bumping Bill. "Have you met Valerie Williams? She's my partner for the fundraiser auction."

"It's been a long time, young lady," Irene said, fluffing her short white perm before holding out her arms for a hug. "Come here."

Valerie gave the woman a tentative embrace, but Irene pulled her closer.

"You two have met?" Brett asked.

"I've run the Candy Shack for nearly fifty years, Bartholomew. Of course we've met."

"It's nice to see you again," Valerie said politely.

Irene turned her attention to Brett. "When are you going to pick up the gift basket I put together for you?"

"I can swing by tomorrow," he said.

"Twenty pounds of candy, Bartholomew. Bring a dolly cart."

Valerie's eyes bugged. "Twenty pounds?"

Irene started ticking off items on her hand. "Dark chocolate cranberries, milk chocolate cranberries, five-pound box of saltwater taffy, one-pound box of cranberry bog frogs, gummy lobsters, sour sharks, sea salt pretzel bars, sea salt caramels, seashell chocolate pops, starfish chocolate pops, sailboat chocolate pops..." She lifted an eyebrow at Valerie. "Need I go on?"

"No. That sounds incredible."

"Bring those boys with you when you come to pick it up. I'll give them a little treat."

"That's kind of you."

Irene got a wistful look in her eye. "I do love the little ones. Never had children myself, but this one—" she playfully elbowed Bill in the side "—at least has a grandson I can dote on."

"And dote on him she does." Bill wrapped his arm around her waist and smiled.

Irene glanced at Brett. "So, when are you breaking ground on the restaurant?"

"Uh…" Hadn't she read Rudy's article? She had to know he was broke. "Once I save up enough money to rebuild."

"And when will that be, young man?" She clapped her hands in a chop-chop fashion. "Time's a wasting. I need my wedding venue back."

"But haven't you picked a new venue?" he asked. "The wedding's just a few months away."

"We're pushing it back again," she said.

"Why? The pandemic's over."

Bill sighed, stroking his salt-and-pepper mustache. "The heart wants what the heart wants. And what her heart wants is…a wedding reception at Half Shell." He took a piece of paper out of his front pocket, unfolded it and handed it to Brett. "So, here. Consider this our deposit."

Brett took the check, his eyes bulging at the amount written in the dollar box. "I can't accept this."

"You can and you will." Irene wagged a finger at him. "I'm not getting any younger. Don't send me to my grave before this one—" she hiked her thumb at Bill "—can put a ring on it."

Beside Brett, Valerie tried—and failed—to hold back a laugh.

Bill, meanwhile, smiled fondly and rolled his eyes, obviously used to Irene's antics. "I've tried, woman. It's not my fault COVID hit when it did. And you won't settle for a small wedding. Nope, you've got to invite everyone in town."

She put her hands on her hips. "Those are our people, Bill. You want them there just as much as I do, so stop sassing me."

Bill grinned, unrepentant. "Yes, dear."

Irene turned to Brett and Valerie. "Do you see what I have to put up with?"

"Irene, you know I want you to have the wedding of your dreams, but—"

"But nothing, Bartholomew," she said. "This town has been investing in my success for more than fifty years, and Bill and I have everything we could ever want or need. Once word gets out that you want to rebuild, I know we won't be the only ones who'll want to pitch in."

Brett shook his head. "You're wrong. That article Rudy wrote—"

"Oh, pish posh. That article was a hatchet job. If Rudy's not scrambling to write a profile about you and your heroism now, I'll start selling chocolate-covered crickets."

Valerie made a face.

"Crickets aren't bad, actually," Bill piped in. "Lots of protein."

Irene gave him an indulgent pat on the shoulder. "No one wants your cricket protein powder, ducky, or your coconut oil coffee or your lemon and kale smoothies."

"His smoothies are pretty good," Brett said, standing up for his gym buddy.

Bill beamed. "Thank you, son."

Irene sighed and reached up to fuss with her hair. "We're getting off track. You need to announce that you're looking for help to get Half Shell back off the ground."

"But I'm not—"

"Don't say no just yet," Irene insisted. "Sleep on it for a few days. Then go cash that check." Brett bit back a sigh. He knew the older woman just wanted to help, even though all she was doing was highlighting just how far he had to go to reach his goal.

When he got back to the inn, he deposited the check in his sock drawer, which would be the only place he deposited it for the foreseeable future. He certainly wasn't about to take Bill and Irene's money when the likelihood of getting Half Shell up and running in time for their wedding was slim to none.

If he could get it back up and running at all, he'd be ecstatic, but until his fingers healed and he could get back to work, he needed to temper everyone's expectations—especially his own.

The next morning, Valerie's boss called during breakfast, and Brett didn't like the way worry lines immediately appeared on her forehead.

"I don't think I'm allowed to do any work right now, Gary. HR was pretty clear about that when I filed my paperwork."

Valerie slid the pendant on her necklace back and forth while she listened. "What about Cole?" Then, a minute later, "Will I get credit for the work?" She nodded. "Okay, give me thirty minutes. If I can find childcare for the twins, I'll do it."

She hung up and turned to Laura. "So… I hate to ask, but my boss just called. He wants me to put in a couple of hours of work this morning to cover for someone who called in sick. Any chance you could watch the twins while I knock out this assignment? I'll be upstairs, but I can't concentrate if I have to keep an eye on them at the same time."

Laura pushed a strand of hair behind her ear. "I thought you were supposed to be on leave?"

"I am, but this promotion is a toss-up between me and the employee who's out sick. If doing this one thing is the difference between getting the promotion and not getting it, you'd better believe I'm going to do it."

Laura gave Brett a meaningful look. "Doesn't she sound like Jonathan when he first got here?"

A spark of hope flared in his chest, but he snuffed it out at the first flicker. Jonathan had been dissatisfied with his life when he'd first made the trip to Cape Cod. Valerie wasn't.

"Why?" Valerie asked. "What brought Jonathan down here?"

Laura moved the baby from one arm to the other. "He was in line to make partner at a big corporate law firm in Boston."

Valerie cocked her head to the side in confusion. "I thought he worked in the juvenile court system."

"He does now. He was supposed to buy the inn for a big hotel chain, but we met and he had a change of heart."

"Wow," Valerie said. "That's a massive career change."

Brett had thought so, too, but his friend had been glad to make it. Once he met Laura, Jonathan hadn't cared what changes he needed to make to his life—he'd been all in.

The same way Steve had been prepared to uproot his life and his business for Chloe.

This situation is different, though, Lord, isn't it? You said it yourself: 'Honour thy father and thy mother.' That's what I'm trying to do.

Besides, after what he went through with Tracy, was it too much to ask for a woman who'd be willing to make some changes for him?

Laura shrugged. "He'd always liked kids, and when he thought about what he really wanted in the long run, being chained to his desk by a pair of golden handcuffs wasn't it."

"Good for him," Valerie said, but her voice sounded choked. "Uh, so…about the twins…?"

"I'm sorry, sweetie. I've got to take Hunter to the pediatrician in half an hour, then I have a potluck with some friends from my Mommy and Me group. Can it wait until we get back?"

Valerie's shoulders drooped, and Brett couldn't take it. He hated to see her unhappy. "I'll do it."

She turned her head so fast he was surprised she didn't get whiplash. "You've been helping us so much this week. I'm sure you want a break."

"What else am I going to do? Sit around and watch TV?"

"Maybe you want some time to plan the big date."

He rolled his eyes, but Laura's spine went as straight as a soldier's. "What big date?"

"Brett's going to be the grand prize at the Cranberry Harvest Festival."

Laura's mouth fell open. "What?"

Valerie smirked. "You should have seen the way the women in the stores at Chatsworth were flirting with him last weekend. He's going to be a hit."

Brett's cheeks heated in embarrassment. There was only one woman whose attention he craved, and she clearly didn't feel the same way. "I'm going to cook the winner dinner," he told Laura. "That's the main attraction."

His friend arched an eyebrow at him. "Very sporting of you."

He shrugged. "I do what I can."

But honestly, he was regretting the whole thing already.

Chapter Nine

The two hours of work that Valerie's boss gave her on Wednesday turned into six. He called again the next day, claiming that Cole was still out of the office, and she ended up spending all day Thursday and Friday in front of her laptop, too.

The only reason she'd been able to do any work at all was because Brett was amazing. He took the boys to the beach all three days and ran them around for hours. She heard from the twins that they built another sandcastle, even bigger than the last one. They collected shells and dug for sand crabs. They played some strange variation of tag in which Brett put seaweed on his head and chased them around the dunes. They ate treats from the ice cream truck and fed bread crusts to the birds.

When she finally finished her work on Friday, she fought off a bout of lightheadedness when she got up from her desk, then descended the creaky stairs from the second floor of the Sea Glass Inn into the parlor. As she stepped onto the wraparound back patio, she inhaled deeply. Cape Cod's briny ocean air was refreshing, and she felt her stress melt away as she looked around at the neighboring homes with their faded cedar shingles and small, cozy rooms.

She hadn't been back to Wychmere Bay much in the last fifteen years. Mostly, her father had visited her. First, in Boston, where she'd gone to boarding school. Then, in New York.

But she couldn't deny that it was comfortable here—clam chowder instead of caviar. A Ford pickup truck instead of a Mercedes-Benz.

Valerie had tried caviar at a couple of fancy restaurants, and she really didn't care for it. Cape Cod lobster rolls, though? Those, she could get behind.

Laura's story about Jonathan's career change was weighing on her mind. She'd actually asked him about it at breakfast this morning, and he'd said that what he liked most about working with kids and families was seeing their lives change in front of his eyes.

Valerie had felt the hot tug of jealousy grip her throat. When she'd dreamed of becoming a doctor back when she was a teen, that was exactly what she'd wanted to do. Make a difference, one patient at a time.

That dream was dead, though. You couldn't be a doctor if you fainted at the sight of blood.

But maybe there was a new dream out there for her, waiting to be found.

Valerie shook the thought right out of her head. She had a plan and she was sticking to it. The fact that she'd be supporting the twins from here on out only made getting that promotion more essential.

Which was why she'd completed those assignments for her boss without pushing back. Her coworker Cole would be back in the office on Monday, so the work she'd just finished should be the last that was coming her way for a while.

Across the dunes, she could see Brett and the boys flying a kite near the waves. The boys had practically been foaming at the mouth to get down to the beach and fly it when Brett had shown them the package this morning.

Chloe had called earlier and told her about the Parents' Night Out event that her day care was hosting tonight. Valerie had immediately booked two spots for the boys—she definitely owed Brett a meal for taking care of the twins for the past three days.

She walked toward the water, the sand gritty between her toes. Now that she was thinking about dinner, she realized she hadn't eaten much all day. Although she'd been in recovery from her eating disorder for a long time, stress could still sometimes mess with her hunger cues.

And taking on all that extra work these past few days had definitely been stressful.

This morning, she'd had about two bites of shredded wheat for breakfast before she'd gotten distracted by another call from her boss, and then—anxious to get everything done and get back to the boys as quickly as she could—she'd worked through lunch without even thinking about it.

Yikes.

She certainly wasn't feeling her best right now, either. Despite the mild temperature, her fingers were freezing and her body felt shaky.

Her blood sugar was probably low. She should go back to the inn and grab a granola bar, but just as the thought occurred to her, the boys caught sight of her, dropping the string of the kite and running to her. Fortunately, Brett held on tight.

"Valwee! We're flying a kite!" Dylan shouted.

"I know, honey. So cool!" She was wearing jeans and a floaty blue top this afternoon, and it ruffled in the breeze. There was a mound of dark green seaweed on the sand between the water and the high tide mark, a tangled mess of the sort she and Vanessa had called mermaid's hair when they were kids.

She touched her necklace, wishing her sister was here with them, and her father, too.

"Mr. Bacon Man gotted it for us! It went *so* high!" Derrick added.

"Amazing! Did you say thank you?"

"Thank you, Mr. Bacon Man!" the boys chorused.

Brett grinned as he flew the kite to Valerie so that she could reel it in. "Tell Valerie what else we did today."

"We raced to da jetty!" Derrick crowed.

Dylan jumped up and down with excitement. "And we beated Mr. Brett!"

"Wow." Valerie widened her eyes. "You must have been fast."

"So fast!"

"Da fastest!"

"And what else did we do?" Brett prompted.

"Fishing!" the boys cried.

Valerie shot Brett a questioning look. "Really?"

He hitched his shoulder. "I bought them a couple of toddler rods. We sat on the jetty and watched the seagulls hunt for crabs, didn't we, guys?"

"Da seagulls drop crabs on da rocks to break da shells!"

"And why did they need to break the shells?" Brett asked.

"So they can eat da crab!" Dylan answered.

"Very good," Brett said.

Dylan beamed.

Valerie's chest went tight. Brett was so good with the boys. So fun and so generous. If she didn't have to head back to New York after the Cranberry Harvest Festival, she'd bid on that date with him herself.

They started walking back to the inn, the boys running ahead. "Tell me how much you spent on the fishing poles and the kite, and I'll pay you back," she said, still feeling shaky on her feet.

Brett gave her a mild look. "Please. It was nothing."

"I know you've got a cash flow problem right now…"

"Valerie." He put his good hand on his hip. "I can afford a couple of beach toys."

Uh-oh. Had she offended him? He wasn't one of those guys

who was intimidated by a financially independent woman, was he? She'd met her share of those kinds of men in New York—lawyers and doctors and software engineers whose noses got bent out of shape when she wasn't impressed with their flashy cars, their expensive clothes and their exclusive restaurant reservations.

But the fact that Brett had spent the last three days babysitting suggested that he was secure enough in his masculinity not to feel threatened by a woman's success. "You really went above and beyond this week. I can't tell you how much you helped me out."

"I'm glad." The light glinted off his sunglasses, and she could smell the sunscreen on his skin. Why couldn't there be men like him in New York?

"I'm taking the boys to the Parents' Night Out thing at Chloe's day care tonight. Can I buy you dinner? As a thank-you?" She stopped and put her hand on his forearm. His very solid forearm.

He stopped, too. "It's really not necessary. But where were you before you came out to get us? Your hands are like ice."

Embarrassed, she whipped her hand away. "I just get cold sometimes."

He tipped his chin down, his warm brown eyes studying her over the top of his shades. "You need to put some more meat on those bones."

Her stomach churned. Bones sounded an awful lot like Sticks. Not wanting him to see how his words had affected her, she dropped her gaze and saw a feather in the sand that the boys might like. She bent down to pick it up, and as she straightened, suddenly all the blood rushed away from her head.

Everything around her dimmed. Little white starbursts popped in front of her eyes. The world took on a weird, pink haze.

"What's wrong?" Brett's voice sounded far away, as though it was coming through a tunnel.

"Nothing," she mumbled, but as she said it, her legs wobbled, and she dropped to her hands and knees on the sand.

"Valerie!" he cried out, and the next thing she knew, she was sitting in his lap.

Brett hadn't been able to catch her. With his arm in this stupid sling, the best he'd been able to do was scoop her up onto his lap after she'd already fallen to the ground.

His heart was racing like he'd just bench-pressed three hundred pounds. He'd never seen someone's face lose all its color like that before.

"Valerie," he said, shaking her shoulder.

She made a small sound but stayed limp in his arms.

The boys were on the inn's back patio, worried frowns on their little faces. "Guys!" Brett called out. "Go inside and find Mrs. Laura. Tell her Valerie needs help."

They ran to comply while Valerie slurred, "I don'… I don'…"

"You don't what, bright eyes?" he asked, relieved to hear her talking, even if she sounded rough.

"I don't need help." Her head lolled back against his chest, but her voice sounded steadier. "I just need to put my head down."

"Go ahead, then."

"Not here. It works better in a chair."

Brett eyeballed the distance from where they were sprawled in the sand to the chairs on the back patio. If she were stable enough to hold tight to his neck, he could probably carry her over there one-handed, but right now, it didn't feel like she had a whole lot of bodily control.

Laura burst out the sliding glass door onto the patio, and Brett waved her over.

"What happened?" she called as she ran toward them.

"I'm fine," Valerie insisted, while Brett said, "She passed out."

"How can I help?"

"She wants to sit on one of the chairs and put her head between her knees." He gestured toward the back patio with his chin. "But I can't carry her over there because of this ridiculous splint."

"We're going to help you up, honey, okay?" Laura crouched and levered herself under Valerie's arm, and Brett shifted her off his lap so he could do the same.

Together, they helped Valerie to her feet, then onto the patio, where she collapsed onto a chair and stuck her head between her legs.

Brett crouched beside her, gently touching her arm, which still felt cool to the touch. "Are you all right?"

She nodded, her head still down. "I'm fine."

"You don't look fine."

Valerie lifted her head. "Sometimes I get dizzy when I stand up too fast, that's all. It's nothing. See? Much better already."

He gave her a wary look. "Have you seen a doctor about it?"

She sighed. "Yes. Several. Don't worry, it's not cancer or anything. It's called orthostatic hypotension. They just tell me to stay hydrated and eat a lot of salt."

"Let me get you a drink."

"I'm fine, Brett. Really," she insisted.

"I'll get it," Laura said. "What do you want? Water? Orange juice?"

Valerie gave her a weak smile. "OJ would be nice."

Laura went inside to grab some.

"You're not diabetic, are you?" Brett asked, because he'd seen someone go into a diabetic coma once when he was in the navy. For diabetics, low blood sugar could be fatal.

Her brow furrowed. "No."

"So it's not low blood sugar?"

"Well…" Valerie chewed her lip. "I didn't really eat lunch today…"

Brett felt a sharp spike of concern spear him. "Nothing? You didn't eat anything?"

She shook her head.

"Why not?"

"I just…forgot."

He shook his head. People didn't just forget to eat lunch. "You're working too hard."

She frowned. "Don't try to mansplain me to myself, please."

"Mansplain? Valerie. I'm worried about you." He couldn't believe how blasé she was being about this whole thing. She'd literally collapsed, and he hadn't even been able to catch her. What if she'd been crossing the street or walking down the stairs?

"Don't be. I'm fine. Seriously. I get lightheaded all the time."

"Do you skip a lot of meals?"

She shot him an aggravated glance, her mismatched eyes flashing in the sun. "I told you. I didn't skip lunch. I forgot."

Laura came outside with Valerie's juice. "Here you go."

She took a sip.

"Better?" Brett asked.

She let out an audible breath before insisting, "I'm fine."

"Have some more to drink."

Another frown flickered across her face. "You're kind of bossy."

"I'm kind of concerned."

Valerie turned to Laura. "Are the twins okay?"

"They were a little freaked out, but I gave them some animal crackers and told them to play with their trucks. They seem fine now."

"Thank you." Valerie smiled at her, and Brett had to admit

that it stung to see her grateful to Laura while she was annoyed at him.

"I'm just glad you're all right," Laura said. "Do you want to go lie down?"

Valerie shook her head. "Walking's better than resting—gets the blood pumping. But I should eat something first. Maybe a granola bar? I've got some in my room."

Brett put his good hand on his hip. "You need to have more than a granola bar."

She glared at him. "I *will*, Brett. Let me start there, though."

The more he expressed concern, the more defensive she got. He needed to flip the script and make her laugh, otherwise they were never going to get anywhere.

"What do you call a fake noodle?" he asked, pausing to let either Laura or Valerie respond. When they didn't, he pulled out the punch line. "An im-*pasta*!"

But it was clear the joke had fallen flat.

"All right, then," Laura said, giving him a funny look.

Time to regroup. He glanced at his watch, then at Valerie. "It's almost five. When you're finished with that granola bar, I'm collecting on that dinner you promised me."

Laura gaped at them. "You two are having dinner together tonight?"

"Yep," Brett said. "She was in the middle of asking me when she passed out. I mean, I know I have an effect on women, but I've never seen anyone actually swoon before."

Laura laughed while Valerie sputtered, "I did not pass out because of you!"

He winked at her. "Just trying to lighten the mood."

"You're bossy *and* annoying," she grumbled.

He cupped a hand behind his ear in a move that always got a rise out of Chloe. "What's that? You think I'm handsome *and* charming? Why, thank you, bright eyes. I think so, too."

She gave him a wry look. "You forgot about modest."

"I didn't forget. I was being humble and leaving it off the list of my many stellar attributes."

That finally got a chuckle out of her. "'Nothing is more deceitful than the appearance of humility. It is often only carelessness of opinion, and sometimes an indirect boast.'"

"What's that from?" he asked.

"Pride and Prejudice."

"The 1995 version or the 2005 version?" He'd had to suffer through both movies on several occasions at his sister's insistence.

Valerie gave him a pert smile. "The book version."

"Old school," he said, tipping his chin down. "I like it."

What he really meant was *I like you.*

"Um…" Laura said, taking a comedically large backward step. "I'll leave you two to it."

Funny—he'd almost forgotten she was there.

Brett knew that, after checking on the baby and the twins, Laura's very next move would be to call Chloe with an update on all of this, but he didn't even care. His sister could give him a hard time all she wanted as long as Valerie had a good meal.

"I'll go get you that granola bar," he said, "then we're going out for dinner."

Valerie sighed. "I thought you said dinner wasn't necessary."

"Well," he countered, "now it is."

She gave him a sarcastic little salute. "Sir, yes, sir."

"Come on." He really didn't want her to be mad at him. "We can go through the list of all the items we have for the auction. And—" he waggled his eyebrows "—plan out my big date."

"Right," she said. "Your date."

Her voice sounded flat, so he poked her in the shoulder. "It'll be fun. And I know just where to take you to eat."

"Where?"

"It's a surprise. But don't worry, you'll love it. It's wild."

She gazed out over the water and sighed. "Sorry if I scared you back there."

"It's okay. I just wish my hand was out of this sling so I could have caught you before you fell down. You didn't hurt anything, did you?"

She shook her head. "Just my pride."

"Nothing to be embarrassed about." He held out his good hand to help her up. "But if it's a known issue, we've got to make sure you're taking care of yourself."

"Thanks for your help." She worried her pendant between her fingers.

He shrugged, pausing for a couple of beats before he replied, "Just doing my civic duty."

She slanted a suspicious glance at him. "Are you making fun of me?"

He grinned. "Yep."

"Okay." She smiled back. "Just making sure."

Chapter Ten

Brett had been right about one thing—the decor in the Irish/Indian restaurant he'd chosen was wild. Valerie noted the lava lamps on the tables immediately, and he pointed out the constellation charts on the ceiling as soon as they walked in.

She was glad for the distraction. Despite the fact that he'd dropped the whole fainting spell thing back at the inn, she was worried that he'd bring it up again. If he did, she didn't know what she'd say.

Aside from her father, she'd never talked about her eating disorder with a man who wasn't a medical professional. It wasn't really something she expected the average guy to understand.

Even her dad, with all his good intentions, had never really grasped what she was going through. "Eat something," he used to beg her. "Please, why won't you just eat?"

As a kid, she'd been unable to articulate her reasoning—all she knew was that the idea of eating the wrong thing at the wrong time or in the wrong amount filled her with intense, crippling fear.

Rules had always given Valerie a sense of control, and her young mind had developed a whole lot of them around her eating. Never mind that her bizarre food rules and rituals never actually gave her what she'd really needed: Peace. Purpose. Acceptance.

Her sister's presence.

Her mother's love.

At the hostess stand, an older Irish lady in an embroidered green sari welcomed them to the restaurant. "Brett, laddie," she said. "How are ya, boyo?"

"Hey, Colleen," he replied, grinning. "Top of the evenin' to ya."

"Oh, you," she said, shaking her head and chucking his cheek before turning her attention to Valerie. "Got to be on yer toes with this one, girlie."

Valerie gave a short laugh. "Yes, I'm getting that."

"Colleen, Valerie. Valerie, Colleen," he said, gesturing between them.

"Table fer two?" Colleen asked.

Brett gave a solemn nod. "Aye."

Colleen snorted and led them to a table by the window. After the older woman walked away, Valerie asked, "You come here a lot?"

He shook his head. "Not anymore. But Colleen and her husband, Shail, were good friends of my parents. We came here a lot when I was a kid."

"Really? She sounds like she's fresh off the boat."

He smiled, the corners of his eyes crinkling. "I think she nurses the accent because it's good for business."

She looked around again. "This place is very…unique."

"Gaudy, right? But fun."

She was still taking in all the nuances of the decor. "For sure."

"Food's good, too," he said, handing her a menu.

"Great." The granola bar she'd eaten back at the inn had hardly made a dent in her hunger. She scanned the menu, which was chock-full of both Irish and Indian dishes. If she ordered a big enough meal, maybe Brett would leave well enough alone and she wouldn't have to talk about her light-headedness again. "What do you recommend?"

"Depends on what you're in the mood for. If you want an appetizer, the seafood chowder's excellent, but so's the potato soup. They also have really delicious samosas and naan. I usually go Indian for the main course. They've got a great shrimp curry, or a tandoori chicken with a mango and cucumber chutney that's out of this world. If you're leaning Irish, though, get the fish pie. Or the corned beef. Or the shepherd's pie."

Valerie giggled. "You're really narrowing it down for me." Brett certainly knew how to make her laugh.

"Can't be helped." He chuckled. "It's all good."

Colleen came over, pen and notebook in hand, and Valerie decided to skew Irish, ordering the seafood chowder, fish pie and a side of soda bread. Brett went for the samosas and the shrimp.

A moment later, Colleen was back with their drinks. Valerie picked up her water and took a sip. Deciding that the best defense was a good offense, she steered the conversation away from herself. "Tell me about being in the navy."

Brett leaned back in his chair. "What do you want to know?"

"Were you stationed in Japan the whole time?"

"After basic training, yup, at the Yokosuka Naval Base in Japan. But I saw a lot of the Pacific. Singapore, South Korea, the Philippines, Indonesia, Thailand, Guam. I've been to Hong Kong, too."

"How cool! What did you think of Hong Kong?" Laura's parents had lived in Hong Kong for nearly two decades, and Valerie had heard lots of interesting stories about it from her friend.

He took a sip of his water. "Crowded. Busy. They have a laser light show every night, and seeing that was fun."

"What else did you do while you were there?"

"There's mountains in Hong Kong, and we took a tram to the top of the highest one and walked around. The trees were cool. All these above-ground roots. It felt like we were in the rainforest. It was summertime, so it was really hot and humid."

She nodded enthusiastically, fascinated, and he went on. "We went to Hong Kong Disneyland, of course, and kicked around downtown, too. Went up and down this giant outdoor escalator, saw the little zoo and the aviary, plus some of the temples and churches."

"You saw a lot."

He shrugged. "Some of the guys just wanted to party, but I wanted to remember where I'd been. See what made each place unique."

She liked that about him. To be honest, she liked a lot of things about him.

"Food there was great, too," he offered.

"What was your job on the ship?"

"Culinary specialist."

She grinned. "That makes sense."

Colleen dropped off their appetizers, and they both dug in. The soup was warm and hearty—exactly what she'd been hoping for.

Brett finished off a samosa, then said, "Honestly, I was disappointed. I had all these dreams of going to the Middle East and coming home a hero, but you're not likely to earn a medal when you're peeling potatoes in the galley below deck."

You might if you run into a burning building and save a little boy's life. She kept that thought to herself, though. She wanted the medal to be a surprise.

"What's the biggest difference between cooking on the ship and cooking at a restaurant?"

He gave her a wry look. "Restaurants don't sway from side to side."

She laughed. "Other than that."

"Quality. Quantity. Being my own boss." He pointed at his plate. "Want to try one of these? I'm willing to share."

She speared one with her fork. "Sure." The savory fried pastry was filled with potato, cheese and spices. It was delicious.

Brett took a sip of his water. "I learned a lot about discipline in the navy. Establishing a daily routine and sticking to it. Building on it."

"Did you go to boot camp?"

He nodded. "Of course."

"Was it as intense as it is in the movies?" she asked.

"It's not quite like what you see in the movies, but yeah, it was pretty intense."

"Did they shave your head?"

"Yup."

She giggled. "I bet you looked funny bald."

He smirked. "Wouldn't you like to know?"

"I would," she said, grinning. "I really would."

When she was young, Valerie used to fantasize about going to boot camp, imagining how easy it would be to lose weight when you were exercising all the time and you had no access to food outside the mess hall.

Boy, was she ever grateful those days were behind her. Now, she just had to make sure that she didn't let stress cause any more episodes like the one she'd had this afternoon.

Maybe telling Brett more about it wouldn't be so bad. He'd clearly been worried about her, and he obviously hadn't been happy with her evasive replies.

She'd never told a man about her eating disorder, but it wasn't something she hid from her friends. And she and Brett were friends, weren't they? If she had to pick up more of Cole's slack at work this coming week, it would be nice to have an ally, someone who was looking out for her and reminding her to prioritize her health…

Colleen brought their main plates to the table, and Valerie took a small bite, then set down her fork. She trusted Brett. Even if he didn't fully get it, she knew he wouldn't turn his back on her the way he had in high school. "About what happened this afternoon..."

He put his fork down, as well, giving her an expectant look.

Was she really about to do this? Her nerves kicked in, and she touched her necklace, asking God for strength.

"I, uh...it's happened to me before."

"You mentioned that," he said. His eyes were kind.

She twisted her pendant around on its chain. It felt like there were bird wings flapping in her chest. It was now or never. She forced the words out. "I had an eating disorder when I was a kid. It's why I left in tenth grade."

"An eating disorder?" he repeated. She couldn't read his tone. She nodded.

The skin between his eyes furrowed. "And we used to call you Sticks. Man, Valerie, I'm so sorry. We were such insensitive jerks."

She gave her head a quick shake. "I'm not telling you to make you feel bad. I just... I wanted you to know."

"Is that why you fainted? Because you didn't eat enough?"

She chewed her thumbnail. "Yes and no. For most people in recovery, the low blood pressure goes away once they're back at a normal weight, but for me, stress and anxiety trigger it, too. So, if I'm stressed, I'm already vulnerable, and then if I forget to eat or if I let myself get dehydrated, it gets even worse."

Brett hesitated for a moment, looking serious. "How old were you when it started?"

"Seven or eight."

He winced. "When your sister died?"

"You'd think so, but no. It took me a lot of therapy to realize that the trigger was my mom leaving. The scared little girl in me believed that if I got sick enough, she'd come take care of me the way she took care of Vanessa."

She dropped her eyes to the table, then dropped her voice to a whisper, too. It hurt to talk about this. Still. After all these years. "I did end up in the hospital a few times, but—" she took a breath to stave off her tears "—she never came back."

"Aw, Valerie." Brett reached across the table and laid his hand on hers, giving it a gentle squeeze. "You're killing me here. Can I give you a hug?"

She laughed a little, wiping the tears from the corners of her eyes. She'd been annoyed with him earlier, but he really did know how to lighten the mood. "You're very understanding."

"So, that's a yes? I can pull my chair over there and give you a hug?"

She laughed harder, his words loosening something inside her. "Yes, you nerd. You can give me a hug."

He scooted his chair all the way around the table, then folded her into a one-armed hug. The scent of his aftershave surrounded her—the zing of lemon, the earthiness of cedarwood and sage.

Too soon, he dropped his arm.

"Are you getting the help you need?" he asked, and there was an earnestness in the way he asked that made her feel warm all over.

"The treatment center I went to when I was a kid was really good, and I kept going to therapy for a long time. I go to support group meetings every so often, but I honestly don't feel like the eating disorder is a problem anymore. That's not why I missed lunch today. It was just the stress."

"I'm glad you're doing better now."

She smiled. "Me, too."

"Did your mom ever come back to explain herself?"

Valerie shook her head. "I haven't seen her since I was seven."

"She didn't stay in touch *at all*?"

She swiped at her eyes again. "No phone calls, no texts, no cards on my birthday...nothing."

"Wow." He shook his head in disbelief. "That's... Wow. And you've never tried to find her?"

"Why? So she could reject me again?"

"No, sweetheart," he said gently. "So you could get some answers."

Her heart hitched in her chest. *Sweetheart.* She liked the way that sounded way too much.

"Do you think she was depressed?" he asked.

She fingered her necklace. As a teenager, she'd spent a lot of time wondering why her mother had left, but not once had the possibility of depression ever crossed her mind.

"I only ask because Chloe got really depressed after our parents died. Like, wouldn't shower, didn't want to get out of bed. It was bad. And losing a child? I can only imagine how much harder that would be."

Valerie mulled that over for a moment. If Dylan had died in the fire, what kind of state would she be in right now?

Still... Her chin wobbled. "I needed her."

"I know, bright eyes. I'm sorry." He put his arm around her again, and she pressed her nose into his shoulder. He was so solid, so strong.

If Brett hadn't been there the night of the fire, if she'd only been able to get Derrick out, she'd have been crushed. Devastated. Even so, she'd never have walked out on Derrick. Not in a million-billion years.

But you have fifteen years of therapy under your belt, and a faith you can rely on.

Did her mother have that? She had no idea.

And for the first time in forever, she kind of wanted to know.

"I don't have the first clue about how I'd go about trying to find her."

"Maybe a simple internet search?"

Valerie picked up her fork again and took a small bite of

her food. "What I meant is I haven't tried hard. I *have* looked online before. No trace."

"Did you search her maiden name as well as her married name?"

"Mmm-hmm."

Brett took a drink of his water. "Huh. I'm not sure. We could poke around the internet together, or maybe talk to a PI. Jonathan used an investigator when he was looking for his dad, and I think his old law firm has a couple of them on staff. I'll ask him if he has any recommendations."

"Okay," she said, unsure whether or not she actually wanted to get serious about looking for her mom. "I'll think about it."

"No pressure. It's completely up to you. And if there's anything else I can do while you're here, you'll tell me, won't you? I might not understand what you're going through, but I'm always willing to listen. Or watch the boys if you need to go to your support group or whatnot."

She tipped her face up. "That's nice of you. Thanks."

"Can I pray for you?"

She nodded.

He wrapped his arm around her a third time, bowing his head and closing his eyes. "Father God, you invited us to come to you with our troubles and burdens. You told us that your yoke is easy and your burden is light, and that in you, we would find rest for our souls. Thank you, God, for helping Valerie gain victory over her eating disorder. Lord, help her find ways to better manage her stress so it doesn't cause physical symptoms. Help her find rest in you. In Jesus's name we pray. Amen."

"Amen," she echoed.

He took his arm back, then eyed her plate. "Now," he said, "how about giving me some of that soda bread? You wouldn't think it would pair well with shrimp curry, but you, mademoiselle, would be wrong."

* * *

In the end, they didn't get to any of their work for the silent auction during dinner, so Brett asked Chloe if she'd watch the twins on Saturday afternoon so he and Valerie could do an inventory without any interruptions.

His sister, of course, was only too happy to help. So, after Chloe, Steve, Laura and Jonathan had taken all the kids down to the beach, Valerie printed out a fancy spreadsheet detailing all the donations they'd collected so far, and they sat down in the dining room of the inn to review it.

The list was impressive. Valerie had been busy with the online requests, and they'd already racked up a four-pack of tickets to a hockey game in Providence, a bunch of museum tickets, an overnight stay at a fancy hotel in Boston, gift cards to chain restaurants like the Cheesecake Factory and Red Lobster, and, in a totally random twist, tickets to a taping of Wheel of Fortune out in Los Angeles.

"Who's going to fly to Los Angeles to watch a game show?" he asked.

"Hey," she pouted. "Wheel of Fortune isn't just any old game show. It's a TV classic. Plus, it's the new host's first season. Everybody wants to see how that's going to go."

"If you say so."

She huffed, and he bit back a smile. Was it weird that he enjoyed giving her a hard time? In fun, of course. Only in fun. He cared about her way too much to actually make her life harder.

Even if she *was* forcing him to take another woman out on a date.

Speaking of which… "Did you submit a request for Patriots tickets? There's a date I wouldn't mind going on."

"What are they, a soccer team?" she asked, all wide eyes and innocent smile.

He gawked at her, trying to figure out if she was serious or not. "You're kidding, right?"

She grinned. "Of course I'm kidding. They're your baseball team."

He gave a strangled laugh. "No, that's the Red Sox. The Patriots are—"

"I know, I know," she said, giggling. "New England's six-time Super Bowl champs. I'm not a total sports novice."

He mimed wiping sweat off his brow. Seemed like she enjoyed giving *him* a hard time, too. "Phew. I was worried there for a second."

"But no. You can't take your date to a sporting event. The men are the ones who'll bid on those. We're not wasting Patriots tickets on you."

"Gee, thanks," he said dryly.

"Seriously, though, do you have any ideas for the date? We've got to make it good. A dream date."

"A dream date?" He fake gagged. "Sounds cheesy."

"Women love cheesy."

Brett did *not* love cheesiness. If he had to outline an ideal date, he'd go with something like their dinner last night. A low-key restaurant—fun, but not fancy—and someone you could talk to for hours without getting bored.

He couldn't admit that to her, though. She was leaving, and there was no point.

And it hadn't been a real date, anyway—the only reason they'd gone out was so she could thank him for babysitting and he could make sure she ate a good meal.

"Okay, you want cheesy?" he said. "How about—wait for it—a long walk on the beach."

She gave him a thumbs-down. "Too cliché."

"Isn't the point of this date the meal I'm going to cook?"

"No, the point of the date is to make the bidder feel special."

"Okay…" He tapped his foot. "What about sea kayaking?"

"*I* think that would be fun, but won't it be too cold for that by then? Plus, it's a workout, right? I don't think most women want to work that hard on a date."

"You might be right about the weather, but if we wait for a nice day, we could take a tandem kayak and I'd do most of the work. We could go to one of the beaches that has a lot of seals, get up close and personal." He could picture Valerie out on the waves with him, sitting up front in shorts and a sun shirt, a ball cap holding back her charcoal hair. A swell of surf would slap against the side of the kayak, spilling into the boat, and she'd squeal in surprise, then brush at the water on her legs and laugh.

Stop it. She wants you to go on a date with some other woman. Not imagine the date's with her.

She tipped her head to the side. "I was thinking something more romantic."

Brett ducked his chin. There was only one woman he wanted to romance right now, and he couldn't. But he wouldn't put it past Irene Perkins or one of the other church ladies to bid on this date, so he'd play along and try to think of something they'd like.

"Shakespeare in the park?" he suggested. It wasn't his idea of a dream date, but Chloe always seemed to get excited for that.

Valerie took out her phone and looked it up. "Nope, it's over for this year." She pursed her lips. "Too bad."

They were both quiet for a minute, thinking. Then he said, "What about glassblowing? There are all those glassblowing studios in Sandwich. Maybe we could take a lesson and make something together."

Sandwich had been famous for its glassmaking since the 1820s, and it had a variety of studios as well as a glassmaking museum. Brett had been there on a field trip in high school, and from what he remembered, the demonstration had been fascinating.

"I love that idea!" She clasped her hands in front of her chest the way she might if she were watching kitten videos on the internet, and a surge of affection swelled inside him. There was something so genuine about her. He wanted to help her with her stress and anxiety, but he wasn't sure there was anything he could do besides pray.

"Better than a bunch of barking seals?"

She smiled. "I'm sure the seals would be a blast, but I like that you guys will have a souvenir from the glassblowing date. The winner will always have something to remember it by."

"Sounds like glassblowing is a definite contender. For comparison's sake, what would *your* dream date be?"

"Mine?" She slid her broken heart pendant back and forth on its chain. "I don't know. I mean, it's nice when the man makes an effort to plan something special, but it's more about the person than whatever we go and do."

She was adorable. "What's the best date you've ever been on?"

"Um…" She cleared her throat. "I haven't really dated that much. And the few dates I've been on—well, let's just say they were generally underwhelming."

Wow, it was bad how happy he was to hear that, wasn't it? *You can't have romantic feelings for her*, he reminded himself. *You just can't.*

Unless…

What if she were open to seeing him long distance? It wouldn't be ideal, but it would be something, at least.

But for how long?

Dating long distance was fine if it led to an eventual commitment. But if he wanted to get the restaurant going again, he couldn't commit to leaving Cape Cod. And there was no way he'd ask her to give up her career.

There are investment banks in Boston, though, aren't there? If things between them went well for a few months, would she be willing to relocate to Beantown so they could meet each other halfway?

It could work.

Maybe.

Possibly.

And she was definitely worth it, even if the chances of it working out in the long run were slim.

"What kind of guys do you usually go out with? Other bankers?" Best to find out now if she'd ever consider going out with a poor slob like him.

She shuddered. "Ha! No."

"Doctors? Lawyers?"

She shrugged. "A few, I guess. I don't really care what someone does for a living as long as he enjoys it and works hard."

Well, that was heartening. "What's the longest relationship you've been in?"

She gave him a funny look. "What is this? The Spanish Inquisition?"

"Just curious. You know all about *my* longest relationship."

She tilted her head to the side. "I think my longest relationship was about a month."

Surprise smacked him in the chest. "That's it?"

"I'm busy. They're busy. It's New York. Everyone's busy, busy, busy." She laughed, but it sounded stilted.

I'd always make time for you.

He pressed his fist to the top of his thigh to stop himself from saying it out loud.

Still, he couldn't prevent himself from asking, "Are you looking for a relationship?"

She threw it back at him. "Are *you*?"

"I'd like to meet someone." He kept his tone loose and easy.

"After you reopen Half Shell, though, right?"

"I mean, if the perfect girl came along…" He opened his palm and spread the fingers on his good hand.

Her lips quirked up in a half smile. "Tough to walk away from perfection."

"That's right." He caught her gaze. "It is."

After two long beats, she blushed and broke eye contact, rolling her necklace between her fingers. "I feel like that, too. If someone amazing comes along, great. If not, I've got my plate full working toward this promotion."

"You're not going to do any more work while you're here, are you?"

She sighed. "We're not back to this again, are we?"

"I don't want to see you get stressed out. You've got enough on your plate with the twins and the auction."

"Cole's never sick. Hopefully he'll be back in the office tomorrow."

"And if he's not?"

She hitched her shoulder. "We'll cross that bridge when we come to it. But, hey. About the auction. I had something I wanted to ask you."

Uh-oh. The last time she'd asked him about the auction, he'd ended up agreeing to put himself on the auction block.

Still, if he could do something to make her happy, he would. "Hit me."

"Wouldn't it be great if we could get some publicity for the event? I know it's a big deal here in Wychmere Bay, and people from some of the surrounding towns have heard about it, but wouldn't it be great if we could make this the biggest fall festival on Cape Cod?"

"That'd be awesome." He'd love for Parents Against Drunk and Distracted Driving to get a huge donation this year.

"Okay, so…" She pulled a business card out of her pocket and tapped it on the table. "What if I gave Rudy Valentini a call?"

Brett's head snapped back. "That guy? No. Absolutely not."

"But we already know he's interested in what we have to say about the fire. We could give him an interview about that and tack on a bunch of stuff about the Cranberry Harvest Festival, too. If I tell him how heroic you were that night, I'm guessing a lot of ladies would make the drive to Wychmere Bay just to bid on you in the auction."

"He'll twist it, Valerie. Make me sound like a joke, which will make the auction sound like a joke. It'll do the exact opposite of what you want it to do."

She leaned forward, all earnestness. "I promise you, with the interview I'd give him, there's no way you'd end up looking like a joke."

"You read that article. You saw what that guy thinks of me."

"I saw him putting a spin on a story that he thought would sell papers. But this isn't the same. He doesn't need spin this time around, because the truth is, if you hadn't showed up, Dylan, Derrick and I might be dead."

There was no way he was bending on this. "If you want to give an interview so bad, find another reporter."

She gave him a steady look with those lovely, kaleidoscope eyes. "Do you know any other reporters?"

"No."

"So…"

"Call around. Put out a press release. I don't care. But I'm not giving Rudy Valentini an interview, and if you do one without me, I'll pull out of the auction altogether."

Her eyebrows slammed together. "You feel that strongly about it?"

"Have you not heard a word I've been saying?"

"I heard you, I just—" She slid her broken heart pendant from one side of her neck to the other. "I think you're wrong about this."

"I'm not."

"Did anyone else contact you for an interview after the fire?"

She looked so hopeful that he couldn't burst her bubble. "Yeah, people called. I've got a bunch of messages I never listened to on my phone."

"Would you consider listening to them and maybe talking to one or two of them? I really think this could be the thing that makes this year's Cranberry Harvest Festival the best one yet."

Against his better judgment, Brett agreed to listen to the messages. There was no way he'd talk to Rudy, but if Valerie thought getting some other press would make the silent auction more profitable for his charity, she was probably right.

He'd do it…for her.

Chapter Eleven

The next week passed quickly. Cole returned to the office, and Valerie's boss left her alone. Brett, however, stepped in to man the Candy Shack for Irene Perkins, who had to go to Boston for a funeral after her goddaughter's husband unexpectedly passed away.

Even though Valerie and Brett didn't see each other much during the day, he was always home to help prep dinner at the inn at six, and he always brought candy home for the kids. After spending six years eating the majority of her dinners at her desk, Valerie could really get used to this.

It was beyond nice to have someone to debrief with at the end of the day.

On Thursday night, Valerie noticed that Dylan had a weird rash, and she made an appointment to take him to the pediatrician the next day. On Friday morning, he was slow to wake up, but once she announced that they could go to the trampoline park before the doctor's office, he was all systems go.

Of course, just as the boys were really getting into their jumping, Valerie's phone lit up. Work. Again.

But not her boss, Gary. This time it was her mentor, Gloria, the only female managing director at their firm.

"Hey, Gloria. What's up?" Dylan and Derrick squealed as they jumped on their respective trampolines, their black curls bouncing.

"Can you get back to the city by Monday?" the older woman asked without preamble.

For a split second, Valerie considered what she'd need to do to make that happen. The drive alone was five and a half hours—and that was only if they didn't run into any traffic, stop for lunch or pull over for a potty break. Before they could leave, though, they had to visit the doctor. And then she'd have to pack and find a babysitter who could watch the twins once they got to New York. "Uh, no. Definitely not."

"Cole quit. And the hiring committee wants to make a decision about the VP role ASAP."

"You're kidding me. Gary told me he was sick."

"He was interviewing with a start-up in Boston's tech corridor. Apparently, they hired him as their head of business development. He put in his notice this morning. I just saw him leave."

"Whoa." Valerie couldn't believe it—her lone competitor for this promotion was no longer part of the equation. "Good for him."

"Sure, best wishes and don't let the door hit you on the way out. He doesn't have your number, does he? If he calls you, don't pick up."

Why would Cole call her? He definitely had her number—all the associates on the health care team at work had each other's numbers on speed dial just in case—but he'd never called her before, and she couldn't imagine why he'd do it now. "Okay, no problem."

"If you have his number, block it."

Valerie paused. That was an awfully strange request. "Is there something you're not telling me, Gloria? Did Cole do something?"

"Of course not," her mentor scoffed. "Just a precaution. It's why when people quit, we have security escort them out immediately. But that's not the point. The point is that the committee wants to announce the new VP as soon as possible, and you're not here."

Oh.

Uh-oh.

"Who else are they even looking at? I thought it was just me and Cole."

"It *was* you and Cole. Now they're throwing Mason's name into the mix."

A pit opened up in Valerie's stomach. "Mason's only been at the bank for three years. I've been there for *six*."

"I know it. You know it. They know it. But again. You're. Not. Here."

Valerie started doing mental gymnastics. If she spent the afternoon on the phone with a nanny agency, could she find someone who'd be available to start watching the twins next week? She only had a one-bedroom apartment in New York, so even if they got there on Sunday, where would the boys sleep?

And what about the Cranberry Harvest Festival? It was only eight days away.

She and Brett were pretty much done with the prep work, though, weren't they? Maybe she could just fly back here the day before the festival to oversee things on-site.

"I'd need to find a nanny and nail down a two-bedroom apartment."

"The firm will put you up in an executive suite until you have time to apartment hunt. I'll have my assistant set it up and email you the details later today. Send her a wish list of what you're looking for in a nanny, and she can handle the interviews for you, too."

Valerie blinked. This was happening fast. "Wow, Gloria. I don't know what to say."

"I've got your back, Valerie. You've worked hard for this, and I'll do my best to hold them off for a couple of days. Get here as soon as you can, and let's not let a little bad timing get in your way."

"I appreciate it," Valerie said, then started chewing on her nails. She'd hate to disappoint Gloria. Her mentor was the closest thing to a mother she had.

"Oh, and I talked to Matt McCarthy from the Marisco Seafood Group about your friend the chef, and he's interested. Put together a pitch. Matt's on the east coast right now. He said he'd try to squeeze in a quick trip to meet the guy."

"That's amazing. Thank you."

"Now wrap it up out there and get yourself back to the city."

Valerie hung up. The boys were still on the trampolines, but only Derrick was jumping. Dylan was lying curled up on his side.

"You okay, Dylan?" she called out. "Did you hurt yourself?"

Dylan didn't move.

"Dilly Dally's sleepy," Derrick said.

That was weird. She toed off her shoes and stepped lightly onto the in-ground trampoline. "Dylan? What's going on?"

Her brother whimpered, his face turned away from her. She crouched next to him and put her hand on his face, which was scorching. His cheeks were bright red.

"Did you jump too much? Are you thirsty?"

He whimpered again.

She looked at Derrick. "What happened? Did he fall?"

Derrick shook his head. "He was jumping, den he layed down on da trampoline, den he shaked all over, like dis." He lay down and started jerking his arms and legs.

Valerie's heart lurched. *No. Please, God. No.*

The same thing used to happen to Vanessa.

Seizures.

She scooped Dylan into her arms and slammed her feet back into her shoes. "Come on, Derrick, we're leaving."

"But Valwee—"

"Now!"

Her brother scurried to obey.

When Valerie's name flashed across Brett's screen, he smiled. She'd be pleased to know he'd just finished a phone interview with a reporter from *The Boston Globe* who'd promised to include mention of the Cranberry Harvest Festival in the article he was writing about the fire.

He picked up the call and said, "Your ears must be burning."

"Brett, we're at the ER. I need you to come and get Derrick."

He shot to his feet. "What happened?"

"Dylan has a fever. He's having seizures."

"Have they checked you in? Are they running tests? Have they given him something for the fever?"

"Yes, yes and yes. Just please come get Derrick. I don't have the bandwidth to watch him while I'm trying to communicate with the doctors and nurses."

He put his phone on speaker so he could book a rideshare while they talked. "Don't worry. I'm on my way."

Chapter Twelve

Valerie and the boys were still in a cubicle in the ER when Brett rushed in. Valerie was sitting on a folding chair with Derrick in her lap. Dylan was on the bed, sleeping, and Derrick was watching monster truck videos on her phone.

"Hey," Brett said, filling the space with his broad shoulders and tall frame.

"Mr. Bacon Man!" Derrick beamed at him. "You camed!"

"Of course I did, buddy. You guys are important to me. But how about you watch a few more of your videos while I talk to your sister?"

"Okay!"

Valerie took her hand away from her mouth—she'd been chewing her fingernails again—and got to her feet. She motioned for Brett to follow her to the far side of the curtain separating their cubicle from the hallway.

Once they were out of Derrick's line of sight, Brett immediately wrapped his good arm around her shoulders and pulled her in for a hug. She sank into it, her arms circling his strong back, her face pressed up against his warm, solid chest.

"Hey," he murmured into her hair.

"Hey, yourself," she answered, breathing in his scent: cedarwood and cinnamon, lemon and sage.

Home.

The thought tripped her up briefly, but then, in the furthest of her far-back memories, she could remember playing at her grandfather's feet while he watched *60 Minutes*, eating old-fashioned candies like peppermints and caramel creams that he slipped her when nobody else was looking. He must have worn the same aftershave as Brett.

That's why she found the scent oddly comforting.

He drew back so he could look her in the eye. "You okay?"

"His temperature was 105.2, Brett." Tears welled in the corner of her eye, but she couldn't start crying. Dylan might be sleeping, but Derrick did not need to see her freaking out.

Brett's eyes bugged. "What is it now?"

"They gave him Children's Advil when we got here. Last time they checked, it was 103.9, so they gave him Tylenol, too."

"When are they going to check again?"

"Half an hour, probably."

"Are they going to admit him?"

"They said they don't usually admit for fever, but since he had a seizure, they'll keep him overnight. They're waiting on the test results before they transfer him to Pediatrics."

"What tests?"

"Flu, COVID, RSV." She ticked them off on her fingers. "Plus a blood count and urinalysis to rule out appendicitis and meningitis."

"That sounds thorough."

Her shoulders slumped. "I guess. I told them about Vanessa, and they said they'd look at his blood count and go from there."

"When did he get sick? He was fine yesterday."

She sniffled. "I don't know. He seemed off this morning, but he rallied when we got to the trampoline park."

"And then…?"

She pulled at her necklace, the chain biting into the back of her neck. "And then I turned my back for a few minutes to take a phone call, and when I hung up, he was lying on the trampoline, whimpering." She was such an idiot. Who put a promotion above the health and safety of their own flesh and blood? "I missed him having a seizure because I was too busy talking to someone from work."

"Hey, hey, hey," he said, taking her hand away from her necklace. "Nobody can keep an eye on their kids 24/7. Don't beat yourself up."

"Vanessa used to have seizures. What if…" The words were so awful they got stuck in her throat. "What if he's been having them for a while, and nobody noticed because my dad was so sick?"

"They're running the tests now, Valerie. Let's not get ahead of ourselves." He tucked a strand of her hair behind her ear with his good hand.

"How'd you get here, anyway? Did Laura drive you?"

He shook his head. "She and Hunter are out at a playdate this morning."

"You didn't drive, did you?"

"I got a rideshare."

"Thanks for coming so fast. I wasn't even thinking about the fact that you still can't drive."

"I'm glad you called. I meant what I said to Derrick. You and the boys are important to me. I want to be here for you. All of you. Whatever you need."

Whew. She didn't know what to say to that. His kindness made her feel a little shaky, as though all the panic she'd been keeping inside since she'd scooped Dylan off that trampoline was trying to punch its way out now that Brett was here to contain it.

But he wasn't waiting for a reply. He took out his phone and glanced at the lock screen. "First things first, it's after one o'clock. Have you eaten anything since breakfast?"

She blew out a wobbly breath. "No." This is what stress did to her: her stomach was in knots, her appetite completely gone. She'd force herself to eat now that he'd reminded her, but it would be a chore.

"But you're feeling okay? You're not going to faint?"

"No, I'm good."

"Okay, Derrick and I are going to go to the cafeteria and get you some lunch. If the doctor comes to talk to you while we're there and you need to head up to Pediatrics or go somewhere else for tests, text me and we'll find you."

She nodded. It was a relief to have someone else here to worry about the day-to-day details. Her whole focus right now was on Dylan, and she'd never have remembered to eat.

"Do you need a minute to freshen up before we go?"

She shook her head.

"I'm going to say a quick prayer." She nodded again, and he put his hand on her shoulder. "God, we love you. We trust you. We know that you're holding Dylan in the palm of your hand. Show us how we can best help him while you work your healing power. In Jesus's name. Amen."

"Amen," she echoed.

He squeezed her shoulder. "It's going to be okay."

"I hope so," she whispered, wishing she had his level of assurance.

Grateful he was there, though, to throw some of his confidence her way.

Brett and Derrick bought Valerie a chicken wrap, milk and a cookie and took the tray back to her in the ER.

"Do you want to give me your keys so I can get Derrick's car seat out of your car? Or should I take him back to the cafeteria for lunch and plan out our next steps after that?"

She dug into her purse for her keys, then held them out to him with shaking hands.

Man, he really didn't want to leave her, but he knew she'd feel better once Derrick was safe at the inn. "We'll be right back," he told her, then led Derrick to the parking garage and grabbed the car seat out of Valerie's car.

Once they'd returned her keys, he took Derrick to the café and bought him a plate of chicken nuggets with carrot sticks and sliced grapes. The boy ate his grapes and nuggets with gusto, laughing when Brett built a log cabin with the carrot sticks he didn't want to eat.

After that, they took a rideshare back to the inn, where Laura met them on the front lawn with a confused look on her face.

She shifted Hunter from one shoulder to the other as Brett set Derrick's car seat down on the grass and then dropped into one of the lawn chairs out front. "What's going on?"

"My brubber's sick. He's in da hospital," Derrick said, climbing into Brett's lap. "Mr. Bacon Man comed to get me."

Laura's eyes lit with worry. "What happened?"

Brett bounced Derrick on his knee. "High fever."

"How high?"

"Scary high. A hundred and five."

Laura's face fell. "Is he okay?"

"They don't know. They're running tests."

"Who's there with her?"

"No one."

"Brett!" Her eyes bugged. "You left her there alone?"

Sometimes being here at the Sea Glass Inn with Laura—Chloe's best friend—felt like having a second sister. And honestly? One sister was plenty for him. "You think I *wanted* to leave her there by herself?"

She pressed her lips together, then shook her head. "I know you didn't. Sorry. I just—the highest fever Emma's ever had was 102. I can't imagine what Valerie's going through right now. And after everything else that's happened, you'd think she could catch a break." She stared at the grass for a second, then added, "But anyway, I'm here now. So get yourself in gear and get back there."

"Will you be okay here with Hunter *and* Derrick? What time does Emma get home from school?"

Derrick climbed off Brett's lap so he could get a better look at Hunter, who was cooing, smiling and gnawing on his fist. "School's out in an hour, but we'll be good. Emma can help entertain Derrick, and Jonathan'll be home by five thirty."

Satisfied that she wouldn't be overwhelmed, Brett texted for yet *another* rideshare. Boy, would he ever be glad once his fingers were healed.

Back at the hospital, he discovered that Dylan had been moved to the pediatric unit, where he'd been placed on an IV. From the doorway, Brett could see Valerie sitting in a chair next to the bed, stroking her brother's hair while he slept.

Brett tapped on the door.

She looked up. Gave him a wobbly smile. "You're back."

"How's he holding up?"

She grimaced. "He was not a happy camper when they put in the IV. Screamed and thrashed so much they needed a couple of orderlies to hold him down. And I had to stand there and watch it happen. It was brutal."

"I'm sorry, sweetheart." He pulled up another chair and sat beside her. "What's in the IV?"

"Fluid and antibiotics. They think he has a urinary tract infection. They're going to keep him overnight to make sure the fever breaks."

"Poor little guy. Are they letting you sleep over?"

She nodded. "Who's watching Derrick?"

"Laura. And Jonathan'll be home by dinnertime."

"He's not used to sleeping by himself. He and Dylan have shared a room since the day they were born."

"I can move up to the empty room beside him, make sure he's not scared during the night."

She gave her broken heart pendant a gentle tug. "Would you? That'd help me sleep better."

"No problem."

She touched his arm, a quick, light brush of her fingers, like a butterfly collecting nectar from a flower. "I really appreciate you being here for us today. It means a lot."

"I'm happy to be here for you. Whenever and whatever you need."

Just say the word and I'll always be here for you. For better, for worse, for richer, for poorer—

Whoa. Wait. Did he mean that?

Was he in love with Valerie?

Just being in the same room with her made him happy, like he was skimming the surface of the ocean at dawn—cool and deep, dark and beautiful. When he was with her, he felt settled. Centered. Essential in some primitive, hard-to-articulate way.

In that moment, Brett knew that he wanted to be the one to take care of her—now and always.

The one who loved her, and the one she loved.

She twisted her hands in her lap. "I don't know how I'm going to cope once I get back to New York. What if one of them gets sick again?"

The mention of New York was like the slap of cold water on his face. "Hate to break it to you, bright eyes, but they're definitely going to get sick again. Hopefully not this sick, but it'll happen. Kids get sick. It's what they do."

"My coworker quit."

"What coworker? The one who was sick last week?"

"Turns out he wasn't sick at all. He was interviewing for a new job. And he got it. So he quit."

That cold splash of water turned into a block of ice. "Congratulations. That means the promotion's yours, right?"

She frowned. "Not exactly. My mentor says they'll give it to me if I can get back to the office ASAP."

"ASAP as in…right after the Cranberry Harvest Festival?"

"She wants me there by Monday."

He flicked a glance at Dylan, who was still sleeping. "What if he's not out of the hospital by then?"

"They said he'd probably only need a short course of the IV antibiotics, and then they can switch him on to a liquid. If the fever breaks, he should be out by tomorrow."

"And then you're going to make him drive to New York the next day?"

She bit her lip. "I don't know what else to do. I need this promotion. After a certain amount of time, if you don't make VP, they force you out."

"They'd *fire* you? For taking care of your brother when you're on a federally protected leave of absence?"

She lifted her shoulder. "They wouldn't fire me right away. And my brothers wouldn't be the official reason. But a few months from now? Definitely. They won't want to keep paying me for work a first- or second-year associate could do."

"And you like working in that environment?"

"I'm good at it, Brett. And I need the money, especially now that the twins are my responsibility."

"What about the Cranberry Harvest Festival?"

"I'll fly back for the weekend. Or not. At this point, there's not much left to do for the auction. I'm sure you can handle it without me."

She must be really scared of losing the promotion if she was considering leaving without fulfilling her promise to her dad.

"Isn't there some other job you could do? Something less stressful?" *Something closer to Cape Cod?*

She gave him a hard stare. "This is what I've had to deal with my whole career. Men thinking I can't handle it. That I'm a delicate flower."

He paused, choosing his words carefully. "It's not that I don't think you can do it. It's that I want you to be happy. And the thought of you going back to a stressful job in a hectic city when you have the boys to worry about, too—it bothers me."

She opened her mouth, then closed it. Opened it, then closed it again. Finally, she conceded, "It's hard to stay mad at you when you say things like that."

Hope rushed through him. "I have feelings for you, Valerie. Real feelings. I wish you didn't have to leave."

"I—" She paled, her freckles standing out from her porcelain skin in stark relief. Dylan's IV beeped and she startled, hopping to her feet to examine the machine.

Had he spoken too soon?

Should he have waited until Dylan was in the clear?

He tried to walk it back a little. "If you have feelings for me, too, we could date long-distance. See how it goes. See if one of us might be willing to relocate at some point down the line."

She frowned and studied the IV harder.

This wasn't promising. Brett started to sweat. Literally. Little droplets of perspiration rolled down his back.

"How would that work, exactly? You know I work eighty hours a week, minimum. And when I'm not working, I'm going to want to be with the twins."

"I like the twins. I'd want to spend time with them, too."

"Would you visit me? You told me you don't even like Providence, and New York's a hundred times more crowded than Providence. There's nine million people living there, and we're all squished together like candies in a little kid's fist."

He didn't love the picture she was painting, but he pressed on. "Yeah, I'd visit you in New York."

"How would you get there? If you hate the traffic in Boston, you'll *really* hate the traffic in New York."

The thought of sitting in traffic with nine million other people made him sweat even more. "I don't know, Valerie. I haven't thought it all through yet. Maybe I'd take the bus."

"Aren't weekends the busiest days for a restaurant? Because

they're the lightest days at an investment bank. Once you get Half Shell back up and running, aren't you going to need to be here on the weekends?"

Why was she so determined to poke holes in his plans to see her? "Most of the time, yes."

"And I can't really take time off to visit you here."

"Ever?"

"I basically never have a full weekend off. And when I do, it's not like they give me advance notice."

Why was he surprised? He knew what her job was like. She'd told him plenty of times. "If I can't make it to New York to see you, we can video chat."

"For how long? A year? Two years? And when we get tired of long distance, who's going to move?"

"I don't know."

She squared her shoulders. "I know you don't think it's good for me, but I'm not quitting my job."

"I'm not asking you to quit your job."

She blinked. "Aren't you?"

They stared at each other. He'd backed them into a corner, and she was calling him on it. He had no one to blame but himself.

Still, though, it felt like his chest was caving in, like she'd cracked it open, reached inside and thrown his heart into a trash compactor.

At least you found out now that you're not worth it to her. At least she didn't publicly humiliate you like Tracy.

But maybe he'd gotten it wrong. Maybe, if she could see herself falling for him, they could find a compromise that would work.

"Do you have feelings for me?" he asked, his voice like gravel. "Romantic feelings?"

Her eyes widened, and she sat up straighter, shifting uncomfortably in her chair. "It's only been a few weeks, Brett. We haven't even kissed."

If she had any idea of how many times he'd had to stop himself from thinking about kissing her... He didn't want to scare her, though, so he simply leaned forward, gave her a mild look and said, "There's an easy solution to that problem."

He wasn't expecting her to take the bait, and she didn't. Instead, her gaze darted to the side. She twisted her hands in her lap. "I'm just trying to be realistic."

"Do you want to keep seeing me?" he pressed. "Should we try to make this work?"

She twisted a strand of hair around her finger, tight enough that her fingertip went red. "I can't deal with this right now."

"You're leaving. I need to know."

"Brett," she said softly, "you've known I was leaving the whole time."

His stomach dropped. It was true. From the very beginning, he'd known she would leave, but he'd let himself fall for her anyway. And he couldn't even claim he'd been blindsided, like he had been with Tracy. Nope, this time it was his own wishful thinking that was to blame.

He was an idiot. Again. In a whole different way.

Valerie wrung her hands. "I'm sorry, but I don't think us getting involved is a good idea. I hope we can still be friends."

He glanced at Dylan, asleep and hooked up to the IV. Swallowing the hurt, he said, "Of course we can still be friends."

"Thank you." Her voice wobbled—with disappointment? With relief? He couldn't tell, and it didn't matter. She didn't want to pursue a relationship with him. That was all he needed to know.

"Of course," he said again, getting to his feet so he could leave. "I hope his fever breaks overnight."

"Me, too." She was squeezing her necklace, holding tight

to that pendant of the broken heart. "For what it's worth, if I lived here, things would be different. I think you're great."

He nodded. It was something, he supposed, but without her, it wasn't worth much.

Chapter Thirteen

Dylan's fever did not break overnight. In fact, it got worse and stayed worse all weekend. When they checked his temperature on Monday morning, it was 105.7.

Every time they gave him medication, it came down a little, but as it wore off, his temperature shot back up. There was no way Valerie could even think about heading back to New York.

She'd have to call Gloria and tell her that this week was looking less and less likely by the second, but she'd rather hold off until Dylan was out of the woods and she had a firm plan for when she'd arrive.

In the meantime, Gloria's assistant had sent her the information about the apartment the firm had booked for her. She'd also requested that Valerie send her a wish list of characteristics she was looking for in a nanny.

But Valerie couldn't concentrate enough to put together a list. When she wasn't worrying about Dylan, she was fretting about Brett.

Brett, her teenage nemesis.

Brett, who'd pulled Dylan out of the fire.

Brett, who had feelings for her but who wanted her to quit her job.

Why had he sprung that on her while Dylan was in the hospital? Didn't he realize she had a zillion other things on her mind?

And she couldn't give up her job. It was the one thing she knew, beyond a shadow of a doubt, that she was good at.

There weren't many things in life that came with a rule book, but her job was one of them. And Valerie liked rules. She liked certainty. There were no guarantees if she let herself explore her feelings for Brett.

It wasn't as though he'd declared his undying love for her, either. He'd said he'd date her long-distance until "one of them" relocated. He'd said they could "see how it goes."

But he'd also said he had feelings for her. And he'd looked crushed when she'd said dating him wasn't a good idea.

Argh! She was so confused.

"Knock, knock."

Valerie looked up. Laura was standing in the doorway, a muffin in one hand and an overnight bag in the other, a newspaper tucked under her arm. "Good morning, sweetie. Thought you could use a change of clothes."

For once, Laura looked fresh and well rested. Meanwhile, Valerie was still in her rumpled clothing from yesterday, and she hadn't yet brushed her teeth or her hair.

Fortunately, the pediatric ward wasn't crowded right now, and she'd been able to sleep in the second bed in Dylan's room. If he'd had a roommate, she would've been relegated to the armchair in the corner. Although the beeping and squeaking and nighttime temperature checks had certainly disrupted her sleep, she had no doubt that if she'd been forced to crash in the chair, the quality of her rest would have been a thousand times worse.

"You're a lifesaver."

Laura smiled and set the bag down by the door, then handed Valerie the muffin. "Brought you breakfast, too."

Valerie took a bite. It was a cranberry-apple muffin. "Where's Hunter?"

"With Jonathan. He took the day off so he could help Brett with Derrick."

Valerie put down the muffin and wrung her hands. "How'd he do last night?" Apparently, Friday and Saturday night had both been rough.

"He was fine, honey. Don't worry. Brett took him and Emma out for ice cream after dinner. Then he read him a ton of stories to get him ready for bed. But how's Dylan?"

Valerie teared up. "Not great. His fever was higher this morning."

Laura's eyes bugged. "Higher than 105? Are they sure it's a urinary tract infection?"

"Now they're saying it's a UTI plus a virus."

"What virus?"

"RSV."

Laura sucked in a breath. "Oof, that's a bad one. Emma had that once. Picked it up at day care. They were worried it would turn into pneumonia."

"They said if the fever doesn't break by Wednesday, they're going to bring in a specialist."

Laura shot Dylan a sad look. "Poor baby. How'd he sleep?"

"Fitfully. But at least he's sleeping now."

"I don't think Brett slept well, either. He was in the kitchen at five this morning when I got up to feed Hunter, making those muffins."

Valerie picked at her muffin again. She didn't have much of an appetite, but it was tasty and she knew she should eat. "No wonder they're so good."

"He's talented, right? Oh, and here." She held out the newspaper. "He wanted me to give you this."

Valerie took the paper. "*The Boston Globe*? Why?"

"He said you should look on page three."

She opened it up, scanned page three and gave a small gasp when she saw the headline of the story on the left side of the page: "Cape Cod Man Saves Toddler Twins from Fiery Death: 'My Parents Taught Me to Put Service Before Myself.'"

She shot Laura a quick glance. "Have you read this already?"

Her friend shook her head.

"I asked him if he'd do some interviews about the fire so we could get a little publicity for the Cranberry Harvest Festival, but he seemed dead set against it. I can't believe he actually did it. And got onto page three of *The Boston Globe*."

Laura leaned in so they could read the article together, which highlighted exactly how courageous Brett had been during the fire. But it didn't stop there. The final paragraphs read:

> In the days since Richardson risked his life to save Williams and the twins, he has devoted much of his time to working with her on Wychmere Bay's upcoming fundraiser, the Cranberry Harvest Festival, which will take place on Saturday, October 5 from 9:00 a.m. to 9:00 p.m. at Tidewater Park.

"We're raising money for a charity that educates teens about the dangers of drunk and distracted driving," he said.

Attractions include carnival games, live music, food trucks, a craft fair and fireworks. Richardson, a chef, is participating in the town's inaugural bachelor auction.

"If you'd like to win a date with me, come to the event and bid," he said. "I'll cook you an unforgettable dinner, and it's for a good cause."

When she finished reading, Laura gave a low whistle. "Watch out, friend. Women are going to be crawling out of the woodwork to come to the Cranberry Harvest Festival now."

Valerie put a hand over her heart, feeling shell-shocked. She'd hoped that Brett would be able to throw in a line or two about the auction if he decided to speak with the press, but she truly hadn't been sure he'd speak with any reporters at all.

This article went above and beyond anything she'd imagined, and she should be ecstatic right now. But the idea of women crawling out of the woodwork to bid on a date with Brett felt like sandpaper on a scab.

God, help me to focus on the facts rather than my feelings. This article was a good thing—no, a *great* thing for the Cranberry Harvest Festival. She needed to hold fast to that and ignore the jumbled-up mess of emotions she had about Brett.

"I can't believe he gave them an interview."

"Well, you asked him to, right? So, of course he did."

Valerie cocked her head to the side. "What do you mean?"

"Everybody can see how he feels about you, sweetie. He can't keep his eyes off you."

Valerie's face heated. "That's not true. You forget that I knew him when he was dating Tracy. He doesn't look at me like that."

Laura snorted. "What planet are you living on? If anything, he looks at you even more schmoopy-eyed than he looked at her."

"Schmoopy-eyed?" Valerie raised an eyebrow.

Laura waved her hand. "You know what I mean. He's head over heels for you, Valerie. You really can't see it?"

"Well, he said he has feelings for me…"

"What! When?"

"On Friday. After he dropped Derrick off with you at the inn."

"And…?" Laura leaned forward in her seat.

"And it's too fast. It's only been three weeks since the fire."

Laura's brow creased. "So? It's not like Brett's a random stranger. You knew him when you were kids. I've known him for more than ten years. He's Jonathan's best friend."

Valerie picked at a loose thread on her shirt. "How come you two never dated?"

"Seriously?" Laura scoffed. "I never had romantic feelings

for Brett. He's like the older brother I never had." She paused for a moment, then asked, "Is that the problem for you? Is it more of a platonic friendship thing on your end?"

Once again, Valerie's cheeks blazed. "It's not a platonic friendship thing."

There was a long beat of silence, and Valerie could feel her friend's eyes on her, but she felt too self-conscious to lift her gaze.

Finally, gently, Laura said, "I know that you're a cautious person, Valerie, and that you like to weigh and measure things before you act. But I think you need to take a chance on this. Brett's the real deal. And if he was willing to risk his life to get you and the boys out of that fire before he even knew it was you, just think about the lengths he'd go to for all of you now."

Valerie shook her head. "I can't. I'm leaving."

"But not for a few more weeks, right? I bet you guys could figure things out before you have to go."

"I'm leaving as soon as Dylan gets out of the hospital."

Laura gasped. "Why?"

"If I don't go, I'm going to lose my promotion." And if she lost the promotion, eventually she'd lose her job.

Laura frowned. "That's terrible. And terrible timing." She nodded at Dylan, who sighed and shifted in his sleep.

Valerie knew it.

But it didn't change a thing.

The last place Brett wanted to be on Wednesday evening was the hospital. But Derrick missed Dylan, and Brett wasn't a big enough jerk that he'd keep a little kid away from his brother just to avoid seeing the woman who'd snapped his heart in half.

He'd had five days to get over himself, and he'd told her they could be friends, so that's what he'd do. Be a friend. A hands-off, arm's-length, chat-for-a-quick-minute-when-we-run-into-each-other kind of friend.

They wouldn't stay long anyway, since Valerie had told Brett—in a short text, which was how they were communicating about the boys these days—that Derrick would have to mask up and talk to Dylan while staying at least six feet away. Regardless, Derrick was excited to see his twin.

And here they were now, at the door to Dylan's room.

"Dilly Dally!" Derrick yelled when he saw his brother in the bed. Dylan was propped up, sucking his thumb and watching a monster truck video on Valerie's laptop, but Valerie was nowhere to be found.

When he heard his brother's voice, Dylan's head whipped to the door. "D-Wex!" he exclaimed happily, although his face was pale and his eyes looked gigantic. He must have lost a bunch of weight over the last few days.

"Mr. Bacon Man bringed me to see you!"

"Hey, buddy," Brett said.

"And he maked you a bacon sandwich!" So far, despite his obvious excitement, Derrick was staying in the doorway to the room, just as he and Brett had discussed.

"I lub bacon." Dylan glanced at the sandwiches Brett was holding.

Brett pulled the wheeled tray table over to the side of Dylan's bed and set the sandwiches down. Dylan was allowed to eat, wasn't he? He imagined he was, but he wanted to know for sure before he fed him. "Where's Valerie?"

"She was sad, so she went in da bathroom."

Uh-oh. Brett didn't like the sound of that. "Let me go talk to her real quick, then you can have your sandwich." He shot Derrick a stern glance. "You stay there, mister."

Derrick gave him a jazzed-up wiggle. "I know. 'Cause of da germs."

The boys started talking to each other about monster trucks, and Brett tapped on the restroom door. "Valerie? You okay?"

She opened the door. Her eyes were red, and she'd clearly just splashed water on her face.

"What's wrong?"

She glanced between the twins, and her face crumpled.

Oh, boy. This wasn't good. Brett took her arm and pulled her into the corridor, then walked a few steps away from where Derrick was dancing around just inside the door.

"What's going on?"

"We…" Her chin wobbled. Tears sprang to her eyes. "We got a diagnosis this afternoon."

Lord, please don't let it be cancer. Let it be something that has a cure.

"And…?"

She twisted her pendant around on its chain. "And they think it's something called Kawasaki disease. He doesn't have all the classic symptoms, but because the fever's lasted so long, it points to inflammation of the blood vessels. It could damage his heart."

Brett winced. "Is it treatable?"

She nodded. "They're going to do an infusion of IV immunoglobulin. They're getting it ready right now."

"That's good, right?"

"It's supposed to reduce the inflammation, but there could still be heart damage."

"How will they know?"

"They're going to do the immunoglobulin, then he'll have to see a cardiologist for an echo and an EKG."

"So, treatment first, then more tests?"

She bobbed her head.

"Will the immunoglobulin break the fever?"

She pulled at her pendant. "That's the hope."

"Okay, this is good." The pep talk was as much for him as it was for her. "He's going to get the treatment he needs."

Her chin wavered again. "They said it can cause aneurysms. Blood clots. Those kids you hear about who drop dead on the football field with no warning? It's almost always from something like this."

"Hey," Brett said, putting his good hand on her shoulder. "Don't jump ahead of yourself. One step at a time."

She leaned her forehead against his chest. "Right. You're right."

He put his hand all the way around her back, holding her close. "Focus on what he needs right now. Future tripping won't help anything."

"Thank you for coming," she said, tipping her head up and creating some space between them. "I wanted to let you know, but I wasn't sure…"

He could guess what she'd been about to say: she wasn't sure he'd want to hear from her after she'd rejected him. "You can call me anytime—especially when it comes to the boys. Forget about what happened last Friday. We're friends, and we always will be."

He meant it, too. He could live with friendship. As long as Dylan was okay and Valerie and the boys stayed in his life in one way or another, he'd take it.

"I read the article in the *Globe*," she said. "Nice job."

Talking to the reporter hadn't been so bad once he'd resigned himself to doing it for the good of the Cranberry Harvest Festival. And he had to admit that the article had turned out well. It might not be enough to sway the local opinion of him, but hopefully it would bring a couple of bidders down from Boston. "Think it'll bring in some more money?"

"I know it will."

"Then it was worth it."

A nurse approached, carrying a couple of IV bags. She looked at Valerie and held the bags up higher. "We're going to get started."

"How long does it take?" Brett asked.

"About three hours," the nurse said, "but he really won't be able to tell the difference between this and the other fluids he's been on."

"Can he eat first?" Brett asked the nurse, then glanced at Valerie. "I brought him a bacon sandwich."

Valerie smiled. "Of course you did."

"He can eat," the nurse confirmed.

Brett gave Valerie a little nod. "I brought you a sandwich, too."

They chatted with both the boys for a few minutes until Steve showed up to drive him and Derrick back to the inn. Brett sent the boy home with Steve, telling his brother-in-law he'd get a rideshare later, once Dylan's treatment was complete.

Valerie gave his arm a grateful squeeze.

She might not love him, but tonight, she needed him. And for a guy who'd spent the better part of the last three months feeling useless, knowing he was needed was the next best thing.

Chapter Fourteen

On Thursday morning, Valerie had to call Gloria and break the bad news. Dylan's fever still hadn't broken. There was no way she'd make it back to the office this week.

"Can't you get somebody to watch him?" her mentor asked, annoyance threaded through each syllable she spoke. "Just for a day or two?"

"Who?" Valerie said. "I came back here because there's literally no one else to take care of them."

"Can't the nurses watch him? He's sick—won't he just be in bed all day? You can fly out of Hyannis in two hours and be back by Saturday afternoon. He'll hardly miss you."

Valerie rubbed her eyes. She hadn't slept well all week. She'd hoped that the immunoglobulin would kick right in, but the attending doctor had told her that sometimes kids with Kawasaki disease needed a second dose. They were going to wait a full twenty-four hours from the start of the last dose, and then make the call.

"No, Gloria." Her voice was weary. "I'm not doing that."

"Let my assistant make a couple of calls. I'm sure she can find you a babysitter who'd come and sit with him while you're away."

Although it was true that Dylan mostly slept or watched cartoon DVDs, there was no way Valerie was leaving him with a stranger while he was sick. "No."

There was a beat of silence. Then, in a hard voice, Gloria said, "I don't think you understand the situation. They'll give this promotion to Mason, and you'll be out of the running. For good."

"I understand."

"Do you?" Her mentor's voice got even colder. "I've had your back from Day One, Valerie. I stuck my neck out for you time and time again, and this is how you repay me? By spitting in my face?"

Valerie shifted uncomfortably in her seat. "That's not my intention at all, but my brother's not even three years old. I'm not leaving him alone in the hospital to go back to work, even if it's only for one afternoon."

"Do you have any idea how many of my kids' events I had to miss? Parent-teacher conferences, sports games, piano recitals, awards ceremonies—all of it. One of them got appendicitis once when I was closing a deal in Dubai, and he had to drive *himself* to the hospital."

Valerie sat speechless for a second. Gloria almost sounded proud of that fact.

Since the day they'd met back when Valerie was in college, Valerie had thought of Gloria as a kind of surrogate mother—one who had stepped up after Valerie's own mother had stepped away.

Gloria might be a great banker, but she wasn't Valerie's mother. And from the sounds of it, she hadn't been much of a mother to own kids, either.

"But you know what?" her mentor continued. "They don't have any student debt. They don't have to worry about supporting me when I'm old and gray. I paid for their weddings. I paid for their honeymoons. And I will pay for *their* children's college educations someday. So, don't do anything stupid. Don't throw your career away because of a few sniffles. Your brother will be fine, and as soon as he is, you'll be kicking yourself for giving up this promotion."

Sniffles, huh? Valerie had told Gloria about the severity of her brother's condition, but it clearly wasn't something the older woman wanted to hear.

Work was Number One in her mentor's life, and she expected it to be Number One in Valerie's life, too.

But it wasn't. Not anymore.

"Maybe," Valerie said, but even as the words left her mouth she felt a thousand times lighter. Financial security was nice. A successful career was nice, too. But they weren't everything. Not even close. "But I'm doing it anyway. I quit."

"Excuse me?"

"I don't want to miss a single second with the boys, Gloria. I'm sorry. I know you've done a lot for me, but I quit."

"You and Cole deserve each other."

"What?" Why would Gloria say something like that?

"You leave for Cape Cod and then he gets an offer from a start-up in Boston? And now you won't come back? It's too convenient. You're seeing each other, aren't you? You planned it this way."

"No," Valerie protested. Although now that Gloria had mentioned it, she wondered which company had lured her coworker away from the bank.

"Whatever. We're done here. I thought you had what it takes to make it in this business, but you don't. Don't ask for a reference. You won't get one from me."

With that, she hung up.

Valerie stared at her phone for a few seconds, waiting for a wave of regret to hit her. It didn't.

Dylan pressed Pause on his cartoon. "Are you leabing, Valwee?"

She reached over and pushed a curl off his face. "No, honey. I'm not leaving."

Dylan turned his attention back to the TV. Valerie wanted to call Brett—he'd been such a big help to her last night, even after she'd told him they couldn't date. But she needed to sort herself out before she talked to him, figure out her next steps now that she'd quit the only job she'd ever had.

Was she going to stay here?

And if she did, would Brett be happy about it? Or would he think it was too little, too late?

So, instead of calling him, she hunted through her address book for Cole's contact details. Ah, there he was.

She shot off a quick text. Heard you got a new job.

She was surprised when he replied almost immediately. Got time 2 talk?

Sure.

Her phone vibrated with his call. "Hey, Cole."

"What's up, Williams? You still on Cape Cod?"

"Yeah. Just quit the firm."

"Seriously? Dude, good timing. This start-up in Boston just hired me to lead their biz dev team, and they're looking for a finance director to work with their CFO. I was thinking of you, but then I was like, *nah*. That girl's getting promoted. No point."

"What's the company?"

"Halprin Technologies. They've developed blood-based early detection tests for, like, fifteen different kinds of cancer and counting."

"Sounds interesting." And it did. A job that would combine her knack for numbers with her passion for medicine? It really, really did.

"It's gonna blow up, Williams, I'm telling you. Insight Capital Partners just gave us a round of Series A funding. You've heard of them, right?"

Of course Valerie had heard of Insight Capital Partners. It was one of the premier venture capital firms in the country, and its primary focus was the health care space.

"The founders are building out the team, looking for people who have a heart for curing cancer. I thought that 'cause of your dad, you might be a good fit."

When she'd told Cole about her father's diagnosis, what she most remembered was him gloating about how he was sure to get the promotion now that she had to go on leave. "I'm surprised, Cole. We were so competitive at work."

"That's *why* I thought of you. You'd put your all into it, and that's what this company needs. Pay's nothing to write home about, but you'd get stock options. And we're gonna crush cancer, Williams. Wipe that bad boy out."

Cole was an overgrown frat boy for sure, but he worked hard, and he seemed excited about his new job. "Would I need to move to Boston?"

"Well, you won't wanna stay in New York, but you inherited a house on Cape Cod, right?" She made a noise of assent. She *had* inherited a house on Cape Cod, even if it was no longer standing. "If they like you and you can make it to the office one or two days a week, they'd probably let you work remote the rest of the time. They're pretty flexible."

"What are the hours like? Better than the bank?"

Cole laughed. "What's *not* better than the bank?"

Valerie laughed, too. "True." Laughing with him was weird, though. She was so used to being his adversary. "You're not messing with me, are you? This is a real opportunity?"

"Yeah, it's real. Let me talk to the team, but bringing you on board will make me look like a rock star. Can I give your info to HR?"

"Go ahead."

"How are those kids, anyway? Your brothers?"

She looked at Dylan, lying on the bed, the IV in his arm. "They're hanging in there."

"You hang in there, too."

* * *

On Friday night, Brett and Jonathan went to Franco's to pick up a couple of pizzas for dinner. When they walked into the pizzeria, Franco started up a slow clap, and then everyone in the restaurant joined in—a few of them offering catcalls and wolf whistles.

Franco grinned. "There he is, Wychmere Bay's most eligible bachelor!"

"Yeah, yeah," Brett said, waving away their nonsense. If Valerie had thought a positive story in the paper would change this town's opinion of him, she'd been wrong. "It's for charity, people. But go ahead, laugh it up."

"When are you reopening the restaurant?" Sarah Jenkins, the owner of a B and B on Main Street, called out.

"Don't know, Sarah," he answered as Franco pulled their chicken ranch pizza out of the oven and slid it into a box.

"I'm dying for some more of your branzino," she said, referring to one of his fish entrées, which he dressed with olives, capers, roasted tomato and saffron sauce.

"Come to the Cranberry Harvest Festival," he said, winking. Might as well lean into this thing while it would still make a difference. After Saturday, the ribbing would just be ribbing; tonight it still had the power to raise money for charity. "I'll make it for you if you win the date."

"Ooh-ee!" someone yelped, while Sarah smiled and said, "I just might."

"Ha," Jonathan said, slapping him on the back. "They love you, man. The auction's gonna be a madhouse."

"If it's not, you'll let Laura bid on me, right? I gave Chloe a hundred bucks so I won't be completely embarrassed."

Jonathan chuckled and paid for the pizza. "You're not going to be embarrassed. I guarantee it. All anyone can talk about is that article of yours in the *Globe*."

Outside, the setting sun had turned the sky purple, and

Brett relished the feeling of the fresh autumn air on his face. "Like I said, let them laugh it up. I will happily fall on my sword for charity."

Jonathan shot him a puzzled look. "What are you talking about?"

"I was the class clown in school. I know how this works."

"How *what* works?" His friend looked genuinely baffled.

"They can laugh all they want. But maybe some Boston socialite will turn up with a fat checkbook, and the joke will be on them."

Jonathan stopped walking, forcing Brett to stop, too. "I don't know why you think anyone's joking. Everyone's excited for tomorrow. They're rooting for you to bring in some big bids."

"From your lips to God's ears," Brett said, but he wasn't convinced. Rudy's article about the fire at Half Shell had highlighted his "sheer stupidity," and that's how Brett felt right now: stupid.

Not just about the auction, either, but about Valerie, too. He'd thought she'd needed him the other night, that she'd appreciated his support while Dylan got the immunoglobulin treatment, but he hadn't heard one word from her since.

Everything he knew about how Dylan had been doing the past two days had come through Laura. Valerie didn't even care enough about him or their friendship to keep him in the loop.

They got back to the inn and Jonathan called out, "Honey, I'm home!" as they went inside.

Laura was right there in the parlor, sitting with a middle-aged man Brett had never met. "Hey, babe," she said, smirking. "We're home, too."

Color rising, Jonathan set the pizza down on a coffee table and stuck out his hand. "Jonathan Masters."

The man smiled and shook his hand. "Matt McCarthy, Marisco Seafood Group." Then he turned to Brett. "And you must be Brett Richardson, hero extraordinaire."

Brett had heard of the Marisco Seafood Group, of course. Practically everyone in the restaurant industry had. It was a multi-brand dining corporation that owned and operated more than six hundred restaurants across the country, including some very high-end chains.

Brett shook the man's hand, although he had no idea what he was doing here.

"Gloria Parker mentioned you to me a few days ago. I was just going to schedule a video call, but after I read the article in the *Globe* about your actions during that house fire, I thought I should come down here and meet you for myself."

Brett scratched his cheek. "I don't know a Gloria Parker."

"From S.J. Morgan Investments? She said one of her mentees knew you personally. That you had a successful seafood restaurant you were looking to get back up off the ground."

"S.J. Morgan is Valerie's bank," Laura said softly.

Of course it was. Of course.

But Brett had told her he wasn't looking for investors. And he certainly wasn't looking to let a huge dining corporation peel away everything that had made Half Shell unique.

Why had she gone ahead and contacted this guy, anyway? Did she think he was incapable? That he still needed her to be his after-school tutor? That he wouldn't be able to accomplish his goals without her help?

"I'm not interested," he told Matt, his voice flat.

"Hey, now," the man said. "You haven't even heard me out."

"Don't need to. Half Shell was my parents' restaurant. I'm not looking to sell a stake to Marisco or anyone else."

"From what I understand, without us, you won't have a restaurant to reopen, be it your parents' or your own."

Brett frowned. What had Valerie told this guy about him? Clearly, she didn't believe in him at all.

No wonder she wasn't interested in dating you. She has no confidence in you whatsoever.

As he'd feared, to her and everyone else in this town, he was just a big joke.

Chapter Fifteen

Dylan's second round of IV immunoglobulin on Thursday night had gone well, and by Saturday morning, the day of the Cranberry Harvest Festival, he was fever-free.

Thank you, God. Please let his heart be okay.

Valerie hadn't seen or spoken with Brett since Wednesday night. She'd been too nervous to tell him about quitting her job over the phone, but she'd been thinking about him nonstop.

The bachelor auction was scheduled for 8:00 p.m. tonight, and she was hoping Dylan would be discharged by then. She wanted to be there to support Brett, but even more than that, she wanted to be the one who put in the winning bid.

She wanted to tell him, today, that she'd quit her job and was leaving New York. That she had real feelings for him, too—he'd quickly become her best friend and her biggest supporter. That he was her dream date, no matter where they went or what they did.

At four o'clock, the doctor came in and let Valerie know that she could take Dylan home. He was supposed to take it easy and take baby aspirin daily to ensure that he didn't develop any blood clots before his follow-up appointment with the pediatric cardiologist in six weeks.

They drove down Main Street on their way back to the Sea Glass Inn, passing Tidewater Park, where the Cranberry Harvest Festival was taking place. Valerie's eyes almost popped out of her head at the sight of the overflowing parking lot and all the people milling around.

At the inn, Laura was playing with Hunter on a play mat in the parlor. She hopped to her feet when Valerie and Dylan walked in. "Dylan! We're so glad to see you, honey. Are you feeling better?"

Dylan nodded, sucking his thumb. "Where's D-Wex?"

Laura shot Valerie a *yikes* look. "Mr. Jonathan took him to the Cranberry Harvest Festival with Emma. I can text him and tell them to come back home."

"I wanna squish da cranberries with my brubber," the boy said. Valerie and Brett had both talked about how much fun the twins would have at the mock cranberry bog at the festival.

Valerie chewed her lip. Dylan had been bouncing off the walls of his hospital room earlier—he was clearly feeling much better. "Maybe we'll walk up there and meet them? Just for a little bit."

Laura nodded. "I'll tell Jonathan to keep his eyes peeled for you."

"Is Brett there, too?"

Laura got a hesitant look on her face. "Uh, he's there, but…"

Valerie cocked her head to the side. "But what?"

"Um, someone from the Marisco Seafood Group stopped by last night. He said your bank sent him? Brett wasn't too happy about it."

Oh, my. The pitch Gloria had told her to prepare right before Dylan went into the hospital—she'd forgotten all about it, and she'd never discussed the opportunity with Brett.

Valerie grabbed hold of her necklace. "What did…what did he say?"

"Not much. He told the guy he wasn't interested, and he didn't really want to talk about it afterward, but it seemed like he was in a weird mood. Jonathan said he made a couple of odd comments earlier, too, when people brought up the bachelor auction when they were picking up pizza at Franco's."

"Odd how?"

Laura hitched a shoulder. "Odd like he thought people were laughing at him. And yes, it'll be kind of funny to see him up there getting bid on, but not in a bad way. Everyone knows he's going to bring in a ton of money for charity."

Remembering how hard she'd had to push Brett to participate in the auction and give an interview to the press, Valerie started to feel sick. Brett had straight-up told her that he felt stupid sometimes—especially since the fire at Half Shell. Had the surprise visit from the Marisco Seafood Group and all of her machinations on behalf of the Cranberry Harvest Festival made that worse?

She needed to find him and set the record straight.

She didn't think he was stupid. He was the best man she knew.

Outside, Dylan was excited to see the squirrels climbing the trees and the birds swooping through the sky. Valerie was just glad to see him out in the fresh air. Hospital living was no fun for anyone, let alone a little kid.

As they got closer to the park, Dylan's excitement ratcheted up a notch. "Will Mr. Bacon Man be dere, too?"

"He'll be there, honey, but I don't know if he'll have a lot of time for us. He has to make sure everything's set up right and keep an eye on the silent auction tables."

She cast a glance in the direction of the big tent where the auction was taking place. Should they go look for Brett now? Or should they find Derrick first?

"Look!" her brother cried. He pointed at a group of people walking by with ice cream cones. "Ice cream!"

"Do you want some?"

He gave an enthusiastic nod, so she took his hand and wove through the crowd in search of the ice cream truck. They quickly found it and got in line. Valerie picked Dylan up, and he rested his head on her shoulder. He was a cuddle bug, that was for sure.

After a minute, a couple of women got in line behind them. "I'm so happy he's going to be here," one of the women said. "I haven't spoken with him since Adam and I divorced."

"Are you going to bid on the date?" her friend asked, and Valerie started paying more attention since, obviously, they were talking about Brett.

"Got to. I don't know if he'll talk to me otherwise."

"Come on, girl, he was hung up on you for a long time."

"The way I broke up with him, though, it was so…heartless."

Valerie took a quick peek over her shoulder. *Oh, man.* She went cold all over. It was Tracy and another one of the mean girls from high school. All grown up.

Brett had wanted to marry Tracy. He'd proposed to Tracy. And now she was here. Available after her divorce.

Dylan's soft breathing in her ear turned into snores, and Valerie stepped out of line. She should find Brett and apologize, warn him that Tracy was here. But what if he didn't want an apology from her? What if he didn't want to be warned?

Dylan shifted in her arms. First things first, she had to get her brother home and check his temperature. Then, and only then, could she come back and find Brett.

The crowd at this year's Cranberry Harvest Festival was massive—probably three times as big as the crowd from the year before. The silent auction was massive, too, and Brett was in awe of the number of items he and Valerie had been able to collect.

Last year, the event had raised about five thousand dollars for charity. This year, he'd be surprised if they weren't able to triple that number, at least.

The auction tables were set up at the back of the main tent, which also housed a stage for the live music, plus a whole sea of folding tables and chairs where people could relax and eat the food they'd purchased from the food trucks lining the parking lot.

Outside, the park was filled with an expanse of vendor booths selling artwork, jewelry, crafts, books and baked goods. Brett could hear squeals of joy and excitement from the kids' area, where there was a big inflatable pool filled with ripe cranberries that the kids could tromp around in, as well as a giant bouncy slide.

Jonathan, Derrick and Emma had stopped by to see him earlier, before they'd headed out to play. Brett had been a little jealous of Jonathan. He wanted to see the delight on the kids' faces when they squished those cranberries. Taking baby Aiden over there last year to watch the fun had been the highlight of his day.

Part of him wished Valerie was here to see the fruits of their labor. But after that visit from Marisco Seafood, he wasn't sure he was ready to see her just yet.

He scrubbed his hand over his face. The auction. He had to focus on the auction. Not Valerie. Not the fact that she didn't think he could resurrect the restaurant on his own.

Chloe and Aiden traipsed over, eating soft-serve ice cream cones. Aiden had ice cream smeared across his face and dripping down his chin.

"Hey, sis. I was just thinking about you two. You been over to stomp the cranberries yet?"

She shook her head. "Nope, I wanted to put a bid in on some tickets for Steve."

"Which ones?" Brett did a quick scan of the clipboards, then pointed. "Sports tickets are over there."

"Thanks, bro." She tossed him a smile. "The Patriots game."

He whistled. "What'd he do to deserve those?"

She shrugged. "I just love him, that's all."

How great would it be to have someone who felt that way about him? "If you really want to win, come back right before the bidding closes at eight."

"Good tip. Thanks."

"Actually, you should come back anyway and collect the bid sheets for me since I have to go up on stage."

"Okay, no prob." She glanced around. "Where's Valerie?"

Brett frowned. "At the hospital. With Dylan."

His sister shook her head. "They got out a few hours ago. Laura said they were heading this way."

Brett's frown deepened. It was really bothering him that he was getting all these updates about her secondhand. "News to me."

"Want to go find them? I can stay here and babysit the bid sheets."

Brett wagged his head. "If she wants to find me, she'll find me."

Chloe shot him an exasperated look. "Why are you being weird? I thought you liked her."

Putting his good hand on his hip, he said, "I *do* like her. But she doesn't like me." Then, under his breath, he added, "Not enough, anyway."

But of course Chloe caught his muttered words. "Enough for what?"

"Enough to go out with me."

"You asked her out?"

"Kind of."

She stared at him. "What does *that* mean?"

"I didn't ask her out on a date, per se… I asked her if she wanted to date me long-distance once she goes back to New York."

Chloe rolled her eyes. "Talk about putting the cart before the horse."

Brett reared back, feeling defensive. "Dylan had just been

admitted to the hospital. It wasn't like she could leave him there to go on a dinner date with me."

"You asked her to date you long-distance after her brother had just been *admitted to the hospital*? Brett, please. You have heard of a little thing called timing, haven't you?"

"Yes, oh wise one, I have. And I only asked her because she'd just told me that as soon as he got out of the hospital, she was heading back to Manhattan. I needed to ask before I lost the chance."

"And she said no?"

"Yeah." His shoulders slumped. "She said no."

Aiden took his last bite of ice cream, and Chloe cleaned his face with a baby wipe. "Why didn't you just tell her that you'd move to New York?"

Brett gave her a startled look. "Um…maybe because I'm *not* going to move to New York?"

"Why not?"

"You're here. The restaurant's here."

"It's not," she said. "The restaurant's gone."

"You know I'm going to rebuild it."

"I know you want to, but why? You're a chef—you can get a job anywhere. And it's going to take you forever to save up enough money to rebuild. Mom and Dad wouldn't want you spending the next ten years of your life chasing the past. They'd want you to embrace the future. Embrace love."

"That restaurant was their life's work," he argued. "Their legacy."

"But Brett," his sister said gently, "they're not here anymore. And sure, the restaurant was important to them, but it's not their legacy. You said it yourself in that newspaper article. We're their legacy—you and me. Their children. Their faith. The values they passed down to us. The lessons we'll never forget."

Brett took a small, involuntary step back. He could remember his parents working together in the kitchen at home on rainy Sunday afternoons—laughing, teasing, sneaking kisses whenever he and Chloe turned their backs.

His dad, sitting at the head of the table and praying over the food. His mom, taping their artwork and schoolwork to the fridge. They'd always been so supportive of each other and their children, always believed the best about each other, put all their hope, love and trust in one another.

They'd seen him join the navy, but they hadn't lived to see him reconnect with his faith.

"I want them to be proud of me."

"They *were* proud of you," Chloe insisted. "But they're gone now. You have to start living for yourself."

He took a breath. In his mind's eye, he could see himself walking away from the burnt remains of Half Shell and boarding a cruise ship to New York. His parents were standing on the dock, waving, his mother blowing kisses over the sparkling expanse of water—both of them urging him on.

Is this what you want for me, God? A fresh start?

He could see Valerie up on the deck of that cruise ship, waiting for him—her pretty face, her kaleidoscope eyes, her trusting smile.

What if she'd simply been trying to help him by sending the guy from Marisco Seafood Group to talk to him? What if that had been her entire motive, and she didn't think he was incompetent at all?

"If you see Valerie, will you come get me so I can talk to her? And if you don't see her, make sure you bid enough to win the date."

Chloe grinned. "Just to be clear, you want me to go above and beyond the hundred dollars you gave me for the auction?"

"Whatever it takes, Chlo. Don't let anyone outbid you. I need you to win the whole thing."

Chapter Sixteen

By the time Valerie got Dylan back to the inn and confirmed that his temperature was normal, it was getting late. Laura texted Jonathan, who brought Derrick home, and the twins had the most joyful reunion she'd ever seen. Now that they were fed, bathed and in their pajamas, they were happily chattering away in the parlor while they played with their trucks.

Jonathan came out of the dining room, drying his hands on a hand towel. "All right, ladies," he said to Valerie and Laura. "I've got the kids. You two head out."

Valerie's jaw dropped. "Seriously? I was going to stay until they went to bed."

"Go," Jonathan said. "You don't want to miss Brett's big moment."

Valerie kissed the boys good night, and then she and Laura speed walked to the park. It was almost eight. The evening air held a definite chill, and it was already full dark.

The crowds were still thick, the lines at the food trucks long. Couples walked by holding lobster rolls in flimsy paper holders, Styrofoam cups full of clam chowder and massive, greasy portions of fish and chips.

Overexcited kids chased each other on the playground, while their overtired parents dutifully stood watch. Teenagers threaded through the booths, where many of the vendors were packing up the last of their wares. From what Valerie could tell, there wasn't much left.

In the main tent, a country act was up on stage, twanging its music into the night. Valerie shivered and pulled her jacket closed. She was nervous about what was going to happen when Brett hit the stage. Had Tracy already found him? Were the two of them going to give things another shot?

She and Laura slipped into the tent just as the emcee announced that the bidding for the silent auction was officially closed. They caught sight of Chloe collecting the bid sheets and made their way to her.

Valerie shot a glance at the papers in Chloe's hands. "How's it looking?"

Her friend smiled. "Incredible. You should see some of these bids!" She flashed the page for the Boston Bruins tickets and—whoa! Incredible was right.

Valerie looked around. "Where's Brett?"

Chloe pointed to the side of the stage. "Right there. Ready for his five minutes of fame."

Tracy, as blonde and bubbly as she'd been in high school, was sitting at a table nearby, touching up her lipstick. Valerie reached for her pendant. "Did Tracy find him? She was looking for him earlier."

Chloe wrinkled her nose. "She found him."

Valerie looked down, the air leaking out of her, while Laura asked, "What did she want?"

"To apologize for the way she reacted to his proposal. She said, looking back, she regretted how she handled it. That she should have talked to him about it before it got to the point where he was down on one knee."

Laura pursed her lips. "How civilized of her."

"Brett was all like, 'Don't worry about it, I'm over it, but there's someone *else* here who deserves an apology from you.'"

"Who?" Valerie said.

Chloe put her hand on Valerie's arm. "You, silly. He told her she needs to apologize to you."

Valerie's gaze shot to where Brett was standing, tall and handsome in his dark jeans and black T-shirt. His fingers were still in a splint, but they wouldn't be for much longer. The cuts he'd sustained breaking the window during the fire were almost fully healed. "Me?"

"You, my friend," Chloe confirmed, grinning. "You have to know that you're pretty much always on his mind."

Hope shot through Valerie from her head to her toes. She opened her mouth to reply, but the emcee chose that moment to announce that the time had come to auction off a date with Wychmere Bay's homegrown hero: Brett Richardson!

Brett jogged onto the stage, holding up his uninjured arm like a victorious boxer. The spectators jammed into the tent erupted into cheers and applause. As soon as the noise settled, the emcee announced, "For those of you who are wondering whether this man truly is a hero, the captain of the Wychmere Bay Police Department is here tonight to present him with the Citizen Award for Valor, which is awarded to individuals who personify courage and self-sacrifice in assisting those in danger. Captain O'Connell, come on up!"

Once again, the crowd went wild as Captain O'Connell placed the medal around Brett's neck. It took a full two minutes for everyone to settle down enough for the emcee to give the rest of his spiel.

Before long, the bidding started, and it was an absolute madhouse. People were yelling out bids all over the place— some were even flashing wads of cash or standing on their chairs to make sure they got the attention of one of the recorders. The bidding quickly moved into the hundreds, and then over a thousand.

Valerie had hoped this would be a successful endeavor, but she'd really had no idea.

Once the bidding reached eleven hundred dollars, it slowed. There were a handful of women still vying for the win, but the vast majority of the room had dropped out.

Tracy called out a bid, and Valerie tensed. Brett might not be interested in his ex-girlfriend, but Valerie sure didn't like the idea of him cooking for her and spending an evening catching up. She raised her own hand and called out, "Twelve fifty."

Beside her, Chloe laughed. "You don't need to bid on him, Valerie. I have it on good authority that he'll take you out for free."

But that just made Valerie more determined to win. Brett had been the one who'd been willing to take a chance on them being together. She'd been the one who'd clung to caution when she should have thrown her worries to the wind.

She had to show him that she was ready now.

Tracy bid again. Valerie couldn't believe it. But before she could call out another bid, someone from the back of the room yelled, "Three thousand!"

Gasps and murmurs shot through the tent. Valerie craned her neck to try to see the bidder, but she couldn't find her in the crowd.

"Going once," the emcee cried.

Valerie's heart was pounding. Technically, she could afford to go higher, but should she? As of this moment, she was the caretaker of two little boys, and she didn't have a job.

"Going twice!"

Before she could think better of it, her hand shot into the air. "Three thousand and twenty-five!"

"Three thousand and twenty-five," the emcee crowed. "We have three thousand twenty-five! Do I hear three thousand fifty? Anyone, anyone? We're looking for three thousand fifty."

The tent was silent. Valerie held her breath.

"Going once! Going twice! S—"

"Five thousand!"

Valerie's stomach dropped. The mystery woman in the back had struck again.

"Sold to the lady in the back for five thousand dollars! Absolutely incredible day for charity, friends! Ma'am, come on up here and claim your prize!"

All the heads in the room swiveled to see who had placed the winning bid. A petite, dark-haired woman with a baseball cap pulled low on her forehead walked up to the stage.

"Who is that?" Laura nudged Chloe.

Chloe squinted and frowned. "I've never seen her before in my life."

The lady strode up the stairs and shook hands with Brett and the emcee.

"Congratulations," the emcee said into the mic. "Our charity this year, Parents Against Drunk and Distracted Driving, truly appreciates your support. Would you like to share your name so we can give you a round of applause?"

The lady leaned forward so she could speak into the microphone. "Hello, my name is Catherine, and I'm glad to be supporting a good cause, but I must admit that the charitable donation isn't the real reason I'm up here tonight."

Valerie went stock-still at the sound of the woman's voice. *Was that...? No, it couldn't be...*

The emcee boomed out a laugh. "I've had the pleasure of dining on Brett's food before, and let me tell you, it is worth every penny."

The woman, Catherine, leaned forward again. "I'm sure it is, but I didn't buy this date for myself. I saw my daughter bidding on it, and I'd like to give it to her as a gift."

Gasps rippled through the crowd. Valerie, meanwhile, was struggling to breathe.

"Well, what's your daughter's name?" the emcee asked. "Tell her to come on up."

"I'm not sure she'll want to," the lady said. "I haven't seen her in over twenty years." Another round of gasps emanated from the crowd.

Laura, eyes wide, covered her mouth with her hand and turned to Valerie. "Is that…?"

Valerie managed a shaky nod. "I think so."

"Valerie, honey," the lady—*her mother*—said into the microphone, "if you don't want to talk to me, that's fine. I understand. But I read about how this young man came to your rescue in an article in *The Boston Globe*, and I thought I'd come down here and see if I could find you and try to make amends."

She choked up, but kept going anyway. "I apologize if I overstepped by bidding on this date, but I promise you, there are no strings attached. I simply wanted to do something nice for you after so many years of not doing anything at all."

Blindly, Valerie reached for a chair, pulling it away from a nearby table so she could sit.

"Thank you," the lady finished stiffly. "That's all I had to say." Then she walked off the stage.

Laura and Chloe both crouched down beside Valerie. "Are you okay?" Chloe asked, while Laura added, "Can I get you some water?"

In all the commotion, Valerie didn't even notice that Brett had vaulted off the stage until he was hunkered down in front of her, too.

"Bright eyes," he said, laying his hand on her arm. "Was that who I think it was?"

She nodded, tears in her eyes. Her mother was here. Her *mother*, after all this time.

"Do you want to talk to her?" he asked. "She's leaving."

Valerie craned her neck, just barely catching a glimpse of her mother's retreating back. She shot to her feet, but a bout of lightheadedness immediately forced her back down.

"Stay there," Brett said. "I'll get her." Then he jogged away.

Laura brought Valerie a water bottle, and she took a few long sips. She wanted to talk to her mother, but she needed to talk to Brett, too.

When he came back, the lady—*her mother*—was following him, trepidation written all over her face.

"Valerie," the woman whispered, her whole body trembling, "is it really you?"

"It's me, Mom." She held out her hand so her mother could clasp it. "Welcome home."

Chapter Seventeen

Brett sat a few tables away from where Valerie was speaking with her mother. Who knew that talking to that reporter from *The Boston Globe* would lead to a reunion that had been twenty-two years in the making?

God, he thought wryly, shooting his gaze up to the ceiling of the tent in gratitude, *you really do have a plan.*

After about a half hour, Catherine got up, gave Valerie's hand one last squeeze and then walked off into the night. Valerie watched her for a few seconds, then glanced at him and waved him her way.

As he got closer to her table, she held out her hand. It was shaking. He took it and sat next to her, then lifted it to his lips. "Hey, beauty. That was wild. You doing okay?"

"I'm good," she said. "Stunned. Shocked. But absolutely okay. Thanks for stopping her before she could leave."

"Of course. What'd she say?"

"That she was sorry. At the time, she thought me and my dad would be better off without her. Sounds like she even—" Valerie winced as she fiddled with her broken heart pendant and took a deep breath "—tried to take her own life a couple of times. Thankfully she's in therapy now, and it's helping. She remarried a few months ago, and her new husband's been encouraging her to look me up and make amends. When they saw the article in the paper, they knew they had to come today."

"Whew," Brett said. "That's a lot."

"It is, but in a good way. I always thought it was something about me that had pushed her away. Like if I'd died and Vanessa had lived, she wouldn't have left." Her hand flitted to her necklace again. "But you were right—it had nothing to do with me. She was depressed."

"Are you going to see her again?"

Valerie nodded. "She and her husband live in Maine. They're driving back tomorrow. I invited them to join us for pizza before they go."

"That's amazing," he said, giving her hand a little squeeze. "And Dylan's doing good since they let him out of the hospital?"

"He's still pretty tired, but no more fever, and that's the main thing."

"Thank God," he said with feeling.

"Amen," she replied. "And, hey, Laura told me about the unexpected visit from Marisco Seafood last night. I'm so sorry. My mentor mentioned that they might be interested in talking to you right before Dylan went into the hospital. I meant to talk to you about it and see if you wanted to put together a pitch, but because of everything that was going on, I completely forgot."

"It's all right. I was taken aback when it happened, but after thinking about it, I realized you were only trying to help."

She let out a breath. "I was worried. I was trying to find you earlier to apologize, but then I ran into Tracy and—" She tugged on her pendant, looking anxious.

"Aw, bright eyes." His heart squeezed. "Were you jealous?"

"So jealous," she admitted.

"Don't be," he said. "I never felt for her the way I feel about you."

Her cheeks pinked. Her hand fluttered. "Really?"

"Really. The feelings I had for her—I was just a boy. I'm

a man now, and the feelings I have for you, they're not going anywhere. So, tell me how much longer you're staying. Now that Dylan's out of the hospital, I know you're anxious to get back to New York."

"Well," she said, a smile spreading all the way across her face, "I can't leave before I redeem my five-thousand-dollar date."

"Five thousand dollars." He shook his head. "Unbelievable."

Now she squeezed *his* hand. "You're worth it."

His heart leaped. He felt the exact same way about her. "What would you say if I told you I was going to move to New York?"

Her mismatched eyes went wide with surprise. "I'd say that's too bad…"

Confusion balled in his stomach. Had he gotten her all wrong—again?

"…because I won't be there anymore. I quit my job the other day. I'm staying here."

Shock flowed through him like a surge of freezing water. "I hope you didn't quit for me. Like Chloe reminded me, I'm a chef. I can get a job anywhere."

She tucked a strand of her long black hair behind her ear and gave him a playful smile. "I quit for me and the twins. You're just a side benefit."

He grinned back at her. "A little presumptuous there, wouldn't you say, bright eyes? It's only been a few weeks. We haven't even kissed."

"Hmm," she said, grabbing hold of the heavy bronze medal around his neck and pulling him closer. "I've heard there's an easy solution to that problem. *If* you're willing to do your civic duty and test it out."

He laughed as he slid his good hand into her hair, which was just as sleek and soft as he'd imagined. "Doing my civic duty's turned out pretty well for me so far. Might as well give it a shot."

Smiling, his hand threaded through her hair, he kissed her, and she kissed him right back.

When he pulled away, he asked, "So? Did I pass the test?"

Wide-eyed, she touched her lips and smiled. "Stellar work, Mr. Bacon Man. An A-plus." Then she studied his medal a little closer, running her fingers over the engraved star. "You should know that I nominated you for a few other awards."

"Did you?" He chuckled. "I should've known you were the one who put the bug in the police department's ear."

"I'm waiting to hear back on most of them, but there's a car dealership that wants to give you a brand-new car."

His eyes popped. "What?"

She pulled up an email on her phone and showed it to him. "See? They said you can take the car or the cash value of the car—your choice."

"Wow." He was floored by the prize, of course, but more than that, he was amazed that she'd spent time and effort trying to help him, despite the many other things that were going on in her life.

My helpmate, he thought. *My love.*

"I thought maybe you could take the money, combine it with that check you got from Bill and Irene and use it to get a start on rebuilding Half Shell. And you saw how crazy everyone went tonight when the police chief gave you that award. I think Irene was right about the town wanting to help. If you want, we can create a crowdfunding campaign so people can chip in and help you get it back off the ground."

He caught her hand and pressed it to his cheek. "I love you, bright eyes."

Gazing deep into his eyes, she took her hand off his cheek and rested it on his heart. "You're my hero, Brett Richardson. I love you, too."

Epilogue

The twins were *not* excited about wearing suits. They kept pulling at their collars and trying to undo their ties.

At a stoplight, Valerie turned so she could face them. "Stop playing with your ties, guys. Don't you want to look nice for Mr. Brett's party?"

That quieted them down for a minute, but by the time Valerie pulled into the parking lot at Half Shell, they were back at it again. Such was life with twins. It wasn't easy, but it was almost always fun.

Before unclipping the boys from their car seats, Valerie took a moment to appreciate the view. The new restaurant had a beautiful walkway lined with vibrant purple hydrangeas leading up to the front door. The architecture was classic Cape Cod, and it looked both elegant and inviting set against the stunning backdrop of Wychmere Bay.

After the Cranberry Harvest Festival, Brett had taken out a commercial real estate loan on the land he owned on the harbor. The loan—combined with the money he'd been awarded by the car dealership, the check from Bill and Irene and the proceeds from the crowdfunding campaign that Rudy Valentini had been happy to highlight in a glowing article in the *Cape Cod Community Times*—had allowed Brett to rebuild Half Shell in a mere eight months.

Today was the grand reopening, and he'd invited everyone

who'd contributed to the crowdfunding campaign to come and eat for free.

When Valerie and the twins walked in, they were greeted by a sea of familiar faces: Laura, Jonathan, Hunter and Emma; Chloe, Steve, Aiden and his new baby brother, Teddy; Bill and Irene, along with Pastor Nate and his son, Hayden; Valerie's mother and her husband, Ron; Cole, and a whole bunch of Valerie's coworkers from the start-up in Boston, where she worked—mostly remotely—as the director of finance; plus countless other friends from in and around Wychmere Bay.

Even Gloria, who'd called to apologize about a week after Valerie resigned, was here, her handsome husband on her arm. Although she and Valerie weren't as close as they'd been when Valerie worked at the bank, they'd met for lunch in Boston a couple of times since, and Valerie still appreciated Gloria's career advice.

Tonight, Brett was serving a fixed menu, and everyone simmered with excitement as they sat for the first course: a bacon-wrapped scallop, served with a small side of arugula, pear and parmesan salad.

After Pastor Nate blessed the food, Valerie cut her scallop in half and lifted a bite to her mouth. Sublime.

Next came a cup of smoked salmon and lobster bisque, which the boys inhaled in no time flat. Finally, the entrée, which was turmeric caramel cod, served with jasmine rice, mint, cilantro and onions. Valerie had to stop the boys from licking the sauce off their plates—it was *that* good.

Once the dinner plates had been cleared, Chloe leaned over, eyes shining, and whispered, "I cannot *wait* to see what he's serving for dessert!"

But before dessert was brought to the table, Brett came out of the kitchen in dark slacks and a white chef's coat. Everyone in the room cheered and gave him a standing ovation. Valerie and the twins clapped louder than anyone, and he winked at her when he saw her, reminding her of the morning she'd first realized he was also staying at the Sea Glass Inn.

What a long, long way they'd come since then.

Brett tapped on a water glass and the room quieted. "Thank you for coming out tonight, everyone. I'm humbled by your support, grateful for your friendship and honored that you're here. Before we bring out dessert—"

"No!" Chloe booed, and everyone laughed. Her sweet tooth was legendary.

"It's coming, Chlo, it's coming," Brett assured her, and everyone laughed again. "I'd like to ask a few special people to come up here for a minute. Valerie? Boys?"

Valerie's cheeks heated. She hadn't been expecting to get up in front of the crowd, so she stayed seated while the boys ran to Brett and latched on to his legs. He lifted them up— Derrick in one arm, Dylan in the other. "These are my little buddies," he said. "We first met in a house fire last year, but now I can't imagine my life without them. Did you like the food tonight, guys?"

"Mr. Bacon Man cooks da best food!" Derrick proclaimed proudly, and everyone chuckled.

"I lub him," Dylan added, and gave Brett a big hug.

"Aw, I love you guys, too," Brett said, giving each of them a kiss on the side of the head before setting them down. "Dylan here had a little health scare last fall, but—" He stopped and looked at Valerie, who was still sitting in her chair. "Can I announce this?"

She nodded, misty-eyed. She and her brothers were all so blessed to have Brett in their lives.

"He had his second follow-up with his cardiologist yesterday, and everything looks good!"

The room cheered again, and Derrick and Dylan started hamming it up by dancing and chasing each other around Brett's legs.

"Some of you might not know this, but Valerie's a twin, too. Unfortunately, her twin sister died when she was just seven years old. She's been wearing a pendant necklace ever since to remember her, but you may have noticed that half of it's missing, and ever since I heard the story behind it, it's made me sad.

"Valerie," he said, "I know your sister will always be one of your best friends, but you're *my* best friend, and I hope I'm one of yours, too. I found a matching necklace and put half of it on a leather bracelet for me—" he lifted his sleeve to show her his wrist "—and saved half of it for you. You've made my heart whole, and I want to do the same thing for you. So—"

He stepped even closer, then took out a necklace and knelt down in front of her chair. "Valerie Williams, I adore you." He gestured at the room around them. "I couldn't have done any of this without you. Will you accept this piece of my heart forever and do me the very great honor of becoming my wife?"

A jolt of pure joy shot through her. If anyone had told her last September that she'd find unconditional love with Brett, she wouldn't have believed it was possible, and yet…he was down on one knee, proposing to her.

Valerie's eyes blurred with tears even as she squealed, "Brett!" and launched herself out of her chair and into his arms.

He laughed as he caught her, wobbled, then steadied them both. "Is that a yes?"

"Yes!"

He put his hands on either side of her face and kissed her. Then he fastened the new necklace around her neck and slotted the two halves of her pendant heart together. It was a perfect fit.

When he held his arms open for the twins, they immediately jumped in for a big, group hug.

"I love you, bright eyes," Brett murmured, tenderness in his voice and his hands and his smile. "Forever."

Then he lifted his head and addressed their family and friends. "And now, before Chloe starts a riot, let's bring out dessert! In honor of the time Valerie and I spent working on the Cranberry Harvest Festival, it's cranberry streusel pie!"

* * * * *

Dear Reader,

You're invited to Brett and Valerie's wedding!

To attend, visit MeghannWhistler.com/newsletter and sign up for my email newsletter. I'll send you the wedding scene right away!

On a serious note, for anyone who could relate to Valerie's history with her eating disorder, I pray that you're getting the help you need. If you or someone you know is struggling, please know that support is available.

The National Association for Eating Disorders has some excellent resources on its website, which you can find at NationalEatingDisorders.org. Additionally, free support groups like Eating Disorders Anonymous and Celebrate Recovery are wonderful places to find strength and encouragement.

I'm always thrilled to hear that someone enjoyed one of my stories. Please feel free to email me anytime at Meghann@MeghannWhistler.com!

Wishing you love and light,
Meghann

ENDORSEMENTS

As I dove into *Higher Authority* by my brother, Bishop Hugh Smith Jr., I felt a surge of pride. Growing up, Hugh mirrored the adventurous spirit of the *Lost in Space* episode "Danger, Will Robinson," always daring to explore the unknown. Hugh fearlessly explores the divine mandate for human evolution, seamlessly blending scripture, science, and spirituality.

Dr. Tino W. Smith

We are once again inundated by the wealth of knowledge and applicable truths from the intellectual mind of Hugh Daniel Smith Jr. as he guides us through God's plan and pattern for human enhancement!

Bishop Roderick Roberts

In *Not for Profit* Nussbaum undercuts the idea that education is primarily a tool of economic growth. She argues that economic growth does not invariably generate better quality of life. Neglect and scorn for the arts and humanities puts the quality of all our lives, and the health of our democracies, at risk.

Not for Profit is especially appropriate for this series, The Public Square. It offers readers a "call to action" in the form of a plan that replaces an educational model that undercuts democracy with one that promotes it. It builds a convincing, if at first counterintuitive, case that the very foundation of citizenship—not to mention national success—rests on the humanities and arts. We neglect them at our peril.

Nussbaum enters The Public Square with this far-reaching and expansive book, which shows us the importance of learning to play well with others—and then how to think for ourselves.

PREFACE TO THE
2016 EDITION

Five years since the last edition of *Not For Profit*, how do things look for the humanities? The first thing to be said is that they are clearly in trouble all over the world. I had no idea that my arguments would seem relevant to so many different countries. With twenty translations either in print or in process, I've been in conversation with people in many different parts of the world who share my sense of urgency about the contraction of an area of study that seems so centrally connected to the future of democracy and good citizenship—particular in a time of heightened anxiety, more or less everywhere, about migration and ethno-religious pluralism, a time when citizens need to communicate better, not worse, than before, if pressing problems are to be solved.

In the U.S., things have improved slightly in K through 12, as the Common Core has replaced No Child Left Behind. The Common Core is far from ideal, but it does place the accent more nearly where it belongs, on student abilities, rather than on stored knowledge uncoupled from critical thought or active imagination. We still need to do much better, demanding forms of assessment that focus far more on what happens in the classroom and on the quality of student-teacher interactions. But disaster is being held at bay, at least. It is also very encouraging to see intelligent public arts programs for young people sprouting up in some of our major cities: in Los Angeles, under the inspiring direction of conductor Gustavo Dudamel, in Baltimore under the equally intelligent entrepreneurship of conductor Marin Alsop, in my own city, Chicago, through the partnership of opera star Renee Fleming with the city government.[1] Similar experiments abound, showing that music and art can foster community, excellence, and an expanded sense of citizenship (as I said, discussing the Chicago Children's Choir).

When we reach colleges and universities, there is some good news to report. First, we simply have new sources of valuable data to study the issues, in the form of reports from the American Academy of Arts and Sciences and the Association of American Colleges and Universities.[2] Although the Academy, unfortunately, focuses primarily on students majoring in the humanities, rather than on the far broader issue of liberal arts courses open to, and frequently required of, students from all majors, the data and analysis, compiled by a high-quality team of administrators and scholars, are extremely helpful. Of particular interest is the finding that two-year institutions are an especially important and growing source of humanities students. In 2012–13, almost forty percent of Associate degrees were in the humanities, a much higher percentage than for four-year BA programs. This is good news indeed, since it would be all too easy for such community college programs to slide toward narrow vocational education, thus creating a class-based, two-tier system, where liberal education is increasingly an opportunity for elites. This has not happened, and it's very important to prevent it from happening.

Moving beyond these valuable data, further good news for the humanities is found in the quality of the new voices that are addressing the issue. Two particularly valuable books are Michael Roth's *Beyond the University: Why Liberal Education Matters* and

Fareed Zakaria's *In Defense of a Liberal Education*.[3] Roth's lucid and highly readable book provides a history of the idea of liberal education in the U.S., showing its deep links to the ideals of democracy in America. He focuses particularly on the role of critical thinking in a free and engaged society. Zakaria's book is especially striking for its moving narrative of his own education. He moved from an India where rote learning and technical training dominated, to a liberal education at Yale where he discovered history and, more generally, a broad-based education that stimulated curiosity, critical thinking, and imagination, and he reflects impressively on what he gained for both life and citizenship. His historical analysis complements Roth's, agreeing that the U.S. democratic tradition has deep links to the practice of liberal education. The high quality of both books, and their favorable reception, give further momentum to the struggle to keep the humanities strong. My book remains distinctive in its international character and its focus on the psychological underpinnings of education, which help us understand why the liberal arts are crucial and why they are frequently under attack. The three books complement one another, and it would be an excellent thing if politicians, trustees, administrators, parents, and students would consult all three.

Turning to politics, however, we find some distressing developments. Not very long ago, conservative politicians used to defend liberal education strongly, differing with liberals primarily over issues such as whether women's studies and the study of race should play a part in it. Today there are increasingly strident calls for the drastic curtailing of the liberal arts. To take just one example: In one of his first acts as governor, in January 2013, Governor Pat McCrory of North Carolina lashed out at liberal arts education. On a national radio program hosted by conservative pundit William Bennett, he said that university curricula are full of "worthless courses" that offer "no chances of getting people jobs." He singled out language study, philosophy, and gender studies as examples. "I'm going to adjust my education curriculum to what business and commerce needs to get our kids jobs."[4] It is not clear that McCrory can enact his ideas, since his office does not give him control over curriculum. UNC, like all distinguished university systems, has a large measure of faculty autonomy and educational control. Even its budget must be passed by the legislature and is not simply created by gubernatorial fiat. But it is ominous that McCrory thinks he can gain popularity by beating up on the humanities. Numerous other politicians have launched similar attacks on the liberal arts. During his unsuccessful campaign for the Republican nomination for president, Marco Rubio claimed, with typical inelegance, "We need more welders and less philosophers."[5] Florida's governor Rick Scott directed his wrath at the anthropologists, saying, "You know, we don't need a lot more anthropologists in the state…I want to spend our dollars giving people science, technology, engineering, math degrees. That's what our kids need to focus all their time and attention on."[6] Note his "all": apparently he disapproves not only of liberal arts majors, but also of general education requirements in the liberal arts. Meanwhile, Wisconsin's governor Scott Walker has proposed to fund departments in proportion to their role as a pipeline into the state's economy—simply assuming that politicians can predict what fields are in fact most beneficial for the state, an assumption that history shows to be highly unreliable.[7] Nor does Walker even consider that a state's system of higher education might have further and broader goals, such as the pursuit of knowledge for its own sake and the formation of citizenship. More recently, many state officials have been offering students financial incentives to focus on STEM fields and not the humanities.[8]

In this context, effective arguments are more needed than ever. I believe that *Not For Profit* remains timely as a reminder of the grave risks we run if we let these development move ahead unchecked.

Not For Profit focuses on citizenship. I argue that the humanities and arts provide skills that are essential to keep democracy healthy. I choose this focus because I believe that most of my readers share the goal of sustaining a healthy democracy, and that even those who do not already favor liberal arts education may be led to support it by the sort of argument I provide. There are, however, two other arguments to be made for keeping the humanities strong. We should remember them and use them.

First, even if we were just aiming at economic success, business cultures around the world are keenly aware of the importance of both critical thinking and imagination for healthy business cultures. Critical thinking builds corporate cultures of accountability in which critical voices are not silenced. And a trained imagination is essential for innovation, a key to any healthy economy: no nation can thrive on the basis of yesterday's skills learned by rote. So business leaders in many parts of the world have given liberal education strong support. For just one example: David Rubenstein, co-founder of the Carlyle Group, one of our most successful private equity firms, said at the World Economic Forum Davos that he worries that American students are losing a valuable skill that can help them succeed in business and life: critical thinking. American policy makers and educators, Rubenstein said, have put too much of a focus on the fields of science, technology, engineering, and mathematics at the expense of the study of literature, philosophy, and other areas in the humanities. Humanities teach problem-solving skills that enable students to contribute to business success. Career-specific skills can be learned later, he said, noting that many of Wall Street's top executives studied the humanities. The reasoning skills that come with a well-rounded humanities education actually contribute more over time, both to individual success and to the success of a nation's business culture.[9]

Striking confirmation of Rubenstein's argument comes from the fact that Singapore and China, two nations that, to say the least, do not aim at the cultivation of critical and independent democratic citizenship, have recently conducted education reforms that foreground the arts and humanities, explicitly in order to encourage innovation and solid corporate cultures. Of course they then must contain those disciplines, preventing them from spilling over into a demand for open political debate, and this they aggressively do. But the very fact that they feel the need to encourage disciplines that they themselves perceive as politically risky shows how important they think they are for business success.[10]

The second argument we should bear in mind, in addition to my citizenship argument, is that the humanities offer insights that are of intrinsic value as we seek to understand our lives. I consider their role in forming citizens to have intrinsic, not merely instrumental, value, but the intrinsic value of the humanities can, and should, be seen more broadly. We all seek a deeper understanding of love, death, anger, pain, and many other themes treated in great works of art, literature, and philosophy. No matter how we earn our living, we all need to confront ourselves, our own life and death. It's easy to forget about these deeper themes when one is young, but it's then that an initial acquaintance plants seeds for fruitful later rumination. It is no surprise that one big growth area for the humanities is in continuing education for adults.[11]

In short, my book focuses on just one part of a three-pronged argument defending the humanities. We can, and should, endorse all three prongs.

As we do so, we should be acutely aware of the advantages offered by the system of liberal arts education that is traditional in the U.S., Scotland, and South Korea, and that is partially present in several other nations, particularly Canada, South Africa, and the Netherlands. (Jesuit universities all over the world also favor this model.) We should not measure the impact of the humanities simply by counting numbers of majors. The whole design of the liberal arts system is that courses in the humanities are required of all students, no matter what their major. In most of the world, students entering a university face a draconian choice of a single subject. So: Either all philosophy or no philosophy. Either all literature or no literature. This system drastically restricts the number of people who study the humanities at the university level, since they must choose a humanities subject as their only field, closing off opportunities elsewhere. (It also means that new disciplines such as gender studies and the study of race have very few adherents, since students have no opportunity to pursue them unless they devote themselves entirely to those subjects, a choice that is probably educationally unsound, given the importance of disciplinary structure: these new programs are intended to provide interdisciplinary learning for all.) Nations with a liberal arts system think differently: Students should have a major subject, which might prepare for a career (although it need not). But they should also take some courses that prepare them more broadly, for citizenship and life. Students can major in computer science or engineering, but in such a system they are also required to take general liberal arts courses in history, philosophy, and literature. This system has striking advantages, preparing students for their multiple future roles in much more adequate way than a narrow single-subject system.

The arguments in my book (insofar as they address college and university education) do have bearing on why students might choose a humanities subject as their major subject. But they are primarily focused on the liberal arts part of the university curriculum, shared (where a nation has made that possible) by all students. And, of course, they also deal with the role of the humanities in primary and secondary education, where specialization has not yet advanced very far. It is not easy to change over to a liberal arts system when a nation's universities have long been structured around the one-subject system. Just adding some huge required courses will not do the job. Good humanities teaching needs small classes, participatory classroom discussion, and copious feedback on frequent writing assignments. It cannot be accomplished in large lectures with multiple-choice examinations. And although MOOCs may have supplementary value, particularly for students who lack direct access to a good university, they are no replacement for live, face-to-face interaction. Good STEM teaching, too, needs student-faculty dialogue, but one can go some distance without that, and there is at least a widespread illusion that some STEM skills can be taught without interactive pedagogy. But if a nation wishes to make a transition to a liberal arts system it will need to think hard about student-teacher ratio and the training of good teachers as part of graduate training. (In the Netherlands, liberal arts programs are currently elective and typically charge an extra fee, which means that they will attract elites, a highly undesirable outcome.) Such changes do not happen right away.

Nonetheless, the progress toward a liberal arts model in nations as otherwise diverse as the Netherlands and India is heartening.

With the mention of India, I now turn to another major issue, the role of private funding in higher education. Politicians, I said, have been increasingly calling for the defunding of the humanities. But politicians have short-term incentives, needing to win election, which lead them to favor easily quantifiable gains (jobs and revenue) over gains less easily quantified (the quality of citizenship, the illumination of the mind and heart). For such reasons, in the U.S., even public institutions of higher education have increasingly sought private funding, and universities elsewhere in the world have been quick to follow suit—often without sufficiently understanding the conditions under which private funding is compatible with academic quality.

Private donors, by contrast, often have long-range incentives (immortality for themselves, the chance to perpetuate forms of study that have enriched their own lives) that lend themselves well to the goals of a liberal arts university or college. However, such a system works well only under certain conditions:

1. A long-standing tradition of liberal arts education: donors have some familiarity with the humanities, no matter what their path in life, and often they look back on liberal arts courses with love, as part of a time of life in which they pursued meaning without financial constraint and were brimming with passion and curiosity. (A wise university will seek to awaken such memories by frequent programs for the community and for potential donors, showing them the excitement of humanities discussions.)

2. A system of tax incentives that reward charitable donations, and, better yet, also threaten loss of one's fortune if one does not give it away, by a large estate tax.

3. Longstanding social norms that give people reputational rewards for such donations.

4. Most important of all: An established and uncompromising system of academic freedom and autonomy, which imposes strict and well-understood limits on donor demands. Donors have to understand that they cannot control the content of an academic program, beyond supporting an area of study in a very general way. They cannot have a voice in faculty hiring or even in the general viewpoint or methodological approach to a subject area. These norms must be publicly understood and inflexibly applied. (My own President says that he spends about half of his time with donors saying no to what they propose to do with their money.)

Under such conditions, private funding can yield excellent results. Where the fourth condition is not well understood, however, disaster easily ensues. In India, the burgeoning demand for higher education has seen a proliferation of private institutions that vary greatly in both academic quality and independence. Although there are some private universities of high quality, there are also many more of low quality. Some are but training programs for future employees in a given corporation. And it is virtually the norm that donors control much more than is consistent with sound academic values. Thus, the idea that the major donor of a university would also hold the post that is the equivalent of a university president is no anomaly, as it should be. Even if this illicit power is used only for good, it always potentially threatens academic freedom and integrity, and the looming presence of donors can have a subtly destructive influence on faculty autonomy even when no threatening demand is actually made. Furthermore, the current government's ominous attack on academic freedom in public institutions, where a high standard of faculty autonomy is the norm, have set the stage for a drastic curtailment of dissent, hence a grave threat to India's admirable democracy.[12]

The humanities have been threatened since their very beginning. Socratic questioning is unsettling, and people in power often prefer docile followers to independent citizens able to think for themselves. Furthermore, a lively imagination, alert to the situations, desires, and sufferings of others is a taxing achievement; moral obtuseness is so much easier. So we should not be surprised that the humanities are under assault, now as ever. The battle for responsible democracy and alert citizenship is always difficult and uncertain. But it is both urgent and winnable, and the humanities are a large part of winning it.

NOTES TO THE PREFACE

1. See http://articles.chicagotribune.com/2013–12–12/entertainment/chi-cps-arts-plan-anniversary-20131212_1_renee-fleming-arts-education-plan-yo-yo-ma. Dudamel's efforts, based on Venezuela's El Sistema, are widely known. For the Baltimore program, see https://www.bsomusic.org/education-community/young-musicians/orchkids.aspx. In Berlin, Sir Simon Rattle's inspiring efforts with inner-city youth are documented in the film *Rhythm Is It*.

2. See http://www.humanitiescommission.org/_pdf/hss_report.pdf and http://www.humanitiesindicators.org/binaries/pdf/HI_HigherEd2015.pdf.

3. Roth (New Haven: Yale University Press, 2014); Zakaria (New York: W. W. Norton, 2015).

4. https://www.youtube.com/watch?v=xUCIkSqXKZ8. The program aired on Jan. 29, 2013.

5. http://www.politifact.com/truth-o-meter/statements/2015/nov/11/marco-rubio/marco-rubio-welders-more-money-philosophers/; Rubio also claimed that welders make more money than philosophers, a claim that Politifact refutes with detailed data, taking as the base group all those who majored in philosophy in college. Philosophy majors make an average first-year salary of $42,200; the average mid-career pay is $85,000. The median pay for philosophy professors is even better, $90,000. On Rubio's remark, see my obituary for philosopher Hilary Putnam at http://www.huffingtonpost.com/martha-c-nussbaum/hilary-putnam-1926–2016_b_9457774.html?1457958169.

6. http://www.motherjones.com/mojo/2011/10/rick-scott-liberal-arts-majors-drop-dead-anthropology.

7. https://www.insidehighered.com/views/2012/11/27/why-scott-walkers-focus-pushing-graduates-specific-majors-wrong-essay. Many of our most successful business leaders have been liberal arts majors, as the article goes on to enumerate at length; and see my discussion of David Rubenstein's analysis, below.

8. http://www.nytimes.com/2016/02/22/business/a-rising-call-to-promote-stem-education-and-cut-liberal-arts-funding.html?_r=0.

9. http://dealbook.nytimes.com/2014/01/23/carlyle-co-founders-formula-for-success-study-the-humanities/.

10. See Martha C. Nussbaum, "Democracy, Education, and the Liberal Arts: Two Asian Models," *UC Davis Law Review* 44 (2011), 735–72.

11. See "The Humanities for Love, Not Money," *New York Times* August 25, 2010, http://mobile.nytimes.com/2010/08/26/education/26HUMANITIES.html.

12. See Nussbaum, *Indian Express*, March 2016, http://indianexpress.com/article/opinion/columns/jnu-row-freedom-of-speech-ekla-cholo-re/.

ACKNOWLEDGMENTS

Because I have been thinking and writing about liberal education for many years, I have more thanks to give than I can properly record here. The many schools, colleges, and universities that have debated the conclusions of my earlier book, *Cultivating Humanity*, must be at the top of the list, as must the Association of American Colleges and Universities, whose members and leaders have been an invaluable source of inspiration and insight. I want to thank Carole Schneider, president of that Association, for involving me in her LEAP report on higher education, and for generously reacting to some of these ideas when I presented them in an earlier form. Mike McPherson of the Spencer Foundation has also been a terrific source of insight, and the year I spent as a resident fellow at the Foundation taught me a lot about this topic, although at the time I was working on a different project. My ongoing association with the Cambridge School in Weston, Massachusetts, where my daughter was educated, gives me optimism about the future of the type of education I defend here. Jane Moulding, the school's head, and all the faculty and trustees are to be honored for their commitment to critical thinking and the arts in an era in which those commitments go against the grain. In a very different way, I get support and nourishment every day from my colleagues at the University of Chicago Law School, an unusual intellectual community where interdisciplinary critical thinking thrives.

One nice feature of working on a topic for many years is that one can trace the ascent of young people one admires to positions of influence. In *Cultivating Humanity*, discussing education for world citizenship, I spoke of a young philosophy professor at St. Lawrence University who pioneered a fine and innovative "intercultural studies" program that involved faculty travel and interdisciplinary teaching. Last April Grant Cornwell became president of Wabash College in Ohio, and I was privileged to deliver a lecture based on the ideas in this book at his inauguration.

Most of all, I have been inspired by the education I received as a child, at the Baldwin School in Bryn Mawr, Pennsylvania. I loved being able to go, every day, from a surrounding community focused on profit and success into a space where critical thinking, ideas, and imagination mattered more than profit. I owe the deepest gratitude to my teachers there. I dedicate this book to three of them above all: to Lois Goutman, our inspiring and emotionally probing drama director, who found ways of getting conventional young women to express capacities we did not know we had; to Marthe Melchior, the tiny, fiery professor of French who taught us how to study France from a multidisciplinary perspective, including history, literature, and the arts, and who helped me and my best friend found a French drama club where we even at times wrote our own plays in French, mine a tragedy on the life of Robespierre (at a reunion about ten years ago, then over ninety, but still fiery, she greeted me with, "Vous voyez, Martha, je suis encore jacobine"); and to Marion Stearns, a superb teacher of English poetry and prose, who taught us how to read and write, terrifying us into getting rid of anything false or egotistical in our writing (so difficult for teenage girls to do).

In India I have learned from all my friends in and from Santiniketan, the home of Tagore's school, especially from the late Amita Sen and Amartya Sen. For other conversations about education in India I am grateful to Gurcharan Das, Mushirul Hasan, Zoya Hasan, Pratik Kanjilal, Krishna Kumar, and Antara Dev Sen.

For comments on earlier drafts or pieces of this manuscript, I am grateful to Andrew Koppelman, Mollie Stone, Madhavi Sunder, and my wonderful editor, Rob Tempio.

NOT FOR PROFIT

I

The Silent Crisis

Education is that process by which thought is opened out
of the soul, and, associated with outward things, is reflected
back upon itself, and thus made conscious of their reality
and shape.
   —Bronson Alcott, Massachusetts educator, c. 1850

[W]hile making use of [material possessions], man has to
be careful to protect himself from [their] tyranny. If he is
weak enough to grow smaller to fit himself to his covering,
then it becomes a process of gradual suicide by shrinkage
of the soul.
   —Rabindranath Tagore, Indian educator, c. 1917

We are in the midst of a crisis of massive proportions and grave global significance. No, I do not mean the global economic crisis that began in 2008. At least then everyone knew that a crisis was at hand, and many world leaders worked quickly and desperately to find solutions. Indeed, consequences for governments were grave if they did not find solutions, and many were replaced in consequence. No, I mean a crisis that goes largely unnoticed, like a cancer; a crisis that is likely to be, in the long run, far more damaging to the future of democratic self-government: a world-wide crisis in education.

Radical changes are occurring in what democratic societies teach the young, and these changes have not been well thought through. Thirsty for national profit, nations, and their systems of education, are heedlessly discarding skills that are needed to keep democracies alive. If this trend continues, nations all over the world will soon be producing generations of useful machines, rather than complete citizens who can think for themselves, criticize tradition, and understand the significance of another person's sufferings and achievements. The future of the world's democracies hangs in the balance.

What are these radical changes? The humanities and the arts are being cut away, in both primary/secondary and college/university education, in virtually every nation of the world. Seen by policy-makers as useless frills, at a time when nations must cut away all useless things in order to stay competitive in the global market, they are rapidly losing their place in curricula, and also in the minds and hearts of parents and children. Indeed, what we might call the humanistic aspects of science and social science—the imaginative, creative aspect, and the aspect of rigorous critical thought—are also losing ground as nations prefer to pursue short-term profit by the cultivation of the useful and highly applied skills suited to profit-making.

This crisis is facing us, but we have not yet faced it. We go on as if everything were business as usual, when in reality great changes of emphasis are evident all over. We haven't really deliberated about these changes, we have not really chosen them, and yet they increasingly limit our future.

Consider these five examples, deliberately drawn from different nations and different educational levels:

- In the fall of 2006 the U.S. Department of Education's Commission on the Future of Higher Education, headed by Bush administration secretary of education Margaret Spellings, released its report on the state of higher education in the nation: *A Test of Leadership: Charting the Future of U.S. Higher Education*.[1] This report contained a valuable critique of unequal access to higher education. When it came to subject matter, however, it focused entirely on education for national economic gain. It concerned itself with perceived deficiencies in science, technology, and engineering—not basic scientific research in these areas, but only highly applied learning, learning that can quickly generate profit-making strategies. The humanities, the arts, and critical thinking were basically absent. By omitting them, the report strongly suggested that it would be perfectly all right if these abilities were allowed to wither away in favor of more useful disciplines.

- In March 2004 a group of scholars from many nations gathered to discuss the educational philosophy of Rabindranath Tagore—winner of the Nobel Prize for Literature in 1913, and leading innovator in education. Tagore's educational experiment, which had wide influence in Europe, Japan, and the United States, focused on the empowerment of the student through practices of Socratic argument, exposure to many world cultures, and, above all, the infusion of music, fine art, theater, and dance into every part of the curriculum. In India today, Tagore's ideas are neglected, and even scorned. Participants in the conference all agreed that a new conception, focused on profit, has taken over—in the process sidelining the whole idea of imaginative and critical self-development through which Tagore had formed so many future citizens of India's successful democracy. Would democracy in India survive today's assault upon its soul? Faced with so much recent evidence of bureaucratic obtuseness and uncritical group-think, many participants feared that the answer might be "No."

• In November 2005 a teachers retreat was held at the Laboratory School in Chicago—the school, on the campus of my own university, where John Dewey conducted his pathbreaking experiments in democratic education reform, the school where President Barack Obama's daughters spent their early formative years. The teachers had gathered to discuss the topic of education for democratic citizenship, and they considered a wide range of educational experiments, studying figures ranging from Socrates to Dewey in the Western tradition to the closely related ideas of Tagore in India. But something was clearly amiss. The teachers—who take pride in stimulating children to question, criticize, and imagine—expressed anxiety about the pressures they face from wealthy parents who send their kids to this elite school. Impatient with allegedly superfluous skills, and intent on getting their children filled with testable skills that seem likely to produce financial success, these parents are trying to change the school's guiding vision. They seem poised to succeed.

- In fall 2005 the head of the search committee for the new dean of the School of Education at one of our nation's most prestigious universities called me for advice. Hereafter I will refer to the university as X. X's School of Education has enormous influence on teachers and schools all over the United States. As I began talking about the role of the humanities and arts in education for democratic citizenship, saying what I took to be familiar and obvious, the woman expressed surprise. "How unusual," she said, "no one else I've talked to has mentioned any of these things at all. We have been talking only about how X University can contribute to scientific and technical education around the world, and that's the thing that our president is really interested in. But what you say is very interesting, and I really want to think about it."

- In the winter of 2006 another prestigious U.S. university— let's call it Y—held a symposium celebrating a major anniversary, a centerpiece of which was to have been discussion of the future of liberal education. A few months before the event, speakers who had agreed to be part of this were told that the focus had been changed and that they should just come and lecture to small departmental audiences on any topic they liked. A helpful and nicely talkative junior administrator told me that the reason for the change was that the president of Y had decided that a symposium on liberal education would not "make a splash," so he decided to replace it with one on the latest achievements in technology and their role in generating profits for business and industry.

There are hundreds of stories like these, and new ones arrive every day, in the United States, in Europe, in India, and, no doubt, in other parts of the world. We are pursuing the possessions that protect, please, and comfort us—what Tagore called our material "covering." But we seem to be forgetting about the soul, about what it is for thought to open out of the soul and connect person to world in a rich, subtle, and complicated manner; about what it is to approach another person as a soul, rather than as a mere useful instrument or an obstacle to one's own plans; about what it is to talk as someone who has a soul to someone else whom one sees as similarly deep and complex.

The word "soul" has religious connotations for many people, and I neither insist on these nor reject them. Each person may hear them or ignore them. What I do insist on, however, is what both Tagore and Alcott meant by this word: the faculties of thought and imagination that make us human and make our relationships rich human relationships, rather than relationships of mere use and manipulation. When we meet in society, if we have not learned to see both self and other in that way, imagining in one another inner faculties of thought and emotion, democracy is bound to fail, because democracy is built upon respect and concern, and these in turn are built upon the ability to see other people as human beings, not simply as objects.

Given that economic growth is so eagerly sought by all nations, especially at this time of crisis, too few questions have been posed about the direction of education, and, with it, of the world's democratic societies. With the rush to profitability in the global market, values precious for the future of democracy, especially in an era of religious and economic anxiety, are in danger of getting lost.

The profit motive suggests to many concerned leaders that science and technology are of crucial importance for the future health of their nations. We should have no objection to good scientific and technical education, and I shall not suggest that nations should stop trying to improve in this regard. My concern is that other abilities, equally crucial, are at risk of getting lost in the competitive flurry, abilities crucial to the health of any democracy internally, and to the creation of a decent world culture capable of constructively addressing the world's most pressing problems.

These abilities are associated with the humanities and the arts: the ability to think critically; the ability to transcend local loyalties and to approach world problems as a "citizen of the world"; and, finally, the ability to imagine sympathetically the predicament of another person.[2]

I shall make my argument by pursuing the contrast that my examples have already suggested: between an education for profit-making and an education for a more inclusive type of citizenship. I shall try to show how the humanities and arts are crucial both in primary/secondary and in university education, drawing examples from a range of different stages and levels. I do not at all deny that science and social science, particularly economics, are also crucial to the education of citizens. But nobody is suggesting leaving these studies behind. I focus, then, on what is both precious and profoundly endangered.

When practiced at their best, moreover, these other disciplines are infused by what we might call the spirit of the humanities: by searching critical thought, daring imagination, empathetic understanding of human experiences of many different kinds, and understanding of the complexity of the world we live in. Science education in recent years has rightly focused on educating the capacities for critical thinking, logical analysis, and imagining. Science, rightly pursued, is a friend of the humanities rather than their enemy. Although good science education is not my theme, a companion study on that topic would be a valuable complement to my focus on the humanities.[3]

The trends I deplore are worldwide, but I shall focus throughout on two very different nations that I know well: the United States, where I live and teach, and India, where my own global development work, much of it focused on education, has been conducted. India has a glorious tradition of humanities and arts education, exemplified in the theory and practice of the great Tagore, and I shall introduce you to his valuable ideas, which laid the foundations for a democratic nation and greatly influenced democratic education in Europe and the United States. But I shall also talk about the role of education in rural literacy projects for women and girls today, where the impetus to empower through the arts remains vital, and the effect of this empowerment on democracy can be clearly seen.

Where the United States is concerned, my argument will range over many types of educational experiments, from the use of Socratic self-examination in schools of many sorts to the role of arts organizations in plugging gaps in the public school curriculum. (The remarkable story of the Chicago Children's Choir in chapter 6 will provide a detailed case study.)

Education does not take place only in schools. Most of the traits that are my focus need to be nurtured in the family as well, both in the early years and as children mature. Part of a comprehensive public policy approach to the questions this manifesto raises must include discussion of how families can be supported in the task of developing children's capabilities. The surrounding peer culture and the larger culture of social norms and political institutions also play an important role, either supporting or subverting the work done by schools and families. The focus on schools, colleges, and universities is justified, however, because it is in these institutions that the most pernicious changes have been taking place, as the pressure for economic growth leads to changes in curriculum, pedagogy, and funding. If we are aware that we are addressing just one part of the story of how citizens develop, we can pursue this focus without distortion.

Education is not just for citizenship. It prepares people for employment and, importantly, for meaningful lives. Another entire book could be written about the role of the arts and humanities in advancing these goals.[4] All modern democracies, however, are societies in which the meaning and ultimate goals of human life are topics of reasonable disagreement among citizens who hold many different religious and secular views, and these citizens will naturally differ about how far various types of humanistic education serve their own particular goals. What we can agree about is that young people all over the world, in any nation lucky enough to be democratic, need to grow up to be participants in a form of government in which the people inform themselves about crucial issues they will address as voters and, sometimes, as elected or appointed officials. Every modern democracy is also a society in which people differ greatly along many parameters, including religion, ethnicity, wealth and class, physical impairment, gender, and sexuality, and in which all voters are making choices that have a major impact on the lives of people who differ from themselves. One way of assessing any educational scheme is to ask how well it prepares young people for life in a form of social and political organization that has these features. Without support from suitably educated citizens, no democracy can remain stable.

I shall argue that cultivated capacities for critical thinking and reflection are crucial in keeping democracies alive and wide awake. The ability to think well about a wide range of cultures, groups, and nations in the context of a grasp of the global economy and of the history of many national and group interactions is crucial in order to enable democracies to deal responsibly with the problems we currently face as members of an interdependent world. And the ability to imagine the experience of another—a capacity almost all human beings possess in some form—needs to be greatly enhanced and refined if we are to have any hope of sustaining decent institutions across the many divisions that any modern society contains.

The national interest of any modern democracy requires a strong economy and a flourishing business culture. As I develop my primary argument, I shall also argue, secondarily, that this economic interest, too, requires us to draw on the humanities and arts, in order to promote a climate of responsible and watchful stewardship and a culture of creative innovation. Thus we are not forced to choose between a form of education that promotes profit and a form of education that promotes good citizenship. A flourishing economy requires the same skills that support citizenship, and thus the proponents of what I shall call "education for profit," or (to put it more comprehensively) "education for economic growth," have adopted an impoverished conception of what is required to meet their own goal. This argument, however, ought to be subservient to the argument concerning the stability of democratic institutions, since a strong economy is a means to human ends, not an end in itself. Most of us would not choose to live in a prosperous nation that had ceased to be democratic. Moreover, although it is clear that a strong business culture requires some people who are imaginative and critical, it is not clear that it requires all people in a nation to gain these skills. Democratic participation makes wider demands, and it is these wider demands that my primary argument supports.

No system of education is doing a good job if its benefits reach only wealthy elites. The distribution of access to quality education is an urgent issue in all modern democracies. The Spellings Commission Report is to be commended for focusing on this question. It has long been a shameful feature of the United States, a wealthy nation, that access to quality primary/secondary education and especially access to college/university education is so unequally distributed. Many developing nations contain even larger disparities in access: India, for example, reports a male literacy rate of only around 65 percent, a female literacy rate of around 50 percent. Urban/rural disparities are larger. In secondary and higher education, there are even more striking gaps—between male and female, between rich and poor, between urban and rural. The lives of children who grow up knowing that they will go on to university and even postgraduate education are utterly different from the lives of children who in many cases do not get a chance to attend school at all. Much good work has been done on this question in many countries. It is not, however, the topic of this book.

This book is about what we should be striving for. Until we are clear about this, it is difficult to figure out how to get it to those who need it.

II

Education for Profit, Education for Democracy

We, the People of the United States, in Order to form a more perfect Union, establish Justice, insure domestic Tranquility, provide for the common defence, promote the general Welfare, and secure the Blessings of Liberty to ourselves and our Posterity, do ordain and establish this Constitution for the United States of America.

—Preamble, *Constitution of the United States,* 1787

WE, THE PEOPLE OF INDIA, having solemnly resolved to . . . secure to all its citizens:
JUSTICE, economic and political;
LIBERTY of thought, expression, belief, faith and worship;
EQUALITY of status and of opportunity
and to promote among them all
FRATERNITY assuring the dignity of the individual and the unity and integrity of the Nation;
IN OUR CONSTITUENT ASSEMBLY this twenty-sixth day of November, 1949, do HEREBY ADOPT, ENACT AND GIVE TO OURSELVES THIS CONSTITUTION.

—Preamble, *Constitution of India,* 1949

> Education shall be directed to the full development of the
> human personality and to the strengthening of respect for
> human rights and fundamental freedoms. It shall promote
> understanding, tolerance and friendship among all nations,
> racial or religious groups.
> —*Universal Declaration of Human Rights,* 1948

To think about education for democratic citizenship, we have to think about what democratic nations are, and what they strive for. What does it mean, then, for a nation to advance? In one view it means to increase its gross national product per capita. This measure of national achievement has for decades been the standard one used by development economists around the world, as if it were a good proxy for a nation's overall quality of life.

The goal of a nation, says this model of development, should be economic growth. Never mind about distribution and social equality, never mind about the preconditions of stable democracy, never mind about the quality of race and gender relations, never mind about the improvement of other aspects of a human being's quality of life that are not well linked to economic growth. (Empirical studies have by now shown that political liberty, health, and education are all poorly correlated with growth.)[1] One sign of what this model leaves out is the fact that South Africa under apartheid used to shoot to the top of development indices. There was a lot of wealth in the old South Africa, and the old model of development rewarded that achievement (or good fortune), ignoring the staggering distributional inequalities, the brutal apartheid regime, and the health and educational deficiencies that went with it.

This model of development has by now been rejected by many

serious development thinkers, but it continues to dominate a lot of policy-making, especially policies influenced by the United States. The World Bank made some commendable progress, under James Wolfensohn, in recognizing a richer conception of development, but things then slipped badly, and the International Monetary Fund never made the sort of progress that the Bank did under Wolfensohn. Many nations, and states within nations, are pursuing this model of development. Today's India offers a revealing laboratory of such experiments, as some states (Gujarat, Andhra Pradesh) have pursued economic growth through foreign investment, doing little for health, education, and the condition of the rural poor, while other states (Kerala, Delhi, to some extent West Bengal) have pursued more egalitarian strategies, trying to ensure that health and education are available to all, that the infrastructure develops in a way that serves all, and that investment is tied to job creation for the poorest.

Proponents of the old model sometimes like to claim that the pursuit of economic growth will by itself deliver the other good things I have mentioned: health, education, a decrease in social and economic inequality. By now, however, examining the results of these divergent experiments, we have discovered that the old model really does not deliver the goods as claimed. Achievements in health and education, for example, are very poorly correlated with economic growth.[2] Nor does political liberty track growth, as we can see from the stunning success of China. So producing economic growth does not mean producing democracy. Nor does it mean producing a healthy, engaged, educated population in which opportunities for a good life are available to all social classes. Still, everyone likes economic growth these days, and the trend is, if anything, toward increasing reliance on what I have called the "old paradigm," rather than toward a more complex account of what societies should be trying to achieve for their people.

These baneful trends have recently been challenged in both of the nations that are my focus. By choosing the Obama administration, U.S. voters opted for a group committed to greater equality in health care and a greater degree of attention to issues of equal access to opportunity generally. In India, this past May, in a surprise result, voters delivered a virtual majority to the Congress party, which has combined moderate economic reforms with a strong commitment to the rural poor.[3] In neither nation, however, have policies been sufficiently rethought with ideas of human development clearly in view. Thus it is not clear that either nation has really embraced a human development paradigm, as opposed to a growth-oriented paradigm adjusted for distribution.

Both nations, however, have written constitutions, and in both, the constitution protects from majority whim a group of fundamental rights that cannot be abrogated even to achieve a large economic benefit. Both nations protect a range of political and civil rights, and both guarantee all citizens the equal protection of the laws regardless of racial, gender, or religious group membership. The Indian list, longer than that of the United States, also includes free compulsory primary and secondary education, and a right to freedom from desperate conditions (a life commensurate with human dignity).[4] Even though the U.S. federal Constitution does not guarantee a right to education, numerous state constitutions do, and many add other social welfare provisions. In general, we are entitled to conclude that both the United States and India have rejected the notion that the right way for a nation to proceed is simply to strive to maximize economic growth. It is, then, all the odder that major figures concerned with education, in both nations, continue to behave as if the goal of education were economic growth alone.

In the context of the old paradigm of what it is for a nation to develop, what is on everyone's lips is the need for an education that promotes national development seen as economic growth. Such an education has recently been outlined by the Spellings Commission Report of the U.S. Department of Education, focusing on higher education. It is being implemented by many European nations, as they give high marks to technical universities and university departments and impose increasingly draconian cuts on the humanities. It is central to discussions of education in India today, as in most developing nations that are trying to grab a larger share of the global market.

The United States has never had a pure growth-directed model of education. Some distinctive and by now traditional features of our system positively resist being cast in those terms. Unlike virtually every nation in the world, we have a liberal arts model of university education. Instead of entering college/university to study a single subject, students are required to take a wide range of courses in their first two years, prominently including courses in the humanities. This model of university and college education influences secondary education. Nobody is tracked too early into a nonhumanities stream, whether purely scientific or purely vocational, nor do children with a humanities focus lose all contact with the sciences at an early date. Nor is the emphasis on the liberal arts a vestige of elitism or class distinction. From early on, leading U.S. educators connected the liberal arts to the preparation of informed, independent, and sympathetic democratic citizens. The liberal arts model is still relatively strong, but it is under severe stress now in this time of economic hardship.

Another aspect of the U.S. educational tradition that stubbornly refuses assimilation into the growth-directed model is its characteristic emphasis on the active participation of the child in inquiry and questioning. This model of learning, associated with a long Western philosophical tradition of education theory, ranging from Jean-Jacques Rousseau in the eighteenth century to John Dewey in the twentieth, includes such eminent educators as Friedrich Froebel in Germany, Johann Pestalozzi in Switzerland, Bronson Alcott in the United States, and Maria Montessori in Italy. In chapter 4 we shall discuss their ideas further. This tradition argues that education is not just about the passive assimilation of facts and cultural traditions, but about challenging the mind to become active, competent, and thoughtfully critical in a complex world. This model of education supplanted an older one in which children sat still at desks all day and simply absorbed, and then regurgitated, the material that was brought their way. This idea of active learning, which usually includes a large commitment to critical thinking and argument that traces its roots back to Socrates, has profoundly influenced American primary and to some extent secondary education, and this influence has not yet ceased, despite increasing pressures on schools to produce the sort of student who can do well on a standardized test.

I shall discuss these educational theories later, but I introduce them now in order to point out that we are unlikely to find a pure example of education for economic growth in the United States—*so far*. India is closer; for, despite the widespread influence of the great Tagore, who tried to build his school around the idea of critical thinking and empathetic imagining, and who founded a university built around an interdisciplinary liberal arts model, India's universities today, like those of Europe, have long been structured around the single-subject rather than the liberal arts paradigm. Tagore's university, Visva-Bharati (which means "All-the-World"), was taken over by the government, and now it is just like any other single-subject-model university, largely aiming at market impact. Similarly, Tagore's school has long ceased to define the goals of primary and secondary education. Socratic active learning and exploration through the arts have been rejected in favor of a pedagogy of force-feeding for standardized national examinations. The very model of learning that Tagore (along with the Europeans and Americans I have named) passionately repudiated—in which the student sits passively at a desk while teachers and textbooks present material to be uncritically assimilated—is a ubiquitous reality in India's government schools. When we imagine what education for economic growth would be like, pursued without attention to other goals, we are likely, then, to come up with something that lies relatively close to what India's government-sector schools usually offer.

Nonetheless, our aim is to understand a model that has influence around the world, not to describe a particular school system in a particular nation, so let us simply pose our questions abstractly.

What sort of education does the old model of development suggest? Education for economic growth needs basic skills, literacy, and numeracy. It also needs some people to have more advanced skills in computer science and technology. Equal access, however, is not terribly important; a nation can grow very nicely while the rural poor remain illiterate and without basic computer resources, as recent events in many Indian states show. In states such as Gujarat and Andhra Pradesh, we have seen the creation of increased GNP per capita through the education of a technical elite who make the state attractive to foreign investors. The results of this growth have not trickled down to improve the health and well-being of the rural poor, and there is no reason to think that economic growth requires educating them adequately. This was always the first and most basic problem with the GNP per capita paradigm of development. It neglects distribution, and can give high marks to nations or states that contain alarming inequalities. This is very true of education: Given the nature of the information economy, nations can increase their GNP without worrying too much about the distribution of education, so long as they create a competent technology and business elite.

Here we see yet another way in which the United States has traditionally diverged, at least in theory, from the economic growth paradigm. In the U.S. tradition of public education, ideas of equal opportunity and equal access, though never robust in reality, have always been notional goals, defended even by the most growth-focused politicians, such as the authors of the Spellings Report.

After basic skills for many, and more advanced skills for some, education for economic growth needs a very rudimentary familiarity with history and with economic fact—on the part of the people who are going to get past elementary education in the first place, and who may turn out to be a relatively small elite. But care must be taken lest the historical and economic narrative lead to any serious critical thinking about class, about race and gender, about whether foreign investment is really good for the rural poor, about whether democracy can survive when huge inequalities in basic life-chances obtain. So critical thinking would not be a very important part of education for economic growth, and it has not been in states that have pursued this goal relentlessly, such as the Western Indian state of Gujarat, well known for its combination of technological sophistication with docility and group-think. The student's freedom of mind is dangerous if what is wanted is a group of technically trained obedient workers to carry out the plans of elites who are aiming at foreign investment and technological development. Critical thinking will, then, be discouraged—as it has so long been in the government schools of Gujarat.

History, I said, might be essential. But educators for economic growth will not want a study of history that focuses on injustices of class, caste, gender, and ethnoreligious membership, because this will prompt critical thinking about the present. Nor will such educators want any serious consideration of the rise of nationalism, of the damages done by nationalist ideals, and of the way in which the moral imagination too often becomes numbed under the sway of technical mastery—all themes developed with scathing pessimism by Rabindranath Tagore in *Nationalism*, lectures delivered during the First World War, which are ignored in today's India, despite the universal fame of Tagore as Nobel Prize–winning author.[5] So the version of history that will be presented will present national ambition, especially ambition for wealth, as a great good, and will downplay issues of poverty and of global accountability. Once again, real-life examples of this sort of education are easy to find.

A salient example of this approach to history can be found in the textbooks created by the BJP, India's Hindu-nationalist political party, which also pursues aggressively an economic-growth-based development agenda. These books (now, fortunately, withdrawn, since the BJP lost power in 2004) utterly discouraged critical think-ing and didn't even give it material to work with. They presented India's history as an uncritical story of material and cultural tri-umph in which all trouble was caused by outsiders and internal "foreign elements." Criticism of injustices in India's past was made virtually impossible by the content of the material and by its sug-gested pedagogy (for example, the questions at the end of each chapter), which discouraged thoughtful questioning and urged assimilation and regurgitation. Students were asked simply to ab-sorb a story of unblemished goodness, bypassing all inequalities of caste, gender, and religion.

Contemporary development issues, too, were presented with an emphasis on the paramount importance of economic growth and the relative insignificance of distributional equality. Students were told that what matters is the situation of the *average* person (not, for example, how the least well-off are doing). And they were even encouraged to think of themselves as parts of a large collec-tivity that is making progress, rather than as separate people with separate entitlements: "In social development, whatever benefit an individual derives is only as a collective being."[6] This contro-versial norm (which suggests that if the nation is doing well, you must be doing well, even if you are extremely poor and suffering from many deprivations) is presented as a fact that students must memorize and regurgitate on mandatory national examinations.

Education for economic growth is likely to have such features everywhere, since the unfettered pursuit of growth is not condu-cive to sensitive thinking about distribution or social inequality. (Inequality can reach astonishing proportions, as it did in yester-day's South Africa, while a nation grows very nicely.) Indeed, put-ting a human face on poverty is likely to produce hesitation about the pursuit of growth; for foreign investment often needs to be courted by policies that strongly disadvantage the rural poor. (In many parts of India, for example, poor agricultural laborers hold down land that is needed to build factories, and they are not likely to be the gainers when their land is acquired by the government—even if they are compensated, they do not typically have the skills to be employed in the new industries that displace them.)[7]

What about the arts and literature, so often valued by democratic educators? An education for economic growth will, first of all, have contempt for these parts of a child's training, because they don't look like they lead to personal or national economic advancement. For this reason, all over the world, programs in arts and the humanities, at all levels, are being cut away, in favor of the cultivation of the technical. Indian parents take pride in a child who gains admission to the Institutes of Technology and Management; they are ashamed of a child who studies literature, or philosophy, or who wants to paint or dance or sing. American parents, too, are moving rapidly in this direction, despite a long liberal arts tradition.

But educators for economic growth will do more than ignore the arts. They will fear them. For a cultivated and developed sympathy is a particularly dangerous enemy of obtuseness, and moral obtuseness is necessary to carry out programs of economic development that ignore inequality. It is easier to treat people as objects to be manipulated if you have never learned any other way to see them. As Tagore said, aggressive nationalism needs to blunt the moral conscience, so it needs people who do not recognize the individual, who speak group-speak, who behave, and see the world, like docile bureaucrats. Art is a great enemy of that obtuseness, and artists (unless thoroughly browbeaten and corrupted) are not the reliable servants of any ideology, even a basically good one—they always ask the imagination to move beyond its usual confines, to see the world in new ways.[8] So, educators for economic growth will campaign against the humanities and arts as ingredients of basic education. This assault is currently taking place all over the world.

Pure models of education for economic growth are difficult to find in flourishing democracies since democracy is built on respect for each person, and the growth model respects only an aggregate. However, education systems all over the world are moving closer and closer to the growth model without much thought about how ill-suited it is to the goals of democracy.

How else might we think of the sort of nation and the sort of citizen we are trying to build? The primary alternative to the growth-based model in international development circles, and one with which I have been associated, is known as the Human Development paradigm. According to this model, what is important is the opportunities, or "capabilities," each person has in key areas ranging from life, health, and bodily integrity to political liberty, political participation, and education. This model of development recognizes that all individuals possess an inalienable human dignity that must be respected by laws and institutions. A decent nation, at a bare minimum, acknowledges that its citizens have entitlements in these and other areas and devises strategies to get people above a threshold level of opportunity in each.

The Human Development model is committed to democracy, since having a voice in the choice of the policies that govern one's life is a key ingredient of a life worthy of human dignity. The sort of democracy it favors will, however, be one with a strong role for fundamental rights that cannot be taken away from people by majority whim—it will thus favor strong protections for political liberty; the freedoms of speech, association, and religious exercise; and fundamental entitlements in yet other areas such as education and health. This model dovetails well with the aspirations pursued in India's constitution (and that of South Africa). The United States has never given constitutional protection, at least at the federal level, to entitlements in "social and economic" areas such as health and education; and yet Americans, too, have a strong sense that the ability of all citizens to attain these entitlements is an important mark of national success. So the Human Development model is not pie-in-the-sky idealism; it is closely related to the constitutional commitments, not always completely fulfilled, of many if not most of the world's democratic nations.

If a nation wants to promote this type of humane, people-sensitive democracy dedicated to promoting opportunities for "life, liberty and the pursuit of happiness" to each and every person, what abilities will it need to produce in its citizens? At least the following seem crucial:

- The ability to think well about political issues affecting the nation, to examine, reflect, argue, and debate, deferring to neither tradition nor authority

- The ability to recognize fellow citizens as people with equal rights, even though they may be different in race, religion, gender, and sexuality: to look at them with respect, as ends, not just as tools to be manipulated for one's own profit

- The ability to have concern for the lives of others, to grasp what policies of many types mean for the opportunities and experiences of one's fellow citizens, of many types, and for people outside one's own nation

- The ability to imagine well a variety of complex issues affecting the story of a human life as it unfolds: to think about childhood, adolescence, family relationships, illness, death, and much more in a way informed by an understanding of a wide range of human stories, not just by aggregate data

- The ability to judge political leaders critically, but with an informed and realistic sense of the possibilities available to them

- The ability to think about the good of the nation as a whole, not just that of one's own local group

- The ability to see one's own nation, in turn, as a part of a complicated world order in which issues of many kinds require intelligent transnational deliberation for their resolution

This is only a sketch, but it is at least a beginning in articulating what we need.

III

Educating Citizens: The Moral (and Anti-Moral) Emotions

A child's first sentiment is to love himself; and the second, which derives from the first, is to love those who come near him, for in the state of weakness that he is in, he does not recognize anyone except by the assistance and care he receives.
—Jean-Jacques Rousseau, *Emile: or, On Education*, Book IV, 1762

If democracy is maturity, and maturity is health, and health is desirable, then we wish to see whether anything can be done to foster it.
—Donald Winnicott, "Thoughts on the Meaning of the Word Democracy," 1950

Education is for people. Before we can design a scheme for education, we need to understand the problems we face on the way to making students responsible democratic citizens who might think and choose well about a wide range of issues of national and worldwide significance. What is it about human life that makes it so hard to sustain democratic institutions based on equal respect and the equal protection of the laws, and so easy to lapse into hierarchies of various types—or, even worse, projects of violent group animosity? What forces make powerful groups seek control and domination? What makes majorities try, so ubiquitously, to denigrate or stigmatize minorities? Whatever these forces are, it is ultimately against them that true education for responsible national and global citizenship must fight. And it must fight using whatever resources the human personality contains that help democracy prevail against hierarchy.

We Americans are sometimes told that evil is something that exists for the most part outside of us. Witness the rhetorical construction of an "axis of evil" that threatens our own good nation. People find it comforting to see themselves as engaged in a titanic "clash of civilizations" in which good democratic nations are pitted against allegedly bad religions and cultures from other parts of the world. Popular culture all too often feeds this way of seeing the world, by portraying the good characters' problems as ended by the death of some "bad guys." Non-Western cultures are not immune from these pernicious ways of thinking. The Hindu Right in India, for example, has long portrayed India as locked in a struggle between the good and pure forces of Hinduism and a set of dangerous "foreign elements" (by which they mean Muslims and Christians, although both groups are no less indigenous to the subcontinent than are Hindus).[1] In the process they have enlisted popular culture, retelling classical epic tales, in popular televised versions, in a way that removes all complexity in their depiction of "good" and "bad" characters and that encourages viewers to identify the "bad" characters with a contemporary Muslim threat.[2]

Such myths of purity, however, are misleading and pernicious. No society is pure, and the "clash of civilizations" is internal to every society. Every society contains within itself people who are prepared to live with others on terms of mutual respect and reciprocity, and people who seek the comfort of domination. We need to understand how to produce more citizens of the former sort and fewer of the latter. Thinking falsely that our own society is pure within can only breed aggression toward outsiders and blindness about aggression toward insiders.

How do people become capable of respect and democratic equality? What makes them seek domination? To answer such questions, we must pursue the "clash of civilizations" at a deeper level, understanding the forces within each and every person that militate against mutual respect and reciprocity, as well as the forces that give democracy strong support. One of our world's most creative democratic political leaders, Mahatma Gandhi, one of the primary architects of an independent and democratic India, understood very well that the political struggle for freedom and equality must first of all be a struggle within each person, as compassion and respect contend against fear, greed, and narcissistic aggression. He repeatedly drew attention to the connection between psychological balance and political balance, arguing that greedy desire, aggression, and narcissistic anxiety are forces inimical to the building of a free and democratic nation.

The internal clash of civilizations can be observed in many struggles over inclusion and equality that take place in modern societies: debates about immigration; about the accommodation of religious, racial, and ethnic minorities; about gender equality; about sexual orientation; about affirmative action. In all societies, these debates give rise to anxiety and aggression. In all, too, there are forces of compassion and respect. Particular social and political structures make a big difference to the outcome of these struggles, but we would do well to work, at least tentatively, with a widely shared narrative of human childhood, in order to locate within it problems and resources that both institutions and social norms can further develop or inhibit.[3] Pinning down the details of any such account is a matter for ongoing research and argument; investigating possible intervention points is equally complex. But we have to begin somewhere, and many proposals for education do not spell out a psychology of human development at all, so it remains unclear what problems need to be solved, or what resources we have for solving them.

Human infants are born, helpless, into a world that they did not make and do not control. An infant's earliest experiences contain a jolting alternation between blissful completeness, in which the whole world seems to revolve around the satisfaction of its needs— as in the womb—and an agonizing awareness of helplessness, when good things do not arrive at the desired moment, and the infant can do nothing to ensure their arrival. Human beings have a level of physical helplessness unknown elsewhere in the animal kingdom—combined with a very high level of cognitive sophistication. (We know now, for example, that even a baby one week old can tell the difference between the smell of its own mother's milk and milk from another mother.) Understanding what the "clash within" is all about requires thinking about this strange sui generis narrative: about human beings' strange combination of competence with helplessness; our problematic relationship to helplessness, mortality, and finitude; our persistent desire to transcend conditions that are painful for any intelligent being to accept.

As infants develop, they are increasingly aware of what is happening to them, but they cannot do anything about it. The expectation of being attended to constantly—the "infantile omnipotence" so well captured in Freud's phrase "His Majesty the baby"—is joined to the anxiety, and the shame, of knowing that one is not in fact omnipotent, but completely powerless. Out of this anxiety and shame emerges an urgent desire for completeness and fullness that never completely departs, however much children learn that they are but one part of a world of finite needy beings. And this desire to transcend the shame of incompleteness leads to much instability and moral danger.

To infants at this early point, other people are not fully real; they are just instruments that either bring what is needed or do not. Infants would really like to make their parents their slaves in order to control the forces that supply what they need. Jean-Jacques Rousseau, in his great work on education, *Emile*, saw in children's desire to enslave their parents the beginning of a world of hierarchy. Though Rousseau did not think children evil by nature—indeed he emphasized their natural instincts toward love and compassion—he understood that the very weakness and neediness of human infants gives rise to a dynamic that can create ethical deformation and cruel behavior, unless narcissism and the tendency to dominate are channeled in a more productive direction.

I have mentioned children's shame at their helplessness—their inability to achieve the blissful completeness that at certain moments they are led to expect.[4] This shame, which we may call "primitive shame," is soon joined to another very powerful emotion: disgust at one's own bodily waste products. Disgust, like most emotions, has an innate evolutionary basis, but it also involves learning, and it does not appear until the time of toilet training, when the child's cognitive capacities are quite mature. Society, therefore, has a lot of room to influence the direction it takes. Recent research on disgust shows that it is not merely visceral; it has a strong cognitive component, involving ideas of contamination or defilement. In disgust, experimental psychologists have concluded, we reject as contaminating those things—feces, other bodily waste products, and the corpse—that are the evidence of our own animality and mortality, and thus of our helplessness in important matters. Experimental psychologists working on disgust agree that in distancing ourselves from these waste products we are managing our anxiety about having, and ultimately being, waste products, and thus animal and mortal, ourselves.[5]

So described, disgust looks like it might give us good guidance, since the aversion to feces and corpses probably has utility, as a rough heuristic for the avoidance of danger. Although disgust tracks the sense of danger very imperfectly—many dangerous substances in nature are not disgusting, and many disgusting things are harmless—avoiding milk that smells disgusting is sensible, and easier than testing it in the lab each time.[6] Disgust soon begins to do real damage, however, in connection with the basic narcissism of human children. One effective way to distance oneself thoroughly from one's own animality is to project the properties of animality—bad smell, ooziness, sliminess—onto some group of people, and then to treat those people as contaminating or defiling, turning them into an underclass, and, in effect, a boundary, or a buffer zone, between the anxious person and the feared and stigmatized properties of animality. Children begin to do this very early, identifying some children as dirty or defiling. One example of this is the common child's game of making a folded paper device called a "cootie catcher," and using it, in play, to "catch" allegedly disgusting bugs, or "cooties," off of unpopular children who are stigmatized as dirty and disgusting.

Meanwhile, children learn from the adult societies around them, which typically direct this "projective disgust" onto one or more concrete subordinate groups—African Americans, Jews, women, homosexuals, poor people, lower castes in the Indian caste hierarchy. In effect, these groups function as the animal "other" by the exclusion of which a privileged group defines itself as superior, even transcendent. A common manifestation of projective disgust is to avoid bodily contact with members of the subordinate group, and even to avoid contact with objects that members of this group have touched. Disgust, as psychological research emphasizes, is full of irrational magical thinking. It is no surprise that ideas of contamination are ubiquitous in racism and other types of group subordination.

Projective disgust is always a suspect emotion, because it involves self-repudiation and the displacement of self-repudiation onto another group that is really just a set of bodily human beings like the ones doing the projecting, only more socially powerless. In this way, the narcissistic child's original desire to turn parents into slaves finds fulfillment—by the creation of a social hierarchy. This dynamic is a constant threat to democratic equality.[7]

This story appears to be universal in some form: studies of disgust in many societies reveal similar dynamics, and we must acknowledge, sadly, that all human societies have created out-groups who are stigmatized as either shameful or disgusting, and usually both. Nonetheless, there are numerous sources of variation that affect the outcome of this story, by shaping people's attitudes toward weakness, need, and interdependence. These include individual family differences, social norms, and law. Typically these three interact with one another in complex ways, since parents are themselves inhabitants of a social and political world, and the signals they send to their children are shaped by that world.

Because stigmatizing behavior seems to be a reaction to anxiety about one's own weakness and vulnerability, it cannot be moderated without addressing that deeper anxiety. One part of addressing it that Rousseau emphasized is learning practical competence. Children who can negotiate well in their environment have less need for servants to wait on them. But another part of the social response has to be directed at the sense of helplessness itself, and the pain it causes. Some social and familial norms creatively address this pain, sending a message to young people that human beings are all vulnerable and mortal, and that this aspect of human life is not to be hated and repudiated, but addressed by reciprocity and mutual aid. Jean-Jacques Rousseau made the learning of basic human weakness central to his whole scheme for education, saying that only cognizance of that weakness makes us sociable and turns us to humanity; thus our very inadequacy can become the basis of our hope of a decent community. He pointed out that the nobles of France did not have such an education; they grew up learning that they were above the common lot of human life. This desire for invulnerability fueled their desire to lord it over others.

Many societies teach the bad lessons that Rousseau's French nobles learned. Through both social and familial norms, they send the message that perfection, invulnerability, and control are key aspects of adult success. In many cultures, such social norms take a gendered form, and the disgust research has found that there is frequently a strong gendered component to the projection of disgustingness onto others. Males learn that success means being above the body and its frailties, so they learn to characterize some underclass (women, African Americans) as hyperbodily, thus in need of being dominated. This story has many cultural variations, which need to be studied closely before they can be addressed in a particular society. Even when a culture as a whole does not contain such diseased norms, individual families may still send bad messages, for example that the only way to succeed is to be perfect and to control everything. So the sources of social hierarchy lie deep in human life; the "internal clash" can never be fought on the terrain of the school or university alone, but must involve the family and the larger society. Schools, however, are at least one influential force in a child's life, and one whose messages we are likely to be able to monitor more easily than others.

A central part of disgust's pathology, we said, is the bifurcation of the world into the "pure" and the "impure"—the construction of a "we" who are without flaw and a "they" who are dirty, evil, and contaminating. Much bad thinking about international politics shows the traces of this pathology, as people prove all too ready to think about some group of others as black and sullied, while they themselves are on the side of the angels. We now notice that this very deep-seated human tendency is nourished by many time-honored modes of storytelling to children, which suggest that the world will be set right when some ugly and disgusting witch or monster is killed, or even cooked in her own oven.[8] Many contemporary stories for children purvey the same worldview. We should be grateful for artists who suggest to children the world's real complexity: the Japanese filmmaker Hayao

Miyazaki, for example, whose wild and fantastic films contain a view of good and evil that is both gentler and more nuanced, in which dangers may come from such real and complex sources as decent humans' relation to the environment; or Maurice Sendak, whose Max, in *Where the Wild Things Are*—which has now become an impressive film—romps with monsters that represent his own inner world and the dangerous aggression that lurks there. Nor are the monsters even entirely hideous; for the hatred of one's own internal demons is a frequent source of the need to project them outward onto others. Stories learned in childhood become powerful constituents of the world we inhabit as adults.

I have spoken of problems; what of resources? The other side of the internal clash is the child's growing capacity for compassionate concern, for seeing another person as an end and not a mere means. As time goes on, if all goes well, children come to feel gratitude and love toward the separate beings who support their needs, and they become increasingly able to imagine the world from these people's point of view. This ability to feel concern and to respond with sympathy and imaginative perspective is a deep part of our evolutionary heritage.[9] Primates of many sorts seem to experience some type of sympathy, as do elephants, and probably dogs. In the case of chimpanzees and probably dogs and elephants, sympathy is combined with empathy, that is, a capacity for "positional thinking," the ability to see the world from another creature's viewpoint. Positional thinking is not necessary for sympathy, and it is surely not sufficient; a sadist may use it to torture a victim. It is, however, a great help toward forming sympathetic emotions—which, in turn, are correlated with helping behavor. The striking experimental work of C. Daniel Batson shows that people who are asked to attend to a vivid narrative of someone else's plight, taking up the other person's point of view, are far more apt to respond sympathetically than people who are asked to listen in a more distanced way. Having responded with sympathetic emotion, they then choose to help the other person—if there is an option presented to them, not too costly, that makes such help possible.[10]

Children who develop a capacity for sympathy or compassion—often through empathetic perspectival experience—understand what their aggression has done to another separate person, for whom they increasingly care. They thus come to feel guilt about their own aggression and real concern for the well-being of the other person. Empathy is not morality, but it can supply crucial ingredients of morality. As concern develops, it leads to an increasing wish to control one's own aggression; children recognize that other people are not their slaves but separate beings with the right to lives of their own.

Such recognitions are typically unstable, since human life is a chancy business and we all feel anxieties that lead us to want more control, including control over other people. But a positive upbringing in the family, coupled with a good education later, can make children feel compassionate concern for the needs of others, and can lead them to see others as people with rights equal to their own. To the extent that social norms and dominant social images of adulthood or masculinity interfere with that formation, there will be difficulty and tension, but a good education can combat such stereotypes, giving children a sense of the importance of empathy and reciprocity.

Compassion is not reliable in and of itself. Like the other animals, human beings typically feel compassion toward those they know, and not toward those they don't know. We now know that even creatures as apparently simple as mice respond with discomfort to the bodily discomfort of other mice—*if* they have previously lived with those particular mice.[11] The pain of mice who are strangers, however, fails to produce the emotional contagion that is a precursor of sympathy. So the tendency to segment the world into the known and the unknown probably lies very deep in our evolutionary heritage.

We may also withhold compassion for other bad reasons; for example, we might wrongly blame the suffering person for her misfortune. Many Americans think that poor people bring poverty on themselves through laziness and lack of effort. Consequently, though often wrong about this, they do not feel compassion for poor people.[12]

These deficiencies in compassion can hook up with the pernicious dynamic of disgust and shame. When a particular subgroup in society has been identified as shameful and disgusting, its members seem beneath the dominant ones, and very different from them: animal, smelly, contaminated, and contaminating. So it becomes easy to exclude them from compassion, and hard to see the world from their point of view. White people who feel great compassion for other white people can treat people of color like animals or objects, refusing to see the world from their perspective. Men often treat women this way, while feeling sympathy for other men. In short, cultivating compassion is not, all by itself, sufficient to overcome the forces of enslavement and subordination, since compassion itself can become an ally of disgust and shame, strengthening solidarity among elites and distancing them yet further from the subordinated.

As young people near adulthood, the influence of the surrounding peer culture increases. Norms of the good adult (the good man, the good woman) make a great impact on the developmental process, as concern contends against narcissistic insecurity and shame. If an adolescent peer culture defines the "real man" as one who has no weakness or need, and who controls everything that he requires in life, such a teaching will feed infantile narcissism and strongly inhibit the extension of compassion to women and other people perceived as weak or subordinate. Psychologists Dan Kindlon and Michael Thompson observed such a culture operating among teenage boys in America.[13] To some degree all cultures portray manliness as involving control, but certainly American culture does, as it holds up to the young the image of the lone cowboy who can provide for himself without any help.

As Kindlon and Thompson stress, the attempt to be that ideal man involves a pretense of control in a world that one does not really control. This pretense is unmasked virtually every day by life itself, as the young "real man" feels hunger, fatigue, longing, often illness or fear. So an undercurrent of shame runs through the psyche of any person who lives by this myth; I am supposed to be a "real man," but I feel that I do not control my own surroundings, or even my own body in countless ways. If shame is a virtually universal response to human helplessness, it is far more intense in people who have been brought up on the myth of total control, rather than on an ideal of mutual need and interdependency. Once again, then, we can see how crucial it is for children not to aspire to control or invulnerability, defining their prospects and possibilities as above the common lot of human life, but, instead, to learn to appreciate vividly the ways in which common human weaknesses are experienced in a wide range of social circumstances, understanding how social and political arrangements of different kinds affect the vulnerabilities that all human beings share.

Rousseau argues that the educator must combat Emile's narcissistic desire to lord it over others from two directions. On the one hand, as he becomes physically mature, he must learn not to be helpless, not to need to be waited on hand and foot. To the extent that he is competent in the world, he will have less need to call on others the way a baby does, and he can less anxiously view them as people with projects of their own, who are not at his beck and call. Most schools, Rousseau thought, encourage helplessness and passivity by presenting learning purely abstractly, in a way that is detached from any practical employment. His educator, by contrast, would teach Emile to negotiate in the world he inhabits, making him a competent participant in that world's activities. On the other hand, Emile's emotional education must continue; through a wide range of narratives, he must learn to identify with the lot of others, to see the world through their eyes, and to feel their sufferings vividly through the imagination. Only in that way will other people, at a distance, become real and equal to him.

This story of narcissism, helplessness, shame, disgust, and compassion lies, I believe, at the heart of what education for democratic citizenship must address. But there are other psychological issues that the educator will need to keep in mind. Research in experimental psychology has revealed a number of pernicious tendencies that seem to be common to a wide range of societies. Stanley Milgram, in his well-known and by now classic experiments, demonstrated that experimental subjects have a high level of deference to authority. Most people in his often-repeated experiments were willing to administer a very painful and dangerous level of electric shock to another person, so long as the superintending scientist told them that what they were doing was all right—even when the other person was screaming in pain (which, of course, was faked for the sake of the experiment).[14] Solomon Asch, earlier, showed that experimental subjects are willing to go against the clear evidence of their senses when all the other people around them are making sensory judgments that are off-target; his rigorous and oft-confirmed research shows the unusual subservience of normal human beings to peer pressure. Both Milgram's work and Asch's have been used effectively by Christopher Browning to illuminate the behavior of young Germans in a police battalion that murdered Jews during the Nazi era.[15] So great was the influence of both peer pressure and authority on these young men, Browning shows, that the ones who couldn't bring themselves to shoot Jews felt ashamed of their weakness.

It is easy to see that these two tendencies lie close to the narcissism/insecurity/shame dynamic I described above. People like solidarity with a peer group because it is a type of surrogate invulnerability, and it is no surprise that when people stigmatize and persecute others, they do so, often, as members of a solidaristic group. Subservience to authority is a common feature of group life, and trust in a leader whom one sees as invulnerable is a well-known way in which the fragile ego protects itself against insecurity. In one sense, then, this research confirms the narrative I have just mapped out.

The research, however, tells us something new. It shows that people who have roughly similar underlying tendencies behave worse if their situation has been designed in a particular way. The Asch research showed that if even one dissenter was present, the subject was able to voice his or her own independent judgment; being utterly surrounded with people who made the mistaken judgment was what stopped the subject from saying what she thought. The Milgram research shows that allowing people to think that they are not responsible for their own decisions, because an authority figure has taken responsibility, produces irresponsible decisions. In short, the same people who might behave well in a situation of a different type behave badly in specific structures.

Still other research demonstrates that apparently decent and well-behaved people are willing to engage in behavior that humiliates and stigmatizes if their situation is set up in a certain way, casting them in a dominant role and telling them that the others are their inferiors. One particularly chilling example involves schoolchildren whose teacher informs them that children with blue eyes are superior to children with dark eyes. Hierarchical and cruel behavior ensues. The teacher then informs the children that a mistake has been made; it is actually the brown-eyed children who are superior, the blue-eyed inferior. The hierarchical and cruel behavior simply reverses itself; the brown-eyed children seem to have learned nothing from the pain of discrimination.[16] In short, bad behavior is not just the result of a diseased individual upbringing or a diseased society. It is a possibility for apparently decent people, under certain circumstances.

Perhaps the most famous experiment of this type is Philip Zimbardo's Stanford Prison Experiment, in which he found that subjects randomly cast in the roles of prison guard and prisoner began to behave differently almost right away. The prisoners became passive and depressed; the guards used their power to humiliate and stigmatize. Zimbardo's experiment was badly designed in a number of ways. For example, he gave elaborate instructions to the guards, telling them that their goal should be to induce feelings of alienation and despair in the prisoners. As a consequence, the findings are less than conclusive.[17] Nonetheless, his findings are at least highly suggestive and, when combined with the large amount of other data, corroborate the idea that people who are not individually pathological can behave very badly to others when their situation has been badly designed.

So, we have to look at two things: the individual, and the situation. Situations are not the only things that matter, for research does find individual differences, and the experiments are also plausibly interpreted as showing the influence of widely shared human psychological tendencies. So we need, ultimately, to do what Gandhi did and look deeply into the psychology of the individual, asking what we can do to help compassion and empathy win the clash over fear and hate. But situations matter too, and imperfect people will no doubt act much worse when placed in structures of certain types.

What structures are pernicious? Research suggests several.[18] First, people behave badly when they are not held personally accountable. People act much worse under shelter of anonymity, as parts of a faceless mass, than they do when they are watched and made accountable as individuals. (Anyone who has ever violated the speed limit, and then slowed down on seeing a police car in the rear-view mirror, will know how pervasive this phenomenon is.)

Second, people behave badly when nobody raises a critical voice. Asch's subjects went along with the erroneous judgment when all the other people whom they took to be fellow experimental subjects (and who were really working for the experimenter) concurred in error; but if even one dissenter said something different, they were freed to follow their own perception and judgment.

Third, people behave badly when the human beings over whom they have power are dehumanized and de-individualized. In a wide range of situations, people behave much worse when the "other" is portrayed as like an animal, or as bearing only a number rather than a name. This research intersects with Kindlon and Thompson's clinical observations. Young men anxiously bent on control learned to think of women as mere objects to be manipulated, and this ability to "objectify" women—encouraged by many aspects of our media and Internet culture—further fed their fantasies of domination.

Obviously enough, these situational features can to some extent become part of a basic education—that is, an education process can strengthen the sense of personal accountability, the tendency to see others as distinct individuals, and the willingness to raise a critical voice. We probably cannot produce people who are firm against every manipulation, but we can produce a social culture that is itself a powerful surrounding "situation," strengthening the tendencies that militate against stigmatization and domination. For example, a surrounding culture can teach children to see new immigrant groups, or foreigners, as a faceless mass that threatens their hegemony—or it can teach the perception of the members of these groups as individuals equal to themselves, sharing common rights and responsibilities.

SCHOOLS ARE BUT one influence on the growing mind and heart of the child. Much of the work of overcoming narcissism and developing concern has to be done in families; and relationships in the peer culture also play a powerful role. Schools, however, can either reinforce or undermine the achievements of the family, good and bad. They can also shape the peer culture. What they provide, through their curricular content and their pedagogy, can greatly affect the developing child's mind.

What lessons does this analysis suggest as we ask what schools can and should do to produce citizens in and for a healthy democracy?

- Develop students' capacity to see the world from the viewpoint of other people, particularly those whom their society tends to portray as lesser, as "mere objects"

- Teach attitudes toward human weakness and helplessness that suggest that weakness is not shameful and the need for others not unmanly; teach children not to be ashamed of need and incompleteness but to see these as occasions for cooperation and reciprocity

- Develop the capacity for genuine concern for others, both near and distant

- Undermine the tendency to shrink from minorities of various kinds in disgust, thinking of them as "lower" and "contaminating"

- Teach real and true things about other groups (racial, religious, and sexual minorities; people with disabilities), so as to counter stereotypes and the disgust that often goes with them

- Promote accountability by treating each child as a responsible agent

- Vigorously promote critical thinking, the skill and courage it requires to raise a dissenting voice.

This is a huge agenda. It must be implemented with constant awareness of local social circumstances, with rich knowledge of local social problems and resources. And it must be addressed not only through educational content but also through pedagogy, to which we turn next.

IV

Socratic Pedagogy: The Importance of Argument

I am a sort of gadfly, given to the democracy by the gods, and the democracy is a large, noble horse who is sluggish in its motions, and requires to be stung into life.

> —Socrates, in Plato, *Apology*, 30E

Our mind does not gain true freedom by acquiring materials for knowledge and possessing other people's ideas but by forming its own standards of judgment and producing its own thoughts.

> —Rabindranath Tagore, in a syllabus
> for a class in his school, c. 1915

Socrates proclaimed that "the unexamined life is not worth living for a human being." In a democracy fond of impassioned rhetoric and skeptical of argument, he lost his life for his allegiance to this ideal of critical questioning. Today his example is central to the theory and practice of liberal education in the Western tradition, and related ideas have been central to ideas of liberal education in India and other non-Western cultures. One of the reasons people have insisted on giving all undergraduates a set of courses in philosophy and other subjects in the humanities is that they believe such courses, through both content and pedagogy, will stimulate students to think and argue for themselves, rather than defer to tradition and authority—and they believe that the ability to argue in this Socratic way is, as Socrates proclaimed, valuable for democracy.

The Socratic ideal, however, is under severe strain in a world bent on maximizing economic growth. The ability to think and argue for oneself looks to many people like something dispensable if what we want are marketable outputs of a quantifiable nature. Furthermore, it is difficult to measure Socratic ability through standardized tests. Only a much more nuanced qualitative assessment of classroom interactions and student writing could tell us to what extent students have learned skills of critical argument. To the extent that standardized tests become the norm by which schools are measured, then, Socratic aspects of both curriculum and pedagogy are likely to be left behind. The economic growth culture has a fondness for standardized tests, and an impatience with pedagogy and content that are not easily assessed in this way. To the extent that personal or national wealth is the focus of the curriculum, Socratic abilities are likely to be underdeveloped.

Why does this matter? Think about the Athenian democracy in which Socrates grew up. In many respects its institutions were admirable, offering all citizens the chance to debate issues of public importance and insisting on citizen participation both in voting and in the jury system. Indeed, Athens went much further toward direct democracy than any modern society in that all major offices, apart from the commander of the army, were filled by lottery. Even though participation in the Assembly was to some extent limited by labor and residence, with urban and leisured citizens playing a disproportionate role—not to mention the exclusion of noncitizens, such as women, slaves, and foreigners—it was still possible for a non-elite male to join in and offer something to the public debate. Why did Socrates think that this thriving democracy was a sluggish horse that needed to be stung into greater wakefulness by the skills of argument that he purveyed?

If we look at political debate—as portrayed, for example, in Thucydides' *History of the Peloponnesian War*—we find that people did not reason with one another very well. Rarely if ever did they examine their major policy objectives, or systematically ask how the diverse things they valued could fit together. Thus we see that the first problem with lack of self-examination is that it leads to unclarity about goals. Plato illustrates this problem vividly in the dialogue *Laches*, when he shows that two of Athens's leading generals, Laches and Nicias, cannot give an account of military courage, even though they think they have it. They simply are not sure whether courage requires thinking about what is worth fighting for, what is ultimately in the city's interest. When Socrates proposes this idea, they like it, and yet their prior thinking had not incorporated it securely. Their utter confusion about one of their own central values might do no harm in a context in which decision-making is easy. With tough choices, however, it is good to be clear about what one wants and cares about, and Plato plausibly links their lack of self-scrutiny with the disastrous military and policy blunders of the subsequent Sicilian expedition, where Nicias was the chief architect of the bruising Athenian defeat. Socratic examination does not guarantee a good set of goals, but it at least guarantees that the goals pursued will be seen clearly in relation to one another, and crucial issues will not be missed by haste and inadvertence.

Another problem with people who fail to examine themselves is that they often prove all too easily influenced. When a talented demagogue addressed the Athenians with moving rhetoric but bad arguments, they were all too ready to be swayed, without ever examining the argument. Then they could easily be swayed back again to the opposite position, without ever sorting out where they really wanted to stand. Thucydides provides a vivid example of this in the debate over the fate of the rebellious colonists of Mytilene. Under the influence of the demagogue Cleon, who speaks to them of slighted honor, the Assembly votes to kill all the men of Mytilene and to enslave the women and children. The city sends out a ship with that order. Then another orator, Diodotus, calms the people and urges mercy. Persuaded, the city votes to rescind the order, and a second ship is sent out with orders to stop the first. By sheer chance, the first ship is becalmed at sea and the second one is able to catch up to it. So, many lives, and such an important policy matter, were left to chance rather than reasoned debate. If Socrates had gotten these people to stop, reflect, and analyze Cleon's speech, and to think critically about what he was urging, at least some would likely have resisted his powerful rhetoric and dissented from his call to violence, without needing Diodotus's calming speech.

Irresolution is frequently compounded by deference to authority and peer pressure, a problem endemic to all human societies, as we have seen. When argument is not the focus, people are easily swayed by the fame or cultural prestige of the speaker, or by the fact that the peer culture is going along. Socratic critical inquiry, by contrast, is utterly unauthoritarian. The status of the speaker does not count; only the nature of the argument. (The slave boy questioned in Plato's *Meno* does better than famous politicians, partly because he is not arrogant.) Teachers of philosophy betray Socrates' legacy if they cast themselves as authority figures. What Socrates brought to Athens was an example of truly democratic vulnerability and humility. Class, fame, and prestige count for nothing, and the argument counts for all.

Nor does the peer group count. The Socratic arguer is a confirmed dissenter because she knows that it is just each person and the argument wrestling things out. The numbers of people who think this or that make no difference. Someone trained to follow argument rather than numbers is a good person for a democracy to have, the sort of person who would stand up against the pressure to say something false or hasty that Asch's experiments demonstrate.

A further problem with people who lead the unexamined life is that they often treat one another disrespectfully. When people think that political debate is something like an athletic contest, where the aim is to score points for their own side, they are likely to see the "other side" as the enemy and to wish its defeat, or even humiliation. It would not occur to them to seek compromise or to find common ground, any more than in a hockey match the Chicago Blackhawks would seek "common ground" with their adversaries. Socrates' attitude toward his interlocutors, by contrast, is exactly the same as his attitude toward himself. Everyone needs examination, and all are equal in the face of the argument. This critical attitude uncovers the structure of each person's position, in the process uncovering shared assumptions, points of intersection that can help fellow citizens progress to a shared conclusion.

Consider the case of Billy Tucker, a nineteen-year-old student in a business college in Massachusetts who was required to take a series of "liberal arts" courses, including one in philosophy.[1] Interestingly, his instructor, Krishna Mallick, was an Indian American originally from Kolkata, familiar with Tagore's educational ideal and a fine practitioner of it, so his class stood at the intersection of two highly Socratic cultures. Students in her class began by learning about the life and death of Socrates; Tucker was strangely moved by this man who would give up life itself for the pursuit of the argument. Then the students learned a little formal logic, and Tucker was delighted to find that he got a high score on a test in this subject; he had never thought he could do well in something abstract and intellectual. Next, they analyzed political speeches and editorials, looking for logical flaws. Finally, in the last phase of the course, they did research for debates on issues of the day. Tucker was surprised to discover that he was being asked to argue against the death penalty, although he actually favored it. He had never understood, he said, that one could produce arguments for a position that one does not hold oneself. He told me that this experience gave him a new attitude toward political discussion: Now he is more inclined to respect the opposing position and to be curious about the arguments on both sides, and what the two sides might share, rather than seeing the discussion as simply a way of making boasts and assertions. We can see how this humanizes the political "other," making the mind see the opposing person as a rational being who may share at least some thoughts with one's own group.

Let us now consider the relevance of this ability to the current state of modern pluralistic democracies surrounded by a powerful global marketplace. First of all, we can report that, even if we were just aiming at economic success, leading corporate executives understand very well the importance of creating a corporate culture in which critical voices are not silenced, a culture of both individuality and accountability. Leading business educators with whom I have spoken in the United States say that they trace some of our biggest disasters—the failures of certain phases of the NASA space shuttle program, the even more disastrous failures of Enron and WorldCom—to a culture of yes-people, where authority and peer pressure ruled the roost and critical ideas were never articulated. (A recent confirmation of this idea is Malcolm Gladwell's study of the culture of airline pilots, which finds that deference to authority is a major predictor of compromised safety.)[2]

A second issue in business is innovation, and there are reasons to suppose that a liberal arts education strengthens the skills of imagining and independent thinking that are crucial to maintaining a successful culture of innovation. Again, leading business educators typically urge students to pursue a broad-based program and to develop their imaginations, and many firms prefer liberal arts graduates to those with a narrower training. Although it is difficult to construct a controlled experiment on such an issue, it does seem that one of the distinctive features of American economic strength is the fact that we have relied on a general liberal arts education and, in the sciences, on basic scientific education and research, rather than focusing more narrowly on applied skills. These issues deserve a full exploration, and it seems likely that, once fully investigated, they will yield further strong support for my recommendations.

But, we have said, the goal of democracies that want to remain stable cannot and should not be simply economic growth, so let us now return to our central topic, political culture. As we have seen, human beings are prone to be subservient to both authority and peer pressure; to prevent atrocities we need to counteract these tendencies, producing a culture of individual dissent. Asch, we recall, found that when even one person in his study group stood up for the truth, others followed, demonstrating that one critical voice can have significant consequences. By emphasizing each person's active voice, we also promote a culture of accountability. When people see their ideas as their own responsibility, they are more likely, too, to see their deeds as their own responsibility. That was essentially the point Tagore made in *Nationalism* when he insisted that the bureaucratization of social life and the relentless machinelike character of modern states had deadened people's moral imaginations, leading them to acquiesce in atrocities with no twinge of conscience. Independence of thought, he added, is crucial if the world is not to be led headlong toward destruction. In his lecture in Japan in 1917, he spoke of a "gradual suicide through shrinkage of the soul," observing that people more and more permitted themselves to be used as parts in a giant machine and to carry out the projects of national power. Only a robustly critical public culture could possibly stop this baneful trend.

Socratic thinking is important in any democracy. But it is particularly important in societies that need to come to grips with the presence of people who differ by ethnicity, caste, and religion. The idea that one will take responsibility for one's own reasoning, and exchange ideas with others in an atmosphere of mutual respect for reason, is essential to the peaceful resolution of differences, both within a nation and in a world increasingly polarized by ethnic and religious conflict.

Socratic thinking is a social practice. Ideally it ought to shape the functioning of a wide range of social and political institutions. Since our topic is formal education, however, we can see that it is also a discipline. It can be taught as part of a school or college curriculum. It will not be well taught, however, unless it informs the spirit of classroom pedagogy and the school's entire ethos. Each student must be treated as an individual whose powers of mind are unfolding and who is expected to make an active and creative contribution to classroom discussion. This sort of pedagogy is impossible without small classes, or, at the very least, regular meetings of small sections within larger classes.

But how, more specifically, can a liberal education teach Socratic values? At the college and university level, the answer to this question is reasonably well understood. As a starting point, critical thinking should be infused into the pedagogy of classes of many types, as students learn to probe, to evaluate evidence, to write papers with well-structured arguments, and to analyze the arguments presented to them in other texts.

It seems likely, however, that a more focused attention to the structure of argument is essential if these relatively mature students are to get the full immersion in active Socratic thinking that a liberal arts education makes possible. For this reason, I have argued that all colleges and universities should follow the lead of America's Catholic colleges and universities, which require at least two semesters of philosophy, in addition to whatever theology or religious courses are required.[3] The course Tucker took at Bentley College is one good example of the way in which such a course might be constructed. Typically, some philosophical texts will provide a jumping-off point—and the dialogues of Plato are second to none for their capacity to inspire searching, active thinking, with the life and example of Socrates up front to inspire. Tucker's course also paid attention to formal logical structure, and this is very useful, because it gives students templates that they can then apply to texts of many different types, from newspaper editorials and political speeches to their own arguments about issues they care about. Finally, getting students to practice what they have learned by debating in class and writing papers—all with detailed feedback from the instructor—allows them to internalize and master what they have learned.

There is no doubt that even well-prepared college undergraduates need this type of class in order to develop more fully their capacities for citizenship and respectful political interaction. Even smart and well-prepared students do not usually learn to take apart an argument without patient training. Such teaching, still relatively common in the United States, demands a great deal from faculty, and cannot be done simply through large lectures. This sort of intensive exchange with undergraduates is difficult to find in most European and Asian countries, where students enter university to read a single subject and do not have liberal arts requirements in the first place, and where the normal mode of teaching involves large lectures with little or no active participation by students and little or no feedback on student writing, a theme to which I shall return in the final chapter.

Tucker was already a high school graduate, but it is possible, and essential, to encourage Socratic thinking from the very beginning of a child's education. Indeed, this has often been done. It is one of the hallmarks of modern progressive education.

AT THIS POINT, we need to pause and think historically, since valuable models of Socratic education have long been developed, as a reaction against passive learning, in a wide variety of countries, and these can and should inform our search. Examining this rich and continuous tradition will give us reference points for further analysis and theoretical sources to enrich it.

Starting in the eighteenth century, thinkers in Europe, North America, and, prominently, India began to break away from the model of education as rote learning and to pursue experiments in which the child was an active and critical participant. These experiments unfolded in different places to some extent independently, but eventually with a lot of mutual influence and borrowing. Socrates was an inspirational figure in all of these reform movements, but they were also inspired, and perhaps more so, by the sheer deadness of existing schools, and by educators' feeling that rote learning and student passivity could not be good for citizenship or for life.

These school experiments all involved more than Socratic questioning. Much of what they proposed will concern us later, when we turn to world citizenship, and, especially, to play and the arts. In this chapter, we will need to lay out the basic ideas of each reform as a whole, in order to convey an overarching sense of each reformer's aims, giving ourselves a framework within which to investigate the idea of critical thinking. As we do this, however, we shall then focus on the Socratic component of each thinker's proposal, returning to other aspects of the education in chapters 5 and 6.

In Europe, a touchstone for all these experiments was Jean-Jacques Rousseau's great work *Emile* (1762), which describes an education aimed at rendering the young man autonomous, capable of his own independent thought and of solving practical problems on his own, without reliance on authority. Rousseau held that the ability to navigate in the world by one's own wits was a key aspect of making a child a good citizen who could live on terms of equality with others, rather than making them his servants. A great deal of Emile's education is therefore practical, and he learns by doing, a hallmark of all subsequent experiments in progressive education. The Socratic element is also prominent, however, as Emile is told nothing on authority from his teacher, but has to puzzle things out for himself, while the teacher simply probes and questions.

Rousseau did not set up a school, and *Emile* tells us little about what a good one might be like, since it depicts a single child with a tutor. In this sense, it is a profoundly nonpractical work, albeit philosophically deep. I shall therefore not dwell on the details of Rousseau's rather schematic philosophical account, preferring to focus on real educational experiments inspired by it. For Rousseau's ideas greatly influenced two European thinkers whose lives overlapped with his and who did establish schools in accordance with their views.

Swiss educator Johann Pestalozzi (1746–1827) took as his target the practice of rote learning and force-feeding, ubiquitous in schools of his day. The purpose of this sort of education, as he portrays it, was the creation of docile citizens who, as grown-ups, would follow authority and not ask questions. In his copious writings on education, some of them in fictional form, Pestalozzi describes, by contrast, an education aimed at rendering the child active and inquisitive through the development of his or her natural critical capacities. He presents the Socratic type of education as engaging and enlivening, and as just plain common sense—if one's goal is to train the mind, and not to produce herdlike obedience.

Pestalozzi's was not a narrow Socratism—he also gave significance, in education, to sympathy and affection. His ideal teacher was a maternal figure, as well as a Socratic challenger. He was ahead of his era in urging a complete ban on corporal punishment, and he emphasized the importance of play in early education. We should bear this larger context in mind as we study his Socratic proposals, although we shall investigate it further only in chapter 6.

In the influential novel *Leonard and Gertrude* (1781), Pestalozzi describes the reform of education in a small town, from an elite sort of indoctrination to a highly participatory and democratic form of mental awakening. Significantly, the agent of this radical change is a working-class woman, Gertrude, who exemplifies the maternal, the inquisitive, and the down-to-earth, all in one. In her village school she educates boys and girls from all social classes, treating them as equals and teaching them useful practical skills. ("Surely it is human beings we are educating, not brilliant mushroom growths," Pestalozzi at one point nicely observes.)

As with Emile's tutor, Gertrude gets the children to solve problems for themselves—Pestalozzi is the inventor of the concept of the "object lesson"—and she always encourages active questioning. Unlike Socrates, however, and to some extent unlike Rousseau's imaginary tutor, Gertrude is also affectionate and interested in cultivating the children's emotional capacities along with their capacity for criticism. In the 1801 book *How Gertrude Teaches Her Children*, Pestalozzi summarizes the principles of good schooling, making it clear that family love is the source and the animating principle of all true education. He suggests that young men and women should both become more maternal and loving; princes, he suggests, have made people aggressive for their own selfish ends, but human nature is in its essence maternal, and this maternal care is the "sacred source of patriotism and civic virtue." The Socratic element in Pestalozzi must always be understood in connection with this focus on emotional development.

Pestalozzi was too radical for his time and place; the various schools he started were all failures, and Napoleon, whom he approached, refused to take an interest in his ideas. Ultimately, however, he had a great influence on educational practice, as people from all over Europe came to visit and talk with him. His influence extended to the United States, and both Bronson Alcott and Horace Mann owe much to his ideas.

Slightly later, German educator Friedrich Froebel (1782–1852) conducted reforms of early education, in the spirit of Pestalozzi, that have changed the way young children in virtually all the world's countries begin their schooling. For Froebel was the founder and theorist of the "kindergarten," the year before "regular" schooling begins in which children are gently encouraged to expand their cognitive faculties in an atmosphere of play and affection, and one that, in a Socratic spirit, emphasizes children's own activity as the source of their learning. Like Pestalozzi, Froebel intensely disliked traditional models of education that viewed children as passive vessels into which the wisdom of the ages would be poured. He believed that education should focus on eliciting and cultivating the child's natural abilities through supportive play. The idea of the kindergarten is just this idea of a place where one learns and unfolds through play. Froebel has a lot of mystical views about the properties of certain physical objects, the so-called Froebel gifts: for example, the ball. By manipulating these symbolic objects, children learn to think actively and to master their environment. Modern kindergartens wisely leave Froebel's more mystical flights to one side, while retaining the core idea that children learn to unfold themselves by active thought, reciprocity, and the active manipulation of objects. Froebel believes that aggression is a reaction to natural helplessness and will drop away of its own accord when children learn to cope with the world around them, while their natural capacity for sympathy and reciprocity will be extended. In terms of our narrative of child development this is a bit too sanguine, but it goes in the right direction.

Because Froebel is concerned with extremely young children, Socratic techniques are not presented in any formal way, but their basis is firmly laid, by encouraging the child to be active, exploring and questioning rather than merely receiving. His idea that each child deserves respect, and that each (regardless of class or gender) should be an inquirer, is also thoroughly Socratic. Children all over the world today owe much to his contribution, since the idea of a type of early education through play in an environment of sympathy and love has created kindergartens more or less everywhere. This healthy idea is under pressure in our world, as children are pressed to drill at skills earlier and earlier in life, often losing opportunities to learn through relaxed playing.

Now our historical search moves to America, where European progressive reforms had a large and formative influence—perhaps explaining why the idea of liberal arts education has flourished here as it has not in Europe. Bronson Alcott (1799–1888) is best known today as the father of novelist Louisa May Alcott, and his school is lovingly depicted in her novels *Little Men* and *Jo's Boys*. Louisa depicts her father (represented as Jo's husband, Professor Bhaer) as following "the Socratic method of instruction"; he mentions that he is strongly influenced by Pestalozzi and Froebel. This appears to be an accurate characterization of Bronson Alcott's orientation, although we must add to these influences that of German idealism and the poetry of Wordsworth.

At the Temple School in Boston, founded in 1834, Alcott taught thirty boys and girls, ages six to twelve. (Teachers, too, were both female and male.) In 1839 the school admitted a black pupil; many parents withdrew their children, and the school closed. But during its brief existence, it carried on and extended the legacy of European progressive education. Alcott's methods are even more clearly Socratic than those of Pestalozzi and Froebel. Instruction always took the form of questions rather than assertions, as children were urged to examine themselves, both their thoughts and their emotions. "Education," he wrote, "is that process by which thought is opened out of the soul, and, associated with outward things, is reflected back upon itself and thus made conscious of the reality and shape [of things]. . . . It is self-realization." This is the language of Hegel, more than of Plato, but the bottom line, in terms of pedagogy, is Socratic. Education proceeds by questioning and self-scrutiny.

Like Froebel and Pestalozzi, Alcott diverged from Socrates in emphasizing emotional development and the role of poetry; classes often focused on the reading and interpretation of poems, Wordsworth being a particular favorite. Argument, however, was not slighted, and children were taught to take responsibility for defending their own ideas. For Alcott, as for his European predecessors, Socrates' approach is incomplete because it does not attend to the emotions and the imagination. Nonetheless, Socrates supplied a major part of what all sought: an emphasis on self-examination, personal accountability, and individual mental activity as antidotes to an education that formed students into pliant tools of traditional authority.

I shall pass more rapidly over a figure of considerable historical significance, Horace Mann (1796–1859). A contemporary of

Alcott's, but in some respects more politically mainstream, Mann might be the most influential figure in the history of American public education, before Dewey. Beginning with his pathbreaking reforms in the Massachusetts public schools, and ending with his work at Antioch College, which he founded, Mann, an abolitionist and a leading defender of women's equality, always stood for inclusiveness: for a liberal education (not just manual training) for everyone, without cost; for free libraries all over the state; and for high standards of teaching in the schools that non-elite pupils attended. As with the figures we have considered, then, Mann was a reformer who detested mere rote learning. His reforms were closely linked to an egalitarian and inclusive conception of democracy. He held that no democracy can endure unless its citizens are educated and active. In matters of inclusion, he was a radical, insisting on equal education of all children regardless of race or sex, on a serious attempt to eradicate class distinctions in education, and even (at Antioch) on equal pay for women in faculty positions. It was under his influence that Massachusetts, in 1852, passed the first state law requiring compulsory school attendance.

In some respects, Mann also shared pedagogical ideas with our earlier reformers; he rejected ineffective and authoritarian methods of teaching, seeking understanding rather than routine. His emphasis, however, was typically on basic competence, literacy, and numeracy; and his critique of authoritarian teachers (especially dogmatic religious teachers who based their teaching on the Bible) was therefore somewhat limited, focusing on the evident nonsuccess of such methods in teaching reading and writing. His insistence on getting children to understand what they were reading was defended less by appeal to the intrinsic worth of questioning and reflection than by pointing to the fact that children simply cannot learn reading by imitation, without understanding.

At Antioch, toward the end of his life, his radical inclusiveness continued (Antioch was the first U.S. college to educate women and men as full equals, and one of the first to educate black students and white students as equals). Meanwhile, his Socratic commitments became clearer: Antioch was the first college to emphasize classroom discussion, and it even offered independent study under faculty guidance.

Mann, in short, was a great practical reformer and a powerful champion of democratic educaton. At least where the schools were concerned, however, he focused above all on basic skills, and his commitment to Socratic and democratic values in the classroom was less central and less reflective than that of the other figures our historical excursus has discussed. With regret, we shall therefore leave him at this point and turn to a thinker who brought Socrates into virtually every American classroom.

Undoubtedly the most influential and theoretically distinguished American practitioner of Socratic education, John Dewey (1869–1952) changed the way virtually all American schools understand their task. Whatever the defects of American primary and secondary education, it is generally understood that stuffing children full of facts and asking them to regurgitate them does not add up to an education; children need to learn to take charge of their own thinking and to engage with the world in a curious and critical spirit. Dewey was a major philosopher, so, with him as with Rousseau, it will not be possible to go deeply into the elaborate ideas underlying his educational practice, but we can at least get a general idea of the connection he made between democratic citizenship and Socratic education.

Unlike all the theorists we have previously considered, Dewey lived and taught in a thriving democracy, and the production of active, curious, critical, and mutually respectful democratic citizens was his central goal. Despite Dewey's wariness of classical "great books"—because he saw such books turned into authorities, and name-dropping substituted for real intellectual engagement—Socrates remained a source of inspiration for him, because he brought lively rational and critical engagement to democracy. Another important inspiration was Froebel—to the exposition of whose ideas Dewey, rarely fond of writing about his distinguished predecessors, devotes considerable emphasis.[4]

For Dewey, the central problem with conventional methods of education is the passivity it encourages in students. Schools have been treated as places for listening and absorbing, and listening has been preferred to analyzing, sifting, and active problem-solving. Asking students to be passive listeners not only fails to develop their active critical faculties, it positively weakens them: "[T]he child approaches the book without intellectual hunger, without alertness, without a questioning attitude, and the result is the one so deplorably common: such abject dependence upon books as weakens and cripples vigor of thought and inquiry." Such a subservient attitude, bad for life in general, is fatal for democracy, since democracies will not survive without alert and active citizens. Instead of listening, then, the child should always be doing: figuring things out, thinking about them, raising questions. The change he wanted was, he said, "the change from more or less passive and inert recipiency and restraint to one of buoyant outgoing energy."[5]

The best way of rendering young people active, Dewey believed, was to make a classroom a real-world space continuous with the world outside—a place where real problems are debated, real practical skills evoked. Thus Socratic questioning was not just an intellectual skill, it was an aspect of practical engagement, a stance toward problems in real life. It was also a way of engaging with others, and Dewey always stressed the fact that in a good school pupils learn skills of citizenship by undertaking common projects and solving them together, in a respectful and yet critical spirit. Cooperative activity had, he believed, the additional dividend of teaching respect for manual labor and other trades; conventional schools often encourage an elitist preference for sedentary occupations. So Dewey's Socratism was not a sit-at-your-desk-and-argue technique; it was a form of life carried on with other children in the pursuit of an understanding of real-world issues and immediate practical projects, under the guidance of teachers, but without imposition of authority from without.

Typically, students would begin with a specific and immediate practical task: to cook something, or weave something, or maintain a garden. In the course of solving these immediate problems, they would be led to many questions: Where do these materials come from? Who made them? By what forms of labor did they reach me? How should we think about the social organization of these forms of labor? (Why is cotton so difficult to prepare for weaving? How did these practical problems interact with slave labor? Questions might fan out in many directions.)[6]

In short, the Socratic questioning grows from a real event, as children are led to treat these events, and their own activity, as "points of departure."[7] At the same time, by learning that producing cotton thread connects to all these complicated questions, children understand the complex significance of manual labor itself, and learn a new attitude toward it. Above all, children are learning through their own (social) activity, not by passively receiving; they thus model, and learn, citizenship. Dewey's experiments have left a profound mark on early education in America, as has his emphasis on the interconnectedness of the world, which we shall discuss in chapter 5, and his focus on the arts, which we shall discuss in chapter 6.

I have spoken so far of a Socratic method that had wide influence in Europe and North America. It would be wrong, however, to think that a Socratic approach to early education was found only there. Rabindranath Tagore in India conducted a closely related experiment, founding a school in Santiniketan, outside Kolkata, and, later, as mentioned, a liberal arts university, Visva-Bharati, to go with it. Tagore was far from being the only experimental educator in India in the early twentieth century. A similar progressive elementary school was set up in connection with Jamia Millia Islamia, a liberal university founded by Muslims who believed that their own Quranic tradition mandated Socratic learning.[8] All these experiments are closely connected to reforms of traditional laws and customs regarding women and children, such as raising the age of consent to marriage, giving women access to higher education, and, ultimately, giving them full citizenship in the new nation. Such reform movements existed in many regions. Tagore's experiment, however, was the most widely influential of these attempts, so I shall focus on it.

Tagore, who won the Nobel Prize for Literature in 1913, was one of those rare people who have world-class gifts in many different areas. He won the prize for his poetry, but he was also a superb novelist, short-story writer, and playwright. More remarkable, he was a painter whose work is valued more highly with the passing years, a composer who wrote more than two thousand songs, which are immensely loved in Bengali culture today—including songs later adopted as the national anthems of both India and Bangladesh—and a choreographer whose work was studied by founders of modern dance such as Isadora Duncan (whose dance idiom also influenced his) and whose dance dramas were eagerly sought out by European and American dancers who spent time at his school. Tagore was also an impressive philosopher, whose book *Nationalism* (1917) is a major contribution to thought about the modern state, and whose *The Religion of Man* (1930) argues that humanity can make progress only by cultivating its capacity for a more inclusive sympathy, and that this capacity can be cultivated only by an education that emphasizes global learning, the arts, and Socratic self-criticism. All these aspects of Tagore's genius made their way into the plan and daily life of his school. It was, perhaps above all, the school of a poet and artist, someone who understood how central the arts all are to the whole development of the personality.[9] Although this aspect of the school will occupy us only later, in chapter 6, it is important to bear in mind that it established the context within which his Socratic experiment unfolded. Both the Socratic and the artistic aspects of the school were inspired by a hatred of dead and imprisoning traditions that kept both men and women, as he saw it, from realizing their full human potential.

Tagore, like many people of his social class, was learned in Western thought and literature. (He translated Shakespeare's *Macbeth* into Bengali at the age of fifteen.) His educational philosophy may well have been influenced a bit by Rousseau, and a lot of his thought shows the influence of cosmopolitan French thinker Auguste Comte (1798–1857), who also influenced John Stuart Mill, who wrote an entire book about Comte.[10] Thus we could call Tagore and Mill cousins: Tagore's idea of the "religion of man" is similar to Mill's notion of a "religion of humanity," and both have their roots in Comte's idea of inclusive human sympathy. Tagore and Mill had a similar hatred of the tyranny of custom, and both were energetic proponents of individual liberty.

If Tagore was influenced by some Western thinking, however, influence went, even more clearly, in the other direction. His school was visited by countless artists, dancers, writers, and educators from Europe and North America who took his ideas home with them. He met and corresponded with Maria Montessori, who visited Santiniketan to observe his experiments. Leonard Elmhirst spent some years at Tagore's school, and then, returning to Britain, founded the progressive arts-oriented Dartington Hall, a school that is still a beacon of the type of education I am defending. Tagore may also have influenced John Dewey. Although such links are difficult to trace because Dewey rarely describes his influences, we know that Tagore spent extended periods in Illinois (visiting his son, who was studying agriculture at the University of Illinois) at just the time Dewey was establishing his Laboratory School. At any rate, whether there was influence or not, the ideas of the two men about critical thinking and the arts are closely related.

Tagore hated every school he ever attended, and he left them all as quickly as possible. What he hated was rote learning and the treatment of the pupil as a passive vessel of received cultural values. Tagore's novels, stories, and dramas are obsessed with the need to challenge the past, to be alive to a wide range of possibilities. He once expressed his views about rote learning in an allegory about traditional education called "The Parrot's Training."[11]

A certain Raja has a beautiful parrot, and he becomes convinced that it needs to be educated, so he summons wise people from all over his empire. They argue endlessly about methodology and especially about textbooks. "Textbooks can never be too many for our purpose!" they say. The bird gets a beautiful school building: a golden cage. The learned teachers show the Raja the impressive method of instruction they have devised. "The method was so stupendous that the bird looked ridiculously unimportant in comparison." And so, "With textbook in one hand and baton in the other, the pundits [learned teachers] gave the poor bird what may fitly be called lessons!"

One day the bird dies. Nobody notices for quite some time. The Raja's nephews come to report the fact:

> The nephews said, "Sire, the bird's education has been completed."
> "Does it hop?" the Raja enquired.
> "Never!" said the nephews.
> "Does it fly?"
> "No."
> "Bring me the bird," said the Raja.
> The bird was brought to him. . . . The Raja poked its body with his finger. Only its inner stuffing of book-leaves rustled.
> Outside the window, the murmur of the spring breeze amongst the newly budded asoka leaves made the April morning wistful.

The students of Tagore's school at Santiniketan had no such sad fate. Their entire education nourished the ability to think for oneself and to become a dynamic participant in cultural and political choice, rather than simply a follower of tradition. And Tagore was particularly sensitive to the unequal burden dead customs imposed upon women. Indeed, most of the searching questioners in his plays and stories are women, since dissatisfaction with their lot prods them to challenge and to think. In his dance-drama *The Land of Cards*, all the inhabitants of that land act robotically, playing out two-dimensional lives in ways defined by the card-picture they wear—until the women begin to think and question. So Tagore's Socratism, like his choreography, is shaped by his passionate defense of women's empowerment, as well as by his own unhappy experience in old-fashioned schools.

The school Tagore founded was in many ways highly unconventional. Almost all classes were held outside. The arts were woven through the whole curriculum, and, as mentioned, gifted artists and writers flocked to the school to take part in the experiment. But Socratic questioning was front and center, both in the curriculum and in the pedagogy. Students were encouraged to deliberate about decisions that governed their daily life and to take the initiative in organizing meetings. Syllabi describe the school, repeatedly, as a self-governing community in which children are encouraged to seek intellectual self-reliance and freedom. In one syllabus, Tagore writes: "The mind will receive its impressions . . . by full freedom given for inquiry and experience and at the same time will be stimulated to think for itself. . . . Our mind does not gain true freedom by acquiring materials for knowledge and possessing other people's ideas but by forming its own standards of judgment and producing its own thoughts."[12] Accounts of his practice report that he repeatedly put problems before the students and elicited answers from them by questioning, in Socratic fashion.

Another device Tagore used to stimulate Socratic questioning was role-playing, as children were invited to step outside their own point of view and inhabit that of another person. This gave them the freedom to experiment with other intellectual positions and to understand them from within. Here we begin to see the close link Tagore forged between Socratic questioning and imaginative empathy: Arguing in Socratic fashion requires the ability to understand other positions from within, and this understanding often provides new incentives to challenge tradition in a Socratic way.

OUR HISTORICAL DIGRESSION has shown us a living tradition that uses Socratic values to produce a certain type of citizen: active, critical, curious, capable of resisting authority and peer pressure. These historical examples show us what has been done, but not what we should or can do here and now, in the elementary and secondary schools of today. The examples of Pestalozzi, Alcott, and Tagore are helpful, but extremely general. They do not tell today's average teacher very much about how to structure learning so that it elicits and develops the child's ability to understand the logical structure of an argument, to detect bad reasoning, to challenge ambiguity—in short, to do, at an age-appropriate level, what Tucker's teachers did in his college-level course. Indeed, one of the great defects of Tagore's experiment—shared to some degree by Pestalozzi and Alcott—was that he prescribed no method that others could carry on in his absence. Prescribing is, of course, a delicate matter when what one wants to produce is freedom from the dead hand of authority. Froebel and Dewey offer more definite guidance because they do not simply theorize, they also recommend some general procedures in early education that others in different times and places have imitated and recast with great success. Dewey, however, never addressed systematically the question of how Socratic critical reasoning might be taught to children of various ages. Thus, his proposals remain general and in need of supplementation by the actual classroom teacher who may or may not be prepared to bring this approach to life.[13]

But teachers who want to teach Socratically have a contemporary source of practical guidance (which, of course, must be only part of an overall program to structure a Socratic classroom in which children are, throughout the day, active and curious participants). They can find very useful and yet nondictatorial advice about Socratic pedagogy in a series of books produced by philosopher Matthew Lipman, whose Philosophy for Children curriculum was developed at the Institute for the Advancement of Philosophy for Children at Montclair State College in New Jersey. Lipman begins from the conviction that young children are active, questioning beings whose capacity to probe and inquire ought to be respected and further developed—a starting point that he shares with the European progressive tradition. He and his colleague philosopher Gareth Matthews share, as well, the view that children are capable of interesting philosophical thought, that children do not just move in a predetermined way from stage to stage, but actively ponder the big questions of life, and that the insights they come up with must be taken seriously by adults.[14]

Lipman also thinks that children can profit early on from highly specific attention to the logical properties of thought, that they are naturally able to follow logical structure, but that it usually takes guidance and leading to help them develop their capacities. His series of books—in which complex ideas are always presented through engaging stories about children figuring things out for themselves—show again and again how this attention to logical structure pays off in daily life and in countering ill-informed prejudices and stereotypes. Two examples from his first book, *Harry Stottlemeier's Discovery*, will illustrate the basic idea. Harry (whose name, of course, alludes to Aristotle and to Aristotle's discovery—and Harry's—the syllogism) is playing around with sentences, and he makes a discovery: Some sentences cannot be "turned around." It is true that "all oaks are trees," but it is not true that "all trees are oaks." It is true that "all planets revolve about the sun," but it is not true that "all things that revolve about the sun are planets." He tells his discovery to his friend Lisa, but she points out that he is wrong when he says, "You can't turn sentences around." Sentences that start with "No" work differently. "No eagles are lions," but it is equally true that "no lions are eagles." The two friends happily embark on more language games, trying to sort out the terrain for themselves.

Meanwhile, real life obtrudes. Harry's mother is talking to her neighbor Mrs. Olson, who is trying to spread some gossip about a new neighbor, Mrs. Bates. "That Mrs. Bates," she says, ". . . every day I see her go into the liquor store. Now, you know how concerned I am about those unfortunate people who just can't stop drinking. Every day, I see them go into the liquor store. Well, that makes me wonder whether Mrs. Bates is, you know . . ."

Harry has an idea. "Mrs. Olson," he says, "just because, according to you, *all people who can't stop drinking* are *people who go to the liquor store*, that doesn't mean that *all people who go to the liquor store* are *people who can't stop drinking*." Harry's mother reproves him for interrupting, but he can tell from the expression on her face that she is pleased with what he has said.

Logic is real, and it often governs our human relations. Lots of slurs and stereotypes work in exactly this way, through fallacious inference. The ability to detect fallacy is one of the things that makes democratic life decent.

Harry and his friend Tony, with their teacher, are working out the difference between "every" and "only." "Every," like "all," introduces a sentence that cannot be turned around. Tony tells Harry that his father wants him to be an engineer like him because Tony is good in math. Tony feels that there is a problem with his father's argument, but he doesn't know quite what it is. Harry sees it: The fact that "all engineers are people who are good in math" doesn't mean that "all people who are good in math are engineers"—or, the equivalent, that "only engineers are good in math." Tony goes home and points this out to his father, who, luckily, is impressed by his son's acuity rather than annoyed by his failure to like his career advice. He helps Tony draw a picture of the situation; a large circle represents people who are good in math. A smaller circle inside this represents engineers, who are also good in math. But there is room for something else in the large circle, clearly. "You were right," says Tony's father with a faint smile, "you were perfectly right."[15]

All this takes place in the first few pages of the first book in Lipman's series, intended for children ages ten to fourteen. The series contains books that progress in complexity, but also cover different areas: mind, ethics, and so forth. The whole sequence, its rationale, and its pedagogical use are nicely explained in a book for teachers, *Philosophy in the Classroom*, which also discusses teacher training and the bare bones of an M.A. degree program in this area.[16] The series as a whole takes students to the point where they might begin to work through Plato's Socratic dialogues on their own, the point, roughly, where Billy Tucker's class begins, although it can be reached earlier by children with regular exposure to Socratic techniques.

This series is aimed at American children. Part of its appeal is familiarity, and the gentle humor that pervades it; so it will have to be rewritten as culture changes, and different versions will need to be devised in different cultures. What is important is to see that something like this is available, and that the teacher who wants to do what Socrates, Pestalozzi, and Tagore all did need not be an inventive genius like them. Some franchised methods are lifeless and excessively directive in themselves. Some become like this because of misuse. In this case, however, the humor and freshness of the books themselves, and their respect for children, are strong bulwarks against misuse. The books obviously do not constitute a complete Socratic approach to education. The whole ethos of the school and classroom has to be infused with respect for the child's active powers of mind, and for this Dewey is an especially powerful guide. They do, however, supply one component of such an education in an accessible and lively way.

The aspiration to make elementary and secondary classrooms Socratic is not utopian; nor does it require genius. It is well within the reach of any community that respects the minds of its children and the needs of a developing democracy. But what is happening today? Well, in many nations Socrates either was never in fashion or went out of fashion long ago. India's government schools are by and large dreary places of rote learning, untouched by the achievements of Tagore and his fellow Socratic educators. The United States is somewhat better off, because Dewey and his Socratic experiments have had widespread influence. But things are rapidly changing, and my concluding chapter will show how close we are to the collapse of the Socratic ideal.

Democracies all over the world are undervaluing, and consequently neglecting, skills that we all badly need to keep democracies vital, respectful, and accountable.

V

Citizens of the World

And so we have to labour and to work, and work hard, to give reality to our dreams. Those dreams are for India, but they are also for the world, for all the nations and peoples are too closely knit together today for any one of them to imagine that it can live apart. Peace is said to be indivisible, so is freedom, so is prosperity now, and so also is disaster in this One World that can no longer be split into isolated fragments.

> —Jawaharlal Nehru, speech on the eve of India's independence, 14 August 1947

Suddenly the walls that separated the different races are seen to have given way, and we find ourselves standing face to face.

> —Tagore, *The Religion of Man*, 1931

We live in a world in which people face one another across gulfs of geography, language, and nationality. More than at any time in the past, we all depend on people we have never seen, and they depend on us. The problems we need to solve—economic, environmental, religious, and political—are global in their scope. They have no hope of being solved unless people once distant come together and cooperate in ways they have not before. Think of global warming; decent trade regulations; the protection of the environment and animal species; the future of nuclear energy and the dangers of nuclear weapons; the movement of labor and the establishment of decent labor standards; the protection of children from trafficking, sexual abuse, and forced labor. All these can only truly be addressed by multinational discussions. Such a list could be extended almost indefinitely.

Nor do any of us stand outside this global interdependency. The global economy has tied all of us to distant lives. Our simplest decisions as consumers affect the living standard of people in distant nations who are involved in the production of products we use. Our daily lives put pressure on the global environment. It is irresponsible to bury our heads in the sand, ignoring the many ways in which we influence, every day, the lives of distant people. Education, then, should equip us all to function effectively in such discussions, seeing ourselves as "citizens of the world," to use a time-honored phrase, rather than merely as Americans, or Indians, or Europeans.

In the absence of a good grounding for international cooperation in the schools and universities of the world, however, our human interactions are likely to be mediated by the thin norms of market exchange in which human lives are seen primarily as instruments for gain. The world's schools, colleges, and universities therefore have an important and urgent task: to cultivate in students the ability to see themselves as members of a heterogeneous nation (for all modern nations are heterogeneous), and a still more heterogeneous world, and to understand something of the history and character of the diverse groups that inhabit it.

This aspect of education requires a lot of factual knowledge that students who grew up even thirty years ago almost never got, at least in the United States: knowledge about the varied subgroups (ethnic, national, religious, gender based) that comprise one's own nation, their achievements, struggles, and contributions; and similarly complex knowledge about nations and traditions outside one's own. (We always taught young people about small parts of the world, but until very recently, we never tried to cover the major nations and regions in a systematic way, treating all regions as significant.) Knowledge is no guarantee of good behavior, but ignorance is a virtual guarantee of bad behavior. Simple cultural and religious stereotypes abound in our world: for example, the facile equation of Islam with terrorism. The way to begin combating these is to make sure that from a very early age students learn a different relation to the world, mediated by correct facts and respectful curiosity. Young people must gradually come to understand both the differences that make understanding difficult between groups and nations, and the shared human needs and interests that make understanding essential if common problems are to be solved.

The task of teaching intelligent world citizenship seems so vast that it is tempting to throw one's hands up and say that it cannot be done, and that we had better stick with our own nation. Even understanding our own nation, of course, requires a study of its component groups, and this was rarely done in the United States in previous eras. It also requires understanding immigration and its history, which would lead the mind naturally to the problems elsewhere that give rise to immigration. Nor should one grant that there is any way of adequately understanding one's own nation and its history without setting that history in a global context. All good historical study of one's own nation requires some grounding in world history. Today, however, we need world history and global understanding for reasons that go beyond what is required to understand our own nation. The problems we face and the responsibilities we bear call on us to study the nations and cultures of the world in a more focused and systematic way.

Think, for example, of what it takes to understand the origins of the products we use in our daily lives: our soft drinks, our clothing, our coffee, our food. In earlier eras, educators who focused on democratic citizenship insisted on taking children through the complicated story of the labor that produced such products—as a lesson in the way their own nation had constructed its economy and its menu of jobs, rewards, and opportunities. This type of understanding was and is important for citizenship, since it prompts awareness of and concern for the different groups that make up our society, their different work and living conditions. Today, however, any such story is of necessity a world story. We cannot understand where even a simple soft drink comes from without thinking about lives in other nations. When we do so, it makes sense to ask about the working conditions of these people, their education, their labor relations. And when we ask such questions we need to think about our responsibilities to these people, as agents in the creation of their daily circumstances. How has the international network of which we consumers are a crucial part shaped their labor conditions? What opportunities do they have? Should we agree to be part of the causal network that produces their situation, or should we demand changes? How might we promote a decent living standard for those outside our borders who produce what we need—just as we usually feel ourselves committed to doing for workers within our borders?

To think about these questions well, young people need to understand how the global economy works. They also need to understand the history of such arrangements—the role of colonialism in the past, of foreign investment and multinational corporations more recently—so that they see how arrangements that in many cases were not chosen by local inhabitants determine their life opportunities.

Equally crucial to the success of democracies in our world is the understanding of the world's many religious traditions. There is no area (except, perhaps, sexuality) where people are more likely to form demeaning stereotypes of the other that impede mutual respect and productive discussion. Children are naturally curious about the rituals, ceremonies, and celebrations of other nations and religions, so it is a good idea to capitalize on this curiosity early, presenting stories of the world's varied traditions in an age-appropriate form, asking children from different backgrounds to describe their own beliefs and practices, and, in general, creating in the classroom a sense of global curiosity and respect. Children can just as well hear a Hindu or Buddhist story sometimes, and not always a classic American story expressing Protestant American values. (In fact, Hinduism and Buddhism are the most rapidly growing religions in the United States, so exposure of this sort will foster not just better global citizenship but better U.S. citizenship as well.) Curricula should be carefully planned from an early age to impart an ever richer and more nuanced knowledge of the world, its histories and cultures.

Our historical examples shed light on this goal as well. Returning to Tagore's school in India, let us ask how he set out to form responsible citizens of a pluralistic nation in a complex interlocking world. Tagore was preoccupied throughout his life with the problem of ethnic and religious conflict and with the need for international cooperation. In *Nationalism* he argues that India's most urgent challenge is to overcome divisions of caste and religion and the unjust, humiliating treatment of people because of their caste and religion. In *The Religion of Man* he extends his analysis to the world stage, arguing that the nations of the world are now face-to-face, and can only avoid cataclysm if they learn to understand one another and to pursue, cooperatively, the future of humanity as a whole. Tagore believed that the horrors of World War I were caused in large part by cultural failings, as nations taught their young people to prefer domination to mutual understanding and reciprocity. He set out to create a school that would do better, forming people who would be capable of cooperative, respectful international discussion.

Accordingly, Tagore's school developed strategies to make students global citizens, able to think responsibly about the future of humanity as a whole. A crucial starting point was to educate children, from an early age, about different religious and ethnic traditions. Festivals celebrated friendship among Hindus, Christians, and Muslims,[1] and children often learned about other customs through enacting festivals in the different religions.[2] Always the effort was to root the student's education in the local, giving each a firm grasp of Bengali language and traditions, and then to expand their horizons to embrace the more distant.

Visva-Bharati, the university founded by Tagore to extend his plan of liberal arts education to the university level, took the idea of world citizenship yet further, thinking of education as aspiring to a nuanced interdisciplinary type of global citizenship and understanding. A 1929 prospectus states:

> College students are expected to become familiar with the working of existing institutions and new movements inaugurated in the different countries of the world for the amelioration of the social condition of the masses. They are also required to undertake a study of interna-

tional organizations so that their outlook may become better adjusted to the needs of peace.[3]

This is but a partial description of the envisaged education, but it indicates that Tagore's goals had a lot in common with what I am recommending, although my proposals focus somewhat more than his on the need for factually accurate historical information and technical economic understanding.

Dewey also aimed education at global citizenship, from the earliest days of the child's schooling. Dewey always emphasized that history and geography should be taught in ways that promoted an adequate confrontation with the practical problems of the present. Economic history was a crucial part of what students needed to learn. Dewey believed that when history was taught with an exclusive focus on political and military aspects, democratic citizenship suffered: "Economic history is more human, more democratic, and hence more liberalizing than political history. It deals not with the rise and fall of principalities and powers, but with the growth of the effective liberties, through command of nature, of the common man for whom powers and principalities exist.[4] This statement seems relatively unsurprising today, since—whatever goes on in elementary school classrooms—most professional historians acknowledge the great importance of economic and social history, and the field has produced a large amount of excellent work concerning daily life and economic interaction. At the time, however, Dewey's was a radical statement, since both instruction and scholarship were preoccupied with "powers and principalities."

Dewey practiced what he preached. In his Laboratory School, for example, even very young children would learn to ask about the processes that produced the things they were using every day.

Weaving cloth, they would learn where the materials came from, how they were made, and what chain of labor and exchange led to the materials being there in the classroom. Typically this process would lead them far from home, not only into regions of their own country about which they previously knew little, but also into many other nations. Children also took care of animals and a garden, learning in that way what it was really like to care for such things on a daily basis, something that Dewey found more valuable than any number of artificial "object lessons" presented in the classroom, and something that also led to curiosity about forms of cultivation and care in other parts of the world. In general, as we have already seen, children learned to see their daily lives as continuous with what they learned in school, and to take from school something meaningful that they could employ in their daily lives. Dewey emphasized that such a focus on real-life activity is pedagogically useful as well; children are more lively, more focused, than when they are mere passive recipients. "[T]he great thing," he concluded, ". . . is that each shall have the education which enables him to see within his daily work all there is in it of large and human significance."[5]

We can see from this passage that Dewey is misunderstood if he is read as denigrating the humanities and suggesting that all learning has to be useful as a mere instrument to some immediate practical end. What Dewey (like Rousseau) disliked was abstract learning uncoupled from human life. His conception of human life, however, was a capacious and nonreductive one, which insisted on human relationships rich in meaning, emotion, and curiosity.

Education for global citizenship is a vast and complex subject that needs to involve the contributions of history, geography, the interdisciplinary study of culture, the history of law and political systems, and the study of religion—all interacting with one another, and all operating in increasingly sophisticated ways as children mature. And such education is also complex in its pedagogical demands. Dewey and Tagore rightly emphasized the importance of active learning for young children. As children grow older, although the connection to real life and activity should never be lost, understanding can become more theoretically sophisticated. There is no single prescription for how to do this, and many good ways in which it can be done. We can at least, however, describe some bad ways.

One bad way was the norm when I was in school: simply not to learn anything about Asia or Africa, their history and cultures, and not to learn anything about the major religions of the world, other than Christianity and Judaism. We did learn a little something about Latin America, but on the whole our eyes were fixed on Europe and North America. This means that we never saw the world as a world, never understood the dynamics of interaction among its component nations and peoples, never understood, even, how the products we use every day were produced, or where. How, then, could we ever think responsibly about public policy toward other nations, about trade relations, about the host of issues (from environment to human rights) that need to be confronted cooperatively in a way that transcends national boundaries?

Another bad way of teaching world history is that chosen by the Hindu Right in India, in the set of history and social studies textbooks they introduced during their brief ascendancy. These books did address the whole world—in a way. But they interpreted world history in the light of an ideology of Hindu supremacy.

Hindus are portrayed as a superior civilization, among the civilizations of the world. When they lived unmixed with other peoples, their society was an ideal one. Muslims, by contrast, are always portrayed as warlike and aggressive, trouble in the Indian subcontinent beginning with their advent. Moreover, so the books related, Hindus are indigenous to the land, whereas other ethnic and religious groups are foreigners. This is a myth, for the ancestors of India's Hindus almost certainly migrated into the subcontinent from outside, as both historical linguistics and the history of material culture demonstrate.[6] Global understanding is never advanced by lies, and yet the whole history of the world and its varied cultures was portrayed through this distorting lens.

These were errors of commission. Equally serious were errors of omission: the books' utter failure to portray differences of caste, class, and gender as sources of social disadvantage in early India, thus suggesting, wrongly, that early India was a glorious place of equality, where nobody was subordinated. The critical spirit that needs to inform all education for world citizenship was totally suppressed.

Finally, the books were pedagogically terrible. They failed to teach students how historical narratives are built up from evidence, and they taught no skills of sifting and evaluating evidence. Instead, they encouraged rote memorization, discouraged critical thinking, and suggested that there is simply one obvious right story (of Hindu glory and perfection) that no respectable person could challenge.[7]

As this bad example, and the good examples of FPSPI and Model UN, show us, world history, geography, and cultural study will promote human development only if they are taught in a way that is infused by searching, critical thinking. (The Model UN is a terrific way of encouraging this sort of learning, as is Future Problem Solving Program International, a multinational program in which children learn to design solutions to global problems using critical thinking and imagination.)[8] Even if the correct facts are presented to students, as was not the case here, history cannot be taught well if it is taught as a parade of facts, an all too common approach. Good teaching requires teaching children to see how history is put together from sources and evidence of many kinds, to learn to evaluate evidence, and to learn how to evaluate one historical narrative against another. Criticism also enters into classroom discussion about what has been learned; when a culture's history and economy are studied, questions should be raised about differences of power and opportunity, about the place of women and minorities, about the merits and disadvantages of different structures of political organization.

In curricular-content terms, the goal of world citizenship suggests that all young people should learn the rudiments of world history (with a focus on social and economic as well as political history), with increasing sophistication as time goes on, and should get a rich and nonstereotyped understanding of the major world religions.

At the same time, they should also learn how to "specialize"—how, that is, they might inquire in more depth into at least one unfamiliar tradition—in this way acquiring tools that can later be used elsewhere. In school this is often done well by allowing students to do research on some particular country. Despite all the defects of my own earlier education, my school was alert to the value of specialized research; in the fifth and sixth grades I was assigned reports on Uruguay and Austria, and I still remember a good deal more about these countries than what I learned in general about South America and Europe. We were even required to study the economies of these nations and their trade relations, though this study was limited to learning major exports and imports and domestic products.

There is no doubt that young children can begin to understand the principles of economics. Dewey had great success getting children to think searchingly about the origins of common products that they used and the mechanisms of exchange governing people's access to them. As children grow older, this knowledge can be made more complex, until at the end of high school children have a grasp of enough about the workings of the global economy to make informed decisions as consumers and voters.

A neglected aspect of learning for world citizenship is foreign language instruction. All students should learn at least one foreign language well. Seeing how another group of intelligent human beings has cut up the world differently, how all translation is imperfect interpretation, gives a young person an essential lesson in cultural humility. European schools on the whole perform this task very well, aware that children will actually need to become fluent in some other language (usually English). Schools in India also do pretty well in this area, in the sense that many children become fluent in English, in addition to learning their own mother tongue, and many of those whose mother tongue is not one of the widely used Indian languages (such as Hindi, Bengali, and Tamil) will often learn one of those in addition. Americans, by contrast, are complacent, used to thinking that English is all they will ever need to know. Our schools therefore begin foreign language learning much too late in most cases, missing the window of opportunity when language is most easily mastered and deeply internalized. Even if the language learned is that of a relatively familiar culture, the understanding of difference that a foreign language conveys is irreplaceable.

I have spoken of the study of other countries: What of one's own? Students should still spend a disproportionate amount of time on their own nation and its history, but they should do so as citizens of the world, meaning people who see their own nation as part of a complex interlocking world, in economic, political, and cultural relationships with other nations and peoples. Where the nation itself is concerned, they should be encouraged to be curious about the different groups that compose it and their varied histories and differential life opportunities. An adequate education for living in a pluralistic democracy must be multicultural, by which I mean one that acquaints students with some fundamentals about the histories and cultures of the many different groups with whom they share laws and institutions. These should include religious, ethnic, economic, social, and gender-based groups. Language learning, history, economics, and political science all play a role in facilitating this understanding—in different ways at different levels.

When students reach college or university, they need to develop their capacities as citizens of the world with greater sophistication. As with critical thinking, citizen-of-the-world education should form part of the basic liberal arts portion of the curriculum, whether the student's focus is business, or engineering, or philosophy, or physics. At this point, history courses can become more searching and complex, and the focus on historical method and the assessment of evidence more explicit. Similarly, courses on comparative religion can become more sophisticated and historically comprehensive.

Also, at this time, all students should acquire a solid understanding of the basic principles of economics and the operations of the global economy, building on earlier grounding. The usual introductory economics course is likely to be a bit insular, detaching principles and methods from a study of alternative economic theories and of globalization, but such courses do at least convey mastery of core techniques and principles. They can be usefully supplemented with a course on globalization and human values, taught from the point of view of both history and political theory. At the same time, all of the ideas involved in the history studied can be appreciated at a deeper level through a course in theories of social and global justice, taught from the point of view of philosophy and political theory. Students who have been lucky enough to have Socratic training in school will be especially well placed to embark on such a philosophy course. But if students get the education I am recommending here, they will all be studying philosophy at the college level as well, so they will be able to enter a more advanced course on justice with a solid preparation.

At the college level the need to "specialize" becomes all the more obvious, since a lot of what students need to learn about an unfamiliar culture requires in-depth familiarity with its history and traditions. Only then can they appreciate how differences of class, caste, and religion create different life opportunities; how urban lives differ from rural lives; how different forms of political organization lead to different human opportunities; how even the family organization and the roles of women and men can be subtly altered by public policies and laws. No student could be expected to learn all this about all the major countries of the world, so an in-depth focus on one unfamiliar tradition is essential. Once students learn how to inquire, and what questions to ask, they can transfer their learning to another part of the world (with which they might be dealing in their work).

Colleges cannot convey the type of learning that produces global citizens unless they have a liberal arts structure: that is, a set of general education courses for all students outside the requirements of the major subject. Nations that, like India, lack this structure can try to convey the same learning in secondary school, but this is really not sufficient for responsible citizenship. The more sophisticated learning that can only be done at a later age is indispensable in forming citizens who have real understanding of global issues and accountability for the policy choices made by their own nation. The need for liberal arts courses is being increasingly recognized in nations that do not have this structure. In India, for example, the highly prestigious Institutes of Technology and Management (IITs) have been in the vanguard of introducing humanities courses for all their participants. One professor at IIT-Mumbai told me that they regard these courses as playing a crucial function in promoting respectful interactions among students from different religious and caste backgrounds, as well as preparing them for a society in which such differences must be respectfully confronted.[9]

Does global citizenship really require the humanities? It requires a lot of factual knowledge, and students might get this without a humanistic education—for example, from absorbing the facts in standardized textbooks such as those used by the BJP, only with correct rather than incorrect facts, and by learning the basic techniques of economics. Responsible citizenship requires, however, a lot more: the ability to assess historical evidence, to use and think critically about economic principles, to assess accounts of social justice, to speak a foreign language, to appreciate the complexities of the major world religions. The factual part alone could be purveyed without the skills and techniques we have come to associate with the humanities. But a catalogue of facts, without the ability to assess them, or to understand how a narrative is assembled from evidence, is almost as bad as ignorance, since the pupil will not be able to distinguish ignorant stereotypes purveyed by politicians and cultural leaders from the truth, or bogus claims from valid ones. World history and economic understanding, then, must be humanistic and critical if they are to be at all useful in forming intelligent global citizens, and they must be taught alongside the study of religion and of philosophical theories of justice. Only then will they supply a useful foundation for the public debates that we must have if we are to cooperate in solving major human problems.

VI

Cultivating Imagination: Literature and the Arts

We may become powerful by knowledge, but we attain fullness by sympathy. . . . But we find that this education of sympathy is not only systematically ignored in schools, but it is
severely repressed.
　　　　　　—Rabindranath Tagore, "My School," 1916

It will be observed that I am looking at the highly sophisticated adult's enjoyment of living or of beauty or of abstract
human contrivance, and at the same time at the creative gesture of a baby who reaches out for the mother's mouth and
feels her teeth, and at the same time looks into her eyes, seeing her creatively. For me, playing leads on naturally to cultural experience and indeed forms its foundation.
　　　　　　—Donald Winnicott, *Playing and Reality*, 1971

Citizens cannot relate well to the complex world around them by
factual knowledge and logic alone. The third ability of the citizen,
closely related to the first two, is what we can call the narrative
imagination.[1] This means the ability to think what it might be

like to be in the shoes of a person different from oneself, to be an intelligent reader of that person's story, and to understand the emotions and wishes and desires that someone so placed might have. The cultivation of sympathy has been a key part of the best modern ideas of democratic education, in both Western and non-Western nations. Much of this cultivation must take place in the family, but schools, and even colleges and universities, also play an important role. If they are to play it well, they must give a central role in the curriculum to the humanities and the arts, cultivating a participatory type of education that activates and refines the capacity to see the world through another person's eyes.

Children, I have said, are born with a rudimentary capacity for sympathy and concern. Their earliest experiences, however, are typically dominated by a powerful narcissism, as anxiety about nourishment and comfort are still unlinked to any secure grasp of the reality of others. Learning to see another human being not as a thing but as a full person is not an automatic event but an achievement that requires overcoming many obstacles, the first of which is the sheer inability to distinguish between self and other. Fairly early in the typical experience of a human infant, this distinction gradually becomes evident, as babies sort out by coordination of tactile and visual sensations the fact that some of the things they see are parts of their own bodies and others are not. But a child may grasp that its parents are not parts of itself, without at all grasping that they have an inner world of thought and feeling, and without granting that this inner world makes demands on the child's own conduct. It is easy for narcissism to take charge at this point, casting others as mere instruments of the child's own wishes and feelings.

The capacity for genuine concern for others has several preconditions. One, as Rousseau emphasized, is a degree of practical competence: a child who knows how to do things for herself does not need to make others her slaves, and growing physical maturity usually frees children from total narcissistic dependence on others. A second precondition, which I have emphasized in talking about disgust and shame, is a recognition that total control is neither possible nor good, that the world is a place in which we all have weaknesses and need to find ways to support one another. This recognition involves the ability to see the world as a place in which one is not alone—a place in which other people have their own lives and needs, and entitlements to pursue those needs. But my second precondition constitutes a complex achievement. How would one ever come to see the world this way, from having seen it as a place where other shapes move around ministering to one's own demands?

Part of the answer to this question is no doubt given in our innate equipment. The natural interplay of smiles between baby and parent shows a readiness to recognize humanity in another, and babies quickly take delight in those recognitions. Another part of the answer, however, is given by play, which supplies a crucial third precondition of concern: the ability to imagine what the experience of another might be like.

One of the most influential and attractive accounts of imaginative play is that of Donald Winnicott (1896–1971), the British pediatrician and psychoanalyst. Winnicott began practicing psychoanalysis after many years of treating a wide range of children in his pediatric practice, which he continued throughout his life. His views are thus informed by a wider range of clinical experiences than are those of most psychoanalytic thinkers, a fact that he often emphasized, saying that he was not interested in curing symptoms, but in dealing with whole people, living and loving. Whatever their origin, his views about play in children's development have had a large and widespread cultural influence that does not depend on any prior sympathy with psychoanalytic ideas. (For example, it seems likely, as Winnicott himself believed, that Linus's security blanket in Charles Schultz's *Peanuts* cartoons is a representation of Winnicott's idea of the "transitional object.")

As a doctor who observed many healthy children, Winnicott had confidence in the unfolding of the developmental process, which would produce ethical concern—and the basis for a healthy democracy—as an outgrowth of early struggles, if things went well enough. He felt that development usually goes well, and that parents usually do a good job. Parents are preoccupied with their infants early on, and attend to their needs well, enabling the child's self to develop gradually and eventually express itself. (Winnicott typically used the word "mother," but he always emphasized that "mother" was a functional category, and that the role could be played by parents of either or both sexes. He also emphasized the maternal nature of his own role as analyst.)

At first the infant cannot grasp the parent as a definite object, and thus cannot have full-fledged emotions. Its world is symbiotic and basically narcissistic. Gradually, however, infants develop the capacity to be alone—aided by their "transitional objects," the name Winnicott gave to the blankets and stuffed animals that enable children to comfort themselves when the parent is absent. Eventually the child usually develops the ability to "play alone in the presence of its mother," a key sign of growing confidence in the developing self. At this point, the child begins to be able to relate to the parent as a whole person rather than as an extension of its own needs.

Play, Winnicott believed, is crucial to this entire phase of development. Having been raised in a repressive ultra-religious household in which imaginative play was strongly discouraged, and having experienced serious relational difficulties in adult life as a result, he came to believe that play was a key to healthy personality growth.[2] Play is a type of activity that takes place in the space between people—what Winnicott calls a "potential space." Here people (children first, adults later) experiment with the idea of otherness in ways that are less threatening than the direct encounter with another may often be.[3] They thus get invaluable practice in empathy and reciprocity. Play begins in magical fantasies in which the child controls what happens—as with the self-comforting games that a young child may play with its "transitional object." But as confidence and trust develop in interpersonal play with the parents or with other children, control is relaxed and the child is able to experiment with vulnerability and surprise in ways that could be distressing outside the play setting, but are delightful in play. Think, for example, of the tireless delight with which small children play at the disappearance and reappearance of a parent, or a cherished object.

As play develops, the child develops a capacity for wonder. Simple nursery rhymes already urge children to put themselves in the place of a small animal, another child, even an inanimate object. "Twinkle, twinkle, little star, how I wonder what you are," is a paradigm of wonder, since it involves looking at a shape and endowing that shape with an inner world. That is what children ultimately must be able to do with other people. Nursery rhymes and stories are thus a crucial preparation for concern in life.[4] The presence of the other, which can be very threatening, becomes, in play, a delightful source of curiosity, and this curiosity contributes toward the development of healthy attitudes in friendship, love, and, later, political life.

Winnicott understood that the "potential space" between people does not close up just because they become adults. Life is full of occasions for wonder and play, and he emphasized that sexual relations, and intimacy generally, are areas in which the capacity for play is crucial. People can close up, forgetting the inner world of others, or they can retain and further develop the capacity to endow the forms of others, in imagination, with inner life. Everyone who knew Winnicott was struck by his unusual capacity to connect with others through play and empathy. With patients, particularly child patients, he had a tireless ability to enter the world of the child's games and cherished objects, their stuffed animals, their fantasies about a sibling's birth. But play, for him, did not cease where the "adult world" began. His adult patients, too, praised his capacity for taking the position of the other. Sixty-year-old analyst Harry Guntrip described this gift in a journal of his analysis with Winnicott: "I could let my tension go and develop and relax because you were present in my inner world." Play was also a feature of Winnicott's non-therapeutic relationships. He and his wife were famous for their elaborate jokes and pranks; his papers contain silly drawings and poems they wrote to each other during boring meetings.[5]

Winnicott often emphasized that play has an important role in shaping democratic citizenship. Democratic equality brings vulnerability. As one of his patients perceptively remarked, "The alarming thing about equality is that we are then both children and the question is, where is father? We know where we are if one of us is the father."[6] Play teaches people to be capable of living with others without control; it connects the experiences of vulnerability and surprise to curiosity and wonder, rather than to crippling anxiety.

How do adults sustain and develop their capacity for play after they have left behind the world of children's games? Winnicott argued that a key role is played by the arts. He held that a primary function of art in all human cultures is to preserve and enhance the cultivation of the "play space," and he saw the role of the arts in human life as, above all, that of nourishing and extending the capacity for empathy. In the sophisticated response to a complex work of art, he saw a continuation of the baby's delight in games and role-playing.

The earlier progressive educators, whose views we described in chapter 4, though unacquainted with Winnicott's writings, understood from their own reflection and experience his basic insight that play is crucial to the development of a healthy personality. They found fault with traditional schools for not comprehending the educational value of play, and they insisted that play be incorporated into the structure of education, both early and late. Froebel focused on the need of very young children to explore their environment through manipulating objects and using their imaginations to endow simple shapes (the sphere, the cube) with stories and personalities. Pestalozzi's fictional heroine Gertrude saw that passive rote learning deadened the personality, whereas practical activities, carried on in a playful spirit, enriched the personality.

Such educators realized early on that the most important contribution of the arts to life after school was that of strengthening the personality's emotional and imaginative resources, giving children abilities to understand both self and others that they would otherwise lack. We do not automatically see another human being as spacious and deep, having thoughts, spiritual longings, and emotions. It is all too easy to see another person as just a body—which we might then think we can use for our ends, bad or good. It is an achievement to see a soul in that body, and this achievement is supported by poetry and the arts, which ask us to wonder about the inner world of that shape we see—and, too, to wonder about ourselves and our own depths.

Technical and factual education can easily lack this cultivation. Philosopher John Stuart Mill (1806–1873), as a precocious child, received a superb education in languages, history, and the sciences, but this education did not cultivate his emotional or imaginative resources. As a young adult, he suffered a crippling depression. He credited his eventual recovery to the influence of Wordsworth's poetry, which educated his emotions and made it possible for him to look for emotion in others. In later life, Mill developed an account of what he called the "religion of humanity" based on the cultivation of sympathy he had found through his experience of poetry.

At around the same time, in America, Bronson Alcott, whose Socratic pedagogy in the Temple School we studied in chapter 4, gave the same idea of poetic education a curricular shape. Drawing on Wordsworth, and using his poems often in the classroom, he held that poetry cultivates a child's inner space, nourishing both imaginative and emotional capacities. In Louisa Alcott's *Little Men*, the imaginative games played at Plumtree School are just as important as the intellectual lessons, and are interwoven with them. Both lessons and games, in turn, are enlivened with a spirit of loving reciprocity, as the school, run like a large family, remarkably anticipates Winnicott's idea that sophisticated artistic play is a continuation of the play between parents and child.

The most elaborate development of the arts as a linchpin of early education, however, awaited the twentieth century and the theoretically sophisticated school experiments of Tagore in India and Dewey in the United States. Dewey wrote a good deal about the arts as key ingredients in a democratic society, and it is clear even today that the cultivation of imagination through music and theater plays a key role in the Laboratory School. Dewey insisted that what is of importance for children is not "fine art," meaning some contemplative exercise in which children learn to "appreciate" works of art as things cut off from the real world. Nor should children be taught to believe that imagination is pertinent only in the domain of the unreal or imaginary. Instead, they need to see an imaginative dimension in all their interactions, and to see works of art as just one domain in which imagination is cultivated. "[T]he difference between play and what is regarded as serious employment should be not a difference between the presence and absence of imagination, but a difference in the materials with which imagination is occupied." In a successful school, children will come to see that imagination is required to deal with anything that lies "beyond the scope of direct physical response."[7] And this would include pretty much everything that matters: a conversation with a friend, a study of economic transactions, a scientific experiment.

Let me focus here, however, on Tagore's use of the arts, since his school was the school of an artist, and one that gave music, theater, poetry, painting, and dance all a central role from the very start of a child's enrollment. In chapter 4 we studied Tagore's commitment to Socratic questioning. But Socratic inquiry can appear cold and unemotional, and the relentless pursuit of logical argument can risk stunting other parts of the personality, a danger that Tagore foresaw and determined to avoid. For him, the primary role played by the arts was the cultivation of sympathy, and he noted that this role for education—perhaps one of its most important roles—had been "systematically ignored" and "severely repressed" by standard models of education. The arts, in his view, promote both inner self-cultivation and responsiveness to others. The two typically develop in tandem, since one can hardly cherish in another what one has not explored in oneself.

As we have mentioned, Tagore used role-playing throughout the school day, as intellectual positions were explored by asking children to take up unfamiliar postures of thought. This role-playing, we can now add, was no mere logical game. It was a way of cultivating sympathy hand in hand with the cultivation of the logical faculties. He also used role-playing to explore the difficult area of religious difference, as students were urged to celebrate the rituals and ceremonies of religions not their own, understanding the unfamiliar through imaginative participation. Above all, though, Tagore used elaborate theatrical productions, mingling drama, music, and dance, to get children to explore different roles with the full participation of their bodies, taking up unfamiliar stances and gestures. Dance was a key part of the school for both boys and girls, since Tagore understood that exploration of the unfamiliar requires the willingness to put aside bodily stiffness and shame in order to inhabit a role.

Women were his particular concern, since he saw that women were typically brought up to be ashamed of their bodies and unable to move freely, particularly in the presence of men. A lifelong advocate of women's freedom and equality, he saw that simply telling girls to move more freely would be unlikely to overcome years of repression, but giving them precisely choreographed moves to perform, leaping from here to there, would be a more successful incentive to freedom. (Tagore's sister-in-law invented the blouse that is ubiquitously worn, today, with the sari, since he asked her to devise something that would allow women to move freely without fearing that their sari would expose their bodies in an inappropriate way.) At the same time, men too explored challenging roles in dance, under the aegis of Tagore, a great dancer as well as a famous choreographer, and known for his sinuous and androgynous movements. Explicit themes of gender equality were common in the dramas, as in *Land of Cards*, described in chapter 4, in which women take the lead in rejecting ossified traditions.

Amita Sen, the mother of Nobel Prize–winning Amartya Sen, was a pupil in the school from her earliest childhood days, since her father, a well-known expert on the history of the Hindu religion, went there to teach shortly after the school's founding. A small child playing in the garden near Tagore's window, she inspired his well-known poem "Chota mai," in which he describes how a little girl disturbed his work. Later, as a young bride, she inspired another well-known Tagore poem, about a young woman "stepping into the waters of life, unafraid." In between, she was a pupil in the school, and she proved to be one of its most talented dancers, so she took on leading roles in those dance dramas. Later, she wrote two books about the school; one, *Joy in All Work*, has been translated into English, and it describes Tagore's activity as dancer and choreographer.[8]

Amita Sen understood that the purpose of Tagore's dance dramas was not just the production of some fine artworks, but also the cultivation of emotion and imagination in his pupils. Her detailed account of the role of theater and dance in the school shows how all the "regular" education in Santiniketan, the education hat enabled these students to perform well in standard examinations, was infused with passion, creativity, and delight because of the way in which education was combined with dance and song.

> His dance was a dance of emotion. The playful clouds in the sky, the shivering of the wind in the leaves, light glistening on the grass, moonlight flooding the earth, the blossoming and fading of flowers, the murmur of dry leaves—the pulsing of joy in a man's heart, or the pangs of sorrow, are all expressed in this expressive dance's movements and expressions.[9]

We should bear in mind that we hear the voice of an older woman recalling her childhood experience. How extraordinary that the emotions and the poetry of the child live on so vigorously in the woman, and what a tribute this is to the capacity of this sort of education for a kind of enlivening of the personality that continues on in one's life when all learned facts are forgotten. Of course, as her book makes clear, this could not be done by simply leaving children on their own to play around; instruction in the arts requires discipline and ambition, if it is to stretch and extend the capacities for both empathy and expression.

Instruction in literature and the arts can cultivate sympathy in many ways, through engagement with many different works of literature, music, fine art, and dance. Tagore was ahead of the West in his focus on music and dance, which we in the United States cultivate only intermittently. But thought needs to be given to what the student's particular blind spots are likely to be, and texts should be chosen in consequence. For all societies at all times have their particular blind spots, groups within their culture and also groups abroad that are especially likely to be dealt with ignorantly and obtusely. Works of art (whether literary or musical or theatrical) can be chosen to promote criticism of this obtuseness, and a more adequate vision of the unseen. Ralph Ellison, in a later essay about his great novel *Invisible Man*, wrote that a novel such as his could be "a raft of perception, hope, and entertainment" on which American culture could "negotiate the snags and whirlpools" that stand between us and our democratic ideal.[10] His novel, of course, takes the "inner eyes" of the white reader as its theme and its target. The hero is invisible to white society, but he tells us that this invisibility is an imaginative and educational failing on the part of white people, not a biological accident on his. Through the imagination, Ellison suggests, we are able to develop our ability to see the full humanness of the people with whom our encounters in daily life are especially likely to be superficial at best, at worst infected by demeaning stereotypes. And stereotypes usually abound when our world has constructed sharp separations between groups, and suspicions that make any encounter difficult.

In Ellison's America, the central challenge for the "inner eyes" was that of race, a stigmatized position almost impossible for the conventional white reader to inhabit. For Tagore, as we have seen, a particular cultural blind spot was the agency and intelligence of women, and he ingeniously devised ways to promote a fuller curiosity and respect between the sexes. Both writers claim that information about social stigma and inequality will not convey the full understanding a democratic citizen needs without a participatory experience of the stigmatized position, which theater and literature both enable. The reflections of Tagore and Ellison suggest that schools that omit the arts omit essential occasions for democratic understanding. An Indian acquaintance of mine expressed frustration that as a child in Indian government schools he never got the chance to explore different social positions through theater, whereas his nieces and nephews in the United States learned about the civil rights movement in part by putting on a play about Rosa Parks in which the experience of sitting in the back of the bus conveyed information about stigma that could not have been fully conveyed without that participatory experience.

So we need to cultivate students' "inner eyes," and this means carefully crafted instruction in the arts and humanities—appropriate to the child's age and developmental level—that will bring students in contact with issues of gender, race, ethnicity, and cross-cultural experience and understanding. This artistic instruction can and should be linked to the citizen-of-the-world instruction, since works of art are frequently an invaluable way of beginning to understand the achievements and sufferings of a culture different from one's own.

In other words, the role of the arts in schools and colleges is twofold. They cultivate capacities for play and empathy in a general way, and they address particular cultural blind spots. The first role can be played by works remote from the student's own time and place, although not just any randomly selected work. The second requires a more pointed focus on areas of social unease. The two roles are in some ways continuous, since the general capacity, once developed, makes it far easier to address a stubborn blind spot.

Both, in order to be stably linked to democratic values, require a normative view about how human beings ought to relate to one another (as equals, as dignified, as having inner depth and worth), and both therefore require selectivity regarding the artworks used. The empathetic imagination can be capricious and uneven if not linked to an idea of equal human dignity. It is all too easy to have refined sympathy for those close to us in geography, or class, or race, and to refuse it to people at a distance, or members of minority groups, treating them as mere things. Moreover, there are plenty of artworks that reinforce uneven sympathies. Children who are asked to cultivate their imaginations by reading racist literature, or pornographic objectification of women, would not be cultivating them in a way appropriate to democratic societies, and we cannot deny that antidemocratic movements have known how to use the arts, music, and rhetoric in ways that contribute further to demeaning and stigmatizing certain groups and people.[11] The imaginative component of democratic education requires careful selectivity. What we should notice, however, is that the way these defective forms of "literature" operate is by inhibiting imaginative access to the stigmatized position—by treating minorities, or women, as mere things with no experiences worth exploring. The imaginative activity of exploring another inner life, while not the whole of a healthy moral relationship to others, is at least one necessary ingredient of it. Moreover, it contains within itself an antidote to the self-protective fear that is so often connected to egocentric projects of control. When people take up the play attitude toward others, they are less likely—at least for the time being—to see them as looming threats to their safety whom they must keep in line.

The cultivation of imagination that I have described is closely linked to the Socratic capacity for criticism of dead or inadequate traditions, and provides essential support for this critical activity. One can hardly treat another person's intellectual position respectfully unless one at least tries to see what outlook on life and what life experiences generated it. But what we have said about egoistic anxiety prepares us to see there is something further that the arts contribute to Socratic criticism. As Tagore often emphasized, the arts, by generating pleasure in connection with acts of subversion and cultural reflection, produce an enduring and even attractive dialogue with the prejudices of the past, rather than one fraught with fear and defensiveness. This is what Ellison meant by calling *Invisible Man* "a raft of perception, hope, and entertainment." Entertainment is crucial to the ability of the arts to offer perception and hope. It is not just the experience of the performer, then, that is so important for democracy, it is the way in which performance offers a venue for exploring difficult issues without crippling anxiety.

Similarly, Tagore's notorious dance performance, in which Amita Sen danced the role of the Green Fairy, was a milestone for women because it was artistically distinguished and extremely enjoyable. So was the even more daring drama in which Amita danced the role of the queen, and the text accompanying her movements was, "Come to my breast." The text ultimately had to be changed to "Come to my heart"—but, Amita told me, "Everyone knew what was really being said." That episode could have set back the cause of women, but it advanced it, because the erotic agency of the queen, beautifully danced by Amita, was delightful. In the end, the audience could not sustain habits of shock and anger, against the gentle assault of beautiful music and movement.

We have touched on images of gender, and perhaps there is nothing more essential to the health of a democracy than having healthy images of what a real man is, and how a real man relates both to women and to other men. This issue was recognized as central from the very beginning of modern democratic culture, in both Western and non-Western nations. In Europe, the philosopher Johann Gottfried Herder, writing in 1792, insisted that good citizens needed to learn that manliness does not require warlike aggressiveness against other nations. Alluding to what he understood to be the custom of Native Americans, he said that the men of Europe, similarly, should put on women's clothes when they deliberate about war and peace, and should in general cultivate a "reduced respect" for warlike exploits and a horror of a "false statecraft" that whips people up into eagerness for conquest. Instead, both men and women alike should cultivate "dispositions of peace"—in the service of which, he suggested, assuming a female role for a time might be very useful.[12]

Similar ideas were explored in India by both Tagore and Gandhi. Tagore's school, through its dance idiom and its emphasis on the arts, cultivated a male personality that was receptive, playful, and uninterested in dominating others. Tagore explicitly linked this goal to a repudiation of the sort of aggressive colonizing nationalism that he associated with European cultural values and norms of manliness. Gandhi, later, firmly linked his nonviolent approach to social change to a repudiation of the goal of domination in sexual relations. He deliberately cultivated a persona that was androgynous and maternal—not to show his followers that they must altogether abandon traditional gender distinctions, but to show them that one can be a real man without being aggressive, that a wide range of gender styles are all compatible with true manliness, so long as the accent is firmly on respect for human dignity in others and compassion for their needs.

In short, children need to learn that sympathetic receptivity is not unmanly, and that manliness does not mean not weeping, not sharing the grief of the hungry or the battered. This learning cannot be promoted by a confrontational approach that says, "Drop your old images of manliness." It can only be promoted by a culture that is receptive in both curricular content and pedagogical style, in which, it is not too bold to say, the capacities for love and compassion infuse the entirety of the educational endeavor.

As with critical thinking, so too with the arts. We discover that they are essential for the goal of economic growth and the maintenance of a healthy business culture. Leading business educators have long understood that a developed capacity to imagine is a keystone of a healthy business culture.[13] Innovation requires minds that are flexible, open, and creative; literature and the arts cultivate these capacities. When they are lacking, a business culture quickly loses steam. Again and again, liberal arts graduates are hired in preference to students who have had a narrower preprofessional education, precisely because they are believed to have the flexibility and the creativity to succeed in a dynamic business environment. If our only concern were national economic growth, then we should still protect humanistic liberal arts education. Today, however, as we'll see in the next chapter, the arts are under assault in schools all over the world.

At this point, a case study will help us see how crucial the arts can be in supplying ingredients for democratic citizenship in an American culture divided by both ethnicity and class. Consider the case of the Chicago Children's Choir. Chicago, like most large American cities, contains huge economic inequalities, which translate into large differences in basic housing, employment opportunities, and educational quality. Children in African American and Latino neighborhoods, in particular, are usually not getting anywhere near as good an education as children in suburban white neighborhoods, or in urban private schools. Such children may already have disadvantages in their homes—only one parent, or even no parents living with them, and no "role models" of career success, discipline, aspiration, or committed political engagement. Schools are not racially segregated by law, of course, but they are largely segregated de facto, so students are likely to have few friends from classes and races different from their own.

To make things worse, the arts, which can bring children together in nonhierarchical ways, have been severely cut back in the public schools, as part of cost-cutting measures. Into this void has stepped the Chicago Children's Choir, an organization currently supported by private philanthropy, which by now includes almost three thousand children, approximately 80 percent of whom are below the poverty line, in programs of choral singing with rigorous standards of excellence. The program has three tiers. First, there are programs in the schools; many of these take the place of programs run by the city that had been cut away. The in-school programs serve some twenty-five hundred children in more than sixty different choirs in fifty elementary schools, focusing on grades three through eight. The in-school program, as the official description of the program states, "validates the idea that music is as important as math and science to the development of the mind and the spirit."

The second tier consists of the neighborhood choirs, eight choirs in different regions of Chicago. These are after-school programs requiring auditions and some level of serious commitment, serving children from age eight to age sixteen. These children perform many times each year and tour to different parts of the country;

they learn a wide variety of music from different countries of the world and develop their musical skills.

Finally, the most advanced level, the Concert Choir, probably the top youth ensemble in the United States, has recorded numerous CDs, toured internationally, and performed with symphony orchestras and opera companies. This group performs works ranging from Bach motets to African American spirituals; the repertoire deliberately includes music from many different world cultures.

This choir system was inaugurated in 1956 by Christopher Moore, a Unitarian minister, who believed that he could change young people's lives by bringing them together through music—across differences of race, religion, and economic class. The system has grown from an initial twenty-four singers to its current size through the dedicated support of many Chicago-area donors; the city gives it free office space but makes no further financial contribution.

Such facts are easy to narrate. What is difficult to describe is the emotional impact of hearing these young people, who do not sing like the church choirs of my youth, motionless with music held in front of them. They memorize everything they sing, and sing everything expressively, at times using gesture and even dance movements to put a song across. Their faces express tremendous joy in the act of singing, and this emotion is a large part of what the program cultivates, in both performers and spectators.

I have observed rehearsals of the neighborhood Hyde Park choir, as well as public performances by the Concert Choir, and even in the highly inclusive activity of the former, one finds immense pride, musical aspiration, and personal commitment. Singers from the Concert Choir typically become mentors to the younger children, giving them role models of discipline and aspiration, and also developing their own ethos of social responsibility.

When I recently interviewed Mollie Stone, conductor of the Hyde Park neighborhood choir and associate conductor of the Concert Choir, I asked her what, in her view, the choir contributes to life in Chicago. She gave me a moving and eloquent set of answers. First, she said, the choir gives children the opportunity for an intense experience side by side with children from different racial and socioeconomic backgrounds. The experience of singing with someone, she said, includes great vulnerability; you have to blend your breath and your body with someone else's, and you have to make the sounds from within your own body, as would not be the case even with an orchestra. So, in addition, the musical experience teaches children love of their own bodies, at an age when they are likely to hate their bodies and feel very uncomfortable; they develop a sense of ability, discipline, and responsibility.

Then, since the choirs sing music from many different cultures, they learn about other cultures, and they learn that these cultures are available to them; they transcend barriers that expectation and local culture have thrown in their way, showing that they can be world citizens. By learning to sing the music of another time or place, they also find ways of showing that they respect someone else, that they are willing to spend time learning about them and taking them seriously.

In all these ways, they learn about their role in the local community and the world, and Stone emphasized that this can lead to many forms of curiosity, as choir alumni go on to study political science, history, language, visual art.

Three stories illustrate what Stone is talking about. One day, she came into the rehearsal room of the Concert Choir and heard a group of African American kids singing a complex passage of a Bach motet they had been rehearsing. "So," she said, "you're getting in some extra rehearsal today?" "No," they said. "We're just chilling. We're just jamming." The fact that these African American kids from ghetto schools felt that a natural way to "chill," to relax together, was to sing Bach, showed that they did not feel confined to "black culture"; they could claim any culture as their own and take membership in it. It was theirs as much as was the world of the African American spiritual.

Stone then remembered her own experience, when she was a young singer in a predominantly African American choir and the choir performed a Hebrew folksong. As the only Jew in the choir, she had a sudden sense of inclusion; she felt that the other kids respected her culture, took it seriously, wanted to study it and participate in it.

Finally, on a recent tour, the Hyde Park neighborhood choir went to Nashville, Tennessee, the home of country music, a place whose culture and values are somewhat alien to most northern, urban Americans—whom residents of Nashville would be likely to regard with suspicion in turn. Hearing a country music group performing outside the Grand Ole Opry, the kids recognized a country song that they had sung in choir, and they surrounded the band, joining in. A celebratory expression of inclusion and mutual respect was the result.

What the choir shows us about the role of the arts in promoting democratic inclusion and respect is not news. It is part of a long American tradition that includes the progressive educators I have mentioned (from Alcott through Dewey). Horace Mann argued that vocal music, in particular, tends to unite people of diverse backgrounds, and to reduce conflict.[14]

I have emphasized, here, the contribution the choir makes to its participants. Needless to say, this contribution is multiplied many times, through the effect on parents and families, on schools, and on audiences who hear the choir both in the United States and abroad.

Unfortunately, such enterprises are not favored by the U.S. educational establishment, local or national. The choir is therefore constantly in debt, and is able to continue to exist only through tireless volunteer donations of both time and money. Chicago is fortunate to have a number of privately funded initiatives through which major arts organizations create programs for the schools—in addition to a great deal of cost-free public art that is typically supported by public-private partnerships.

Since I have mentioned money, let's face up to this issue. The arts, it is said, are just too costly. We cannot afford them in a time of economic hardship. The arts, however, need not be expensive to promote. If people will only make room for them, they can be fostered relatively inexpensively—because children love to dance and sing, and to tell and read stories. If we think of art in the way that Dewey criticized—as highbrow "Fine Art," requiring expensive equipment and objects for its "appreciation"—we can easily be led to the conclusion that in a cost-conscious time there is not enough money for it. I have heard such arguments from educators in Chicago, and I do not buy them. I have been in rural areas of India, visiting literacy projects for women and girls that have no equipment at all—not even chairs and desks, no paper, no pens, perhaps only a slate passed from hand to hand—and there, the arts are flourishing, as young girls who are just beginning to read express themselves much more fully by putting on plays about their experiences, or singing songs of their struggles, or drawing pictures of their goals and fears. Dedicated activist teachers know that the arts are the way to get kids to come eagerly to school, to want to learn to read and write, to want to think critically about their situation in life. So often, as a visitor, I have been asked if I will teach them a song of the American women's movement—and when I volunteer "We Shall Overcome," they already know it, in every regional language. Music and dance, drawing and theater, these are powerful avenues of joy and expression for all, and it does not take much money to foster them. Indeed they are the backbone of the curriculum in rural literacy programs because they supply both children and adults with motivation to come to school, positive ways of relating to one another, and joy in the educational endeavor.

Why can't we use the arts this way in the United States? Recently I visited a program for troubled young teens at Morton Alternative, a public high school in Cicero, a city just outside of Chicago. Teens who have been kicked out of another public high school must go to Morton Alternative—unless they drop out entirely (since some are over sixteen). The school has a total of only about forty students, so individual attention is feasible. Thanks to a remarkably astute and compassionate principal, who focused on each child's history as if that child were his own son or daughter, and thanks to an arrangement with a volunteer organization of psychotherapists and social workers, all children receive a lot of individual mentoring and regular group therapy in groups of four or five. I was deeply impressed by the changes that were taking place just because some adults are listening. The school was as close to the family environment of Alcott's Plumtree School as it was possible to be when children had to return home to families that were often dysfunctional and even violent. What do you do with the arts, I asked. The principal and the head therapist seemed surprised. They had not thought of this as something helpful.

But why on earth not? These adolescents, most of them Mexican American, come from a culture with enormously rich music and dance traditions. Through these, and through theater, they could have found powerful ways to express their conflicts and aspirations. Group therapy is already a type of theater, but it does not involve the sort of disciplined achievement that putting on a play would. There was no economic reason why they were not doing this. They just had not thought about it.

Four weeks later, the head therapist sent me a poem that one of the girls in the therapy session I had observed had written as a result of his new determination to incorporate the arts into his efforts at Morton Alternative. A halting, yet extremely powerful account of her growing love for her baby, written by a teen mother who was having enormous struggles in that role, the poem did seem to me to mark a new stage in her progress toward pride and self-mastery, and the therapist supported that conclusion. It makes so much sense, and it did not cost an extra dime.

The education I recommend requires that teachers do things differently. Implementing it would require major changes in teacher training, at least in most districts in the United States and most nations of the world. It would also require most school principals (though not the principal at Morton Alternative) to change the ethos of their schools. In this sense, this education is costly. But the costs are, I believe, transition costs; there is nothing intrinsically more expensive about doing things this way. Once the new ways are in place, they will perpetuate themselves. I would even argue that a type of education that gets both students and teachers more passionately involved in thinking and imagining reduces costs by reducing the anomie and time wasting that typically accompany a lack of personal investment.

VII

Democratic Education on the Ropes

But the danger lies in this, that organised ugliness storms the mind and carries the day by its mass, by its aggressive persistence, by its power of mockery directed against the deeper sentiments of heart. . . . Therefore its rivalry with things that are modest and profound and have the subtle delicacy of life is to be dreaded.

—Tagore, *Nationalism*, 1917

And whoever walks a furlong without sympathy walks to his own funeral drest in his shroud.

—Walt Whitman, *Song of Myself,* 1855

How is education for democratic citizenship doing in the world today? Very poorly, I fear. This is a manifesto, not an empirical study, so this chapter will not be filled with quantitative data, although the data support my concern.[1] The disturbing trends I am describing must simply be summarized, and illustrated by telling and representative examples.

The argument I have been making is intended as a call to action. If it should turn out that things are less bad than I believe them to be, we should not breathe a sigh of relief; we should do exactly what we would if we believed things were pretty bleak. We should redouble our commitment to the parts of education that keep democracy vital. Even if it should turn out that they are not as profoundly threatened as I believe them to be, they are clearly vulnerable and under great pressure in an era of economic globalization.

EDUCATION OF THE TYPE I recommend is still doing reasonably well in the place where I first studied it, namely the liberal arts portion of U.S. college and university curricula. Indeed, this part of the curriculum, in institutions such as my own, still attracts generous philanthropic support, as rich people remember with pleasure the time when they read books they loved and pursued issues open-endedly. During the recent economic crisis, we have even seen an increase in commitment as donors who value the humanities dig deeper in order to preserve what they love.

It is possible to argue, indeed, that the liberal arts portion of college and university education in the United States now supports democratic citizenship better than it did fifty years ago.[2] Fifty years ago, students knew little about the world outside Europe and North America. Nor did they learn much about minorities in their own nation. History, whether world or U.S., was typically taught with an eye on large political events and dominant political actors. The story of minority or immigrant groups was rarely emphasized; nor was economic history a part of the grand narrative.

Today all this has changed for the better. New areas of study, infused into liberal arts courses for all students, have enhanced their understanding of non-Western nations, of the global economy, of race relations, of the dynamics of gender, of the history of migration and the struggles of new groups for recognition and equality. Curricula have been increasingly fashioned with an eye to good citizenship in a world of diversity, and these changes are paying off. Young people these days rarely leave college as ignorant about the non-Western world as students of my own generation routinely did.

Similar changes have taken place in the teaching of literature and the arts. Students are exposed to a far wider range of materials, and their "inner eyes" (to borrow Ellison's phrase) are cultivated by being exposed to the experiences of people of many different types, both within their own nation and abroad. The history of music is now taught with a far greater recognition of the world's many musical traditions and their interactions. Film history recognizes contributions outside the Hollywood mainstream.

We in the United States cannot be complacent about the health of the humanities, however. Despite continued support from donors, the economic crisis has led many universities to make deep cuts in humanities and arts programming. Other areas also have to make cuts, to be sure. But the humanities are widely perceived as inessential, so it seems fine for them to be downsized, and for some departments to be eliminated completely. At one of our largest public universities, there has been talk recently of selecting a few humanities disciplines that are supposedly at the "core" of an undergraduate education, and eliminating the rest. The university's topnotch department of religious studies was informed that philosophy is part of the "core" but religious studies is not.[3] These changes are still under discussion, but they are typical of the sort of cost-cutting measures that are being contemplated in universities and colleges of many kinds. Even where cuts do not threaten whole departments, they threaten the health of departments, since faculty who cannot fill vacancies become overworked and are unable to do their job well.

To some extent, these threatening changes are externally imposed. We should not blame them all on outsiders, however. Too often, our universities have taken short-cuts—for example, by teaching large courses without sufficient critical engagement with students and without enough feedback on student writing; too often faculty allow regurgitation to lead to success. To the extent that universities fail to achieve the goals that I have defended, it becomes much easier for outsiders to depreciate humanistic studies.

The liberal arts, then, are threatened, both from without and from within. In a recent article, Harvard's president Drew Faust reports, and laments, "a steep decline in the percentage of students majoring in the liberal arts and sciences, and an accompanying increase in preprofessional undergraduate degrees." Have universities, she asks, "become too captive to the immediate and worldly purposes they serve? Has the market model become the fundamental and defining identity of higher education?" Faust concludes with a ringing defense of the liberal arts model and its role in our nation:

> Higher learning can offer individuals and societies a depth and breadth of vision absent from the inevitably myopic present. Human beings need meaning, understanding, and perspective as well as jobs. The question should not be whether we can afford to believe in such purposes in these times, but whether we can afford not to.[4]

Liberal arts education, then, is endangered in the United States, although it still has many strong defenders and a good chance of surviving. Outside the United States, many nations whose university curricula do not include a liberal arts component are now striving to build one, since they acknowledge its importance in crafting a public response to the problems of pluralism, fear, and suspicion their societies face. I've been involved in such discussions in the Netherlands, in Sweden, in India, in Germany, in Italy, and in Bangladesh. As I have observed, it is precisely in the Indian Institutes of Technology and Management—at the heart of the profit-oriented technology culture—that instructors have felt the need to introduce liberal arts courses, partly to counter the narrowness of their students, but partly, as well, to cope with religious- and caste-based animosities.

Whether much reform in this direction will occur, however, is hard to say, for liberal education has high financial and pedagogical costs. Teaching of the sort I recommend needs small classes, or at least sections, where students discuss ideas with one another, get copious feedback on frequent writing assignments, and have lots of time to discuss their work with instructors. European professors are not used to this idea, and would at present be horrible at it if they did try to do it, since their graduate education includes no training in teaching and this is not regarded as an important part of preparing their job file; in the United States, by contrast, graduate students are teaching assistants, frequently teach their own tutorials or small classes, and are supervised by faculty, since one all-important part of a job file is a "teaching portfolio," including professorial recommendations and student course evaluations. European faculty, lacking this systematic preparation, all too often come to expect that holding a chair means not having to grade undergraduate writing assignments. Graduate students, too, are often treated distantly and hierarchically.

Even when faculty are keen on the liberal arts model, bureaucrats are unwilling to believe that it is necessary to support the number of faculty positions required to make it really work. At Södertörn's Högskola, a new university in Stockholm where a high proportion of the students are immigrants, Vice-Chancellor Ingela Josefson wants to create a course called Democracy for all undergraduates, which would realize some of the goals of critical thinking and world citizenship that I have discussed here. She has sent young faculty to spend a year in liberal arts colleges in the United States so that they can learn the style of teaching that is needed to make this project work. Government bureaucrats, however, have so far refused to give the funding to create a course for all students that can be broken up into sections of twenty to twenty-five students. The course exists, but on a reduced level, not serving the needs of the entire student body. Meanwhile, an aggressive attempt to form partnerships with the various institutions for art education in Stockholm—schools that focus on theater, film study, dance, circus training, and music—is still in its infancy, and has not yet had the public support to influence the undergraduate curriculum at Södertörn.

Another problem that European and Asian universities have is that new disciplines of particular importance for good democratic citizenship have no secure place in the structure of undergraduate education. Women's studies, the study of race and ethnicity, Judaic studies, Islamic studies—all these are likely to be marginalized, catering only to the student who already knows a lot about the area and wants to focus on it. In the liberal arts system, by contrast, such new disciplines can provide courses that all undergraduates are required to take, and can also enrich the required liberal arts offerings in other disciplines, such as literature and history. Where there are no such requirements, the new disciplines remain marginal. I vividly remember attending a conference entitled "Religion and Violence against Women" sponsored by the women's studies program at Berlin's distinguished Humboldt University. The program was exciting, the topics urgent. Such a conference, at my own university, would probably have attracted almost 50 percent males, as my courses on topics such as feminist philosophy typically do. At Humboldt, however, apart from a few of the invited speakers, there was not a single male in the audience—with the exception of Sweden's ambassador to Germany, an old friend of mine whom I had invited. This is a typical experience in Europe, because the requirement to take a course on women's issues is often the only thing that destigmatizes the field for young men and makes it socially acceptable to show an interest in it.

Meanwhile, the pressure for economic growth has led many political leaders in Europe to recast the entirety of university education—both teaching and research—along growth-oriented lines, asking about the contribution of each discipline and each researcher to the economy. Take Britain, for example. Ever since the Thatcher era, it has been customary for humanities departments in Britain to be required to justify themselves to the government, which funds all academic institutions, by showing how their research and teaching contribute to economic profitability.[5] If they cannot show this, their government support will drop and the number of faculty and students decline. Whole departments may even be closed down, as numerous classics and philosophy programs have been. (British faculty do not have tenure any longer, so there is no barrier to firing them at any time; so far, though, the norm has been to transfer them to some nonclosed department until they retire.) These problems are closely related to the absence, in Britain and in Europe generally,[6] of a liberal arts model. Humanities departments cannot justify themselves by pointing to their role in teaching required liberal arts courses for all students, as they can in the United States.

Where departments are not closed, they are often merged these days with other units whose contribution to profit is more obvious—thus putting pressure on the merged discipline to emphasize those parts of its own scope that lie closer to profit, or can be made to seem to. When, for example, philosophy is merged with political science, it puts pressure on philosophy to focus on highly applied and "useful" areas, such as business ethics, rather than the study of Plato, or skills of logic and critical thinking, or reflections about the meaning of life—which might ultimately be more valuable in young people's attempts to understand themselves and their world. "Impact" is the buzzword of the day, and by "impact" the government clearly means above all economic impact.

Academic research, too, is increasingly driven by the demand for "impact." The current Labor government has recast all research, including humanities research, on the model of research in the sciences. It has to be supported by grant money, and researchers have to go out and find that money, usually from government bodies. Humanities research has not previously been funded in this way; it has traditionally been funded by stable direct funding because it has been understood that humanities research contributes to human life in a global way, not by producing this or that immediately useful discovery. Humanities professors in the United States get a certain amount of research leave as part of their standard contract. Typically they need to show that they are actively engaged in research and publication during that time, but they show this to peer faculty who understand what humanities research is about. British humanists have to continue filling out grant applications for government agencies, a great time killer, and also a great distorter of research topics, since the government agencies who screen grant applications are looking for "impact" and are often deeply suspicious of humanistic ideas. (Nor is Britain the most extreme in this regard. In some parts of Europe, one has to apply for a grant even to support one's own graduate students—who, in U.S. nonscience fields, and in many other countries as well, are funded by a standard agreement between an academic department and the university administration. Thus they can pursue their own education in an open-ended way, rather than being slotted into some professor's "research team" from the start.) One cynical young philosopher, in one of these recently merged departments of philosophy and political science, told me that his last grant proposal was six words under the word limit— so he added the word "empirical" six times, as if to reassure the bureaucrats that he was not dealing in mere philosophy—and his application proved successful.

These baneful trends have recently been formalized in a proposal by the Labor government for a new system of research assessment called the Research Excellence Framework. According to the new guidelines, fully 25 percent of the rating of a research proposal will depend on assessment of its "impact." Distinguished historian Stefan Collini has presented a devastating analysis of the scheme's likely impact on the humanities in "Impact on Humanities: Researchers Must Take a Stand Now or Be Judged and Rewarded as Salesmen." (He notes that responsibility for higher education in Britain is now part of the Department of Business, a dispiriting development.) Collini worries about the lack of protest against the cheapening vocabulary, which depicts research as a type of hucksterism: "Perhaps our ears no longer hear . . . how ludicrous it is to propose that the quality of scholarship can be partly judged in terms of the number of 'external research users' or the range of 'impact indicators.'" Academics in the humanities must insist, he argues, that their research is "a collection of ways of encountering the record of human activity in its greatest richness and diversity," and is valuable for this reason. If such a protest does not take place, humanists in Britain will devote more and more of their time "to becoming door-to-door salesmen for vulgarized versions of their increasingly market-oriented 'products.'"[7]

British humanists tell me that part of the problem is government's insensitivity to humanistic values when it assesses grant proposals; private foundations sometimes do better. Still, they feel, justly I believe, that the system of applying for grant money, though it may work well for the sciences, is not suited to the humanities and tends to corrupt the mission of humanistic scholarship. They consequently fear for the future of a humanities supported by no powerful public constituency. The British situation is typical of current developments in Europe.

In India the denigration of the humanities began long ago with Nehru's emphasis on science and economics as the linchpins of the nation's future. Despite his own deep love for poetry and literature, which informs every corner of his political analysis, Nehru concluded that modes of emotional and imaginative understanding must take a backseat to science, and his views prevailed.[8] Some humanities disciplines do not exist at all. Thus the study of comparative religion and the history of religions is not an academic subject in Indian universities. Other disciplines, such as philosophy, have long been weak and are stigmatized on that account; bright young people would not be encouraged to go into them, because "philosophy" has long been thought to mean something merely historical and linked to traditional religion, and is for this reason unpopular. The prestige disciplines are the sciences and engineering, economics, and to a certain extent empirical political science.

The hottest competition for entrance is for places in the Institutes of Technology and Management, where (apart from the required humanities general-education courses that have wisely been introduced) only technical education is on offer. A prominent research scientist of Indian origin at my own university—himself educated at IIT Delhi—described the whole IIT experience as one of "de-education," in the sense that students focus narrowly on preprofessional skills and are discouraged from learning independent research techniques. Moreover, he emphasized, this narrowing begins far earlier. Since entrance to the IITs is by nationwide competitive examination, the victorious students are from towns all over the country. Most have been raised to think that getting a good job is the main aim of education. The idea that people should learn things that prepare them to be active, thoughtful citizens is an idea that has "never crossed their path." As I have mentioned, and my science colleague agrees, the humanities courses—which students actually enjoy—supply a temporary and partial corrective to the narrowness of the rest of the education, but, given the overall structure of incentives in the students' situation, their effect is rarely lasting.

What of the interdisciplinary university that Tagore created, called "All-the-World"? Visva-Bharati was running short of money, so it turned to the government for help. The price of financial support was a loss of independence, and Visva-Bharati rapidly lost its distinctive liberal arts curriculum. Now it is a university like every other, only with somewhat lower standards than many.

Although this is not my topic, we in the United States should pause at this point to be thankful for our traditions, which combine a liberal arts model with a strong cultivation of humanistic philanthropy and a basically private-endowment structure of funding. (Even the stronger U.S. state systems, such as the University of Michigan and the University of California, are increasingly relying on private endowment money.) We did not deliberate and wisely choose this system, but we can be happy that it has evolved and that we can all rely on it.

At my own university, for example, we do not have to go hat in hand to bureaucrats who lack all sympathy with what we do. Instead, we go to wealthy alums whose educational values pretty well match our own since they are by and large alums who loved their undergraduate liberal arts education, whatever else they went on to do. They love the life of the mind, and they want others to enjoy it. It would not be easy for another country to arrive at our system, because ours rests on broad-based liberal arts education at the undergraduate level, with lots of individual attention from faculty—something people value and want to pass on to future generations—and also on tax incentives for charitable donation and a long-established culture of philanthropy. Building such a system, if another country wanted to do it, would take many years. (Britain is now trying, but it is unclear how far the effort will succeed.) We in the United States can be grateful for our good luck, since our politicians are no more friendly to the humanities than those of other nations.

Even here, in what might seem to be a secure bastion of the humanities, there are signs of trouble. A recent controversy here at the University of Chicago concerns the fact that the Viewbook for prospective students has been revised to show lots of students in gleaming laboratories, and no students sitting and thinking. Campus tours, too, have apparently been instructed to bypass the traditional bastions of humanistic learning to focus on parts of the campus associated with medicine, science, and preprofessional studies.[9] Apparently someone thinks that our undergraduate programs will look more attractive if they are represented as less focused on philosophy, literature, history, and other subjects that have traditionally been staples of our core curriculum.

The universities of the world have great merits, then, but also great problems. They are far from preparing young people for citizenship as well as they might, although some still do a very good job.

By contrast, training for citizenship is doing poorly in every nation in the most crucial years of children's lives, those known as K through 12, where the demands of the global market have made everyone focus on scientific and technical proficiencies as *the* key abilities, and the humanities and the arts are increasingly perceived as useless frills that we can prune away to make sure our nation (whether it be India or the United States) remains competitive. To the extent that the humanities and arts are the focus of national discussion, they are recast as technical abilities that ought to be tested by quantitative multiple-choice examinations, and the imaginative and critical abilities that lie at their core are typically left aside.

In the United States, national testing (under the No Child Left Behind Act [NCLB]) has already made things worse, as national testing usually does, for critical thinking and sympathetic imagining are not testable by quantitative multiple-choice exams, and the skills involved in world citizenship are also poorly tested in such a way. (Consider how world history would have to be assessed on a standardized test; all that I have said about learning to examine evidence, criticize a historical narrative, and think critically about differences among narratives would have to be omitted.) "Teaching to the test," which increasingly dominates public school classrooms, produces an atmosphere of student passivity and teacher routinization. The creativity and individuality that mark the best humanistic teaching and learning has a hard time finding room to unfold. When testing determines a school's entire future, forms of student-teacher exchange that do not have a payoff on tests are likely to be squeezed out. Whether a nation is aspiring, like India, to a greater share of the market, or struggling to protect jobs, like the United States, the imagination and the critical faculties look like useless paraphernalia, and people even have increasing contempt for them. Across the board, the curriculum is being stripped of its humanistic elements, and the pedagogy of rote learning rules the roost.

Notice that part of the issue here is content, and part is pedagogy. Curricular content has shifted away from material that focuses on enlivening imagination and training the critical faculties toward material that is directly relevant to test preparation. Along with the shift in content has come an even more baneful shift in pedagogy: away from teaching that seeks to promote questioning and individual responsibility toward force-feeding for good exam results.

The No Child Left Behind Act was prompted by a real problem; we have tremendous inequalities in our schools. Some children get vastly greater educational opportunities than others. What should we do, if we think that we need national assessment in order to promote greater educational equality, but reject the current form of national assessment for the reasons I have given? It is not impossible to create a nuanced, qualitative form of national assessment. Indeed, the United States had the ingredients for one in previous years, and an excellent recent book about accountability, Richard Rothstein's *Grading Education: Getting Accountability Right*, proposes a multilayered state and federal program that tests a variety of cognitive and behavioral outcomes in a far more sophisticated way than NCLB, focusing in particular on skills needed for good citizenship.[10] This sensible and well-argued book is an excellent starting point for a really helpful national debate about accountability.

Although I have just criticized the British approach to the humanities at the university level, it seems clear that in the high schools the British have done better with assessment than we have.[11] The GCSE (formerly O-level) and A-level exams that students take in a variety of subjects in their high school years are essay exams read by multiple readers and graded the way one would grade a student paper. Philosophy is one of the high school subjects that is rapidly growing in popularity, and philosophers seem to agree that it is not some terrible travesty of philosophy that is tested (for example, facts about the lives and "doctrines" of famous philosophers), it is really Socratic philosophical ability: the ability to analyze and think critically about a wide range of philosophical issues. In other areas, similarly, testing is ambitious and qualitative. So testing can be good, preserving humanistic values. If good teachers know how to grade their students' work in class, there can be a test devised to measure what is graded. The only problem is that this sort of testing will be much more expensive than the standardized type, and we will have to devote a lot of attention to recruiting a competent bunch of assessors and paying them well, something that nobody currently seems willing even to discuss.

The Obama administration has a chance to change the current modus operandi, promoting a richer conception of education and, if desired, a richer, more qualitative conception of testing. President Obama's own personal values would seem to lead toward supporting such changes; he is famous for his interest in hearing and sifting the arguments on all sides of an issue, and he declares his great interest in "empathy" as a characteristic pertinent to an office as high as that of Justice of the U.S. Supreme Court. His own education clearly had the characteristics I have been praising here, and it produced a person who knows how to think critically, who thinks with rich information about a wide range of world situations, who repeatedly displays a robust ability to imagine the predicaments of many types of people—and its corollary, the ability to think reflectively about himself and his own life story. Very likely, Barack Obama's home life contributed a great deal to this process, but his schools must have done their part. And we know that when the time came for college, he attended two institutions famous for their commitment to the liberal arts model: Occidental, a fine liberal arts college, and Columbia University, where the undergraduate humanities curriculum is well known for its comprehensiveness and for the engaged, enterprising teaching with which material is presented.

Nonetheless, so far at least, President Obama has not given any signals of support for the humanities or a reform of national education efforts in a liberal arts direction. His choice for secretary of education, Arne Duncan, inspires no confidence, since as head of the Chicago public schools Duncan presided over a rapid decline in humanities and arts funding. And the indications are that rather than decreasing the focus on the type of national testing pioneered under No Child Left Behind, the administration plans to expand it. In his speeches on education, the president rightly emphasizes the issue of equality, talking about the importance of making all Americans capable of pursuing the "American Dream." But the pursuit of a dream requires dreamers: educated minds that can think critically about alternatives and imagine an ambitious goal— preferably not involving only personal or even national wealth, but involving human dignity and democratic debate as well.

Instead of such important and generous goals, however, President Obama has so far focused on individual income and national economic progress, arguing that the sort of education we need is the sort that serves these two goals. "[E]conomic progress and educational achievement have always gone hand in hand in America," he insists. We should judge any new idea in education by how well it "works"—presumably with reference to these goals. He defends early childhood interventions by saying, "For every dollar we invest in these programs, we get nearly ten dollars back in reduced welfare rolls, fewer health care costs, and less crime." Never in this entire lengthy speech does he mention the democratic goals I have emphasized. And when he mentions critical thinking—once—it is in the context of what businesses need for profitability. We need, he says, to develop tests that measure "whether they possess 21st century skills like problem-solving and critical thinking, entrepreneurship and creativity." This one gesture toward the humanities—in a speech largely devoted to the praise of science and technology—is clearly a narrow allusion to the role of certain skills in business advancement. And the proposed assessment—a strengthened form of NCLB—shows very clearly that the humanistic parts of the sentence are not the core of the proposal.[12]

Even more problematic, President Obama repeatedly praises nations of the Far East, for example Singapore, which, in his view, have advanced beyond us in technology and science education. And he praises such nations in an ominous manner: "They are spending less time teaching things that don't matter, and more time teaching things that do. They are preparing their students not only for high school or college, but for a career. We are not." In other words, "things that matter" is taken to be equivalent to "things that prepare for a career." A life of rich significance and respectful, attentive citizenship is nowhere mentioned among the goals worth spending time on. In the context of his speech, it is difficult to avoid the conclusion that the "things that don't matter" include many of the things that this book has defended as essential to the health of democracy.[13]

The U.S. system of public education contains huge inequalities. It is tempting to think that national testing offers a solution to this problem. Nonetheless, one does not solve the problem of unequal opportunity through a type of testing that virtually ensures that no child has the opportunity for a stimulating education or adequate preparation for citizenship.

What of India? I have spoken of India's disdain for humanistic content at the university level. Very much the same is true of elementary and secondary schools, since these are heavily influenced by prevailing social norms and national trends. Tagore's school in Santiniketan still exists, but, as we saw, its focus on the arts makes it very unfashionable in the present climate. Once a highly sought-after destination for the most talented students from all over India—Nehru's daughter Indira passed her only truly happy years of schooling there, for example—it is now stigmatized as a place for problem children, and parents are not proud to send a child there. Such a school does not offer the type of preparation that is likely to lead to success in the IIT entrance examination. At those same Institutes of Technology and Management, meanwhile, instructors lament their students' deficient humanities preparation.

Humanistic content, then, is in decline—from a position that was already insecure. What of pedagogy? Throughout the nation, the pedagogy of rote learning has dominated for many decades. It is in a sense not surprising that a nation struggling to produce mass literacy from a position of low literacy would focus on drilling and would neglect the empowerment of the individual student through questioning, sifting of evidence, and imaginative expression. Such a result is even more understandable when we remember that rote learning dominated in colonial times. The schools that Tagore briefly attended and rapidly left all utilized this sort of boring cramming, and it was this that motivated him to try to create something different. But to understand is not to condone. Again and again I have heard Indian Americans express regret about the stultifying quality of their own education, by contrast to the good things they observe in the schools their children attend.

Rote learning dominates, then, in government schools. So too do many forms of corruption; in some states the teacher absenteeism rate is as high as 20 percent.[14] Equally damaging to children is the infamous practice of "private tuition," where teachers accept a fee to teach well-off kids in their homes after school—a practice that creates incentives not to teach well during the normal school day. Teachers all too rarely try to innovate, to inspire children. Their highest hope is to stuff them full of facts so that they perform well on national examinations.

Ironically, such bad practices dominate in the very places—government elementary and secondary schools—where we would suppose that students, being at least in school and, after a while, literate, have already had relatively good luck and seem to have a realistic hope of attaining an influential position in society. (Literacy rates in the nation as a whole still hover around 50 percent for women, 65 percent for men, so anyone who progresses even to secondary education is privileged.) At the "bottom" of society, however, something more promising is often on offer. Thousands of rural literacy programs funded by nongovernmental organizations teach basic literacy and basic skills. The ones I know well focus on women and girls, but such programs come in many varieties. What many of them have in common, however, is resourcefulness and imagination. Working women and girls will not come to class unless they get something out of it, and so teachers are forced to be innovative, warm, experimental. They use drawing, dance, and music; they involve students in mapping and talking about the power structure of their village, or in reflecting about how they might get a better deal from the landlords for whom they work as sharecroppers. They communicate excitement about what they are doing, something that few government teachers manage to do.

What these programs show us is that improving the bleak situation of the arts and humanities requires, above all, human investment. Money is nice, but committed people, and strong support for such programs, are the main factors.

We in the United States can study our own future in the government schools of India. Such will be our future *if* we continue down the road of "teaching to the test," neglecting the activities that enliven children's minds and make them see a connection between their school life and their daily life outside of school. We should be deeply alarmed that our own schools are rapidly, heedlessly, moving in the direction of the Indian norm, rather than the reverse.

DURING THE ERA in which people began to demand democratic self-governance, education all over the world was remodeled to produce the sort of student who could function well in this demanding form of government: not a cultivated gentleman, stuffed with the wisdom of the ages, but an active, critical, reflective, and empathetic member of a community of equals, capable of exchanging ideas on the basis of respect and understanding with people from many different backgrounds. Rousseau, Pestalozzi, Froebel, Alcott, and Tagore differed in many ways, but they all agreed that the passive pedagogy of the past offered little to the nations of the future, that a new sense of personal agency and a new critical freedom would be needed if participatory institutions were to be sustained.

Today we still maintain that we like democracy and self-governance, and we also think that we like freedom of speech, respect for difference, and understanding of others. We give these values lip service, but we think far too little about what we need to do in order to transmit them to the next generation and ensure their survival. Distracted by the pursuit of wealth, we increasingly ask our schools to turn out useful profit-makers rather than thoughtful citizens. Under pressure to cut costs, we prune away just those parts of the educational endeavor that are crucial to preserving a healthy society.

What will we have, if these trends continue? Nations of technically trained people who do not know how to criticize authority, useful profit-makers with obtuse imaginations. As Tagore observed, a suicide of the soul. What could be more frightening than that? Indeed, when we consider the Indian state of Gujarat, which has for a particularly long time gone down this road, with no critical thinking in the public schools and a concerted focus on technical ability, we can see clearly how a band of docile engineers can be welded into a murderous force to enact the most horrendously racist and antidemocratic policies. (In 2002 Hindu right-wing mobs, egged on by propaganda purveyed in the schools—Hitler, for example, is portrayed as a hero in state history textbooks—murdered approximately 2,000 Muslim civilians, a genocidal assault that has been condemned around the world and has led to the denial of a U.S. visa to that state's chief minister, who masterminded the whole campaign of religious hatred.[15]) And yet, how can we possibly avoid going down this road?

DEMOCRACIES HAVE GREAT rational and imaginative powers. They also are prone to some serious flaws in reasoning, to parochialism, haste, sloppiness, selfishness, narrowness of the spirit. Education based mainly on profitability in the global market magnifies these deficiencies, producing a greedy obtuseness and a technically trained docility that threaten the very life of democracy itself, and that certainly impede the creation of a decent world culture.

If the real clash of civilizations is, as I believe, a clash within the individual soul, as greed and narcissism contend against respect and love, all modern societies are rapidly losing the battle, as they feed the forces that lead to violence and dehumanization and fail to feed the forces that lead to cultures of equality and respect. If we do not insist on the crucial importance of the humanities and the arts, they will drop away, because they do not make money. They only do what is much more precious than that, make a world that is worth living in, people who are able to see other human beings as full people, with thoughts and feelings of their own that deserve respect and empathy, and nations that are able to overcome fear and suspicion in favor of sympathetic and reasoned debate.

Afterword to the Paperback Edition: Reflections on the Future of the Humanities— at Home and Abroad

Since the publication of *Not for Profit* in the spring of 2010, I have traveled extensively, both in the United States and abroad, talking about the ideas of the book and current developments in the places I've visited. In the United States, I've been to liberal arts colleges, large state universities, religious universities, and large private universities. Outside the United States, I've spoken about the future of the humanities in Australia, Britain, Canada, Finland, France, Germany, India, Ireland, Italy, Korea, the Netherlands, and Spain. The book has already appeared in translation in Spanish, Italian, French, and Dutch, and a total of twelve translations are planned or complete. A lot of media coverage has accompanied these publications, so one can see that the book has struck a chord and helped to galvanize a public conversation.

The first response I have to these experiences is hope and gratitude. I remain deeply worried about the future of the humanities, but I've met so many people in all walks of life who care passionately about that future and who are investing great energy in shaping it that I now feel less pessimism. I wrote the book in order to give people something to grasp onto as they fought for a future they believed in, something that might help many people in many different places make their case for the humanities. And I do believe that it has helped many people make arguments to administrations, communities, legislators, alumni, parents, and the public at large. This is a struggle that, to be successful, must be waged locally, and I have come back from my travels deeply impressed with the efforts I've seen.

I've also learned a huge amount. In the United States, what I've seen is that liberal arts colleges and the liberal arts portions of private universities are in a reasonably healthy state, thanks to ardent support from parents and alumni and a competitive economic situation that makes these prestigious schools more hotly sought-after than before. Public universities, on the other hand, face a much shakier future. Notorious cuts in humanities at SUNY Albany and the University of Nevada at Las Vegas are just two examples of what the economic downturn is doing to the humanistic part of state campuses, and I have not seen any state system that is not deeply shaken—except for those that saw the danger looming long ago and have become, in effect, private universities. The University of Michigan, for example, is one of the best places in the country to study and teach humanities, with innovative interdisciplinary programs of many kinds and standard departments of superb quality; and this is thanks to a large private endowment that renders the university largely independent of the political process and its pressures. Since candidates running for election to that state's board of regents had been known to campaign on the promise to defund areas of scholarship such as sexuality studies and women's studies, independence is crucial. Of course, many private donors won't support those fields either, but one can look until one finds donors who do wish to support the scholarly agenda that educators deem wise and fruitful.

Both these observations and the need to explain these developments in other countries have led me to think a lot about public versus private funding. There's no doubt that politicians have incentives that bode ill for their judgment when making decisions about higher education. They have to stand for election soon—right now at a time of deep economic anxiety—and so they reach for tangible economic achievements, such as "I've generated n jobs for the state of S." More abstract achievements, such as "I've laid the groundwork for the long-term health of democracy," are not likely to play well at the polls, particularly in our time, so politicians are led by the very structure of their incentives to prefer a model of education geared to short-term economic achievement. This is true all over the world.

A comical example of this problem surfaced during a visit I paid to a very prestigious liberal arts college that is part of the public university system of a large state. I gave a talk about the value of the humanities based on the book for a large audience of students and faculty. The next day, at a large public ceremony, the state's governor, a rising politician of some influence, put in an appearance and made a little speech about education. Unfortunately, it was a caricature of the position I had been opposing—so much so that students burst out laughing. It's truly a sign of the times that a politician would not only choose a narrow economic message but would not even do enough homework to realize that this message might not go down well at a liberal arts college.

Private donors, by contrast, have a much more diverse set of goals. In the United States, where a liberal arts tradition is deeply entrenched, wealthy donors usually have had a liberal arts education themselves, and they often recall it with pleasure as a time when they pursued ideas open-endedly and with the excitement of youth. This nostalgia is often rekindled by seminars for alumni, which most private colleges and universities offer in some form—and all should offer more. So they are often moved simply by love, and by the desire to perpetuate what they love for their grandchildren. They also seek personal immortality, and in the United States the immortality of having your name on a building or a name chair is our only surrogate for the immortality of the entailed estate. Donors may also have aims to improve the world in a variety of ways, or to strengthen some field dear to them, and so forth. What is essential is that faculty and administrators remain firmly in control of these goals and say no to any that seem frivolous or partisan, or where the donor wants too much control. But U.S. universities are used to this: the job of being president of a major university involves spending a lot of time saying no to wealthy donors. In that situation, with those norms securely entrenched, donors often yield, allowing academic administrators to shape their initially weak proposals. It's quite different elsewhere. In India, for example, I've heard of corporations setting up entire universities whose aim is to maximize the profit of that corporation. Here, private funding is undermining not only liberal education but even high-quality scientific and technical education, since academic freedom is key to high quality in all areas.

In short, there is no simple answer to the question of whether private funding of universities is good for the humanities. It can be, if four conditions are in place: (1) a working liberal arts system, which ensures that donors come out of that culture and know what its joys and rewards are; (2) a system of strict academic control of academic values and choices, which keeps donors on a short leash; (3) a tradition of social norms giving high prestige to donations to nonprofits; and (4) a tax system that makes such donations attractive. (Universities love the estate tax and fight against its repeal.) Most countries do not have these four features, so it would be unwise of them to rush into private funding.

A further condition is desirable if private funding is to yield good results, and it doesn't hurt for public funding either: that is, fruitful connections with donors and the larger public. Universities and colleges need, I think, to do a lot more to bring in the larger community, showing them what we do and why it is worthwhile and exciting. There are many ways of doing this, speakers' programs being the most obvious. Better still, however, are weekends when people can come to a campus and sign up for miniclasses, reminding themselves how much fun it is to read a poem or discuss a Socratic dialogue. For our more active alumni, we also offer a range of ongoing seminars and retreats with faculty, and it is crucial to do this, I believe, in order to show vividly how engagement with ideas opens and refines the mind, and how much more exhilarating respectful debate is than the culture of insult that so often reigns in the media.

I have spoken of the liberal arts system. One of my major conclusions, as I've traveled and talked, is that this system has huge pedagogical and practical benefits. Students with different major subjects, sharing a common set of general courses, learn from each other in pedagogically significant ways. It's a lesser philosophy education when only philosophy majors are present in philosophy classes. More important, a mixed liberal arts education recognizes that higher education prepares students in two distinct ways: for a career, but also for citizenship and life. The liberal arts system does not force any student to make a bitter choice between studying all humanities and studying no humanities, and it does not force parents to subsidize what looks like a dead-end major. You can get your valuable engineering degree while still reading Plato and Tolstoy. And this allows parents to relax: their child can pursue the humanities while still doing something useful that prepares them for career success.

Will the liberal arts system spread beyond Scotland, where Mill first praised it, and where it clings to life despite the uniformities imposed by the European Union, and the United States, where it has become deeply entrenched? Korea has by now also invested deeply in liberal arts education, with great enthusiasm. Law has even become a postgraduate degree there, very recently, requiring a prior liberal arts degree. Some other countries are moving in the liberal arts direction: Holland now has some very popular liberal arts programs in Leiden, Rotterdam, and Utrecht, and India's prestigious Institutes of Technology and Management have required humanities courses. Whether we'll see more movement in this direction, however, depends a great deal on pedagogy: Will faculty in Europe and elsewhere be willing to do the type of labor-intensive teaching of undergraduates that this model requires, with lots of classroom discussion and frequent essay assignments returned with copious comments? Will politicians and bureaucrats be willing to hire enough faculty to offer such instruction in small classes? We must wait and see, and study these experiments as they unfold.

So the United States has a relatively favorable position, at least in higher education, although there are many signs of strain. Outside the United States, all countries report some anxiety about the future of the humanities and some degree of cutting. Beyond this, there is great variety. It has been fascinating for me to learn more about current developments in Singapore and China, so often touted as successes because of their emphasis on technological education. In fact, however, both of these nations have recently conducted massive educational reforms in order to give a larger place, in both schools and universities, to both critical thinking and the arts.[1] The reason is hardly a desire to cultivate democracy. It is, instead, the demands of a healthy business culture in a mobile world economy. Both nations have recognized that critical thinking is a very important part of a healthy business culture: huge mistakes go undetected when nobody raises a critical voice. Moreover, the literary and artistic humanities are essential to cultivate the capacity for creativity and innovation. So despite their fear of the democratic potential of these disciplines, both nations are bolstering them—while trying to ensure that the critical thinking doesn't touch on government policy, the experimental films don't generate protest outside the film school, etc. This somewhat bizarre way of showing respect for the humanities is testimony to the power of these studies in generating wealth. Although this has not been my primary argument, it is itself a point worth noting.

But, sticking to the more traditional roles of the humanities as I describe them, there is enormous variety in the extent of support. The "best cases," I would say, are Korea, Ireland, and Holland. The worst case by far is Britain, with Australia perhaps close. Italy, France, Germany, and the Nordic countries are somewhere in the middle. What makes for a best case? One crucial variable is a long tradition of thinking the humanities a part of national identity. The Irish tell me that of course they are a nation of poets, talkers, music-makers: and the humanities remain enormously popular, although they are being cut along with everything else in the present dire economic situation. The fact that they, like Scotland, take pride in being different from England in this regard is a contributory factor.

In Holland, philosophy has long been a mainstay of public culture. With a high-quality philosophy magazine that sells ten thousand copies or more per month, with excellent coverage of philosophy on television, with philosophical consultants in the police academy and in virtually every walk of life, and with serious attention to teaching philosophy in schools from elementary school on, there are many sources of energy and optimism, despite recent government cuts. There is even a popular television program on philosophy for children ages 10 to 15, on which I've been a guest. People just like philosophy, and their enthusiasm is contagious, so young people get into the culture early. The origins of this widespread public interest in philosophy go back a long way and are complex, but by now philosophy's place is secure, and one can take delight in lecturing to a public so diverse, so informed, and so passionate. If even here the humanities face adversity, as they do, they certainly do not acquiesce, but wage a real war against those agents of a for-profit approach to education who have managed to gain political power.

Korea is perhaps a nation where the humanities are on the rise and are not declining.[2] I used to be more definite about this, but recent news suggests that even here cuts are under way. At any rate, here too the issue is one of national identity. During the Japanese occupation, the Japanese made it illegal to study Korean language and literature or Confucian philosophy. They wanted Koreans to be a technically trained set of peons to execute the will of the masters. Of course this generated a reaction, and the forbidden subjects were taught illegally, sometimes with the help of American missionaries. The result is a culture of higher education that is liberal arts–based, looking to the United States for norms and increasingly for a pedagogy to go with them, and that values the humanities a great deal. Korea also has a huge variety in types of institutions of higher education, public and private, liberal arts colleges and large universities, and this diversity itself helps the humanities find a strong place.

In my "worst cases," by contrast, the nation sees itself as primarily commercial and the humanities as peripheral to national identity, elite frills. One might have thought that England's tradition, which produced so much great literature and philosophy, was one that valued the humanities in education. But already in Mill's time this was no longer true, if it ever had been. By contrast to Scotland, he said, the English think of higher education as primarily instrumental. Mill was never kind to the culture in which he lived (he was buried in France, as he requested). In his inaugural address as rector of St. Andrews University in Scotland, he imputes England's narrowness in education to a combination of commercialism, which instrumentalizes everything, and Puritanism, which shrinks from the exploration of deep emotions and desires. Whatever the accuracy of this diagnosis, England, at least since the Thatcher era and perhaps long before, has devalued the humanities more aggressively than any other educational culture, demanding that they show that they can contribute to narrowly commercial goals. My visit there was the most depressing point in my travels. Lecturing both at the British Academy and at a forum at the London School of Economics called "Valuing the Humanities," I did meet committed souls who came from both the humanities and the sciences (one being Lord Rees, the Astronomer Royal), but my impression was that they believed that their chances of being influential were virtually nil. That has led to a gloomy silence and resignation all around, rather like the gloomy endurance with which people used to queue during the miners' strike for buses that never arrived. The spirit of protest lacks fuel.

Australia, like Britain, has long thought of education as commercial and instrumental, and there is a further issue in that profoundly egalitarian society: people have grown used to thinking of the humanities as elitist. So a large part of what I found the need to do there was to answer that charge, talking about different attitudes to teaching humanities and the difference between an elitist "great books" model and the more Socratic and democratic approach I recommend. It was an uphill battle, given that even the arts, and reading, are often viewed as elitist. In the United States, by contrast, at least since World War II and the GI Bill, there has been a very successful effort to reimagine the humanities in a non-elitist way, as part of a general education for all citizens. This effort was renewed and enhanced in the 1970s by the introduction of the study of race, the study of women, and the study of human sexuality to the undergraduate curriculum. I found myself making these points in Australia, and one could see that an opening for both arts and humanities has been created by the urgently felt need to show respect for the aboriginal people and their traditions, as well as to confront the best ideas of social justice more generally.

These "best" and "worst" cases contain lessons for public debate: anyone who wants to commend the humanities to a particular society needs to know that society and its traditions well, and needs to choose the arguments that are most likely to prevail, given the society's conception of national values. That's why, although I'm happy that my book has aroused interest in many places, I'm also convinced that its main function is to be a catalyst for the more precise and immersed arguments of others.

NOTES

I. The Silent Crisis

1. *A Test of Leadership: Charting the Future of U.S. Higher Education*, available online. A valuable counterreport is *College Learning for the New Global Century*, issued by the National Leadership Council for Liberal Education and America's Promise (LEAP), a group organized by the Association of American Colleges and Universities (Washington, DC, 2007), with whose recommendations I am largely in agreement (not surprisingly, in that I participated in drafting it).

2. I first explored these abilities in *Citizens of the World: A Classical Defense of Reform in Liberal Education* (Cambridge, MA: Harvard University Press, 1997), a book concerned only with developments in higher education in the United States, and with just the required "general education" portion of higher education.

3. One valuable project that focuses on these ingredients in basic science education is Project Kaleidoscope, www.pkal.org.

4. On education and flourishing lives, see Harry Brighouse, *On Education* (New York: Routledge, 2006); the LEAP report (above, n. 1); and the related discussion of self-development in Kwame Anthony Appiah, *The Ethics of Identity* (Princeton: Princeton University Press, 2005).

II. Education for Profit, Education for Democracy

1. This has been shown with particular clarity by Jean Drèze and Amartya Sen in *India: Development and Participation* (New York and Oxford: Oxford University Press, 2002), and in the earlier edition, which has the title *India: Social Development and Economic Opportunity* (New York and

Oxford: Oxford University Press, 1996). The data come from studies of different Indian states that have adopted different policies, some favoring economic growth without direct support for health and education, some favoring direct government action to support health and education (which the Indian Constitution leaves to the states). The field studies are gathered in Drèze and Sen, editors, *Indian Development: Selected Regional Perspectives* (Delhi, New York, and Oxford: Oxford University Press, 1997).

2. See Drèze and Sen, *India: Development and Participation*.

3. Jobs in health and education are under state control according to the Indian Constitution, so the national government can affect development in these areas only indirectly.

4. Article 21 of the Indian Constitution speaks only of "life and liberty," but "life" has since been interpreted to mean "life commensurate with human dignity." The South African Constitution has gone much further, however, in giving constitutional form to basic welfare rights.

5. Rabindranath Tagore, *Nationalism* (New York: Macmillan, 1917).

6. See Nussbaum, *The Clash Within: Democracy, Religious Violence, and India's Future* (Cambridge, MA: Harvard University Press, 2007), ch. 8, for a detailed account, with references and citations.

7. See Nussbaum, "Violence on the Left: Nandigram and the Communists of West Bengal," *Dissent*, Spring 2008, 27–33.

8. Thus, in West Bengal, it was the arts community that earliest and most strongly opposed government policies of kicking rural laborers off their land without skills training or job opportunities; see ibid.

III. Educating Citizens: The Moral (and Anti-Moral) Emotions

1. The history of the Indo-European languages shows us that Hindus almost certainly migrated into India from outside. (If there were any truly indigenous people, these were the Dravidian people of southern India.) Muslims and Christians arrived from outside, later, in small numbers, but the bulk of contemporary Indian Muslims and Christians are converts from Hinduism. In any case, the idea that the date of one's arrival in a place—1500 B.C.E., say, rather than 1600 C.E.—gives one a claim to more citizenship rights should be vigorously rejected.

2. See my discussion of televised versions of the *Mahabharata* and *Ramayana* in *The Clash Within*, ch. 5. For a totally different use of the *Mahabharata* for purposes of contemporary social reflection, see Gurcharan Das's wonderful book, *The Difficulty of Being Good: On the Subtle Art of Dharma* (Delhi: Penguin, 2009; London: Penguin, 2010; and New York: Oxford University Press, 2010). Das is profiled in chapter 2 of my *The Clash Within*.

3. I argue for this account in detail in Nussbaum, *Upheavals of Thought: The Intelligence of Emotions* (Cambridge: Cambridge University Press, 2001), ch. 4.

4. For a more extensive analysis of both shame and disgust, see Nussbaum, *Hiding from Humanity: Disgust, Shame, and the Law* (Princeton: Princeton University Press, 2004).

5. See the references in ibid. to the experimental work of Paul Rozin, Jonathan Haidt, and others.

6. Rozin's experiments make clear the gap between disgust and the sense of danger.

7. See *Hiding*, chs. 2 and 4. My psychological account owes a large debt to the concepts and arguments of Donald Winnicott.

8. Did the beloved story of Hansel and Gretel, made fashionable in the opera by Humperdinck, himself a disciple of Wagner, who sought to extol the pure German *Volk*, contribute to fantasies that led, later, to the perhaps unconscious selection of a mode of extermination? At the opera's end, the blond German children come to life, freed from the witch's spell, and cheer her incineration.

9. See Frans de Waal, *Good Natured: The Origins of Right and Wrong in Humans and Other Animals* (Cambridge, MA: Harvard University Press, 1996).

10. C. Daniel Batson, *The Altruism Question* (Hillsdale, NJ: Lawrence Erlbaum, 1991).

11. See Dale J. Langford, Sara E. Crager, Zarrar Shehzad, Shad B. Smith, Susana G. Sotocinal, Jeremy S. Levenstadt, Mona Lisa Chanda, Daniel J. Levitin, and Jeffrey S. Mogil, "Social Modulation of Pain as Evidence for Empathy in Mice," *Science* 312 (2006), 1967–70.

12. See Candace Clark, *Misery and Company: Sympathy in Everyday Life* (Chicago: University of Chicago Press, 1997).

13. Dan Kindlon and Michael Thompson, *Raising Cain: Protecting the Emotional Life of Boys* (New York: Ballantine, 1999).

14. For a concise summary of Milgram's and Asch's research, see Philip Zimbardo, *The Lucifer Effect: How Good People Turn Evil* (London: Rider, 2007), 260–75.

15. Christopher R. Browning, *Ordinary Men: Reserve Police Battalion 101 and the Final Solution in Poland* (New York: HarperCollins, 1993).

16. Reported in Zimbardo, *The Lucifer Effect*, 283–85.

17. See my review of Zimbardo, *Times Literary Supplement*, October 10, 2007, 3–5.

18. Again, my summary is based on a wide range of research described in Zimbardo.

IV. Socratic Pedagogy: The Importance of Argument

1. See Nussbaum, *Cultivating Humanity: A Classical Defense of Reform in Liberal Education* (Cambridge, MA: Harvard University Press, 1997), ch. 1.

2. Malcolm Gladwell, *Outliers: The Study of Success* (New York: Little, Brown, and Co., 2008).

3. See *Cultivating Humanity*, chs. 1 and 8.

4. See Dewey, "Froebel's Educational Principles," in *The School and Society and The Child and the Curriculum* (Chicago: University of Chicago Press, 1990), 116–31.

5. Dewey, *The School and Society*, 112–15.

6. See ibid., 20–22, where Dewey shows how many complex historical, economic, and scientific ideas can be elicited from the apparently simple task of producing cotton thread.

7. Ibid., 19.

8. See Nussbaum, "Land of My Dreams: Islamic Liberalism under Fire in India," *Boston Review* 34 (March/April 2009), 10–14.

9. See Kathleen M. O'Connell, *Rabindranath Tagore: The Poet as Educator* (Kolkata: Visva-Bharati, 2002).

10. *Auguste Comte and Positivism* (London: Westminster Review, 1865).

11. Translated in V. Bhatia, ed., *Rabindranath Tagore: Pioneer in Educa-*

tion (New Delhi: Sahitya Chayan, 1994). All references in the rest of the chapter are to this translation.

12. Cited by O'Connell, *Rabindranath Tagore*.

13. Maria Montessori (1870–1952), a great educator, follower of Pestalozzi and in conversation with Tagore, made such minute prescriptions for the conduct of the school day that the worldwide educational movement she inspired has to some extent been hampered by the degree of guidance she offered and the sense of authority she imposed.

14. See Gareth Matthews, *Philosophy and the Young Child* (Cambridge, MA: Harvard University Press, 1982), and *Dialogues with Children* (Cambridge, MA: Harvard University Press, 1984).

15. Matthew Lipman, *Harry Stottlemeier's Discovery* (Montclair, NJ: Institute for the Advancement of Philosophy for Children, 1982), 1–14.

16. M. Lipman, A. M. Sharp, and F. S. Oscanyan, *Philosophy in the Classroom* (Philadelphia: Temple University Press, 1980).

V. Citizens of the World

1. O'Connell, *Rabindranath Tagore*, 148.

2. Amita Sen, *Joy in All Work* (Kolkata: Bookfront Publication Forum, 1999).

3. O'Connell, *Rabindranath Tagore*, 148.

4. John Dewey, *Democracy and Education* (New York: Macmillan, 1916, reprinted Mineola, NY: Dover, 2004), 207.

5. Dewey, *The School and Society*, 89, 11, 15, 24.

6. See Nussbaum, *The Clash Within*, ch. 7.

7. For a detailed analysis of specific passages, see Nussbaum, *The Clash Within*, ch. 7.

8. See www.fpspi.org.

9. Conversation with D. Parthasarathy, March 2008 (at a conference in Delhi on affirmative action in higher education).

VI. Cultivating Imagination: Literature and the Arts

1. See Nussbaum, *Cultivating Humanity*, ch. 3.

2. See F. Robert Rodman, *Winnicott: Life and Work* (Cambridge, MA: Perseus Publishing, 2003).

3. Donald Winnicott, *Playing and Reality* (London and New York: Routledge, 2005, originally published 1971).

4. See Nussbaum, *Poetic Justice: The Literary Imagination and Public Life* (Boston: Beacon, 1995), ch. 1.

5. See Rodman's extensive discussion. For Guntrip's analysis with Winnicott, see J. Hazell, *H.J.S. Guntrip: A Psychoanalytical Biography* (London: Free Association Books, 1986).

6. Donald Winnicott, *Holding and Interpretation: Fragments of an Analysis* (New York: Grove Press, 1986), 95.

7. Dewey, *Democracy and Education*, 226, 227.

8. Amita Sen, *Joy in All Work*.

9. Ibid., 35.

10. Ralph Ellison, *Invisible Man* (New York: Random House, 1992 Modern Library edition, with Introduction by Ellison, added 1981; originally published 1952), Introduction.

11. On the use of play and the arts by the Hindu right, see Nussbaum, *The Clash Within*.

12. Johann Gottfried Herder, "Letters for the Advancement of Humanity" (1793–97), translated by Michael Forster, in Forster, ed., *Herder: Philosophical Writings* (Cambridge: Cambridge University Press, 2002), Letter 119, 404–409.

13. See arguments and references in the LEAP Report, *College Learning for the New Global Century*.

14. See discussion in Richard Rothstein, with Rebecca Jacobsen and Tamara Wilder, *Grading Education: Getting Accountability Right* (Washington, DC: Economic Policy Institute, 2008), 18.

VII. Democratic Education on the Ropes

1. Focusing only on the arts and only on pre-college education in the United States, good summaries of trends can be found in the CNN.com article "Budgets Cut Student Experience," http://www.cnn.com/2003/

EDUCATION/08/13/sprj.sch.cuts/, discussing the effects of the No Child Left Behind Act. See also "Cuts in Arts Programs Leave Sour Note in Schools," http://www.weac.org/news_and_publications/at_the_capitol/archives/2003-2004/arts.aspx. For the drastic impact of the California budget crisis on music and art (which are basically gone), see "L.A. Schools Budget Cut, 2,000 Teachers Gone," http://www.npr.org/templates/story/story.php?storId=105848204.

2. See Nussbaum, *Cultivating Humanity.*

3. Personal conversation with religion faculty at Arizona State University, March 2009.

4. "The University's Crisis of Purpose," *New York Times Book Review*, September 6, 2009, 19.

5. One part of this shift, but only one, is the mandatory research and teaching assessment, which measures faculty research and teaching effectiveness in mechanical ways (number of pages, whether the instructor uses PowerPoint, and so forth). The more insidious aspect is the demand—once implicit, now quite open—that research be shown to have "impact," meaning contribution to national economic goals.

6. Scotland used to have a four-year B.A. degree, with the first year devoted to liberal arts courses. The commitment of Scottish universities to the liberal arts was famous even in the nineteenth century: John Stuart Mill's Inaugural Lecture at the University of St. Andrews praises the suitability of the Scottish university system for democratic citizenship, by contrast with England's narrower curriculum, focused on theology. The standardization of higher education imposed by the EU's Bologna scheme, however, has made Scotland assimilate to the rest of Europe, rather than vice versa.

7. *Times Literary Supplement*, November 13, 2009, 18–19.

8. For Nehru's ambivalence about the humanities, see Nussbaum, "Nehru, Religion, and the Humanities," in Wendy Doniger and Martha Nussbaum, *India: Implementing Pluralism and Democracy* (New York: Oxford University Press, forthcoming 2010).

9. "Tour Guides Take Route Less Traveled," *Chicago Maroon*, October 16, 2009. The "apparently" in my text is there because the *Maroon*, a student newspaper, is not always totally accurate, but the data it presents are convincing.

10. Rothstein, *Grading Education*. For the earlier assessment model, in the National Assessment of Educational Progress (NAEP) in the 1950s and 1960s, see ch. 6.

11. For other aspects of the British assessment system, see Rothstein, *Grading Education*, ch. 7.

12. Barack Obama's speech on education, *Wall Street Journal* blog, March 10, 2009.

13. Ibid.

14. See *The Pratichi Education Report: The Delivery of Primary Education, a Study in West Bengal*, by the Pratichi Research Team, Kumar Rana, Abdur Rafique, Amrita Sengupta, with an introduction by Amartya Sen, no. 1 (2002) (Delhi: TLM Books, 2002).

15. See Nussbaum, *The Clash Within*, especially chs. 1 and 9.

Afterword to the Paperback Edition:
Reflections on the Future of the Humanities— at Home and Abroad

1. I study this in detail in "Democracy, Education, and the Liberal Arts: Two Asian Models," *UC Davis Law Review* 44 (2011), 735–72.

2. See my discussion of Korea in that same article.

INDEX

The Public Square Book Series
PRINCETON UNIVERSITY PRESS

With Thanks to the Donors of the Public Square

President William P. Kelly,
the CUNY Graduate Center

President Jeremey Travis,
John Jay College of Criminal Justice

Myron S. Glucksman

Caroline Urvater

Printed in the USA
CPSIA information can be obtained
at www.ICGtesting.com
JSHW082350240624
65300JS00006B/346